FLOCK

THE

BOOK 1

KATE STEWART

USA TODAY BESTSELLING AUTHOR

"There is a legend about a bird which sings just once in its life, more sweetly than any other creature on the face of the earth. From the moment it leaves the nest it searches for a thorn tree, and does not rest until it has found one. Then, singing among the savage branches, it impales itself upon the longest, sharpest spine. And, dying, it rises above its own agony to outcarol the lark and the nightingale.

One superlative song, existence the price. But the whole world stills to listen, and God in His heaven smiles. For the best is only bought at the cost of great pain... Or so says the legend."

–Colleen McCullough, *The Thorn Birds*

Prologue

I GREW UP SICK.

Let me clarify. I grew up believing that real love stories include a martyr or demand great sacrifice to be worthy.

My favorite books, love songs, movies, the ones that resonated with me, have kept me grieving long after I turned the last page, the notes faded out, or the credits rolled.

Because of that, I believed it, because I *made* myself believe it, and I bred the most masochistic of romantic hearts, which resulted in my illness.

When I lived this story, my own twisted fairy tale, it was unbeknownst to me at the time because I was young and naïve. I gave into temptation and fed that beating beast, which grew thirstier with every slash, every strike, every blow.

That's the novelty of fiction versus reality. You can't re-live your own love story because, by the time you've realized you're living it, it's over. At least that was the case for me.

All these years later, I'm convinced I willed my story into existence due to my illness.

And *all* were punished.

That's why I'm here, to feed, to grieve, and maybe to cure my sickness. It's here that it started and it's here where I have to end it.

It's a ghost town, this place that haunts me, this place that made me. A few weeks shy of my nineteenth birthday, my mother had sent me to take up residence with my father, a man I'd previously only spent a few summers with when I was much younger. Upon my arrival, I'd quickly learned that his stance hadn't changed on his biological obligation, and he doled out the same rules as he had when I was small—to rarely be seen and never heard. I was to uphold myself to the strictest of morals and excel in school while executing his standard of living.

In the months that followed, a prisoner of his kingdom, I naturally did the opposite, ruining myself, and further tarnishing his name.

Back then, I had zero regrets, at least when it came to my father until I was forced to deal with the aftermath.

Now at twenty-six, I'm still living in it.

It's clear to me that I'll never outgrow Triple Falls or outlive the time I spent there. After years of fighting it, this is the conclusion I've drawn. I'm a different person now, but I was before I left too. When everything happened, I was determined I'd never return. But the infuriating truth I've discovered is that I'll never be able to move on. It's the reason I'm back. To make peace with my fate.

I can no longer disregard the greedy demand of the vessel beating in my chest or the nagging of my subconscious. I'll never be a woman capable of letting go, of leaving the past where it belongs, no matter how much I want to.

Navigating my way through the winding roads, I roll down my window, welcoming the cold. I need to numb. Since I hit the highway, my mind has been reeling with memories I've desperately tried to suppress during waking hours since I fled.

It's my dreams that refuse to set me free, my dreams that keep the war raging in my head, the loss shredding my heart, forcing me to re-live the hardest parts, over and over in an agonizing loop.

For years, I've tried to convince myself that life exists after love.

And maybe it does, for others, but life hasn't been so kind to me.

I'm done pretending I didn't leave the largest part of me between these hills and valleys, between the sea of trees that hold my secrets.

Even with the cold whip of the wind on my face, I can still feel the warmth of the sun on my skin. I can still sense his frame blocking out the light, feel the prickling of surety the first time he touched me, and the goosebumps that touch left in his wake.

I can still feel them all, my boys of summer.

All of us are to blame for what happened—all of us serving our sentences. We were careless and reckless, thinking our youth made us indestructible, exempt from our sins, and it cost us.

Snow drifts toward my windshield in a lazy fall, dusting the trees and covering the surrounding ground as I exit the highway. The crunch of my tires in the gravel has my heart pounding in my throat as my hands start to shake. I sweep the endless evergreens lining the road while trying to convince myself that facing my past head-on is the first step in confronting what's plagued me for years. All I have left is dwelling within the prison I've built. It's the truth I'm determined to face that's the most definite, the most crippling.

Most consider knowing all-consuming love a blessing, but I consider it a curse. A curse I'll never be able to lift. I'll never know love again as I did here all those years ago. And I don't want to. I can't. I'm still sick with it.

There is no question in my mind that for me, it was love.

What other pull could be so strong? What other feeling could addict me to the point of insanity? Of doing the things I did and living with these memories within this ghost story.

Even when I'd sensed the danger, I gave in.

I didn't heed a single warning. I went in a willing captive. I let love rule and ruin me. I played my part, eyes wide open, tempting fate until it delivered.

There was never going to be an escape.

Stopped at the first light at the edge of town, I press my head against the steering wheel and inhale calming breaths, hating the fact that I'm still so powerless to the emotions this trip has stirred within me, even as the woman I've become.

Exhaling, I glance back at the bag that I tossed in the backseat after my decision mere hours ago. I thumb my engagement ring, rotating it on my finger as another stab of guilt runs through me. All hope of the future I spent years building was lost the minute I ended my relationship. He'd refused to take the ring, and I have yet to take it off. It hangs heavy, a lie on my finger. The time I spent here before has caused another casualty, one of many.

I was engaged to a man capable of keeping his vows, a man worthy of commitment, of unconditional love—a loyal man with a steadfast heart and warm spirit. And to him, I'd never been fair. I could never love him in the way a wife should love a husband.

He was a consolation, and accepting his proposal meant settling. One look at his face when I called off our upcoming nuptials let me know I had destroyed him with the truth.

The truth that I belong to another. That whatever remains of my heart, body, and soul belongs to a man who wants nothing to do with me.

It was the agony on my fiancé's face that aided to my breaking point. He'd given me his love, his devotion, and I'd thrown it away. I'd done to him what was done to me. Disobeying my heart, my master and monster had cost me Collin.

Minutes after I liberated us both, I packed a bag and left in search of more punishment. I drove straight through the night, knowing there was no significance of time, that it doesn't matter. Nobody is waiting for me.

Well over six years have passed, and I'm back to square one, back to the life I fled, my feelings running rampant as I reason with myself that leaving Collin wasn't a mistake, but a necessary evil to free him from the lies I told. I'd wronged him making promises I could never keep, and there was no way I was making more, to love and cherish in both sickness and in health because I hadn't disclosed just how sick I am.

I never told him how I allowed myself to be used, ravaged, and at times debased to the point of depravity...and that I'd loved every second of it. I never told my fiancé how I'd blood-let my heart—starved it—until it had no choice but to beat in a distinct rhythm that only matched the thrum of one other. In doing so, I'd sabotaged my chances of recognizing and accepting the kind of love that heals, rather than hurts. The only love I've ever known or craved is the kind that keeps me sick, sick with longing, sick with lust, sick with need, sick with grief. The distorted kind that leaves scars and jaded hearts.

If I can't grieve enough to cure myself in my time here, I'll remain sick. That will be my curse.

There may never be a happily ever after for me because I gave my chance away by becoming attuned to the dark parts.

Accustomed because of the year I freed my inhibitions, reacting to rejection and pain and losing all moral sense of myself.

These are things you don't say aloud. These are the type of confessions women who command respect are never supposed to give voice to. Not ever.

But it's time to confess, to myself more so than any other, that I'd hindered my chance of a normal and healthy relationship because of the way I was built, and because of the men who built me.

At this point, I just want to make peace with who I am, no matter what ending I get.

The hardest part of all of this isn't the fiancé whose heart I broke. It's the knowledge that the one and only man my heart's ever been faithful to, I will never have.

Trepidation engulfs me as more memories surface. I can still smell him, feel the swell of him inside me, taste the drop of salt in his cum, see the satisfied look in his hooded eyes. I can still feel the unmistakable rush from the looks we shared, hear the rumble of his dark chuckle, feel the wholeness from his touch.

The closer I get, the more memories come crashing over me. My resolve to face what haunts me beginning to break away piece by jagged piece. Because I have some idea of what the true end looks like, and I can't escape it anymore.

There may be no cure, no moving on, but it's time to deal with unfinished business.

Let the ghost hunt begin.

PART 1

THEN

Chapter One

PULLING UP TO THE MASSIVE IRON GATES, I PUNCH IN THE
code Roman gave me and gawk as the sprawling estate
comes into view when I drive through. Acres and acres of
neon grass littered with trees surround the massive house in
the distance. The closer I get, the more I feel like a foreigner. To
the left of this palace sits a four-car garage—which I forgo—
choosing to park in the circular drive at the foot of the porch.
Exiting the car, I stretch my legs. The drive wasn't long, but my
limbs grew heavier with every mile as I got closer. Though the
house is impressive, it feels more like a prison to me, and today is
the first day of my sentence.

Opening the trunk, I gather a few of my bags and head up
the steps, scanning the pristine deck. Nothing about this place
feels inviting, aside from the land it sits upon, and everything
about it reeks of money.

fortune. His grudge for her clear in that sense. Add that to the fact he's given the minimum over the years, keeping Mom in her respective place in his food chain makes it easy to see he has no lingering feelings for her.

For a brief time, I've lived on both sides of poverty due to their night and day lifestyles, and to spite his wishes, I'll take the stock and money and go against every one of them. The minute I'm able, my mother will never work again. Any amount of success I have, I'm determined to earn for myself, but the fear of failing along with the possibility that gambling on myself would ultimately cost *her* is what brought me here. But in order to carry out my plan, I have to play along with his, and that includes being 'appreciative and respectful enough to learn the business, even if it's from the ground level.'

The hardest part of that will be to tame my mouth and silence my resentment, which is front and center since he could have spared us both an awkward year together by simply having a fucking heart with the woman who has done both their jobs as my parent.

I don't exactly hate my father, but I don't understand him or his unapologetic cruelty, and never will. I'm not about to spend the next year trying to figure him out. Any communication on his part has always felt mandatory and rushed. He's always been a monetary provider, not a dad. I respect his work ethic and success but have zero understanding as to the whys of his lack of empathy and the chill of his sub-zero personality.

"I'll come home every chance I can," I tell Christy, unsure I can make it a promise due to my schedule.

"I'll come up too."

Opening the top of my chest of drawers, I toss in a pile of socks and undies, "Let's see how Adolf feels about you occupying a guest room before you gas up, okay?"

"I'll rent a hotel with my mom's card. Fuck your dad."

I laugh, and it sounds odd in the massive room. "You really aren't feeling my parents today."

"I love your mom, but I don't get it. Maybe I need to go by and see her."

"She moved in with Timothy."

"Really? When?"

"Yesterday. Just give her time to get settled."

"Okay…" she pauses, "why am I just now hearing this? I knew things were getting bad, but what's really going on?"

"Honestly, I don't know." I sigh, giving in to the resentment I'm starting to feel. It's not like me to hide anything from Christy. "She's going through something. Timothy is a decent guy, and I trust him with her."

"But he wouldn't let you move in."

"To be fair, I'm an adult, and he doesn't exactly have the space."

"I still want to know why she's okay with letting you live with your dad *now*."

"I told you, I have to work at the plant for a year to get her set up. I don't want to worry about her while I'm at school."

"It's not your job."

"I know."

"You're not the parent."

"We both know I am. And we'll resume our plans the minute I get back."

It was a surprise to me that my father agreed to let me attend community college here for a couple of semesters, rather than make me take a sabbatical to start a year late at a more acceptable school. It's his dime, and he's the sole source of my college fund, so that win during negotiations let me know he wanted his way enough to compromise—a departure from his controlling personality.

I glance around the room. "I haven't spent more than a day with him or summered here since I was eleven."

"Why is that?"

"It was always something. He claimed it was overseas trips and expansion that kept him from being able to care for me for weeks or months at a time. The truth is, I got my period, boobs, and an attitude, and he couldn't deal. I don't think there's anything Roman fears more than being a real parent."

"It's weird you call your dad by his first name."

"Not to his face. When I'm here, it's Sir."

"You never talk about him."

"Because I don't know him."

"So, when do you start your job?"

"My shifts will be from three to eleven, but I've got orientation tomorrow."

"Call me when you get off. I'll let you unpack."

It strikes me when we disconnect that I'll be stuck with the silence in the room, of the house, and utterly alone. Roman didn't even have the decency to meet me here to get me settled.

"Cee?" Christy's voice sounds as uncertain as I feel.

"Uh, shit. Okay, I'm feeling it now." I open the French doors that lead onto my private balcony and stare down at the pristine grounds. In the distance is nothing but a blanket of the greenest grass cut in a diagonal shaped pattern, beyond is a thick forest of trees that surround a cell tower. Closer to the house is a well-kept garden that screams southern opulence. Wisteria covers several trellises that canopy statuesque fountains. Hedges covered in trimmed honeysuckle trickle over sporadic fencing. The scent of several blooms wafts to my nose as the breeze hits me in hushed welcome. Plush seating is placed strategically throughout the manicured garden, which I decide will be my reading nook. The large, sparkling pool looks inviting, especially due to the budding summer heat, but I feel too ill at ease as a new resident of the palace to think of it for personal use. "God, this is weird."

"You've got this."

Her nervous tone is unsettling, and we're both unsure at this point, which instills more fear in me.

"I hope so."

"A little over a year and you're home. You're almost nineteen, Cee, if you hate it, you *can* leave."

"True." It is the truth, but my agreement with Roman is a different story. If I go back on spending my time at the plant, I lose a fortune, a fortune that could erase my mother's debt and set her up comfortably for the rest of her life. I can't—won't—do that to her. She's worked herself stupid to care for me.

Christy reads my hesitation.

"This isn't on you. It was her job to raise you, Cee. That's the obligation of a *parent*, which you should never feel obligated to repay."

It's true, and I know it, but as I survey Roman's lifeless palace, I find myself missing her more than ever. Maybe it's the distancing and treatment from my father that makes me feel such gratitude for her. Either way, I want to care for her. "I know my mother loves me," I say more for myself than for Christy. Mom's withdrawal, from life, from *me*, after all our years together was a cruel and confusing surprise.

"Well, I for one, wouldn't blame you if you liberated yourself. I love your mom and all, but they both seem worthless at this point."

"Roman is tolerable, strict, but we managed a few summers. Well, we managed to avoid each other for a few summers. I'm not looking to bond, just survive. This place feels…cold."

"You've never been there?"

"No, not this house. He didn't build it until after I stopped coming for the summers. I think he lives mostly out of his condo in Charlotte." Across from my bedroom door a few feet away sits another. I open it, relieved to see it's a guest room. To my left at the top of the stairs is a mezzanine overlooking the bottom floor foyer leading to a long corridor with more closed doors. "It's going to be like living in a museum."

"I hate this." She lets out a sigh, which is more like a whine, and I can feel her bitterness. We've been friends since middle school and haven't been separated a day since we met. I don't know how to do life without her, and quite frankly, I don't want to. But for my mom's well-being, I will. A little over a year in a sleepy town nestled in the middle of the Blue Ridge Mountains and I'm free. I can only hope the time flies.

"Just find yourself a distraction. Preferably one with a penis."

"That's your solution?" I make my way back into my bedroom and onto the balcony.

"You would know if you would give just *one* the time of day."

"I have, and you saw how that worked out."

"Those were boys, find a *man*. Just wait, girl. You're going to tear that town up when they get a look at you."

"I couldn't give a shit right now," I stare at the spectacular mountain view just beyond the private forest. "I'm officially living on the opposite side of the coin. This is so weird."

"I can only imagine. Chin up. Call me after orientation tomorrow."

"'K."

"Love you."

Chapter Two

CURSING LIKE A SAILOR, I PARK IN THE LAST ROW AT THE plant and quickly make my way through a sea of cars into the lobby. The last thing I need is a lecture on timeliness after a stale and uneventful dinner with my father last night. That hour or so I was forced to spend under eagle-eyed scrutiny was enough to make me thankful for my new schedule, which will have me working most nights. The warmth of the sun disappears the second I pull open the glass doors. The building itself feels ancient. Though polished, the tile floors are cracking and peeling after decades of use. There's a large potted fern in the middle of the lobby that gives a pretense of life somewhere inside, but upon closer inspection, I realize it's fake and littered with cobwebs. A lone security guard that looks past his prime stands idly by as an older, well-dressed woman with shrewd grey eyes greets me from behind a front desk.

"Hello, I'm Cecelia Horner. I'm here for orientation."

"I'm aware, Ms. Horner, last door on the left," she replies, her eyes assessing my dress as she directs me to a long corridor. Dismissed, I take the steps, pass a few vacant offices and just in time, slip past a woman holding the door for the last of the newcomers. She greets me with a warm smile—the only warmth in the building apparently—as I shiver from the frigid indoor climate. She instructs me to fill out a name tag, and I do, sticking it on the sundress I opted to wear today before being bound to the drab uniform that waits in my closet. I feel the heavy stares of those already seated and choose the closest open desk.

The room is dark, the only light from a projection screen that says 'Welcome' in bold letters with the Horner Technologies company logo across the bottom.

I've never taken pride in my last name. As far as I can tell, I was a spill Roman made years ago that he had enough money to clean up. I have no illusions we'll ever be close. He doesn't look at me with the same cruel indifference as he does my mother from what I've gathered in the few encounters I've witnessed, but I'm most definitely an afterthought.

Dinner last night was awkward to say the least, our conversation forced. Today I'm here to do his bidding. Another worker ant to add to his industrial farm. It's like this is some attempt to teach me a life lesson that hard work pays off, but I'm no stranger to that. I've paid my way since I've been able to work, bought my first car, and made the insurance payments while balancing my own checkbook. I've got nothing to learn from him, that much I know. I have little doubt the longer I comply with his demands and agree with his plans for me, the more my resentment will grow.

This is for Mom.

The woman who greeted me at the door steps up to the

front of the room and smiles. "Looks like most of us are here, so let's begin. I'm Jackie Brown, yes like the movie," none of us laugh, "and I've been working for Horner Tech for eight years. I'm the HR director, and I'm excited to welcome you to orientation. In an effort to get to know everyone, I would very much like if each of you stood and briefly introduced yourselves."

I'm in the first seat upfront, and she nods toward me. I reluctantly stand, not bothering to face the rest of the room and speak directly to her. "I'm Cecelia, *not* like the song. New in town. I'm just going to clear the air now and let you know my father owns this place, but I want no special treatment. And I promise not to narc if you take an extra cigarette break or like your afternoon delight in the janitor's closet."

My introduction doesn't go over well with Jackie Brown as she gapes at me, while a chuckle sounds up behind me. Taking my seat, I curse my inability to get through the first few minutes of orientation without my grudge rearing its ugly head. I should know better than to poke the bear on my first day and have no doubt my father will hear about this. But other than the inevitable repercussion, I'm having a hard time regretting it. I remind myself for the hundredth time that this is for Mom and vow to keep my attitude in check, at least until my probation period is over.

"Next, you, behind her."

With the movement behind me, I catch a whiff of cedar before he speaks. "Sean, no relation to the man upstairs, and this is my second time working for Horner Tech. I left briefly. And I would very much enjoy some afternoon delight in the janitor's closet." Muffled laughter sounds throughout the room as the first smile I've been capable of in days, spreads over my face.

I half turn in my seat and look over my shoulder to meet amused hazel eyes. The drag of his gaze over me has my skin prickling with awareness. Feet away, in the dim light, I'm able to appreciate the alluring outline of his features along with his incredible build, the stretch of his T-shirt across his pecs, and snug-fitting dark jeans before he takes his seat. We play a short game of stare off where I wait a few seconds past the awkward point before I turn back to face Jackie Brown.

"Welcome back, Sean. Let's refrain from making any more comments like that, shall we?"

It takes a lot of effort to hide my grin, and I can still feel his gaze on me as one by one the room stands to introduce themselves.

Maybe this won't suck so bad after all.

Chapter Three

"**H**EY, AFTERNOON DELIGHT!" AN AMUSED CHUCKLE
sounds up behind me as I make my way through the
parking lot, "Wait up!"

Frown in place, I turn to see Sean sauntering toward me between a row of cars. Hands on my hips, I stare him down as he approaches, and then am forced to look up at him when he gets closer due to our difference in height.

In the sparkling light of day, he's far more impressive than I gave him original credit for, and I'm careful to control my gawk. His looks are—paralyzing—spiked two-toned dirty blond and platinum hair, sun-drenched skin, insane build, and hazel eyes with undecided dominance, a strong nose with a slight bump along the ridge ending with just the right flare. And his mouth, his mouth is enough in and of itself to keep my thirsty eyes busy. His tongue darts out, sliding against the ring tucked in the corner, showcasing his full bottom lip. His gaze glitters over me, along with a building smirk as I take my fill and then drift to his pronounced Adam's apple, broad shoulders, and lower, and lower. A large tattoo covers the majority of his left arm, the dark black tip of a wing and feathers starting just above his elbow and looks like it ends at the base of his neck.

"That's not my name."

"Sorry," a flash of teeth, "couldn't resist."

"Try harder."

His chuckle sends a flutter across my skin. "Will do. That was pretty brave back there."

"Yeah, well, I'm not looking forward to the job. It's a condition of my sentence."

He frowns. "Sentence?"

"Because of my last name. I'm being forced to work here for a year, so I'm deserving of it, I guess." I shrug as if my bitterness hasn't said too much on my behalf.

"Hmm, you aren't alone. I'm not thrilled about being back here either." He's older, I'm guessing somewhere in his mid-twenties, his presence impossible to ignore due to his insanely good looks and his scent is just as tempting—cedar and something else I can't put my finger on. The vibe he's throwing off is irresistible. The more he stands in the golden sun, the more he seems to absorb. It's alarming just how much looking at him is unnerving me. But I don't berate myself for it because his gaze is equally shameless. This morning, though my mood was grim, I'd dressed up, and I'm glad I made an effort as I face off with Sean in a knee-length halter sundress, black with small white polka dots. I'd left my hair down, and it lays straightened over my shoulders. I'd spent extra time on my lashes and heavily glossed my lips, which I lick under his stare, and his eyes drop.

"Cecelia, right?"

I nod.

"So, what are you doing now?"

"Why?"

He runs a hand through his messy spiked mane. "You're new in town, right? My roommates and I have a spot a few miles away. We're having a few friends over today, and I thought you might want to come."

"Yeah, I'm going to pass."

He tilts his head, amused by my fast answer. "Why?"

"Because I don't know you."

"That's the point of the invite." His mouth might be moving with pleasantries, but his eyes are devouring me in a way I'm not entirely comfortable with.

"That crack I made back there might have given you the wrong impression about me."

"I'm making no assumptions, swear," he holds up his palms, where a heavily inked ace on his right wrist poses as a permanent top card up his sleeve.

Clever.

He winks, and it feels like a kiss on the cheek. All I have to look forward to at home is a swim and a book. And I have a feeling I'll be doing that for most of the summer. I look him over carefully and hold out my hand.

"Let me see your driver's license."

Thick blond brow raised, he pulls out his wallet and hands me his license. I take the offered card and eye it and him as a cigarette appears, dangling between his lips before he strikes a black titanium Zippo, and I flick my attention back to his ID.

"You are aware you're the last smoker, right?"

"Someone's got to keep up my old man's bad habits," he says on an exhale.

"Alfred Sean Roberts, twenty-five, and a Virgo." I take a picture of his license and shoot off a text to Christy.

If I wind up dead, this dude did it.

The response bubbles start immediately, and I know she's going insane. The picture does little credit to the real thing. His looks are jarring and seem out of place here.

"Sending out a safety net?" he asks, reading my move.

"Exactly," I hand him back his license. "If I don't make it home, you're suspect number one."

He seems to mull over my statement. "*Do you party?*"

"In what sense?"

"In every sense."

"Not really, no."

He looks at me with such…intensity, new hesitation in his posture, as if weighing whether or not to take back his invitation. Despite being slightly offended, I decide to make it easy on him. "I guess that's a dealbreaker? Don't worry about it, see you around—"

"It's not that, just…" He cups the back of his neck. "Jesus, I'm fucking this up good. It's just the guys, they'll, well, they're—"

"I've been to plenty of parties, Sean. I'm no Little Red Riding Hood."

This earns me a grin before he stomps out his cigarette with a greased-stained tan boot. "Good, because we don't want to let the wolf get a whiff."

"Where exactly are you taking me?"

He flashes a blinding smile that feels like a bat to the chest.

"I told you, my spot."

I should be wary, especially because of his hesitation, but I'm intrigued more than anything. "I'll follow you."

We pull up to a two-story house, the only one in a tiny cul-de-sac. The rest of the houses on the street spaced just far enough apart to allow a fair amount of privacy. It's a far cry from the inch between houses neighborhood I grew up in. I get out of my Camry and meet Sean at his car, an old classic that I struggled to keep up with on the ride over. It's fire engine red, looks newly polished and seems to suit him perfectly. The rest of the parking spots in the circle and lining the street are cars of the same nature, mostly classics, shiny metal with powerful engines—either that or huge trucks that require some effort to climb in.

"This is beautiful," I tell him as he gets out and closes the door, eyes hidden due to a pair of vintage Vegas Elvis style shades. Sunglasses that would look ridiculous on anyone else but work effortlessly on him. Darting my eyes away, I run my fingers along the glossed exterior of the car.

"What is it?"

"'69 Nova, SS."

"I love it."

A flash of teeth. "Me too, come on."

I glance up the driveway, and it's easy to see the tan-sided house is suited for bachelors. It's nothing special, the lawn manicured enough to make it clean, but lacking a personal touch. There's a group of people gathered on the porch, a few of their heads already turned our way.

A twinge of social anxiety keeps me idle as Sean walks a few steps ahead of me to follow. When he senses I'm not at his side, he turns back, and I latch my wrist to the arm draped loosely at my side. "Who all lives here?"

"Me and two others, they're like my brothers, and both will bite."

"That's reassuring."

He pushes his shades up to his crown and eyes me skeptically. "Maybe we should go somewhere else."

"Should we?"

Sean takes the few strides towards me, his voice level when he speaks.

"Look, I'll admit back at the plant I thought you were a bit more bulldog than pup."

I give him a dead stare.

He points to my expression, a new grin in place. "See, now *that*, that mean mug right there, is what will keep you alive in this house. Think you can keep that up while you're here?"

"I don't understand. Aren't these your friends?"

He lifts a steady hand between us before pushing some hair away from my shoulder. I don't shy away from his touch. "If you had flinched, I'd take you somewhere else, you've got this. Just don't take any shit like you didn't from me back at work and you'll be fine."

He takes my hand and we walk through the crowd on the porch, stopping short of the front door. "Who's this?" The voice comes from the porch swing, out of the mouth of a guy draped around a girl who looks at me with the same interest. I can practically see the 'we don't do well with strangers around here' in both their expressions.

"She just started at the plant. Cecelia, this is James, and that's his girl Heather," he jerks his chin to the others crowded by the porch fence who scrutinize me while sipping their beers, "Russell, Peter, Jeremy, Tyler." They all give me the lift of their chins while a strange sensation rolls up my spine, and it's not a bad one. If anything, it feels a little like déjà vu. Tyler holds my gaze the longest after our introduction, and I can't help but notice the wing tip beneath the cuff of his T-shirt when he lifts his beer. Our eyes stay locked until I'm led into the house.

Despite my hesitation in coming, I feel more comfortable here than I have after one night at my father's, and I use that to fuel each step. Once inside, I scan the spotless house. The walls look freshly painted, and the furniture new. The living room is empty of people, save the loveseat where a couple talks animatedly, the guy giving me a once-over before giving Sean a nod while he guides me through a sliding glass door. It's when I step through onto the patio that my hackles rise, and the hairs on the back of my neck stand at attention. I feel like I'm on display, which isn't far from the truth because the back yard is bustling with people, smoke billowing from a nearby barbecue, and out of the mouths of a few next to the fence bordering the yard. To our left is a long patio table full of people taking shots and playing cards. The gathering seems to be just a few heads shy of a full-on party. Sean leads me to the middle of the yard where rows of coolers sit fully stocked with beer next to a picnic bench.

"Nice place."

"Thanks, we're working on it. Beer?"

"I..." I pause, intent on trying to fit in despite standing out like an inexperienced sore thumb. The last time I drank, it didn't end well. "Yeah, I'll have one."

He twists the lid on a hard cider. "I think this is chick beer." I take a sip and then another, liking the taste. Sean's lips lift in a sultry smile. "Like that?"

"It's pretty good."

"I guess I should've asked how old you are."

"Old enough to vote, but not to legally drink."

He hangs his head.

"Not *that* young. I'll be nineteen in a few weeks."

"Shit," he eyes me. "I thought I was going to be trouble for *you*."

I double tap my brows. "I'm tricky like that."

"You are trouble," he says, his eyes searching mine. "I can tell."

"I'm harmless."

"No, you're more," he shakes his head slowly. "A lot more." He takes a beer from the cooler and pops off the top, his eyes never leaving me. "Hungry?"

"Starving," I say honestly, my stomach rumbling from the smell permeating the yard.

"Should be ready soon." One of the guys playing cards on the porch waves him over, his curious eyes trained on me. "You okay here for a second?"

"I'm good."

"Be right back." He stalks off, and I zero in on his ass. A feminine laugh sounds behind me and I turn as she approaches. She's beautiful, with long blonde hair, baby blue eyes, and in my opinion, the perfect physique. Petite with soft curves. My last growth spurt puts me hovering above her at 5'9. I got my blue eyes and reddish-brown hair from my father, and work with the slightly disproportionate build I inherited from my mom. What I lack in my border B cup breasts I make up with a double D butt.

She grins. "Can't blame you, you could bounce a quarter off that ass."

"Was I that obvious?"

"A little," she plucks a cider from the cooler, twists off the top and takes a sip. "But we *all* stare at that ass. I'm Layla."

"Cecelia."

"So, how do you know Sean?"

"I don't. I met him at orientation today."

She wrinkles her nose. "You work at the plant?"

"First shift starts tomorrow. Just moved here yesterday."

"I only worked there for a few years after high school, and I couldn't stand it. Most everyone here works there or has at some point. The owner is an asshole, though. He lives in a castle somewhere around here." She turns to me. "I get the townies having that job, but why would *you* take a job there?"

"I'm the daughter of the asshole."

She tilts her head, her clear blue eyes widening slightly before darting past me in the direction Sean left. "No shit?"

"Yeah, and trust me, I'm dreading it."

"I already like you," she takes another sip of her cider and glances around the yard. "Same shit, different day."

"They do this often?"

"Oh, yeah—" she flutters her fingers as if the subject isn't worth entertaining. "So where did you move from?"

"Peachtree City, just outside of Atlanta."

"Why would you want to move here?"

I shrug. "Single parents, and they passed the baton this year."

"Sucks."

"It does."

She looks past me, lifting her chin to the same guy who summoned Sean from the porch, this time, his eyes only for her. He's got nothing on Sean looks-wise, but there's something about him that commands attention, especially hers. She gives him a knowing grin and turns to me. "Can't leave your man alone too long, even with his friends. Well, a man that can't do without you. And my man doesn't like my attention divided." She rolls her eyes as his jaw ticks with impatience. "Do you have a boyfriend back home?"

"No."

Her eyes are still on his as they pass a look that displays ownership of the other on both parts before she turns to me.

"Well, hopefully you find something in Triple that keeps you entertained."

"Maybe." I lift my bottle to sip my cider and find it empty.

She plucks us each a new one from the cooler, passing one to me. "I better get over there. Join us if you want."

"Thanks, I'm going to wait here for Sean. Good meeting you."

"I'll see you around, Cecelia."

She saunters off, retreating onto the lap of her man and wraps herself around him as he plays his hand. He subtly, but possessively caresses her thigh with his thumb as she whispers in his ear. I dart my eyes away, a little envious. It's been a while since I had a steady boyfriend, and I sometimes miss the ritual.

The more I look around, the more I recognize these people are family. I seem to be the only outsider here, which I assume is the reason for the seconds long glances that are coming at me from all sides. Not the type to mingle, I find myself missing Sean, who's been gone for what seems like forever as I stand in the middle of the yard, a fish out of water. Music filters down from an open window on the second floor of the house as I walk over to the fence, overlooking a partial mountain view. I might have moved from the suburbs of Atlanta to the mountains in Bumfuck, Nowhere, but even I can appreciate the spectacular scenery.

Do you party?

No. Though I attended a few in high school, I always opted to leave early. I'm fully aware of the protocol and behavior necessary to blend in at these types of gatherings, but I've never really become comfortable in the way Christy is, who's never met a stranger. Christy is always the buffer for me, and I find myself wishing she was here. I've never been the one to dance on a table after taking too many shots or give in to a random hookup. My record is squeaky in that sense. I've always been more of an introvert, an onlooker, bearing witness to the goings-on while too afraid of making any mistakes and losing face.

In hindsight, I wished I'd made a few worthy missteps and been a little bit braver. But weeks ago, I crossed that stage for my diploma unmemorable, the 'what's her name?' girl in the background of a few yearbook pictures. It dawns on me now, here amongst strangers, I can be anyone. Aside from Sean's easy read on me during our first encounter, no one knows me. Christy's right in a lot of ways about my role in my relationship with my mom. She's been begging me for years to loosen up. Maybe it's not too late to make those notable blunders, make myself more of an 'in the moment' gal, and less of a wallflower.

More of a wishful thinker than executioner, I perch against the fence and am halfway through my second cider, lost in the view of the evergreen drenched mountains when I sense I'm not alone.

"Sean desert you already?" A voice rumbles from next to me. I turn to see Tyler standing just feet away, his arms crossed over the edge of the fence, his expression and brown eyes warm.

"Yeah," I wave my bottle. "No complaints, I'm a fan of whomever's playing DJ, and I've got a drink and a view. Tyler, right?"

His answering grin reveals a dimple. "Right."

"Do you work at the plant, too?"

"Nope, I work at a garage for now, just got back from Greensboro, had a job out there the last four years of my reserves."

"Really?"

He runs his hands through his half-inch hair. "Really."

"What branch?"

"Marines."

"Did you like it?"

He smirks. "Not enough to make a career of it. Four years in, another four years on standby, but I guess I consider it time well spent."

"Welcome back, Marine. Thank you for your service."

"Most welcome."

We clink bottles.

"Do you own one of those cars outside?"

"Yeah, the '66 C20 is mine."

I draw my brows, and he grins.

"The neon green pickup with the black top." Pride oozes from his lips as I take him in. He's a bit smaller in stature than Sean, but just as shredded physically. He's got the sweetheart eyes, a rich brown surrounded by black, naturally curled lashes. Clearly, there's no shortage of hot men in the mountains. Christy will be thrilled. Though entertaining, and highly appealing, I'm just not sure any of them are my type. But with each sip of cider, I feel like I'm forming an opinion. And so far, I haven't met a bicep I haven't liked. That thought—combined with the cider—makes me giggle.

"What were you thinking, just then?" Tyler's lips tug up at the corners, amping his smile to the next level.

"Just… Yesterday I lived somewhere else, and now I'm in a stranger's yard."

"Crazy where a day can take you, huh?"

"Exactly."

"That's nothing unusual around here, trust me," he says, inching closer. His predacious gaze sends a shiver along my neck.

"What do you mean?"

"Stick around long enough, you'll see for yourself."

"Well, I don't hate it so far," I drawl, knowing the cider is starting to speak on my behalf.

"Good to know," he crowds me a little against the fence. It's not threatening, but enough to feel some of the summer sun radiating off his skin.

"Back off, jar-dick, she just got here," Sean says, nudging his way between us and looking at me with a lifted brow. "Where's that mean mug?"

I lift my cider to indicate where it all went wrong, feeling warm all over as he takes it from me. "Let's get you fed."

Tyler grins at me over Sean's obstructive shoulder. "See you around, Cecelia."

"Hope so," I tilt my head past Sean, so he can see my answering smile.

"Knew you were trouble," Sean drawls out, shaking his head before leading me by the hand over to a fully stocked picnic bench table full of mixed barbecue and endless sides. Sean and I eat together and it's hard not to avoid the looks we get huddled in our little bubble, isolated from the rest of the party.

"Ignore them," he says through a mouthful. "And," he points to me, playfully ordering, "mean mug."

"Is there a reason we aren't eating with everyone else?"

Lazy hazel sweeps me. "How about I want to keep you to myself for now?"

"That so?" I take a bite to hide my smile, unsure of the signals I want to send. Only inches apart when we started eating, our knees touch now as we lean toward each other. As we feast, we slide into easy conversation and he reveals he moved to Triple Falls when he was five, and met the friends he's since taken up residence with. Sean, Tyler, and their other roommate moved into the house a week ago, which I assume is some of the reason for this gathering, along with Tyler's homecoming. Sean's worked between the plant and a garage since he graduated high school. And his family owns a restaurant on Main Street, which is a Triple Falls community staple. Though Sean speaks like he's an open book, his eyes hold so much mystery as if his words oppose his thoughts.

A full plate of barbecue later, my limbs grow heavy from every look we exchange. Unable to fully play immune, I steal glances at him when he becomes distracted by the late arrivals pouring into the back yard. The party is getting more aggressive as the sun threatens to set, and conversations grow louder. Another half-drained cider in hand, I stand in the middle of the yard by his side, the backs of our hands brushing as Sean chats with Tyler and Jeremy.

Rattling with anticipation, I'm only half-listening to their conversation, too swept up in the 'what if' these stolen touches could lead to, and the circulating warmth from the booze. It's when Sean purposely slides a finger along the side of my hand that I feel that prickle again. It's a distinct and unshakable feeling that I'm being watched.

Newly paranoid, where I was just at ease, I look in every direction for the source, searching through the crowds until my blue eyes collide with slicing silver-grey…but it's not just the eyes that bind me where I stand—it's the predatory look inside them.

Sean's words drift through my cloudy head. *"We don't want to let the wolf get a whiff."*

I have a feeling it's said wolf who's caught my scent and is eyeing me from feet away.

The party bustles around him as we stare off and he comes into full view. It's the third time I've been hit today with attraction, and I stand awestruck by just how much I'm feeling it.

I still can't make it past his intense stare as he considers me like he's contemplating his next move.

And in the next second, he's coming right for me.

Holy Shit.

I lift my chin, as he treads through the yard, a dark haze shrouded in masculine beauty. Just past a prominent widow's peak, lays long waves of rich-looking, thick onyx hair, equally dark brows above silver eyes filled with auspicious intent. Between high-cut cheekbones is a sleek nose and…his mouth.

Looking fresh off the runway, he's dressed in black from his

T-shirt to his lace-free army boots, the tongue in them falling limp, much like mine, the closer he gets.

My body spikes with adrenaline, and I fight myself not to look away but lift my chin higher to spite the unspoken threat dancing in his eyes. But no mean mug I could ever muster could save me from the dominance in this man's swagger and the chill that emanates from his stare.

"Shit," I hear Sean mutter when he finally reaches us. "I told you I have her, bro."

Soul stealing eyes break from mine, freeing me from their hold before he speaks, his voice deep and full of authority. "She's a fucking baby, your boss's daughter, and she's done drinking. Here anyway." He turns to me. "Time to go."

I frown. "Don't be a pooper."

I go over the words in my head. *Yep. That's what I said.*

I swear I see his lips twitch before he barks at Sean. "She's leaving."

"Chill, man. Cecelia, this is Dominic."

"Dominic," I say, utterly mystified.

Jesus, Cecelia, tweens have more game.

"My brother made an error in judgment bringing you here. You need to leave."

"You're brothers?" They couldn't be more different in appearance.

"Not exactly," Sean corrects from my left.

"You're really going to kick me out?" I ask Dominic, lingering in the jolt I felt in those seconds. Maybe it's the stout cider, but my palms are still tingling from the exchange.

"Are you, or are you not, Roman Horner's *eighteen-year-old* daughter?" His lips curl around the words in disgust, a tinge of an accent lacing each one. Our audience grows, and I audibly gulp as the air around us becomes thick with tension.

"I'm sure I'm not the first underage girl to drink at one of your parties," I snap, feeling the eyes of everyone on me. He could have taken Sean aside and told him to get rid of me, instead he's decided to openly embarrass me. "And I turn nineteen in two weeks," I add with the weakest of arguments.

Dominic's expression morphs into one of boredom.

"Have I offended you in some way, and anyway, how old are *you?*" I ask as he gives Sean a withering stare while some unspoken communication passes between them.

"Why?" his gaze cuts back to me. "So you can write it in your butterfly and diamond-studded diary?" I hear the echo of laughter around me and my cheeks heat.

Jesus, Cecelia, stop talking.

"Let her stay, Dom," Layla speaks up from the patio. "She's not bothering anyone."

His eyes scour me from head to foot before he jerks his chin in a silent order.

"Dom, come—" Sean speaks up next to me, and I hold up my hand.

"Whatever, I'll go," I glare at Dominic, shifting my weight from one foot to the other, thoroughly humiliated. This pleases him, and I see my cowardly reflection mirrored in his cold steel eyes.

He turns to walk off, and I stop him, my hand on his forearm while I down the rest of my cider before dropping the empty bottle at his feet.

"*Oops,*" I say in my best bottled blonde imitation.

Gritting his teeth, like my touch is blistering, his eyes slowly drift up to mine, his dark brows slashed in a 'what the fuck?' expression.

"You know, you could say it was nice to meet me. You are kicking me out of your party. It's the polite thing to do."

"Never been accused of being polite."

"It's not an accusation," I snap, as Sean curses and starts to drag me off. "It's common decency, arsehole." Clearly, cider gives me a drunken British pirate accent when I've had too much of it, or I've been watching too much BBC. I giggle with the rush of a buzz as Sean lifts me into a fireman's hold.

"And what a pretty arsehole you are," I drawl.

Laughter comes from all sides as Dominic's full lips twitch in something close to a smile, and I struggle against Sean to let me down. "I am trouble, you know," I smart, as a catcall sounds from my left. "Just ask your *brother*." Sean's chest bounces against my thigh as I'm carted through the living room and out the front door.

Once he's carried me to the driveway, he sets me on my feet, an apologetic smile already in place as he glances over his shoulder.

"What the hell is his problem?"

"I warned you," Sean says with a grin. "He's mostly bite, no warning bark."

"He didn't have to embarrass me."

"He gets off on it, I have to admit, that went a lot better than I thought it would."

"I thought it went pretty shitty." I slur, realizing just how hard the cider has hit me.

He frowns, studying me carefully. "I'm going to drive you home, okay? I'll pick you up to get your car in the morning."

"Fine," I huff as he opens the door for me. Sitting in his seat, I cross my arms, furious. "I feel like I just got put in timeout." I turn to him. "I'm not a confrontational person, like at all. Sorry, I don't know what came over me."

"Dominic could bring the claws out of a nun."

"You don't say."

Sean chuckles, shutting his heavy door before looking over to me with sympathy.

I sink in my seat. "It's my dad, isn't it?"

He nods. "He employs nearly half the people at that party."

"It's not like he deals with the day-to-day at the plant."

"He's got a long reach."

"Yeah, well, I make it a point not to tell him a damn thing. You can trust me. And I am an adult."

He taps the lip I hadn't realized I'd pushed out. "You're fucking adorable. And beautiful. But let's be honest, a little too young and good of a girl to be hanging out with us assholes."

"I've been to plenty of parties, I just never really partake. And I *like* you assholes. Just not *that arsehole*."

"Sure about that?"

"Not a fan." That's not entirely true, I appreciated the hell out of him until he'd opened his mouth.

"No?"

I slowly shake my head as he brushes the hair away from my shoulder. Sean's effect on me is potent, and I feel the draw to lean into his touch as he gazes at me. I know my guard is down because of the booze, but I can't blame it all on the alcohol. He's disarming, and the attraction is definitely there.

"Then you're stuck with me," he says, his voice dropping as he cups my jaw and brushes his thumb over the small divot in my chin.

"Fine with me." When he slowly withdraws his hand, I feel the loss of his warmth and busy myself buckling my seatbelt, my head spinning from the turn of events. "Thank you for today. I had fun."

He turns the engine over, and the feel of the vibration against my bare legs sparks a fire inside me. Sean reads my excitement.

"Like that?"

"Hell yes." I bob my head. "Never been in one of these."

He studies me, the air in the car growing dense.

"Tell me, what were you just thinking?" I ask, stealing the earlier question from Tyler, my voice a little hoarse from the inhalation of all the smoke and this sun god's rapt attention.

"Some other time."

He tears out of the driveway as I giggle in my seat—the ride home as exhilarating as the last few hours. Windows down, the wind whips my hair around my face as Sean speeds down the deserted roads that lead to my father's palace. Heavy bass thuds throughout the cabin, old southern rock wafting out of the speakers. I stick my hand out my window and air surf, my chest bubbling with possibilities as I steal a glance at Sean and see a promising gleam in his eyes while a subtle smile graces his lips.

It's the start of a great summer.

Chapter Four

"**G**OOD MORNING, CECELIA," ROMAN SAYS AS I JOIN HIM in the dining room. He sits at the polished table in a high-backed chair. The rest of the room is empty, save robin's egg and cream draperies that I know are worth a fortune. He's dressed in some designer or another as he skillfully plucks some grapefruit onto his fork.

"Good morning, Sir."

"I heard you arrive last night. Is there something wrong with your car?" He's displeased.

Tough shit.

"I'm having it serviced, and I'll be picking it up this afternoon." It's the only lie I can manage as I fight the urge to press my hands to my temples.

I had no idea that cider could be so potent. Passing on the small breakfast display, I duck into the kitchen—a Michelin star chef's dream—pull a bottled water from the fridge, gather some of the yogurt I requested his housekeeper buy, and snatch a few grapes. Back in the dining room, I peek out the window to see the front of the property lit up with the new day's sun. The house would be perfect for a family that enjoyed each other's company. It saddens me that it's wasted on a man who doesn't appreciate it.

"Your first day is today."

"Yep," I take the seat opposite him.

"Your word choice is not appreciated, nor is your lack of enthusiasm," he says dryly, scrolling through his phone.

"Sorry, Sir, I'm still a little shell shocked from the move. I'm sure I'll have more when I'm fully awake."

He eyes me, and I see some of myself in our shared dark blue, along with my inherited chestnut hair. "Do you have everything you need?"

I nod. "Anything I don't, I can grab myself."

He sets his phone down and regards me with the authority of a parent, which is both laughable and irritating. "I want you to take advantage of this year. *Really* weigh your options. Have you decided on a major?"

"Not yet."

"It's getting late."

I glance at my new Apple Watch, a first-day gift he had waiting on the threshold of my door last night when I got home. I'm still deciphering if it was a hint on the schedule I agreed to keep or a kind gesture. "It's only eight a.m."

"Don't be coy."

I wink at him. "Learned from the best." That's a lie. I haven't learned a thing from this man, except time is money for him, and both seem to be better spent elsewhere. I pop a grape in my mouth. "Thank you for the watch."

He ignores my appreciation, his jaw tensing. "I got a call from HR."

I slump in my seat and swallow. "Oh yeah?"

"What were you thinking with that comment?"

"I wasn't, Sir. And I assure you, it won't happen again." And it won't. I've spent the majority of my life on the right side of things, and it's always been by choice. Sean was right. I'm far more good girl than rebel by decision. I've seen one too many of my peers go the other way, and it did not fare well for them. Not at all. However, nothing about this exchange is sitting well with me. Any authority my father has right now over my life, I'm granting him, and hating it. It would be so easy to push away from the table and claim my life back, and the year he's stealing. But it's more than money, it's my mother's welfare dangling over-head, so I straighten my posture. "I'm looking forward to it, hon-estly. I just may have overdone it a little last night."

"Not really what a father wants to hear."

It's on the tip of my tongue to say, 'where's this father you speak of?' but instead I play nice.

"Just blowing off a little post-grad steam. If it eases your mind, I only had three girl beers, and I'm not much of a fan of drinking, or anything else for that matter."

"Good to know."

You know nothing.

"Who brought you home?"

"Just a local."

"Ah, does he have a name?"

"He does. Friend."

And that's the end of our discussion. I make sure of it.

Coast is clear.

Sean: I'll be there in thirty.

I'll be out back swimming. Join me if you want. The gate code is 4611#.

My first jump in the pool is glorious. I make sure of it by do-ing a cannonball and screaming a curse at the top of my lungs. It just seemed like the right thing to do. I don't know enough about my dad to discern if he's satisfied with his life, but I'm pretty sure he's not happy.

Happy people can't pick up pennies with their ass cheeks. He's too high strung, a trait I've inherited, and am determined to try and rectify. But if this year is all about getting into his good graces and being on my best behavior, I'll wait until I'm left to my own devices to ensure a quiet rebellion. Everything about my time here so far feels calculated, like everything is in its place, the feel and look of perfectly combed hair that I'm dying to ruffle up. If I'm a rebel at all, my fight is against the monotony. Maybe that's why I felt so at home at that party. Everything about that group screamed lawlessness, at least in the parental sense. And this time—my time—between graduation and college should be the time I have the same freedom. I spend the first half of my morning deliberating on how to steal some of what's being stolen back.

My dilemma has a simple solution. From now on, I'll say yes more often. To whatever and whomever I choose. Playing it safe my first eighteen years has proven to be flavorless, if not a bit fruitless. I don't want to move into the next phase of my life or the one after regretting chances I didn't take. So, this summer I'll trade no for yes. I'll trade playing it safe for playing, period. I'll toe the grey area, which includes my obligations to my parents and figure out a way to swirl in a little color for myself.

I'll take this year of confinement and mix it with some much-needed liberation, not only from my responsibilities, by from my own self-inflicted moral code.

Free time will take on a whole new meaning for this wallflower.

I seal that deal with myself with a leap into the pool.

I'm several laps in when I see the blurry reflection of my new arrival. Breaking the surface, I manage to stifle the gasp that threatens when I spot Sean in swimming trunks, a lit cigarette in hand, standing at the edge of the pool.

From the mere sight of him, I have the urge to cross myself in the Holy Trinity and send up a prayer of thanks. He's ripped, in every sense, from head to toe, from the razor-sharp cut of unruly hair to his obscene pecs, to the extra pebbled muscle flaring just next to his ribs. The delicious trail of golden hair leading past the waistband of swimming trunks accentuated by arrows of his deep V. It's as if the devil himself and his physique made a deal, giving him zero room for anything other than golden flesh and muscle. Hovering above, he oozes with sex appeal on dry land as I drown in the sight of him. Even with his chunky gold glasses covering his eyes, I can feel his stare, and it's a shot of adrenaline straight to the chest.

"Miss me, Pup?"

"Maybe."

He leans down cupping water to snuff out his cigarette, and it's the first time I can clearly see the tattoo on his arm. The feathered tips belong to a raven with stretched wings taking up the whole of his upper arm, the head and beak rest against his bicep, facing away from him as if watching his back. The menacing and lethal claws at the foot of the body embedded in such a way it's as if they're anchored painfully into his skin. The ink is so vibrant, so bold.

It's as if it's a separate entity from him. Like if you were to reach out and touch the intricately defined feathers, the bird will react.

"Nice place."

"Thanks, I'll tell the owner."

He looks around. "You really don't want to stake any claim in all this?"

I shrug. "I didn't earn it."

He shakes his head and lets out a low whistle, scanning the grounds. "So, *this* is how the one percent lives."

"Yep, and trust me, it's just as foreign to me as it is to you."

"How so?"

"We've been estranged for years. I had to outgrow my adolescence before *he* decided we could have a relationship again."

"That's shitty."

"Enough about Roman. You swimming or not?"

Dropping his T-shirt and smokes, he dives in, and I turn in time to see him emerge, a river pouring from his thick blond strands, sliding down his impressive chest.

He lifts to stand, towering above the water line, marking his height an inch or two above six feet.

"How you feelin' today, lightweight?" He asks, his faint drawl distinct, like perfectly edited punctuation.

"I feel…like I got drunk off a few chick beers. And maybe a little embarrassed."

"Don't be. You made an impression."

"Couldn't have been much of one, I got kicked out." I tread water, feeling the burn of the sun on my back.

"That wasn't you, it was Dom, trust me."

"So, tell me why you quit the plant the first time."

"I was working at the garage, but Dom graduated from college and came back to claim my spot."

"Dominic just graduated?"

He hikes a brow. "You judged him that hard, Pup?"

"Maybe, but he's a dick. Where did he go to college?"

"Just got his masters from MIT. Computer geek. He's an evil genius with a keyboard."

My interest only grows. "Really?"

He lifts one side of his mouth. "You impressed?"

I stand stunned, not at all able to picture Dominic on any school campus just as Sean cuts his hand along the water creating a tidal wave that drenches me.

I sputter out the water in surprise. "You ass!"

"You're in a pool." He lifts a thick brow. "Bound to get wet."

His statement is loaded with insinuation, and I know Christy would have a field day if she saw this guy. I can hardly believe he's standing in Roman's pool.

I move to engage in his play and turn swiftly instead, pulling myself from the water before adjusting my bikini to make sure I'm covered. I picked the less revealing of the two I own, but I might as well be naked with the feel of his eyes on me.

"Where are you going?"

"I'm thirsty? You?"

His eyes dip to the water dripping from my neck. "Sure."

"Water? Tea? Grape juice?"

"Surprise me."

"Surprise," I say, stripping the water from my hair with a towel before wrapping it around me and widen my eyes. "It'll be grape juice."

"Living it up today, huh?" His smile is blinding. I fight the urge to ask him to take off his shades. Walking toward the house, I can feel the tension coiling, and I know the goosebumps on my skin have little to do with the air hitting my wet body. Once inside, I carefully trek over the sea of polished marble and peek outside to see Sean hoist himself up on the side of the pool, lighting a cigarette, waiting for me. Fighting the urge to text Christy, I bury my face in my hands and feel a smile building beneath. Though I've only had two partners, I'm not an innocent girl. In fact, when I became sexually active, I surprised myself with my thirst, my sexuality, with my fascination for the act itself, and the unexpected cravings after, but this attraction is on another level.

Opening the fridge, I grab two bottles of grape juice and again glance outside. When I was seventeen, I had a horrible crush on Brad Portman. The feelings that stirred in me when the attraction was returned were some I knew could never be topped. Later, when he kissed me for the first time and fire exploded in my chest and belly before trickling to my core, I was sure nothing could come close to that euphoria, nor the feeling of when he closed his eyes tight with pleasure and pressed inside me, claiming my virginity.

Those feelings and memories, I swore would remain the hottest moments of my life, until I walked outside, juice in hand, to see Sean lift his sunglasses.

Chapter

Five

"**B**LUE MADONNA" BY BØRNS CROONS FROM MY CELL phone on the lounger as I wade through the water at the deep end. Sean stands propped against the wall on the opposite end. His powerful arms stretched along the concrete behind him, his eyes trained on me as mine drift to the midnight ink on his arm.

"So, what's the deal with the tattoo?"

"Deal?"

I roll my eyes. "Some of your friends have it too, *a lot* of them. What does it mean?"

"It's a raven."

"I'm aware of that," I say, my thighs and calves starting to burn from lack of exercise. "But what does it symbolize? Is it like a…best friend thing?" A giggle escapes me.

"You makin' fun of me, Pup?"

"No, but you don't think it's a little weird you share a tattoo with *that* many grown men?"

"Nope," he pops the 'p' sound. "Think of it as a promise."

"A promise of what?"

He shrugs. "Whatever promise it needs to be."

"Do you always answer questions in riddles?"

"It's the truth."

His eyes dip as I swim to the middle of the pool, my chest inches above the waterline, before lifting back to mine, the look in them enough to have me taking a mental picture.

"You want to tell me what you're thinking all the way over there?" His question dries my tongue.

"I'm thinking I don't know a lot about you."

"Not much to tell. I told you I moved here when I was young. It's a small town. As you can imagine, we came up with creative ways to occupy our time."

"That's when you met Dominic? When you were kids?"

He grins. "I was wondering when you'd bring him up again."

"Is he always like that?"

"Like what?"

I wrinkle my nose. "Abrasive?"

This earns me a chuckle. "I think you know the answer."

"So, what's his problem? Mom didn't hug him enough?"

"Probably not. She died when he was young."

I wince. "Shit, I'm an asshole."

"So is he. And he doesn't apologize for it, so you shouldn't either."

"So, you're all just friends with a promise? Why a raven?"

"Why not?"

I roll my eyes. "I'm getting nowhere with you."

His smooth voice clouds my vision. "Why don't you stop hiding behind the water and come a little closer, then I can get a better look at you."

"I'm not hiding," I hear the squeak in my voice and want to drown myself.

He lifts his chin in silent order, and I slowly inch my way closer. His posture stays relaxed as he sinks into the water so that his lips crest just above the smooth surface.

He's still feet away, but his effect is lethal, my arms feel like lead now as I swim toward him. Predatory hazel eyes roam over me as if he's deciding where to sink his teeth in first. I love it, the draw, the sizzle growing in the chlorine perfumed air. I'm in way over my head with this one, and we both know it.

"Penny for your thoughts?" My voice is shaking. The tension is too much. When I'm within reach, he strikes, capturing me by the waist and pulling me to stand before him. I yelp and then giggle as his eyes glitter over my chest, his breath hot on the triangle between my thighs skimming the surface. My nipples draw tight as his fingers ghost along my hip. He's still crouched in the shallow end, while I stand above him, his every exhale hitting the thin material at the apex between my legs, whispering over my clit. I fight a moan.

"You want my thoughts?" He whispers roughly, "Is that what you want?"

I slowly dip my chin.

The rumbling of an approaching car snaps me out of my stupor, but Sean drags me right back in when his knuckles drift in a light dance along my stomach.

"I'm thinking we don't have enough time for this discussion." His voice is jagged as he tilts his head, his hand pushing the soaked hair away from my chest as he slowly stands to tower above me. He's so close, the droplets of water like diamonds on his skin. My eyes trace a few scars on his pecs and biceps as I run my tongue along my lower lip, my core tightening in anticipation.

He leans in and presses a kiss to my temple, his fingers

sliding down my shoulder with his whisper. "Thanks for the swim."

Drawing my brows, I hear the repetitive roar of an engine out front.

"Wait…what about my car?"

"Parked out front."

"You drove my car here? But you don't have a key."

"Worked at a garage, remember?"

"So, you're a locksmith too?"

His mouth hitches in a smirk. "Sure."

"Well then, thanks, I guess."

"You're welcome, I *guess*," he mimics me perfectly, including the disappointment in my tone. I'd wanted him to kiss me, and the arrogant bastard knew it. I can sense his high from my frustration. He's playing games. It should anger me, but I like this game too much already. He lifts himself from the pool, grabs his T-shirt and pulls it on. Disappointment thrums through me as he slips on his glasses, pulls a cigarette from his pack, tilts his head, and flicks his Zippo to light it. Glancing down at me, he lets out a plume of smoke. "See you at work."

"**W**HAT SWEET HELL IS THIS?" I MUTTER BENEATH MY breath as I grab another tub. I'm making calculators. Correction, I'm doing quality control on Horner Tech's newly manufactured calculators. It only took an hour into my shift to make the decision not to piss away college and start critically thinking about my future. This is not my dream job, not by a long shot. Not long after I started my shift, I formed a respect for my co-workers. I'm sure it's not their dream job either, but they do it religiously to provide for their families, and in no way can I fault them, nor judge them for that, regardless of how unsatisfying the work is for me.

But this can't be my future.

I'll go fucking insane. Three hours in, I'm glancing at my watch and again cursing the position I'm in. A year of this?

Not only that, I've been commissioned to work with the

Chatty Cathy next to me, who appears to be the plant gossip and works at the speed of light, making me look like a fumbling toddler. All I have to do is give her a nod and she seems satisfied with the return conversation.

It's when I'm in my fourth hour that I smell the familiar scent of cedar and nicotine. His breath hits my ear.

"How's it going, Pup?"

I turn to see Sean mirroring me in wardrobe, khakis, and a short-sleeved collared button-down, which doesn't do a damn thing to take away from his appeal. He's got a clipboard in hand as he grins down at me. Ms. Chatterbox's eyes volley between us, her interest piqued at the exchange.

"Pure adrenaline," I deadpan, and he laughs as I scratch my ear beneath my hairnet.

"You need tunes," he says, eyes widening at the woman beside me. He must be aware she's got a motor mouth.

"I thought those weren't allowed?"

"We might be able to work around it."

Sean is technically my supervisor, which will make the job more bearable. He told me he worked at the plant for several consecutive years prior, earning him seniority, which he didn't lose when he left. He'd only attended orientation that day as a formality and to brush up on plant policies. And right now, I can't think of a better position to be in than beneath him.

We silently stare off until he nods past my shoulder. "Missed one."

"You're distracting me," I say cheekily.

"Good to know," he gifts me a slow wink. "See you in a bit."

When he's at a safe distance, Chatty, whose real name is Melinda, gives me the side-eye as she grabs another tub from the stack just dropped off at our station. "How do you know Sean?"

I shrug, stacking up the empty tubs. "We met yesterday at orientation."

"You be careful with him. And steer clear of his friends, that dark one they call the Frenchman," she leans in, "I've heard... *things* about him."

"Really?"

The Frenchman.

It has to be Dominic she's speaking about. I detected a hint of an accent when he spoke and have little doubt there's truth to her warning. I'd been introduced to that infuriatingly gorgeous, dark cloud last night. He's the mirror opposite of the spiked sun-ray that's been taking up my thoughts today.

Melinda looks to be in her early forties. Everything about her screams of southern values. From her old school perm to her high-waisted mom jeans to the cross draped around her neck. After just a few short hours of listening to her, my conclusion is that she's not only the plant gossip but the town gossip as well, and no secret of mine will ever be safe with her. I have no doubt I'll make it into her future dinner conversations.

"Yeah. They don't mess around. Fast cars, parties, drugs, and girls." She leans in close. "I hear they *share* women."

This bit of news is far more interesting than her dear friend Patricia's boating accident last year and the fate of her eleven-year-old cocker spaniel. "Really?"

She leans in even closer. "I hear they smoke the weed."

I can't help my giggle. "That wacky tobacky, huh?"

She narrows her eyes at my condescension. "I'm just saying, be careful. One of them got ahold of my cousin's goddaughter, and let me tell you, it wasn't pretty."

I can't help my bite.

"What happened to her?"

"No one really knows, and no one has heard from her in

months. That boy broke her heart so bad she rarely comes home anymore."

She pulls her cell phone from her pocket, darting her eyes around because phones are forbidden on the plant floor. She scrolls through before she lifts a picture. It's from a social media profile and the girl displayed on the screen is gorgeous. I tell her as much.

"She was the pride of my cousin, but once he got his hooks into her, she changed. I don't know." She glances over her shoulder. "Those boys, pretty as they are, I think might have the devil inside them."

From my first and second impressions, I find it hard to believe that's true of Sean, but Dominic might be a different story.

As wrong as it may be, I sidle up to Melinda for the rest of the shift, suddenly in the mood for conversation.

Chapter
Seven

BACK ACHING FROM LONG HOURS ON MY FEET, I UNLOCK MY car and practically fall into the seat, turning on the AC to get out some of the humidity in the interior. Tilting the vents my way, I let the warm sticky air dry on my face before I pull my phone from my purse and see I missed a text from Christy. I can't help my smile when I see I also missed one from Sean.

> **Sean: Come to the garage. I'll ping you.**

> **It's been a long day. I think I'll just go home.**

> **Sean: Bullshit. You can sleep in tomorrow. Pizza's on me.**

Sean pings me the location and I weigh my fatigue against the rush of seeing him again. Decision made, it takes me ten minutes to get there, and when I pull up, I'm shocked by the size of the garage. Next to a glass-enclosed lobby are six bay doors, the largest at the end, I assume for commercial machine repairs. It's nothing like I imagined. A few of the cars I saw at the party sit outside in a large lot. Stepping out of my car, I hear music blaring from the other side of the dented bay doors. Clearly, business hours are over, with little sign of life inside aside from a dim light in the lobby. As I approach, an unmistakable smell invades my nose.

These devil boys are smoking 'the weed.'

I giggle as I take down my hair and run my fingers through it. There's absolutely nothing to be done about my uniform. I approach the door to knock and see Dominic on the other side of the double-paned window with a King's Automotive logo in bold, shielding much of the glass. The sight of him stops my curious footing as I drink him in. A lock of dark hair cascades over his forehead as he furiously clicks the side of the mouse on his computer underneath a stuttering yellow light, a lit joint between his perfect lips, and an open beer next to his monitor.

His lashes are so thick. I can see them dancing over his high cheekbones from feet away. He's a fucking marvel to look at. His broad chest is cloaked in a grey T-shirt with the logo along with a few grease spots that trail down to his dark jeans. I can't see this man looking bad in anything. Studying his hands, I imagine the damage they could do or the pleasure they could give. As if he can sense me watching, he looks up, and our eyes meet.

Bang.

It's a shot right to the chest and my blood pumps overtime to keep up with the oxygen I'm now deprived of.

He studies me just as intensely for a few seconds before he moves toward the door. Jerking it open, he stares down at me, his expression unreadable, the joint hanging loosely from his lips when he speaks.

"What are you doing here?" His voice is slightly raw as if he's been yelling all day, then had a hot shot of whiskey after.

"I was invited."

"Allow me to uninvite you."

"Why?"

He blows a plume of smoke from his lips, and I turn my head to avoid it.

"You don't belong here."

I'm not leaving. That much I know. Thinking on my feet, I pluck the joint from his lips and pinch it between my fingers. His eyes deaden as I take a timid pull on it, fanning my hand repeatedly to get the rest of the smoke away from me as quickly as possible.

"This tastes…" I inhale, "fucking awful." I choke, and cough on my exhale.

His lips quirk slightly before the smile is gone. "That's because you're trying to be someone you're not. You can't stay, Cecelia."

"I won't drink."

He takes his joint back. "Do what you will, sweetheart, but not here."

He moves to shut the door, and I stick my foot in it. "If this is about my dad, then you should know I'm not his biggest fan either, okay? I'm just a result of his *sinful fornication*," I mock in my best preacher man voice. "And them's the breaks," I glance around the lobby, "pun intended. He doesn't *own* this town. Or me."

He crosses his arms, my words not making a dent in his stance.

"He's not the sheriff, okay? Since I'm *new* in town, bored out of my mind and stuck here for a year, I could use some friends. Now, let me in before I play girl and whine to your brother."

"See that window?" He jerks his chin to the large window behind me.

"Yeah."

"What does that say?"

"King's Automotive." I roll my eyes, reading his intent. "Fine, you're the shot caller, right? Then let's barter, Mr. King." I take a step up, so that we're close, not quite nose-to-nose due to his height, but so that I'm invading some of his space. It's a bold move and I do the best to hide the shake in my voice. I pull a twenty from my pocket. "Beers on me tonight."

Another jerk of his chin. His spoon colored eyes unwavering.

I shove the money back in my pocket. "Come on, Dominic, let's be friends." Batting my lashes in exaggeration, I glance past his shoulder, hoping Sean will see me and intervene, but I come up empty. "What's it going to take to get in here?"

He doesn't move or speak but robs my confidence piece by piece by just standing there as I try my best to muster up some sort of alter ego worthy of this opponent. I can see by his unimpressed gaze that I'm failing miserably.

But he's right. I'm a wallflower trying to impersonate a mighty oak. However, I made promises to myself that I intend to keep. So, I do the only thing I can, I pluck the joint from his fingers and take a bigger hit before blowing it right in his face.

I'm so high from just two hits I swear I can see space. A deep rumble comes from his throat as he lets out an annoyed exhale.

To my surprise, the door opens, and in my spacesuit, I take a wobbly step inside. His voice covers me in goosebumps as he speaks when I move to walk past. "Don't make me regret this."

I present his joint back to him with pinched fingers, and he takes it. "I won't, but don't let me hit this again." I make it halfway to the door leading to the bay on the other side when he stops me.

"Cecelia." I could live every day of my life listening to the curl of his faint accent around my name. I glance back and see the warning in his eyes. I spent half my shift being lectured to about tangling up with these men, and it did nothing but intensify my curiosity. "I'll say this *once*. It's not smart, you being here."

"I know."

"Can't know much."

"Oh, mais j'en sais déjà beaucoup, Français." *Oh, but I know a lot, Frenchman.*

I may have taken French in high school, but I'm far from conversational. However, the payoff of those classes is well worth it to see the mild twitch of his lips and muted surprise in his eyes.

"Je ne parle pas français." *I don't speak French.*

He smirks, and I could die. It's utterly perfect coming out of his full lips. The indifferent ire in his eyes licks me with every second that passes before I break our stare due to the intensity alone. Turning back to the garage, I stumble a little as I make my way toward the door seeing the guys huddled at the far end in the last bay, shooting pool on an old coin table. Sean finally spots me, his warm grin lighting me up. "See you in there?" I look back at Dominic, whose eyes are on me, his take on me impossible to read.

All I get is a nod.

Chapter Eight

AFTER EATING MY WEIGHT IN PIZZA, NO DOUBT DUE TO the buzz, I steal another look at Dominic, who went straight to work on a Chevy after entering the garage. His shirt has ridden up, giving me the perfect view of the ripples in his stomach along with a hint of his V while he lays on a roller on his back. The bay I assumed was for commercial use turned out to be an after-hours lounge set up with leather couches that surround the ancient, ratty green pool table.

Tonight's gathering consists of Sean, myself, Russell, and Jeremy, whom I've learned also works at the garage with Dominic. I sit tucked into the corner of a long, beat-up, pleather couch next to Sean as Jeremy and Russell shoot a game. Southern rock croons softly in the background at Sean's insistence. He's to the left of me, his muscular thigh touching mine, arm draped behind me along the back of the couch. Between the heat of his body, his smell, and the sight of Dominic's bare midriff just feet away, I'm having a horrible time keeping my hormones and accompanying imagination in check. But my pheromones must be working overtime because I can't seem to escape the stares of the men I'm keeping company with either. I don't flatter myself they're interested, but just as curious about me as I am them and their collective raven tattoos.

Sean had said they were a promise, but I can't imagine what that means.

I've timed my glances at Dominic, feeling a little like a creeper with the amount of attention I'm giving him. He's the quietest, making him the most enigmatic of the four.

Much like Sean, it's just not natural for a man to be so fucking enticing. As many times as I've glanced over, I haven't managed to find a single thing my eyes disagree with.

"So, you hate the plant, huh, Pup?" Sean drawls as I watch Dominic sift through his toolbox.

"Stop calling me that," I say, elbowing him in the ribs.

"Nope, the nickname stays."

"It's just...so fucking boring," I sigh. "Good thing I'm a creative daydreamer." I dart my eyes away from Dominic, just as his cold gaze lands on me from where he lays beneath the truck.

I look over at Sean still perched next to me. "But, I do like my supervisor."

"Oh yeah?"

"Yeah."

I have little time to appreciate the tension from our exchanged look when the door opens on the opposite side of the garage. Tyler stands in the threshold with a twelve-pack in his arms. "'Sup, fuckers?" His gaze zeroes on me, and his smile grows as I lift my hand in a little wave. He strides past the bays, lifting his chin in greeting.

"Hey, beautiful, you slummin' it again tonight?" He pulls a joint from Jeremy's fingers and takes a hit as Russell grabs the beer and adds it to a large cooler to ice it down.

"Not at all. And for the record, I grew up in a small ass house, not with a silver spoon in my mouth."

Tyler's eyes shine with interest as he moves to steal Sean's place next to me.

"No room," Sean says with an edge to his voice. A protective edge, and I can't help the increase in my pulse because of it.

"You forget, I'm the problem solver," Tyler lifts me easily and places me in Sean's lap, and I sink into it.

I feel right at home with these guys, as if I've known them for far longer than two days. It's the oddest thing. The only thing that feels out of place is the sensation coming from the man a few feet away. I'm overdue for a look when I let my eyes wander and see he's watching Sean's hands, his fingers, and how they're casually curling around me.

And when he slowly lifts his gaze to mine—static.

Tyler glances down at Dominic. "When you going to cut out, Bro? It's way past quitting time."

He darts his eyes away from mine. "Twenty."

"Is that exact?" I ask Dominic, who ignores my question.

"Probably," Sean whispers on his behalf.

"Let's clock him, shall we?" I set my watch to time him and Dominic shakes his head in annoyance. "So how long have you owned this garage?" I ask Dominic, trying to get him into the conversation.

"It's a family thing," Sean answers for him to spare me the rude silence of his reply. "Been around for years. Kind of like *your family business.*" There's a hint of a grudge on his tongue. It's becoming more apparent that my father isn't the most loved man in Triple Falls. It's really not a surprise. The looks I got today at the plant alone were enough to have me thinking of myself as an out-cast. Not even in high school had I felt as much like one as I did today. I was thankful for merciful Melinda and Sean being there, otherwise I might have locked myself in the bathroom until my shift was over.

Coming out and announcing I was the boss's daughter was a stupid move, but I can't take it back.

Head down, Cecelia. One year to freedom.

The second my watch goes off, Tyler moves from his seat next to me to shoot a game and Dominic takes his place, a maga-zine and leather bag in hand.

"Twenty minutes on the nose," I compliment him as he un-zips the bag and pulls out the contents, only to be met by more silence.

I heard they share women.

It's been echoing in my head since Melinda said it. But with Dominic's disposition, I can't imagine any scenario like that. Or is it my presence that offends him to the point he's closed off? He's got an obvious problem with me, and that's been evident since the moment we met.

Was that only last night? It seems like a lifetime ago, and yet I feel totally comfortable on Sean's lap.

Dominic sets the magazine across his lap before pulling out blunt wraps and a large bag of 'the weed.'

Growing up, I've never let myself get close enough to a group like this one. Always fearful of the repercussions. To them, this is just another night, to me, it's like entering a whole new world.

"Where did you go and what are you thinking about?" Sean whispers from beneath me, his fingers brushing my arm, launch-ing shivers in their wake.

I glance over my shoulder and our lips are only inches away when I answer. "Nothing, it's been a long day."

I feel him tense slightly as our eyes dance over each other in a dare. If he kissed me tonight, I would return it. That much I know. But the electricity surrounding me is enough. I'm drowning in testosterone, unsure where it's all coming from. For the first time ever, I'm being a little reckless with my signals, and I'm not sure I care. Sean is the first to look away, but his finger runs down my arm, and I sense he got my message. It's then I know, if he makes a move, it will be in private. I turn to scan the garage as they land in natural conversation, calling each other out like only family does, while Dominic skillfully rolls a blunt in his lap. I'm entranced while he soaks the paper with precise licks of his tongue, his eyes cast down, dark lashes flitting over his sculpted cheekbones. When his cloudy eyes lift to mine, and he runs his tongue carefully along the blunt seal, my lips part.

Fuck me.

Sean pulls me tighter to him, causing my legs to shift and Dominic curses, trying to save the weed spilling from the magazine resting in his lap. His eyes narrow on a laughing Sean. I sink into Sean's hold, a wall of hard muscle behind me as Dominic's tongue darts out again, skillfully re-wetting the paper.

Once it's lit, the music is turned up, and the conversation gets louder. From that moment on, I get high, but I'm not sure from which part of contact. Probably all three.

Chapter Nine

WAKE TO THE GENTLE CARESS OF KNUCKLES THAT SWEEP away the hair covering my face. I open my eyes to see Sean squatting before me, his hazel eyes filled with tenderness. I have no idea when I dozed off, but I catch the small amount of drool that threatens at the corner of my mouth as he gazes down at me.

"I'm going to let Dominic drive you home, and Tyler's going to follow in your car."

"What time is it?"

"A little past three."

"Shit, I was out that long?" I straighten, running my hands through my hair. I'm trying to collect my wits when I get an inkling of being watched and glance up to meet Dominic's stare. He's observing our exchange closely. I reply to Sean with my eyes still on Dominic. "Why is *he* taking me?"

He follows my line of sight. "I live just a few miles away and I need to close this place down," he replies gruffly.

I avert my gaze to him. "You don't sound happy about it."

He gives me that beaming smile as if he's shaking off some irritation. "I wanted to take you."

"So, you take me," I say, hoarsely clearing the rest of the sleep from my voice. "You don't work here anymore, right?"

"It's just tonight," he says, his jaw tightening.

"Okay." I stand. "But I can drive myself."

"Just let him take you," he says insistently. "You were out for a while. That's some potent shit you inhaled. Just to be safe."

I feel a slight unease. My brain still a bit cloudy from being inside the garage bong for so many hours, so I nod. I haven't mastered the mountainous roads, especially after nightfall, and I decide not to risk it.

Once outside, the fresh air hits as I follow a silent Dominic to a sleek black old body Camaro.

"Nice," I say as he opens the passenger door and I glance over and meet Sean's watchful gaze from where he's standing in the doorway of the shop. I smile and wave goodnight and see his gaze drift from Dominic to me before he feigns a smile back at me. I've seen enough genuine smiles from Sean at this point to know the difference. He's pissed. I glance over to Dominic and see his unforgiving stare on Sean before he ushers me inside his car and shuts the door. I've barely registered the exchange when Dominic slides into the driver's seat and starts the Camaro. Loud music blares, making me jump in my seat as the engine's purr tickles my senses. Dominic doesn't bother to turn it down, but does the opposite, cranking it up to ears bleeding volume, ruining any chance of conversation.

Prick.

Screeching guitar fills the cabin of the car as I shift my gaze over to him while he backs out of the driveway, his hand on the gear shift. He doesn't bother checking the rearview to look for oncoming traffic and whips us out like he owns the road.

Wide-eyed, I look back to where Sean was standing and see he's gone.

And then Dominic floors it, tearing out like a bat out of hell, his speed reckless. The transition smooth as he switches gears and floors it down every straightaway. It's the scariest fifteen seconds of my life from the time I decide to let the crippling fear go and embrace the ride. By then I'm caught up, wrapped in the exhilaration, my heart pounding as I throw my head back and a loud laugh escapes me.

I look over to where Dominic sits, controlling the car like an expert, knowing the give and take of every inch of the pavement, hugging the yellow lines like he's memorized every one of them. He doesn't so much as look my way, but I swear I see his lips twitch at the sound of my laughter. It curbs as I study him in the dim light of the cabin, the music pulsing through me, along with the feel of the motor dancing beneath me. Dominic is in his element, in complete control as he drives on through the pitch-black night. I can faintly see my own headlights behind us before they flutter out.

"Bundy" by Animal Alpha blares out of his speakers, a contrast to the eerily quiet night amongst the evergreens surrounding us. I place my hands on the dash, the feel of the stealthy car eating the road a lot like flying. Soaking in every moment, I swear I feel a shift in the air as I rock myself a little to the devilish beat. If driving this way is to intimidate or scare me, much to my surprise, he's failing miserably.

And in the length of a song, I let go, uncaring of his perception and let myself enjoy those few minutes of not being in control, of leaving my fate in someone else's hands. Since I've been in

Triple Falls and felt the space between my mother and me, I've realized my role in her life has been more of a reversal than I wanted to admit. I admit it to myself now, that I've been more like the parent than she has in the last nineteen years. I've been stricter on myself than she ever has been on me. I've willingly never given her a reason to worry. I've pulled the wine out of *her* hand, and ground out her ash-ridden cigarettes, and covered her with a blanket more times than I can count. I saved my virginity for someone I thought loved and respected me while secretly shaming her for her blatant promiscuity during my younger years. From the stories she's told me, she was the original party girl, and daily, I bore witness to the aftermath of her life choices. I've lived the opposite of her decisions, which I know gave her relief. But in this moment, just for a few minutes, I let all that go. With the wind in my hair, I close my eyes and just…fly.

And it feels fucking liberating. So much so that I find myself disappointed when the car begins to slow and Dominic turns onto the isolated road that leads to my father's estate.

Coming down from an unimaginable high that's far exceeded many of the adolescent thrills preceding it, we sit waiting until my headlights light up the otherwise abandoned road. When Tyler pulls up behind us, I punch the gate code in to allow both cars to pass. The arch-shaped iron gates open, and Dominic surveys the house in the distance as he slowly creeps down the driveway before circling the entrance. Stopped just short of the staircase leading to the porch, he turns to me, expectant.

"I don't know whether to slap you or thank you."

"You loved it." His tone is limp, but his eyes contradict it. He's looking at me with a mix of curiosity and dare I think, interest?

I decide not to thank him or encourage his rude behavior and exit the car, shutting the heavy door and meet Tyler, who now stands at the driver's side of my Camry with my keys hooked on his finger. I grab them and give him a soft, "Thank you." I'm suddenly drained from the white-knuckled car ride home and the long day behind me.

He gives me a wink. "No problem, see you around."

"Hope so." I glance back to Dominic who's scanning my house, his jaw set, his expression unreadable. I've never seen a man wear such an impenetrable mask. Christy's words ring in my ears.

Those were boys, find a man.

These guys aren't anything like the guys I knew back home. Sure, they seem just as arrogant, some of their routines the same, but there's something oddly different about them. I'm wondering now as I peer at Dominic if that's such a good thing. Sean's smile comes to mind, the brilliance of it, the light in his eyes and the way he takes care of me when I'm around him, whether I need it or not, and it puts me at ease. Dominic senses my intense stare and barely spares me a glance before jerking his head to Tyler to join him.

"Night, Cecelia," Tyler walks the short distance to Dominic's Camaro, taking my seat in the car. It's when he pulls the shiny black door closed that I'm snapped from the spell. The car is already speeding off into the distance by the time I make it up the porch and through the front door, thankful my father isn't there to greet me.

That night, I slip into bed and leave my balcony doors open. I feel the crisp night breeze flow through the room and it blankets my skin while bringing me back to the inside of Dominic's Camaro.

I fall asleep and dream vividly of hazel eyes, upturned lips, of blurring trees, and endless roads.

THE NEXT MORNING, WEARING A GIDDY SMILE FROM THE recollection of my dreams in the shower, I tread down the staircase with a rehearsed excuse on my lips, nerves firing off as I cross the foyer and walk into the dining room. I'm relieved when I find it empty. But that relief is short-lived when I hear the ping of my phone and see an email from my father, and the subject line, visitors. Roman Horner doesn't text—that's much too personal. He corresponds with his child through email.

> You're a grown woman, and I realize the conditions of your stay with me might be a bit stifling on your extracurricular activities due to your late schedule. That said, this is the second night I've lost sleep due to your late-night appearance and the noise of your arrival outside of my front door. From here on

out, do your best to see yourself home at night and be respectful of my house, Cecelia. Visitors are to be kept at a bare minimum. Also, I will be staying in Charlotte for the next few days due to my schedule. The housekeeper will be in today. Please let her know if there is anything you may need.

Roman Horner
CEO Horner Technologies

I fight the urge to send back an eye roll emoji. Instead, I fire back a 'Yes, Sir.'

I'm just about to FaceTime Christy when my phone rings.

"Hey, Mom," I say, making my way toward the kitchen to grab my yogurt.

"It's been two days and not a peep."

"I've been busy. I haven't called Christy much either."

"And that's supposed to make me feel better?"

"Yes. She's my first and last call of the day."

Silence. I'm guilting her and being a shit about it. She knows she hasn't been there for me since her life hiatus.

"How is it there?"

"It's fine."

"You know I hate that word."

"So far Roman is predictably absent. I really have no idea what you saw in him."

"It was a long time ago. A different life," her tone is somber, and I wonder if I'll ever understand how my existence came to be.

"You two are nothing, and I mean nothing, alike. How are you feeling?"

"Fine." I can hear the smile in her voice.

"Oh, shut up."

We share a laugh, and after it dies, her lingering silence puts me on edge. "Mom, you okay?"

"Does he talk about me?"

"No. We don't even discuss the weather. Why?"

"I just don't want him saying negative things about me."

"I wouldn't believe him anyway. He's not the one who raised me."

I hear her sigh. "That makes me feel better, I guess."

"You sure you're okay?"

"Yeah. I hate that you're there. I feel like I failed you."

"It was a spell. You're entitled to have one. We all are now and then, right?"

"Right. But if you hate it there—"

"I don't. I'm keeping to myself. It's like staying at an employee-free resort. I can handle this."

"You sure?"

For you, I can. That's what I want to say. "I'm sure."

"I love you, kid."

Chapter Eleven

MY FIRST TWO WEEKS AT THE PLANT ARE BEARABLE DUE to my supervisor and the extended breaks he grants me. Still, I hear the whispers of a few as I walk by, and there's no mistaking the sneer of a group of women who more than likely hate me for my last name. One in particular, a beautiful Latina named Vivica, constantly eyes me like my day is coming. The news must have spread fast throughout the plant that I was the owner's daughter because more and more of my smiles go unreturned.

The pacifist in me tries hard to ignore it, turn the other cheek and keep my head down. If I didn't already think of my time here like a sentence, now I have every reason to. Sean senses their looks as well, but no one questions him when he whisks me off the line, including Melinda, who may not verbally object but doesn't spare me her skeptical looks when I'm taken from our collective workstation. Though I seem to be public enemy number one, everyone at the plant seems to love Sean, and he has an easy rapport with most of the employees. The irony is that because I'm with him, I'm managing to get by, and it has nothing to do with my last name.

We haven't spent much time apart since we met. Whether sunbathing before our shifts poolside or spending our nights at the garage where the boys take turns teaching me how to shoot a game. Russell, Tyler, and Jeremy are always there, but Dominic is mostly absent. Even when he does make a rare appearance, he doesn't give me the time of day. Yet every time I catch him looking at me, his expression keeps me on edge. It's always a mix of curiosity and disdain. More than once, I've tried to summon the nerve to ask him what his issue is, and every time I've chickened out.

Since I arrived in Triple Falls, I've been wrapped up and around Sean, literally and often, in the oasis in my father's back yard. Each time we've gotten close to anything intimate, he presses a kiss to my temple, not my lips, and releases me. Several times, he's leaned in with his lips taunting me, and each time I'll catch my breath waiting, hoping his lips will drift from my temple or cheek to where I've spent ample daydreams imagining them. It's as if he's waiting for something other than the permission in my eyes to make a move. I've caught him numerous times, gliding his tongue along his lip ring while he's watched me in the way that says we're anything but friends. Butterflies swarm me when he's around, and my body draws tight every time he pulls me close. I've memorized his body, aching daily to shift our relationship from friends to more. His refusal to act on our chemistry is driving me up the wall. At the same time, I love the delicious anticipation, the feel of his eyes on me as I take a shot at the pool table, the feel of his fingers tracing the water on my skin. It's been frustrating and enthralling, and I find myself on the line often in the midst of a daydream while Melinda prattles on about her church friends, mostly the pastor's wife. And not in a flattering way. But since Sean's unexpectedly come into my life, when I hit the pillow, he's often with me in my dreams too. Opening my eyes, I find myself grinning as I recall the latest image of him wading toward me in the water, the sun dancing around him, illuminating him as he prowls toward me. Briefly, I entertain trying to sink back into that blissful sleep to continue our rendezvous when my phone vibrates with an incoming message.

Sean: Thinking of you.

What are you thinking?

Sean: All kinds of thoughts.

Care to get specific?

Sean: Some other time.

Coast is clear if you want to swim.

Sean: Good, cause I'm already in your driveway.

Tumbling out of bed, I race down the stairs and open the door to see Sean, his hair damp from a shower and laying in a beautiful mess at his crown, his arms crossed as he leans against his Nova. He's dressed in boots, shorts, and a black tank, and I take a mental picture as I stand there looking like God knows what.

I blush, combing my fingers through my hair. "I just woke up."

"You're beautiful," he stalks toward me.

I nod over my shoulder. "You can come in. My dad won't be home until later on today."

He moves to greet me with a kiss on the cheek and I shy away. "Morning breath."

"I don't give a fuck." He leans in and plants a soft kiss on my jaw, lingering while the air grows thick between us.

Breathless, I resist the urge to pull him closer.

"Do you have hiking boots?"

His question throws me. "Uh, yeah."

"Dress light and put them on. I've got something I want to show you."

"You're taking me on a hike?"

Hiking is the last thing I want to do with him.

"It will be worth it."

"This is beautiful," I pant out as we climb another set of boulders at the edge of the mountain. Muscles I haven't used in years scream as the foreign feel of moss brushes my shin while I try to scale the rock. Behind me, Sean spots my every move, his breath hitting my thighs as I glance down where he trails my lower half taking care to help me, in case I lose my footing.

"Couldn't agree more," he cups my ass with a hand to help me over a ledge of large rock. The clear insinuation of his tone spreads to my toes as I make it over.

"Where are you taking me?" I ask when I clear the last step and take in the view before he hauls himself up to where I stand, the large backpack strapped to him doing nothing to weigh down his climb. He grips my hand, lacing our fingers when he reaches me. "Not too far now."

I glance at my watch. I'm supposed to meet Roman for dinner, and I hate the trepidation I still feel when it comes to him. I'm eleven years old all over again. After several meals, we're no more comfortable together than we were when I arrived.

"What time is it?" Sean asks, eyes flashing my way.

"It's early."

"Do you have somewhere to be?"

"No, sorry, it's just my father," I release a stressed breath. "I'm supposed to have dinner with him later."

"But that's later."

"Right," I draw the word out to make it more of a question.

"So, your free time is now, here, with me."

I stop and draw my brows. "Uh-huh."

"So, you should be here, *with me.*"

"I am?"

"Is that a question?"

"No. I'm with you."

"But you're thinking about your dad."

"Can't help it."

"Sure about that?"

I frown. "Is this a test?"

"They say land of the free and the home of the brave," he mutters, shaking his head as he resumes our walk.

"Yeah, they do," I follow behind him. "Your point?"

He turns back to me. "I say, it's the land of the mentally inept, electronically dependent, and brainwashed media slaves."

"You just insulted me. Gravely, I think."

"Sorry, I'm just saying why waste *now* time worrying about later?"

"*Now* time?"

"It's the only measure of time that matters. Time itself is just an invisible line, a measure people made up, right? You know that. And while it's good for reference, it's also a major stress trigger, because you're letting it control you."

I can't even deny it. The idea of dinner with Roman is ruining my time with Sean.

"Okay, sorry."

"Don't be sorry. Just don't give it power. Now is now, later will eventually be *now*. Don't be a slave to the insanity of keeping time and keeping up. *Now* is the only thing you have control over, and even so, it's an illusion."

"You are one strange man," I laugh, shaking my head.

"Maybe, or maybe everyone needs to wake the fuck up and snap out of business mode. But they won't, because they're too cozy in the down comforters they bought from an Instagram ad."

"Now you're saying I'm too comfortable?

"Depends." He draws my arm to him, slowly unfastens my Apple Watch, drops it to the ground, and smashes it with his boot.

"Holy fucking," I gape at him, fish mouthed "...not nice!"

"How did that feel?"

I recover the destroyed watch from the ground and answer honestly. "It stung."

"Yeah, but what time is it?"

"Obviously, I have no idea," I snap, shoving the useless watch into my cutoffs.

"Congrats, baby, that's freedom."

"That's unrealistic."

"For you. You're still on a schedule," he presses a finger to my temple, "in there."

"I get it. You're saying I need to unplug, yadda, yadda, I'm sure there was a less painful way to make your point."

"Yeah, but you don't get it, you need to retrain your brain. I bet you would draw the line if I tried to drive my boot through your cellphone."

"Damn right I would."

"Why?"

"Because I need it."

"For what?"

"For...everything."

He pulls a cigarette from his pocket and lights it, pointing at me with it between his fingers. "Think about it critically. How many times have you needed it today?"

"To text you back, for one."

"I could have easily rung your doorbell. But I know you would get the phone before you ever got the door, and do you know why?"

"I was on it."

He nods.

He starts our trek again, and I reluctantly follow, still miffed about my watch. "So, I'm thinking you don't have social media?"

He sighs. "Fuck no. Hell no, the worst thing we've ever done is give everyone a microphone and a place to use it."

"Why?"

He pauses at a clearing and turns to me, his eyes void of any humor. "A hundred easy reasons."

"Then give me the best one."

He considers my question briefly, taking a long drag of his cigarette. "All right," he exhales, "aside from the slow and inevitable defilement of humanity, I'll give you a scenario."

I nod.

"Imagine a person born with an unparalleled gift of retaining knowledge. And in finding out they had this gift, they go straight to work, schooling themselves for years and years to hone that gift and turn it into a superpower, becoming a wealth of knowledge like no other, to the point they're well respected, a reckoning force, someone to *really* listen to. You with me?"

I nod again.

"And maybe that person suffers a loss. Maybe someone close to them dies, and that death poses a question they have no answer to, and so they make it their mission to answer that question and refuse to quit until they have irrefutable proof of *where* their loved one went. So, they live, eat, breathe every minute of every day of their life for the answer to that one question. And one day it happens. They succeed, and in doing so, they transform their theory to fact, and if they share that proof, they know they could change life as we all know it. And say this person could not only prove there was a hereafter, but could prove the very existence of God, no more faith necessary. He's real. So they have their proof, their life isn't meaningless, the death they've grieved isn't pointless, they have the answer, and they want to give it to others." He takes another drag of his cigarette and exhales a steady stream before lifting hazel eyes to mine. "They post it on social media so the world will *finally* have the answer to a question that's plagued people for endless centuries. What would happen?"

"We wouldn't believe them."

He slowly nods. "Worse. Betty Lou would debunk it in ten minutes, whether she was right or wrong because she's got millions of followers, and her opinion *is* God. Then this other person, the person with proof, facts, video, is nothing but another quack on the internet because Betty said so. So, millions of people didn't listen, and neither did their friends because Betty is *always right*. And still that quack who is so certain about *their truth*, who has bulletproof evidence, begs all the other quacks to listen but no one does because *everybody* is quacking because of all the microphones. And now, none of us will ever know God exists, and many will still live daily with the crippling fear of dying."

"That's so sad and..." I draw my brows, "so true."

With another exhale, he flicks the cherry off his cigarette

and grinds it out. "The sadder truth is that the only way to conquer the fear of dying is by *dying*."

"Jesus."

Sean grins. "You sure? Is *He* listening?"

I roll my eyes. "You're killing me."

"Why the turn of phrase? Does death scare you?"

"Stop playing on my words," I swat at his chest.

He chuckles, then shrugs while unscrewing his water bottle. "You asked. Just relaying a message."

"That whole spiel wasn't yours?"

He takes a healthy swig and then recaps it, darting his eyes away. "No. Not mine. Just another quack."

"But this is what you believe?"

His eyes meet mine, his gaze intent. "It's the one that makes sense to me. Rang true for me. It's how I live." He leans in. He's close, so close. "Or maybe," he pushes the sweat-matted hair away from my forehead and widens his eyes before giving me a blinding smile, "I'm just another quack."

"Probably," I say softly. "And you *do* obey the clock because you have to be on time for work," I point out.

"Got me there. But my free time is *mine*. I'm not a slave to time. And if I'm honest, my work time is mine, too."

"How so?"

He nudges me forward with his hand on my back. "Almost there."

"You aren't going to answer me?"

"No."

"You're unbelievable," I grumble. This man is absolutely nothing like I expected, and yet I can't get over what comes out of his mouth or the fact that I know he means and believes what he says. I don't think I've ever met anyone so confident in their skin, so sure of their place. My eyes glide over the perfection that is

Alfred Sean Roberts as he walks in contemplative silence beside me.

"So, what's your superpower?" I ask, a little breathlessly while keeping his pace.

"I'm good at reading people. Anticipating what they want. Yours?"

I spend a few seconds thinking about it. "I don't know if it's necessarily a superpower, but most mornings, I can remember my dreams...vividly. And sometimes, if I wake abruptly, I can resume them. Other times I will myself back into them."

"Pick up where you left off?"

"Yeah."

"That's cool, I sleep so hard, I never really remember mine."

"Sometimes they hurt," I admit, "so much so that it can ruin a day of my life just from the feelings they evoke. So, it's not always good."

He nods, his eyes scouring the trees before looking over at me. "Every superpower has a price, I guess."

We've been off the beaten path of the specified trails at the mouth of the mountain for what seems like forever. Once we clear the next set of rocks, I marvel at our surroundings and my new back yard. I've spent weeks driving around the narrow roads and steep inclines of the mountains and not once thought about breaching the trees to see what's inside. Fully submerged, I never expected to be so enamored by the tranquility, the cool air, the organic smell, or the sweat covering my skin. I look over to Sean with fresh eyes.

"You'll make a mountain hippie out of me yet."

"Let's hope so."

Somewhere between the time I saw him standing at his car this morning and the few hours we've spent on our hike, I've let a part of me I've kept locked away for years, my romantic heart, begin to hope. Sean's made it far too easy to give it a reason to peek around the corner of the bitterness I've buried it behind. With every look, every touch, every easy exchange of words I feel that beckoning, letting me know it might be safe to come out and take a look around.

But we haven't been in this long, whatever this is blooming between us. Even if Sean declared time our enemy, I'm all too aware that trust is fragile and can shatter in an instant. Time has told me it only takes seconds to be made a fool. In my short experience with men, I've been cheated on, lied to, and humiliated, and I have no intention of letting that happen again if I can help it. I don't at all have a good track record with trusting my instincts when it comes to men. And after my last disaster, I promised myself I would be more cautious. The next man who wins my heart, my affection, will have to do a lot more to deserve it than offering pretty words and petty promises. Yet that promise I made to myself and my new determination for a temporary jailbreak don't mesh well. Sean is one tempting apple in my celibate new garden. Physically, I want him. And it's clear the feeling's mutual. Maybe I shouldn't think past that.

"What are you thinking?"

"Just glad I'm here."

He gives me a side-eye. "I'm calling bullshit."

"I haven't...dated in a while." I'm not sure it's the right word to use.

He glances over at me. "And?"

"And it's been a while, that's all."

"What happened with the last one?"

"You first," I say as he steps over a fallen tree limb and easily lifts me to clear it.

"My last girl was Bianca. She was manipulative, so it didn't last long."

"Manipulative how?"

"She wanted to control me. I don't do well with that. She wanted to manipulate my now, but I found myself trying to escape her more than I wanted to tolerate her. I ended it. Your turn."

"He cheated on me in a club bathroom, on my eighteenth birthday."

"Ouch."

"Yeah, he was an asshole. To be fair, I was warned about him. My best friend Christy hated him, but I didn't listen," I give him a pointed look. "And I was warned about you too."

He rolls his eyes. "I knew I should have gotten you earbuds."

"Melinda sure does like to talk."

"She only knows what she thinks she knows."

A few more steps in and I pause at the sound filtering through the trees. "What is that?"

"Come on," he guides me through another clearing of thick brush and around a corner. My jaw drops and my eyes widen when I see a waterfall looming a story above us, behind it sits a hollow cave, if it can be called that. The interior of it is completely visible behind the water, making it more of a nook.

"Oh my God, I've never seen one of these."

"Pretty cool, huh?"

In minutes we're standing behind it, the water flowing into a shallow pool at the bottom. I turn to see Sean setting down his pack, laying out a thick blanket.

"We're picnicking behind a waterfall?"

"Cool, isn't it?"

"So awesome." I step back as he unpacks, refusing my help and eyeing the spread as he pulls out different containers. Cheese and crackers, granola bars, fruit. It's simplistic, but the gesture alone sets my heart aflutter. He pulls out a few water bottles before stretching out a hand to me. It's a dream, a living dream, this gorgeous man with sun-drenched skin and luminous eyes, reaching for me, along with the scene surrounding us. Resisting the urge to tackle him, I join him on the blanket a few rocks digging into my butt as I settle in at his side, drinking in the view.

"This is incredible."

"Glad you like it. There are other falls around, but this one is private."

"It's private because we're trespassing in a state park," I point out with a grin. "In case you missed the 'No one past this point' sign."

He shrugs. "Just more imaginary lines."

"Like time, huh?"

"Yeah, like time." He pushes the sweaty hair away from my forehead. His voice coated in warmth when he speaks. "Happy Birthday, Cecelia."

"Thank you. It's cool you remembered."

"You said you had one coming up, and I checked with HR on what the date was."

"This is so much better than what I had planned," I say, breathing in the cool mist drifting from the waterfall. A small cloud of a rainbow shines below on the rocks and I take a mental picture. I wouldn't want to be anywhere else.

"What did you have planned?"

"Reading." I glance around. "But you sure make that seem like a sad plan." I gaze over at him and free the question I want answered most. "Are you for real?"

He frowns, pulling open a container and popping some cheese into his mouth. "What do you mean?"

"I mean…are you really *this* nice? Are you going to turn into some raging dick in a couple of weeks and ruin all of this?"

He seems completely unfazed by my question. "Is that what you're used to?"

I don't hesitate. "Yes."

"Then, I guess it depends."

"On what?"

"Can you keep a secret?"

"Yeah," I lean in, my fingers itching to return the gesture and brush the sweaty blond hair from his forehead.

"Good."

"That's it?"

"Yep."

"You're talking in riddles again. Are *we* the secret?"

He reaches out and pulls me to him, my back to his front and grabs a piece of cheese, offering it to me. I take it and chew, leaning into him, enjoying the view and the feel of him behind me. He's so attentive, so disarming, so incredibly good at putting me at ease that I loathe the thought he's anything but the guy he's shown me to be.

It's then I feel his hesitation.

"Whatever it is, please tell me now. I'm serious. I would rather know."

His breath tickles my ear. "I don't do things the way most people do when it comes to *any* aspect of life. I follow my gut, my instincts on everything, and answer to very few."

"What does that mean exactly?"

"It means I belong to *myself*, Cecelia, at all times. And I choose carefully who to spend *my* now with. I'm selfish with my time and sometimes, about the things I want."

"Okay."

"But whatever choices I make, I work with, with little regret, no matter the consequence."

"That sounds…dangerous."

Another beat of silence.

"It can be."

Chapter Twelve

After our picnic, we dozed off on the blanket. I'm the first to wake on Sean's chest where he lays now, sprawled out on his back, hands tucked behind his head, eyes closed, breathing deep and even as I quietly pack up the containers and scrape my hands free of debris.

Cleaning up is the least I could do. It's been the perfect birthday, though some of his truth stung a little. If I'm interpreting him right, he's not the boyfriend type, or the commitment type, though his actions in the last few weeks of knowing him have been contradictory. He's still a mystery even though we've spent a good amount of time together. But it's no longer my need to define us that has me staring down at him in wonder. It's the ache, the throb, the need to get closer that has me studying the definition of his biceps, the muscular expanse of his chest. My fingers itch at my sides to trace the ring glistening on his lush mouth. It's my tongue that's eager to trace the Adam's apple at his throat. I want him, in the worst fucking way, and I find myself resenting him for the fact that I'm this strung out, while he seems completely at ease.

I pull off my top, leaving on my sports bra and bring it to the cascading water drenching my shirt before I wipe off the sweat and dirt I collected on our hike. Sean lays content on the blanket as I brush myself down all the while imagining what it would be like to touch him the way I want to, to kiss and be kissed by him.

He says he's a man who takes what he wants, who follows his gut with little regret and doesn't worry about the consequences. I wonder how he would feel if I were to be so bold with my body's current demand. I resume my seat on the blanket, just watching.

I'm creepy. Right now, I'm the creepy girl watching him sleep. I turn away, heat flushing my cheeks as I run a hand down my face. We're completely alone. Did he want it that way? But we've been alone before, many times.

My head says don't embarrass yourself, but I decide to take his advice. In one swift move, I straddle him, lean down, and tentatively run my tongue along his lip ring.

His reaction is instant, his hand shoots up and grips the back of my head as he lifts and holds me just an inch away, running his nose along mine, as my breath catches. His eyes penetrate as he drinks in the look on my face, his voice filled with pure lust when he finally speaks. "Took you long enough." Then his mouth is on mine, his groan filling me as he thrusts his tongue past my lips, kissing me so deep, wetness floods my core. Mouth never leaving mine, he flips us easily, transitioning me so I'm on my back. As he tugs at the button on my shorts, his erection presses into my hip while he slowly pulls down my zipper. Utterly confused by his fast pace and his reaction to my kiss, I open for him, his hot mouth drawing me in. He rips his lips away and moves a hand between my shorts and panties, one finger gliding along my clit. Mouth parted, he hypnotizes me with that lone finger, moving it slowly up and down.

Up and down.

The pad of his finger alone sends shockwaves throughout my body as he pulls away, and gazes down at me with crippling intensity.

A loud moan erupts as he keeps his touch feather-light, and I grip his hand, urging him for more, bucking my hips for friction.

"Please," I whisper. "Please."

"No fucking way, I'm taking my time. You took yours."

"I didn't know that's what you wanted."

"The hell you didn't. I was letting you make the decision."

"You were," my eyes roll back with the next stroke of his finger, "waiting for me?"

"I wanted you sure."

My body thrums with white-hot desire as I gaze up at him. "I'm sure."

He grins as I grip his hand with my fingernails and dig in, urging him on. "Sean, please."

Finally, he slips that thick finger underneath my panties and groans when he finds me soaked. I go blind with need and feel my thighs shake as he resumes his ministrations with the same gentle assault. It's not enough friction, and he knows exactly what he's doing.

I grip his hair and pull it, and he smirks, his eyes lit with lust, his finger still teasing. It's not enough, not nearly enough. I thrust my hips and groan in frustration, just before he starts to pull himself away.

I'm being punished for my impatience.

Bastard.

"I'll stop. I'll stop. Please don't." I give no fucks about begging. It's been way too long since I've been touched, and never in the history of all my nows have I ever been so attracted to a man.

"Sean…" I whisper as he reads the desire in my eyes before he leans down kissing me deeply, so thoroughly, that emotion stirs within me. In seconds I'm drunk, my need raging out of control as I clutch him to me.

It's too much.

And when I'm blazing under his touch, he finally presses a finger into me, watching intently as my back bows.

"Goddamn," he murmurs, before leaning down and sucking my neck before trailing his kiss just below my ear. "Tell me what you want, birthday girl."

"I want your mouth."

"Where?"

"On me."

"Where on you?"

"Anywhere."

He moves to withdraw his finger.

"Between my legs. Right now."

He lifts, jerking my shorts down and discarding them behind him before spreading my legs. Lowering his head, he licks me smoothly over the silk between my thighs.

"S-s-Sean!" I stutter out as he teases me, drawing my clit into his mouth through the fabric as I pound on his biceps, my need getting the best of me.

His eyes dart to mine, an infuriating smirk on his lips. "Is this what you want?"

"I want your mouth on my pussy, your tongue inside me."

Painfully long seconds later, my panties sit somewhere on the rock behind me as he pushes my thighs apart, stroking the skin with his fingers before dipping his head and tasting the whole of me with one swipe of his tongue. I let out a welcoming shriek as he digs in with precise licks, nothing behind them but wicked intent. Writhing on the blanket, I let out an arsenal of curses as he slips a finger in, crooking it along my G. It took me months to figure out how to orgasm alone, practice to pinpoint the parts of my anatomy that set me off, and this man has managed to find them all within mere minutes. Superpower on full display.

He laps me up, stealing my ability to communicate, my shaking legs draped on either side of his head. Hazel eyes peer up at me as I grip the blanket in my hands and squirm due to the workings of his magic mouth. He licks me furiously as I buck in response, heart hammering, covered in a sheen of sweat. He rubs his fingers along my walls, teasing, torturing, before shoving them into me in beckoning. I explode, convulsing as I lose myself, calling his name as he jackhammers his tongue along my clit. He continues to lick as I shudder until I'm begging for him to stop, too sensitive for any more. And despite my tightening thighs around his head, he sucks my folds into his mouth, taking in every last drop of my orgasm. It's filthy and perfect, and when he lifts to kiss me, I lick his mouth, sucking his tongue with fervor. I run my hand along the length in his shorts, feeling his reaction. Dipping my hand in, I glide my fingers along his taut stomach and moan when I discover a smear of precum. He wants me just as much, and it shows as I wrap my hand around his impressive length for only a second before he lowers his body, denying me access. Satiated but intent on more, I stare up at him with the longing I feel.

He shakes his head. "Today is about you."

"Trust me. It would be for me. It's okay to be selfish," I reply breathlessly.

He stops the hand I reach for him with and kisses the back of it.

"Sean, I'm not innocent."

He threads our fingers. "No, but you're *more*. A lot *more*."

"You truly mean that? Considering what you confessed earlier?"

"You took that the wrong way."

"Meaning what?"

He peers down at me, cupping my cheek with a warm hand, sliding his thumb along my mouth. "Meaning with you, right now, I'm feeling a little selfish."

"Is that a bad thing?"

"It's a very bad thing."

"How so?"

He drops his head on my stomach and groans.

My heart blossoms when he lifts his head to peer up at me, and we exchange a look, the rawness in his eyes lets me know I've made as much of an impression on him as he has me. In exchange for his silent confession, I give him an ounce of my trust. No more words necessary.

It's on the return hike back to his car, where he takes great care to lift me into his hold, stopping me here and there for a kiss, lulling me with deep strokes of his tongue that I know I could fall for Alfred Sean Roberts. And today, a small part of me does.

Sean: Thinking of you.

What are you thinking?

Sean: All kinds of thoughts.

Care to get specific?

Sean: You're beautiful and completely unaware of just how much. And you taste so fucking good.

What are you doing to me?

Sean: Not nearly enough. Come to the garage.

I'll be there in an hour.

It's been days since the waterfall and he's barely touched me intimately since. He's wrapped up in me constantly when we're around the guys but leaves me every night with a chaste kiss, his mixed signals driving me up the wall. It's as if he's waiting for... something I can't put my finger on. But instead of complaining about it, I've played along because, honestly, I'm enjoying the ache and anticipation. I've never been much of a fast girl, but my attraction to him makes my inhibitions hard to hold. The boys of my past have nothing on this man. Nothing. And these days, when I look at my reflection, I see the noticeable afterglow of the weeks spent draped in his attention. It's a high I'd almost forgotten about, a high that's more addictive to me than any drug could ever be. My heart has some scar tissue, but it beats steady, constantly letting me know that playing his game leaves it vulnerable, and somewhere in the back of my mind, I hear the warning. For now, I'm playing blissfully ignorant, all too ready for another hit.

"Can you put the phone down while we dine?"

I tense in my seat, feeling Roman's stare and shove my phone into my pocket before lifting my fork.

"Sorry, Sir."

"You are clearly distracted this evening."

Because I'd much rather be in the now with Sean. I don't know why Roman insists we dine together. Conversation is forced, our shared meals unbearably uncomfortable, at least for me. It's hard to gauge what makes Roman uneasy because the man is impenetrable stone. He's always annoyed, but that seems to be his only discernable emotion—if he's even capable of emotion. The longer I'm in his house, the more like a stranger he feels to me.

"What were your parents like?"

I've never asked about them before. Not even when I was younger. Even when I had my youth to fall back on for false bravery, I knew better than to ask. They were both deceased, that's the extent of what both Mom and I know.

Roman draws a perfect bite of pasta onto his fork. "What specifically do you want to know?"

"Were they as outgoing as you?"

His jaw clenches and I congratulate myself but steady my features.

"They were socialites, and my father kept regular attendance at the golf course."

"How did they die?"

"They drank."

"Poison? They go out in a Shakespearean way?"

"You find death amusing?"

"No, Sir." *I find this conversation amusing.*

"They died not far apart. Three years. They had me when they were in their forties."

"You got a jump on them in that sense, huh?"

My mother was twenty when she had me, and Roman was older by twelve years. He'd dipped into the honeypot.

"I never planned for children."

I give him jazz hands. "Surprise. It's a girl."

Not even a twitch of a smile.

"Tough room," I sip my water. "Sorry about the diapers, couldn't be helped." I'm positive the man never changed one of my diapers. Not one.

"Cecelia, do you plan on behaving this way all night?"

"One can only hope." *That you don't destroy my soul with your death glare.*

"So, no parents, no girlfriends. Do you have a friend to hang out with?"

"I have associates. Plenty of them."

"So, what does Roman do to let his hair down?"

Another side-eye. I'm getting nowhere.

"Dinner was delicious, but I do have some pressing plans tonight. May I please be excused?"

He doesn't hesitate. "Yes."

As I flee the dining room, I swear I hear him echo my sigh of relief.

A little over an hour later, I enter the garage, and Tyler's dimple greets me first. His eyes roam over me as I delight in his attention. I took special care tonight, soaking my body in lotion mixed with juniper essential oil. I styled my hair in beach waves and bronzed my skin so it shimmers, even in the muddled yellow lamps above. I went light with my makeup, so the freckles Sean told me he loves, shine through. But my lips I colored hot pink to match my new sundress.

"Damn, girl, you're smoking," Tyler says, greeting me with a warm half hug as Sean converses with Dominic on the far side of the garage away from everyone else. Even with the purposeful distance, their aggressive voices are muffled as Steve Miller croons out, "The Joker." The conversation looks tense, so I decide to leave them to it. Jeremy greets me next with the lift of his chin and an appreciative sweep of his eyes as he takes his shot at the table. Jeremy is shorter in stature, but I can tell his second home is the gym. He's bulky, solid muscle beneath his simple clothes, but he wears them well. He's got the trendy man beard thing going on and sports suspenders over his T-shirt. His brown hair is cropped shorter, unlike Sean's, who's got that struck by God's lightning hair.

"Up for a game, Cee?" Jeremy drawls before he taps the nine-ball in.

"You mean another ass whooping?" I ask as my eyes roam from his raven tattoo to the black beanie hanging from his back pocket. Even though the temperature cools considerably after sundown, it seems out of place for the start of summer.

"You planning on robbing someone tonight, Jeremy?"

He pauses and then resumes chalking his cue before shoving the beanie deeper into his pocket. "Already did."

"Oh yeah?"

He winks, and Tyler chuckles. "The only thing you robbed tonight is your mom's dresser."

Jeremy glares at Tyler. "Are we doing your momma tonight? Because I think we know how that ends. And for me, it's always a happy ending."

"Shut the fuck up," Tyler snaps. Russell, who I consider the second mute next to Dominic, grabs a stick and chalks it. "Tyler, you know *no one* can do *your* momma quite like Jeremy can."

I look to Tyler, who seriously looks pissed. "Is there really a story there?"

"No," Tyler snaps, more toward the others than to me. "They're just fucking with me."

"If that's what you have to tell yourself to sleep tonight, *son*," Jeremy smirks and turns to me. "He's a Momma's boy. But I think we need some more quality time to remedy that. Daddy knows best."

Grinning at their back and forth, I look up to see Dominic watching me as Sean talks a mile a minute. A spark runs through me at his scrutiny. We haven't spoken since the night he let me into the garage. Every time I get close enough, he shuts me down, blatantly ignoring me as if I'm not speaking directly to him. Sean tells me not to take it personally, but with his constant shunning, and the looks he gives me, it grates at me. I shift my attention to Sean, despite the awareness of Dominic's stare and study him, remembering the feel of his kiss, the look in his eyes, the way he'd consumed me with his mouth, with the promise of more. And that's what I see when he finally turns in my direction. His hazel gaze travels appreciatively down my body before a faint smile graces his lips.

Shivers run down my spine when he looks at me this way. It's as if we know what's coming, and we aren't the only ones aware of it.

"You two need a moment alone?" Russell snarks snidely, catching our latest exchange before lining up his cue to the ball and taking his shot.

"Here's an idea, shut the fuck up," Sean says easily, just as he reaches me, pulling me to him. The man has confidence in spades, a smile that could melt the panties off a nun, and eyes that convey everything without him speaking a word. Every day I become more drawn to him, and every day I feel the tie that's beginning to bind us. Actions over words, that's what I'm taking with a grain of salt over Sean's cautious words on my birthday.

"Missed you," he holds me to him tightly as I bask in his arms, my eyes meeting Dominic's behind his shoulder before he pushes out the back door of the garage without a word.

"Why does he hate me?"

"Ignore him."

"Kind of hard to."

"He's good at that," he says, softly pressing a brief kiss to my bare shoulder. "You look beautiful," he leans in and inhales, damn near drawing a moan from me. "Smell good too."

I turn my head so our lips are close. "Thank you."

"This for me?" His knuckles run up the side of my dress, and the ache starts at my core with the memory of rocks digging into my back, cascading water, and his wicked mouth. He reads my thoughts, his eyes flaring, and this time I'm the one who's brandishing the canary-eating smile.

"Maybe."

"Trouble," he murmurs. I bite my lip and I swear I hear a faint groan.

"We playin' or what?" Russell snaps us out of our intimate bubble. Sean rolls his eyes as we break apart and he fishes two beers out of a nearby cooler. I accept one, knowing I'm not going to drink much of it. The minute he cracks his beer, and the music gets turned up, I grab my stick and the games commence.

And I'm horrible. Despite my best efforts, my depth perception is off, way off to the point it's embarrassing. And the guys have no issue razzing me about it. After scratching my way into another loss to Jeremy, I push my lip out and head for a seat on the couch, instead opting for Sean's lap. He allows it, running a welcome hand down my back.

"I suck."

"You do," he agrees.

I grind my elbow into his side.

"Easy now. It takes practice," Sean murmurs as I lean back into the stroke of his hand. The rhythmic feel of his fingers lulls me into a state of want as I watch him crack up with his friends. After another few games or so, I'm completely absorbed, in his smell, his hands, the timber of his voice, the feel of him. Everything about Sean turns me on, not just the way he looks but also the workings of his mind. It's a draw that has me dizzy, aroused continuously, and enraptured in a way I'm not used to. Sean, in a way, is a new drug. More potent. More addictive and altogether just…more.

He turns to me, seeming to read my thoughts and his grin widens. "Something on your mind, Pup?" He's well aware of exactly what I'm thinking, but I don't play into it.

"I'm… Will you teach me how to drive?"

"You know how to drive."

"No, like you drive."

My eyes rake his face and lower. And we share a second or two, lost in those seconds in that cave. I know he's there. His body draws tight as I lean into him.

"Please?"

Wordless, he stands, holding me to him as he nods at Tyler. "We're going to take off."

Grinning, I wave goodbye at the guys before following him out of the garage and into the parking lot. He pulls his keys from his pocket and tosses them to me, I catch them easily, as a thrill runs through me.

"You're really going to let me drive?" I eye his prized possession.

"Let's see what you got."

Amped, I slide into his car, loving the feel of the wheel at my fingertips.

Sean glides in next to me. "Know how to drive a stick?"

I nod. "My mom had one. I learned on it."

I check the car is in neutral and turn the engine over, giving it a chance to warm up.

In my sundress, I appreciate the cool feel of the bench seat beneath the material on my thighs.

"How did you guys manage to find all these classics?" I glance around the cabin in awe of the state of it. It's been perfectly restored.

"They were all in my family, my uncle collected them, and when he died, we restored them. That's how we all got started fixing cars."

"They're so rare. Aren't you guys ever afraid to wreck them?"

"What's the point of having something if you don't use it?"

"Good point," I say, securing the ancient seatbelt around my waist and run my finger over the SS on the wheel. Doubt creeps in and he drowns it out, his reassurance falling easy from his lips. He's not nervous, which makes me less so.

"It's just a car. Easy on the turns, these weren't made for mountain roads."

"That's true, so why do you drive them?"

A flash of teeth. "Because we fucking can."

I shake my head at the pride in his eyes.

"You're such a man."

"Thank you. Now, you'll get used to the give on the wheel, but take your time in figuring it out."

I nod, studying the gear shift and frowning. "This isn't like the one I learned on."

"Take it slow," he says, running a finger over the hand I have on the shift, "we've got all the time in the world."

I grin over at him, and my breath gets stolen by his expression, the thump in my chest a sign of growing invitation. The cabin fills with tension, the good kind, as he rests comfortably on his side of the car.

"Ready?"

"So fucking ready," he murmurs, before pulling his hand away.

Within a few grinding seconds of the clutch and a wince on my part, we're off.

Sean guides me through the first few minutes, his voice gentle and assuring as he helps me navigate my way through the winding roads. Once we're safely away from sharp turns, I give it some gas, and he gives me a few more pointers, while I memorize the clutch pattern.

"You've got it."

"Not quite."

"No," he says, running a hand down my shoulder. "You've got it. Open it up." I shiver under his touch and glance over at him catching his wink in the dim cabin.

Music thrums low through the speakers and Sean lifts from where he sits, turning the dial on the dash. "Good one," is all he says as he cuts all communication letting me know the lesson is over and I'm on my own.

The Black Crowes begin to bellow, "She Talks to Angels," as I'm granted my freedom, and I take it, anxious for the high. Between the music and steady buzz of the car, my whole body erupts in goosebumps. I can feel the smile on my face as the wind whips through my hair.

We're flying, my heart soaring as I switch gears, surprising myself with the ease in the transition before I hammer the gas.

Sean doesn't flinch, doesn't move next to me, his trust mine as I begin to sing along with the lyrics, with him. I'm somewhere between screaming and singing when his fingers push away the thick hair at the nape of my neck and stroke down my arm. Senses heightened, my body sighs into his caress. He covers my neck, my arm, and slides his hand down to where his hand covers mine on the gearshift before drifting back up, and then he strokes my chin with his knuckle. My pulse skips when he slides the spaghetti strap of my sundress down, his fingertips ghosting over my skin.

My lips part at the touch, as I begin to slow and peek over at him. One second passes, then another, before I'm turning onto one of a dozen deserted roads and shoving the gear into neutral and pulling the brake. We sit there, feet apart, his fingers stroking, coaxing me into a frenzy as I wait.

"Look at you," his voice needy and urgent.

"Sean," I moan hoarsely, already soaked as his fingers draw me further under his spell.

Hesitation coils off him, and I can clearly feel it as he toys with me, leaving me wanton and on the verge of snapping.

The tension builds along with the heartbeat at my core as my eyes implore him to do precisely what he's thinking. I see the decision in his eyes a second before he says, "Fuck it." In the next, I'm in his arms for a breath before we collide. His kiss is anything but gentle as he pushes his tongue past my lips and wholly explores my mouth with deep thrusts. It's as if every look, every touch, every subtle exchange has led us up to this moment. Rightfully starved, I allow my hands to roam, gripping the T-shirt at his biceps as he pulls me flush to him, and I lift my leg and straddle him, wanting to get closer, the rush of adrenaline clashing with insatiable need. We kiss and kiss, alone in the car on a nameless road, hearts hammering, our fast breaths mingling as he hikes my dress up to my hip and I grind on his lap, licking into his mouth, tracing his piercing with my tongue.

"Fuck," he grits out on a breath between kisses. He flicks the other spaghetti strap of my dress down a second before he yanks the material freeing my breasts, my pebbled nipples drawing tight, the ache unrelenting. He cups each in his calloused hands, his kiss deepening to level insane as my clit pulses, begging. I grip his hand and move it to my thigh beneath my skirt and feel only a second's worth of hesitation before he knuckles the silk and lace fabric between. He dips into the elastic, shoving my panties to the side and I gasp into his mouth as he roughly shoves two fingers inside me. My moan fuels him as he twists his fingers, fucking me roughly with them.

"Sean," I gasp out, hooking my arm around his neck to ride his hand. Reaching down, I palm and squeeze his erection and feel his groan as he pushes me back against the dash, ripping my arm from around him. He rests me on his knees as I set my elbows on the dash, just watching him. Dress still hoisted around my hips, he grips the flimsy triangle of material between my thighs and rips the crotch away. Eager, I move in to release him, but he swats my hand, unbuttoning his jeans and freeing his cock before pumping it in his fist. My mouth waters at the sight of it, the sight of him coming undone.

He lifts, pulling out his wallet and plucking a condom from it before he hands it to me. I rip it open and grip his silky skin in my hand, pumping him from base to oozing tip before I roll the latex onto him. Once fitted, he runs a finger between my folds, playing with the gathered wetness at my core. A cool breeze drifts through the car as he grips my head with his palm and pulls me in for a kiss, a second before pushing me onto my back, twisting to settle between my legs and driving into me until he's buried. I quake at the feel of him as he thrusts into me mercilessly. The slapping sound fueling me, I lift my hips to meet his. He grips my hair with his fist as he drives into me and I moan at the sting and the reward of his fucking. Lifting his T-shirt, I run my hands over his muscled chest as he gazes down at me, his eyes lava, his heart pounding against my palm.

"Damn...you..." he grunts, picking up his pace, "you are so much trouble."

Filled to the brink, I fumble to get his shirt off and he discards it with ease. Free to roam, I take in every detail, the timber of his grunts, the feel of his skin, every nuance of his build and lock my legs around him, meeting his hips before tossing my head back. He's deep, so deep. I can only hold onto him and allow myself to be ravaged. He consumes me wholly, with his scent, his face, his body, his cock. He pushes my crooked thigh against the seat, diving deeper and I scream his name as he goes feral, his hips picking up at an unimaginable pace as he burns through me.

I blink and his hand dips between us, his fingers kneading my clit as he pounds his cock along my walls, lifting and angling himself just so. The orgasm sneaks up and I explode, the entirety of my body shuddering with release as he drives in once, twice and comes, his jaw slack, eyes firing emerald in the soft light of the cabin. I run my fingers along his biceps as he gazes down at me, wordless. His golden smile returns before he covers me in a soft kiss, his fingers loosening their grip on my hair and I'm lifted from the seat by the sweep of his arm and brought to his chest.

"That escalated quickly," he says with a chuckle.

"Mmhmm," I murmur, hearing the fatigue in my voice.

"We have a problem," he mumbles into my neck, as I massage his sweat slickened shoulders.

"What's that?" I ask, unbelieving I let it, no, *willed* it to go that far.

He lifts his head, peering up at me where I gather myself in his lap. "I only had that one condom."

"We have all the time in the world, right?" He nods into my shoulder, a haunted hint shadowing his eyes when they meet mine.

"Right."

"What's wrong?" His gaze clears and he shakes his head, his shoulders going lax.

"Nothing," he strokes my skin, cupping my breasts, "nothing at all," he repeats, before claiming my mouth possessively. In his claiming kiss, I get lost.

Chapter Fourteen

LAUNDRY.

For the past fifteen minutes, that's what Sean and I have been sorting. And not just Sean's laundry, but Tyler and Dominic's as well.

"Is there a reason we're washing your roommate's clothes too?"

"Why not?"

"Because it's their laundry, that's why."

"You do shit for your friends, right?"

"Yeah, like picking up the dinner check once in a while or painting their nails. I don't spray and wash their thongs."

"This is better."

"How so?"

"Because who likes doing laundry?"

I do. I like doing laundry, because of Sean. He makes menial tasks a hell of a lot more fun, especially when he runs his crotch along mine where I sit perched atop a washer, leaving me wanton, wondering if it was purposeful before his lips lift.

Bastard.

He plays mind games with me all the time, which keeps me on my toes. A lot of the time it's wordplay, most of the time sexual suggestion I would miss if I wasn't paying attention. But I don't miss it, because Sean edges me, constantly, sometimes to the point of tears, until I'm begging.

He's a bit of a sadist, and I love it.

Every part of the last week has felt like the honeymoon phase of our relationship, or whatever this is. I haven't spent much time thinking about it because he's given me no reason to worry. Though he's shit at phone conversations, rarely ever keeping his phone on him, leaving my texts unanswered for hours, we spend most of our *now* time together.

He loads coins into the slots as I glance around the rundown room full of battered machines. "You do have a laundry room at home, right?"

"Your point?"

"Just saying, you guys probably would save money, in the long run, buying used machines off the web or something."

He locks his strong arms around me and leans in, running his nose along mine. His sunglasses rest on the crown of his head, a heather grey T-shirt stretches along his muscular chest as he crowds me. Fingering the waistband of his jeans, I inhale his sunshine scent deep, lost in the feel of him and almost forgetting about our conversation. Indecent as it may be, I lock my legs around him, my shorts riding high up my thighs.

He looks down between us, running his knuckles along the flesh of my inner thigh. "I love your long legs and this place right…" he grips my hair and gently tugs, exposing my neck before placing a soft kiss at the hollow of my throat, "here."

"Hmmm, what else?"

"I'll give you the CliffsNotes."

He kisses the skin just below my ear and then lifts my hand, pulling my wrist to his lips. He runs a finger along the top of my tank, just above my cleavage and traces it slowly before cupping my face, running his thumb along my cheek.

"This face of yours," he murmurs, planting soft kisses on my forehead, my eyelids, tracing the faint freckles on my nose before settling on my lips. His gentle kiss draws me in before he deepens it, capturing my moan as I melt into his hold. He doesn't give a damn about the perception of others. He's constantly touching me in public and private—no holds barred, no shits given. He claims me daily and holds little back now as he possesses my mouth fully, while I sink into him. I've never known affection like this, not ever.

He's made every man preceding him a liar and shamed them within just weeks of his attention, his affection.

This is why I love doing laundry—or *anything*—with Sean.

With him, I'm in a constant state of arousal and intrigue. The man is oddly fascinating, and I'm never sure what's going to come out of his mouth next.

"I don't save money."

Case in point.

"Why is that?" I pull away.

He does little more than lift a brow in reply.

"Ahh, let me guess, there's no other time than the present. You're a man who lives without a single thought of the future."

"I'm pressing that in more ways than one," he murmurs into my neck.

I draw my brows, and before I can question him, he speaks again. "I'd much rather give it away than save it."

"Why? Is money imaginary too?"

He pulls back, grinning at me. "Now you're getting it."

I cup the back of his neck, running my fingers through spiky swirls of blond. "Is there any law you abide by?"

"My own."

"A lawless man with no future. And you say *I'm* dangerous."

"You have no idea how much," he says, hauling me off the machine. "Come on. I want a cigarette."

We sit in his car, facing the shopping center, our view between watching the traffic of the laundromat and the Mexican restaurant next to it. Inside, a woman stands in a corner on the other side of the glass, rolling out fresh tortillas. Smiling, she kneads the dough before flattening it out and tossing it on a burner next to her work-top. I get a little lost just watching her as Sean flicks his Zippo, his one cigarette turning into two and then three before he excuses himself from the car to tend to the laundry. I offer to go with him, but he tells me to sit tight. I do, lost in the monotony of watching the older woman make tortillas. Her job is just as repetitive as mine is at the plant. But where I steadily watch the clock until the proverbial whistle blows, her serene smile hasn't budged, even when she's not talking to her coworkers or the patrons that constantly greet her. She's content, happy, and seems completely at ease with her task. I envy her, wishing I had the same peace at my job. Sean rejoins me and—without a word—lights another cigarette, the sharp slap of his Zippo the only sound in the car.

"This woman has been making tortillas the whole time."

"She does it all day and all night."

"That's crazy."

"It's what she does. There are a ton of people out there with jobs just like it."

"I know, I work one."

"Yeah," he exhales a cloud of smoke, "but she doesn't begrudge her work."

"Got me there. She hasn't stopped smiling."

We sit for endless minutes, just watching her. "I can't imagine why she's so happy."

"It's a decision," he says easily.

"A decision." I consider his statement and see he's watching her just as intently. "Do you know her?"

"Her name is Selma. She brings her van into the shop sometimes."

"Does she pay with imaginary money?" I joke.

"You could say that. We don't charge her. The clothes are ready."

"I'll help."

He opens his car door and jerks his head. "Sit tight."

"Sean, I've been watching this woman make tortillas for like two hours."

"So, keep watching," he shuts his door.

I slump in my seat, annoyed with his orders but nonetheless stay put. In minutes I'm lost in thought, mulling a little over our earlier exchange in the laundromat.

"You're a man who lives without a single thought of the future."

"I'm pressing that in more ways than one."

Dominic. It's the only conclusion I can draw. He's been a total prick since I showed up at his house. He's going to be a problem, I can tell, just by his hostile stare and blatant disposition. I decide to ask Sean about it later while I watch Selma finish turning a fresh batch of tortillas with her fingers over the flame. When she's done, she scoops a fair amount of them up and places them in a bag before gathering the few bills in her tip jar. She makes her way toward the cash register on the other side of her counter, carefully counting each dollar before exchanging it for what I assume are the bigger bills on the far side of the drawer. My jaw drops when I see her scope out the immediate area around her and take more before she furtively shoves the money into the tortilla bag. It's then she begins to tend the few customers coming up to pay. Fixated, I watch as she keeps the drawer open, making change before tucking their tickets in her apron. She's covering her tracks. Once she's left alone at the drawer, she takes a few more bills, makes some change, and I know the numbers will add up at the end of the night.

Smiling Selma is a tortilla making *thief*.

And this ain't her first rodeo.

I've spent hours of my day watching this woman, admiring her for her ability to find joy in her solitude only to find out she's a thief.

Well, ain't that some shit?

Sean won't believe it, and I find myself itching to tell him as a van pulls up beside me. A guy who looks to be in his thirties exits before opening the back door. Attached to it sits an electric chair making it wheelchair accessible. My attention locked on the van, I don't notice Selma until she too is peering in the van, the bag in hand, her soft voice crooning out hurried Spanish just as the back seat is turned and a young boy comes into view. He's severely disabled, his legs and arms shriveled at his sides, his eyes searching and searching, darting left and right. He's blind. Selma steps up into the van, showering him with kisses and tosses the bag of tortillas and cash onto the seat next to him. My heart sinks.

She does it for him.

She steals for him.

My eyes drift back to the boy, who looks to be eleven or twelve. Her grandchild, maybe?

For a minute or two, I wish I'd taken Spanish instead of French so I could understand the conversation between her and the man who stands behind her, watching her shower the boy with affection. It's so painfully clear she lives for him. The man speaks to her softly as if she's breakable, so much gratitude shining in his eyes as she rains kisses on the boy's forehead, nose, and cheeks.

Guilt gnaws me when I think of all the assumptions I made in those few seconds after I'm fairly sure I saw her steal the money.

Sean's car door opens and closes, but I keep my eyes on the boy. What type of life does he live, confined that way, unable to see, unable to move his arms and legs, his body a prison?

"He's partially deaf too," Sean says as my eyes sting and tears threaten. When Selma steps out of the van, the man hugs her, shame and guilt in his eyes. He pulls back from her embrace, evident worry etched all over his features as he studies her and glances back at the restaurant. It's obvious he doesn't want her to do it.

"She steals for her son and her grandson?"

"Son-in-law. Her daughter gave birth and then left him to raise him alone. He gets a check, but it's not enough. Selma has severe arthritis, but every single day she pounds that dough for her boys, and it makes her happy. The saddest part is that she's a staple at that restaurant. It wouldn't be the same without her. And the assholes that own it haven't given her a raise in eight years."

I swallow. "I couldn't wait to tell you she was stealing. I didn't think you would believe me. I almost didn't believe it myself until I saw it happen." He lifts a tear from my cheek and I turn to look at him. From the look he's giving me I gather the rest. "You *knew*, you *knew* I would see this."

"How did that feel?"

"It stung a lot worse than the watch." Something close to satisfaction shines in his eyes before he gazes past me as the man drives his son away. In minutes, Selma is back behind her counter, pounding out tortillas with a smile on her face. I turn back to Sean and scrutinize him.

"Who in the hell are you?"

What twenty-five-year-old man does his friends' laundry, genuinely cares about Selma's cash flow problem and disabled grandson, hates money, hates time, has zero regard for status, and lives without a single worry for the future?

Alfred Sean Roberts.

That's who.

It's then I give myself permission to trust him a little more. But it's also then that the budding feelings give me pause. He's made it far too easy to like him. This man who bats away rules and boundaries, he may be dangerous for *me*. Sensing my fear, he leans in to kiss me for endless seconds. When he pulls away, I feel myself sinking further, more drawn in, and even more conflicted about it.

"Seriously, Sean, who are you?"

"I'm a man with clean laundry, and I'm starving. In the mood for Mexican?"

All I can do is nod.

Chapter Fifteen

SEAN GUIDES ME INTO THE DARK BAR BY THE HAND, OUR bellies full after feasting on fajitas, our collective pockets lighter after tipping Selma profusely. Uneasy, I fidget behind him as I take in our new surroundings—neon lights of every color line the walls, the floor littered with overused cocktail tables. The only thing that looks new is a jukebox sitting in the far corner. The bar has the shape of a shoebox and smells a lot like a soured dish rag.

"'Sup, Eddie?" Sean greets the man behind the bar. Eddie looks to be in his early thirties and rough around his every edge. His eyes are the color of midnight and his size is intimidating to say the least. I can't help but note the presence of a familiar tattoo on Eddie's arm as he drapes a soiled towel over his shoulder.

"Hey, man," he replies, eyeing me over Sean's solid frame. "I can see what you've been up to."

Sean gives him a lopsided grin. "This is Cecelia."

I give him a little wave behind Sean's bicep. "Hi."

"What are you drinking?"

I grip Sean's arm, hesitant. He knows I'm not of age. He runs his thumb over the back of my hand.

He's got this.

Of course, he does.

"I'll take a beer." He turns to me. "You?"

"Jack and Coke."

I damned near giggle when Sean's brow lifts. I lean in. "I've always wanted to order one. The alternative is a martini, and I don't think Eddie would make one of those."

He grins. "You thought right."

Sean pays for our drinks and leads us to a table on the far side of the bar closest to the jukebox. He pulls out the leftover stash of quarters from our laundry run and hands them to me. "Choose wisely, or Eddie will throw us out on our asses."

I take the money and make a few selections before joining Sean at the table. He lifts my drink to me, and I thank him before taking a huge sip. My eyes widen as the whiskey latches to the back of my throat and I start to choke. Sean winces and turns back to Eddie, who raises a skeptical eyebrow.

Even with the burn threatening imminent death, I know I need to play this underage drinking thing off a lot better. With watering eyes, I clear my throat as Sean chuckles.

"First time drinking the hard stuff?"

"Piece of cake," I say, as the warm liquid starts to filter through my veins.

He shakes his head, a rueful smile on his lips. "Where exactly did you grow up again? I'm thinking there's a *ville* on the end of it."

"Shut up. And you're calling me small town? There's like four stoplights in this one."

"Twelve."

"I told you I didn't party much in school."

"Or ever," he jests.

"I just…" I sigh.

"Just what?"

"Well, my mom was a mess and lush enough for both of us. One of us had to be the grown-up."

Sean's hazels soften and I decide they're far more green than brown. "Don't get me wrong. I wouldn't trade her for the world. She was a lot of fun."

"Was?"

"Yeah. I learned how to drive when I was eight."

He leans forward. "Come again?"

"That's right. I had mad skills," I boast, braving another drink of my whiskey with a splash of flat Coke.

"Sure you did."

"We didn't have a lot of money, so we made do. My mom was creative. She always found a way to make that extra twenty dollars a week work. One sunny Saturday, she had this brilliant idea to take me on an abandoned road and let me go nuts." I smile, lost in the memory. "She put a phone book in the driver's seat and just let me at it, for hours. She let me two-wheel our mini-van. Then afterward, she would take us to this roadside barbecue shack that had the best tater tots with cheese. So, for a year or so that became our Saturday ritual. Me, my mom, a phone book, our minivan, and tater tots with cheese."

Sean leans back in his seat, his beer halfway to his mouth. "I love that."

"She had this way about her, a way I'm envious of some-times. She could make something out of nothing, made ordinary days spectacular." I study Sean as he nods. "You remind me of her in that way."

He winks. "It's all about the company we keep."

"Don't credit me for being the fun one. We both know I'm not. I'm a 'stay-in-the-lines' kind of girl and you're, well, you're the red crayon."

He kicks back and shrugs. "Don't be so hard on yourself. Nothing wrong with being responsible and taking care of the people you love."

"It's insanely boring," I take another swig of my drink. "My friend Christy saved me from being a total introvert." I dart my eyes down. "I've never wanted to be the center of attention, you know? But I always envied those people who could make ordinary days, extraordinary. Like you, and Christy, and my mom."

"You have it in you."

I shake my head. "No, I don't. I'm just meant to be a fan of those who do. Anyway, what about your parents? Tell me about the restaurant."

"I'll do one better; I'll take you there sometime soon. I want them to meet you."

"I'd love that."

"They're my idols—both of them. Good people with strong opinions, big hearts, all about family and loyalty, married for over thirty years. They work side by side every single day. They live out in the open, fight out in the open, and make up out in the open."

"They love each other out in the open, huh? Maybe that's why you're so openly affectionate with me?"

"Probably."

"Well, those are good idols to have," I drawl, my fourth mouthful of drink going down a lot smoother. "This isn't so bad. Maybe I'm a whiskey girl."

"Easy, killer." He peels at his beer label. "You don't talk much about your dad."

"That's because I have no idea who the man is. I really have no clue why he wants me to be in his life at all. Appearances are deceiving. I may be here, but he's not. Half of the weeks I've been here, he stays in Charlotte. After nineteen years, he's still a mystery to me. An iceberg. It's pretty bad when you can't see any humanity in the man responsible for half your created life. When I got here—and although I was pissed about it—I tried to keep an open mind, but it's proven pointless. If I had to choose one word to describe him and our relationship, it would be evasive."

He nods and takes another sip of his beer.

"And your mother?"

"Absent," I say softly, shaking off the threatening emotion and muster up a smile. "Painfully so, as of the last six months."

He turns my hand over on the table and runs the pads of his fingers on the inside of my palm. "I'm sorry."

"Don't be. It's life. I'm all grown up now. Mom did her job. Dad at least helped pay some of the bills. I really have no reason to complain." But it's hurt that seeps into me as I recall a time where I felt like my mother's priority.

"I miss her," I admit as I pull my hand away and shake my head. "*They* say she was born in a directionless generation. I honestly have to agree with that assessment. For years, she lived this big abundant life, always looking for more, wanting more and never really carrying any of her grand plans out. I admired her so much, and something—something—must have happened along the way. I still can't figure it out. It's like she forgot who she was and just...gave up."

"She's what, in her early or mid-forties?" Sean asks.

I nod. "She had me when she was my age. I guess you could say we grew up together."

He shrugs. "So, she's close to halftime. She's probably trying to figure out how she wants to live out the second half."

"Probably," I rub at my nose to try and stop the budding burn. "I just wish she would let me help her figure it out."

"That's not your job."

"I know."

He gently nudges me. "Doesn't make it any easier though, does it?"

"No."

He doesn't offer me anything more. He just sits there with me, letting me grieve, his touch reassuring as he squeezes my hand.

"So, besides your parents, who is your hero?" I ask, taking another sip of my drink.

"If I had to name one, Dave Chappelle."

I rack my brain. "The comedian?"

"Yep."

"Why?"

"Because he's fucking brilliant and real. He uses his platform in an incredible way, and his genius shines through. He says the shit many are too afraid to say and then tosses in some insight here and there that will stun you, make you think. He walked away from fifty million dollars, refusing to sell his soul in a way so many others would."

"That's so far from any answer I thought you would give."

"Yeah, well, he's flawed too, and he makes no apologies about it."

My phone buzzes with an incoming message from Christy and Sean nods toward it. "Look up some of his stand-up on your little computer when you get home."

"Maybe I will."

"But do yourself a favor, never research your heroes."

"Why?"

He tips his beer. "Because you'll find out they're human."

He takes my phone away when I lift it to check the message.

"New rule. No phones with me."

"What?" I jerk my head back. "Not ever?"

"Never. Not in my car, not in my house, not in the garage. When you're with me, you leave your phone at home."

"You're serious?"

"It's all I ask. But I am seriously asking you for this." His tone is severe, leaving little room for negotiation.

"Why?"

"A few reasons, one of them being this is *my* time. I'm choosing to spend it with you, and I want the same from you."

"It sounds controlling to me."

He leans in. "Hand to the Messiah, I promise you, baby, the last thing I want to do is control you."

"Then what's with the rule?"

"If I asked you to please trust me enough and that an explanation will come later, would you?"

Jade eyes prompt mine. He's serious, so much so that I can't look away.

"Why can't I get an explanation now?"

"We aren't there yet."

"You're talking in riddles again."

"I know, but it's a dealbreaker for me."

I gape at him. Never in our time together has he taken such an air of authority. It irks me to no end, but is it really too much to ask?

"It's a slippery slope. If I give you this, the explanation damn well better be worth it."

"It will be."

"Okay. Fine, *for now*, no phone."

"Good," he leans in. "Two words to describe you…" he chucks the underside of my chin, "beautiful and buzzing."

I give him a begrudging grin. "Nah, not yet."

"Sure." He puts his beer down and grips my hand, pulling me from my chair just as "So What'Cha Want" by the Beastie Boys starts to play. "Good one."

"There are perks to being raised by Generation X," I follow his lead. My eyes drink him in.

"What's that?"

"The music, of course."

"Can't argue with that."

"I learned how to dance to this song. But I didn't think this would be your thing."

"What do you know about my thing?" He taunts me, pulling me onto the sad patch of a dance space.

"I know a thing or two about your thing, baby," I quip just as he starts swaying his hips, his upper body relaxed. He's good, better than good. Stunned by the sight of him moving with such ease, I hesitate, just watching until he pulls me closer to him, urging me with the gentle thrust of his hips. Cheeks heating, I size up the bar to make sure no one's watching. There are only a few others in the pub that time forgot, and it's apparent none of them give a shit. And with the warm buzz flowing through me, I decide I don't either. I follow Sean's lead and start rocking my hips because this girl has a little rhythm. Sean's eyes light up with delighted surprise as we dance through the song, and the next, and the next.

I drink another Coke splashed whiskey.

We dance.

I grip his T-shirt as he hitches my leg on his hip, slowly hiking my shorts up my thigh.

We grind.

He leisurely sips droplets of sweat from my neck and blows the rest dry with his lush lips.

We dance.

Shamelessly wrapped around him, I lick the divot in his throat.

We grind.

He takes a shot of tequila before licking the salt from my wrist, never once taking his eyes off mine.

We dance.

I tease, pressing my ass into his erection, lacing my hands around his neck as he snakes a possessive arm around my waist.

We grind.

Back on the floor, he watches me intently as I taunt him to Ciara's "Oh" with a circle eight movement of my hips.

We drink some more.

Mid-song and covered in sweat, our pores seeping with alcohol, he stops my movement, cups the back of my neck, and yanks me to him, boldly kissing me like a man possessed.

We leave.

And race to his car as it starts to rain.

Doors closed, we collide, tongues dueling for dominance.

He rips at the straps of my halter as I lift, unbutton, and toss my shorts.

I straddle him.

His groan vibrates my tongue as I latch my lips to his neck.

He frees his cock from his jeans, rolls on a condom, shoves my panties to the side, impaling me in one sure thrust.

Right there in the crowded parking lot, feet away from the bar...

We fuck.

Chapter Sixteen

ROUSING IN PURPLE HUE, I GO FROM A BLACKOUT SLEEP TO a pounding head, slightly disoriented until I feel the warmth of the body wrapped around me. I've damn near forgotten what it was like to be cocooned in masculine arms, and last night was the first time Sean brought me home with him.

Something unspoken happened between us yesterday.

The feel of Sean surrounding me is everything this morning, despite the riot in my head.

These past weeks I've spent with him have been some of the best of my life.

It's just…Sean.

He's everything I didn't know I wanted in a man and so much more than I ever hoped to have. He's considerate, thoughtful, and ridiculously smart, and my attraction to him is boundless on so many levels. With him, I feel lucky, like I won some sort of man lottery. And in a way, that makes me fearful.

My heart is no longer hiding in the shadows, it's dancing in the open now, much like we were in the bar last night.

And the sex, I've never had it so good. His brand of fucking is both blissful and tortuous. We'd spent our time diving into each other with heated whispers. It had been a marathon of moans and groans, and I'd never wanted it to end. We'd had drunken sex, which was a first for me. I'd let my inhibitions go and it had paid off in spades.

I damn near moan as I recall him driving into me from behind, his hands covering me, spreading me to take him deeper as he spoke filthy words at my back.

When he came, raking his nails on my scalp, I surprised myself by going with him without the help of a hand between my legs—another first.

We slowed down, unable to stop, reaching for the other minutes later. I called his name repeatedly out of fear of the chest he was cracking wide open, of what he was able to see. His kiss, his touch, the slow thrust of his hips soothing me with soft words of "I know, baby, I'm with you."

With me. And he was. For so long, I've been in hiding, and in a month of knowing him, it's like he's freed me.

He surrounds me with his embrace. The deep exhale of his breath lulling me back into a peaceful state even as that voice in my head screams, 'what in the actual fuck, Cecelia?'

I burrow into his hold, enjoying the warmth coupled with the sting between my legs as more of last night's memories envelop me.

Spending a few silent minutes in his arms, my body reminds me of why I woke, the strain in my bladder commanding me to break away from him. Lifting his inked arm, I slither out of bed before staring down at him as he sleeps, his spiky hair thoroughly disheveled from my fingers, his golden body encased by his faded denim comforter. Ogling my new man, I give myself another second to appreciate him, softly shutting his door before padding down the hall to his bathroom. Tyler and Dominic have the bedrooms with bathrooms. Sean had given his away freely.

Of course, he had. He's selfless.

Another reason to want to trust him.

His needs are so basic, and yet I feel like I'm starting to become one of them. He's making me believe it.

Once I relieve myself, wincing the entire time, I wash my hands and study my reflection, noticing the faint bite marks on my neck. Anxious for a painkiller for the budding migraine, but more anxious to get back to Sean, I open the door and am met with the sight of Dominic in the bedroom on the opposite side of the hall.

Naked.

Sleeping naked.

The sight of him knocks the breath from me as I stand frozen, somewhere between in and out of the bathroom.

He's on his back, stretched out, his head tilted due to the propped position of his pillow, his muscular arm tucked beneath it.

I. Can't. Look. Away.

His chest rises and falls in a steady rhythm as I stand immobile to the sight of him. One of his legs is drawn up and resting on the edge of his bed while the other lay straight out, the position itself like an offering. My eyes dip to where his cock rests between his muscular thighs.

Jesus, he's beautiful. I don't know how long I stand, just watching him, drinking him in, I only know that when my eyes drift from his impressive cock back to his face, I'm met with a silver stare.

My palms tingle while my face blanches with shame and humiliation, and I still can't look away.

Instead, I just stare...and he stares back at me. I know I should apologize and bolt, but I'm unable to form words, not even to offer the apology he rightfully deserves.

Or does he?

He had to have heard us last night. Did he leave his door open knowing I would see him?

Caught in the moment, in my utter stupidity, the morning light in his bedroom lifts as he lowers his eyes. I follow his gaze and see he's hard.

Get out of here, Cecelia!

"Sorry," I whisper, barely audible.

I don't wait for a reply before I dash away back to the safety of Sean's room, relieved to see him still sleeping soundly. Guilt eats me alive as he pulls me back into his hold once I hit the mattress. I lay next to him, staring through the inch view in his blinds, my heart pounding with fear and my body thrumming with exhilaration. I flip over in Sean's arms and study him. He's the most beautiful man I've ever been with. Ever. Our courting has made me feel things I've only dreamed about.

He's been nothing short of incredible with me, to me.

Riddled with shame, I run my fingers through Sean's hair before pulling him closer.

So what, I'm attracted to Dominic. Of course, I'm attracted to him. He's got that beautiful asshole vibe thing that makes women stupid.

And this morning, though thoroughly fucked and sated, I behaved like one of them.

For the record, Dominic's not attractive on any ordinary level. No, his looks demand attention, appreciation, much like Sean's.

Beautiful naked man.

Of course, I'm going to look.

Because he was naked.

It means nothing.

So, all I need to do is forget about those hostile steel eyes and the fact that just minutes ago, they weren't hostile at all. Not in the slightest.

That look was something else entirely.

"So, do I tell him?"

"That you stared at his roommate's dick so long you got busted?"

Christy laughs on the other side of the line, enjoying herself at my expense as I unpack the grocery bags, mostly trying to find a place for the guilt cloud I've been under all day.

I'm completely inexperienced with the 'I saw your roommate's dick, and I liked it so much I gave you a guilty morning blow job' confession. Christy is doing little to help me as I search the bachelors' kitchen for what I need, having spent half a paycheck on a steak dinner while frosting the 'I really only want you, but I couldn't resist' carrot cake I baked to make up for the lingering remorse. Because they, whoever the hell *they* are, say that the way to a man's heart is through his stomach. I'm hoping it's also the way to a sincere apology. One that I will give as soon as I can figure out how to explain myself.

I don't want to ruin any part of what we have going for being a peeping Thomasina.

"Yeah, girl, tell him his roommate needs to cover his junk and make it sound convincing."

"That's lying."

"That's the truth. It's not your fault you walked out of the bathroom and got eye fucked."

"Yeah, but I'm the one who—"

"Babe. He doesn't need to know that. I'll be honest though, if you had spoken up this morning, it would have seemed a lot more convincing."

We were out of the house within minutes of waking up, and I was thankful because it meant escaping Dominic. After we picked up Sean's car from the bar where Tyler retrieved us drunk last night, we went hiking. I bitched the first half-hour because of my pounding head but felt a lot better halfway in after a lot of hydrating. Sean hates being inside. Whether I stand by and talk to him while he's screwing with his car, or we swim or hike, the outdoors is his happy place. He's a restless man from what I can tell, definitely not a fan of Netflix and chill, and the chill part is *never* chill. The man is magic with his mouth, hands, and cock, and he would much rather bend me over a tree stump in the woods than take me on his living room couch.

The upside to that is there's never a dull moment. Even our earlier grocery trip was an adventure. He forced me to stand on the lip of the cart while he sped us down the aisles popping grapes into our mouths. Though he's agreed to let me cook for him on our day off, I have zero doubt he will get us out of the house after. It's as if he has to exhaust himself before he hits his pillow. Despite his warnings that he doesn't do things in the traditional sense, this period in our new relationship feels a lot like nesting, which is why I'm playing house with him today, and I don't want to screw it up. Finding a boyfriend after only a day in town was not at all what I expected, but finding Sean was a miracle.

The fact that my feelings are getting involved has made this betrayal far worse in my mind. Especially after this morning.

Sean doesn't seem the jealous type, but if I'm wrong, my admission could be disastrous.

"I need to get my ass up there if they're as hot as you say."

"Focus," I order, looking for a cutting board. "New man. Saw other man's member."

"You said they share, right?"

"It's a rumor. Has to be."

"Why?"

"Because…I don't know. I just can't picture it."

"Freaks hide in plain sight, baby. You're living proof."

"Shut up. Shut up! I don't know why I called you."

"Because you lurve me, and because you were dying to tell me you had multiples. *Finally.*"

"Christy. Listen to me. I could fall for this man."

"Damn, already?"

"I know, I know, it's too soon and so stupid. But he's incredible."

"I believe you from what you said. Just be careful, okay?"

"How do you do that?"

"I don't know. That's the advice I'm supposed to give you. Once you start falling it's kind of impossible to stop, isn't it?"

"Exactly. This is a disaster."

"Don't be so dramatic. Tell the man you saw his roommate naked and be done with it."

"Fine. I will."

"And take a fucking picture, for Christ's sake, God invented camera phones specifically for shit like this."

"Sean doesn't want me to have my phone when we're together. I'm going to have to hide it before he gets back." I wince, knowing how damning it sounds and I'm met by a moment of complete silence on the other end.

"That's a little controlling, don't you think?"

"He just hates the distraction of it. He wants me present when we're together."

"That's kind of hot."

"He's different, I'm telling you."

"Well, just rip the Band-Aid off now. If he goes psycho, at least you find out now, rather than later."

"Good point. Christy, I'm in over my head already with this guy. He just makes me think...differently, makes me feel...gah, what the hell am I doing?"

"I know you're scared, but don't let the past dictate what could be good for you. Lord knows I've been praying for this. Love you. Call me tomorrow."

"Love you." After hanging up, I dash to my car and put my phone in the glove box resentful of the deal but opting to honor it after today. I have no doubts Sean meant what he said about it being a dealbreaker. After returning to the kitchen, I add a few spices to the salad mix and begin to chop up the tomatoes while trying to reason it out.

Christy's right. It's not a big deal. I'm making a mountain out of a molehill.

Dominic should not be sleeping naked if he doesn't want to be seen, and I have to get over it. Sean will probably think it's funny.

Sure, he'll think it's as funny as you thought it was walking in on Jared mid-thrust.

But Sean is not my ex, and I'm trying my best not to make him pay for a boy's mistakes. Deciding to admit the truth before dinner, I chop up an onion on the plastic cutting board I found and grin when I hear the front door close. Sean had double backed to the store to grab the beer we forgot during our first trip.

"That was fast," I round the corner and run smack into Dominic. His eyes widen as he grips my wrist, shaking the knife out of my hand a split second before impact. I sputter as he glares down at me while ripping his earbuds out.

"What the fuck?!"

"I'm s-s-sorry, I thought you were Sean and you heard me."

"Obviously, I fucking didn't." I gawk as he glances around the kitchen. "What are you doing?"

"Obviously, I'm cooking," I snap. "You don't have to be so rude."

My anger amuses him. "I like my steak rare."

"That's Tyler's steak."

"Mine now," he reaches behind me and pops a cherry tomato in his mouth.

"I'm not cooking a damn thing for you."

He yanks me to him, and I lose a little bit of breath as he eyes my mouth. "My house, *my rules*. You cook for one of us. You cook for *all* of us."

"Also, Sean's house, my hands, and my fucking prerogative."

His smile is cruel. "You like playing house?"

"I'm not playing house. I'm cooking for my—"

"Boyfriend? Cute. You think Sean's your boyfriend?" He sets me loose, and I pick up the knife between us, tempted to use it as I backtrack. "I didn't say that. I didn't say he was my boyfriend."

"You didn't have to. Word to the unwise, careful about getting attached, sweetheart."

"Yeah, what do you know?" I snap, slapping the knife on the counter behind me.

He smirks, opening the fridge and grabbing a water bottle. He downs it as my eyes glide over him. His thick onyx tresses are askew, his bare chest covered in a sheen of sweat, droplets trickling down his eight-pack dispersing into a faint happy trail. I dart my eyes away but feel his gaze weighing heavily on me. "He fucks you in the woods, doesn't he?" My eyes snap to his, but I clamp my mouth closed. "Let me guess. He took you to a pretty waterfall."

I feel slapped. Worse than that, I feel...played. But I rise to the occasion.

"Actually, no. He fucked me in his Nova first."

His answering chuckle is infuriating. "Oh yeah, a backseat Betty?"

"What are you, jealous? I don't see any girl around here clamoring to cook for you. There's probably not a dumb enough woman alive."

He steps toward me, placing the drained bottle on the counter behind me, crowding me to the point I'm forced to lift my chin. "Such nasty, hateful words from a filthy, cum-coated mouth."

I rear back, and in a second flat, he's controlling the hand meant to slap him to cover the bulge in his shorts. "Careful, violence makes me *hard.*" He tilts his head and his eyes flare, the sight of them like the glint of a knife. "I'm a psychiatrist's wet dream."

I struggle against him as he runs my hand along his dick, which is very, *very hard.* It also makes it almost impossible not to estimate the size of it. That sick rationalization makes my stomach turn.

"Too bad for them, I'm not weak."

"I'm not weak."

Though drenched in sweat, his clean scent invades me. "Do you come when he fucks you against the trees?"

I look past his shoulder, praying for Sean to appear and come up empty.

"Eyes on me, *Pup,*" he spits with disgust.

"Let me go."

"I already have, but you're doing a good job." It's then I realize my fingers are running along his dick of their own accord. I jerk my hand away, and his dark chuckle fills the room.

"Why are you acting this way? I've done nothing to you."

"Maybe I just don't like you."

"Well then, maybe I just won't give a fuck."

He leans in and grips my chin, hard. "But you do."

I rip my face out of his hold just as the door slams. I'm shaking from head to toe when Sean rounds the corner. One look at my face wipes his greeting smile away.

"Your girl just rubbed on my dick," Dominic says as if reporting the weather while he snags a beer from Sean's bag, twists off the cap and flicks it toward the sink. My jaw goes slack and Dominic shrugs, "She likes watching me sleep, too. Thought you should know."

I shake my head furiously, tears threatening as I look over to Sean. "That's not true, Sean, that's not true."

Setting his bag down, Sean curses and holds up a finger muting my defense before following Dominic up the stairs. Perplexed, I stand in the kitchen while my carefully planned apology dinner goes up in flames.

Chapter Seventeen

'M ALREADY OUT OF THE HOUSE AND HALFWAY TO MY CAR when Sean catches up to me.

"Cecelia."

"He's the fucking devil," I'm feeling guilty, humiliated, and furious.

"Trust me. He's not."

I open my car door and Sean slams it. "Don't let him fuck us up."

"I didn't touch his dick." I'm lying. I'm lying to him. "I did, but not that way." Sean's mouth quirks as I groan in frustration. "Not in a sexual way. He…I did see him naked. This morning. He had his door wide open and he was lying there. Naked. And I saw him."

Sean's lips twist up further into a smile. "That bastard would work naked if he could. He's a nudist. Don't worry about it."

"Really?"

"Yeah, really. Is that why you've been jumpy today? You thought I'd be pissed?"

"Well, I didn't know..." I shake my head. "It's a weird position to be in."

"Dominic is a master of flipping a situation. It's nothing new." He watches me carefully. "Did you like what you saw?"

"W-what?" I gape at him.

"There's no other way to ask that question, Cecelia."

He's not backing down and he can read me, so it's pointless to lie. I don't want to lie to Sean.

"He's attractive, but—"

"The blow job this morning?" He lifts both brows and his smile goes a mile wide. "That was either guilt, or you were hot, or both."

"Can we talk about how your roommate is the Son of Satan for a second?"

"Deflecting," he laughs. "Interesting."

"Shut up. He's attractive, and he knows it. He's also several other choice adjectives."

Sean grips the back of my neck and pulls us nose to nose. "I'm fucking crazy about you. You know that, right? Last night was incredible."

I return his grin. "Feeling's mutual. I just didn't know how to tell you without—"

"It's okay to look, Cecelia," he drawls. "And I rather enjoyed that guilty blowjob."

"I really, really don't like him."

"Doesn't matter." He releases me. "He lives here, so get in there and finish cooking or he wins."

"Are you crazy? I'm not going back in there. He twisted my words—"

"You need to stand your ground with him and do it early, or he'll walk all over you." It's an unapologetic order and his tone is borderline militant, much like last night. I deflate a little.

"Sean, how did he know we went to the waterfall?"

Sean's eyes deaden and he stares on at me blankly. "So, you're going to let him win."

"Are you going to answer me?"

His silence is answer enough. I try and read into the look in his eyes, but he's not backing down. He's not going to apologize for someone else's actions. And he damn sure doesn't want me to play victim. As pissed as I'm getting, he's absolutely right. If I leave and let everything Dominic says and does get in the way of Sean and me, he *will* win.

Tossing my shoulders back, I make my way through the cars and head back inside.

"Get 'em, baby," I hear Sean chuckle behind me.

Dominic glares at his well-done steak as I bite into a mouthful of salad, not bothering to hide my smile at all.

His eyes meet mine and he lets out a low whistle. Brandy, Sean's spitz bounds down the stairs as Dominic tosses the whole steak over his shoulder.

"She can't chew that, asshole," Sean objects, picking up the steak and tossing it on the counter, using his silverware to slice it up without a cutting board.

Animal.

"Then maybe you should have gotten a real dog, not a fucking shower poof," Dominic fires back.

I can't help my giggle. I hadn't expected such a lady dog when Sean introduced me to Brandy, and I gave him hell for it.

"At least she's amusing," Dominic sizes me up. "Do you do tricks too?" He stabs into his broccoli.

Sean gazes on at me expectantly and I briefly entertain throwing my plate at Dominic, but I decide not to waste a good steak.

And anyway, what in the actual fuck is going on? I look between them and see no sign of conspiracy, but why is Sean not defending me? Not even a little. I get that he wants me to stand my ground, but where's the backup? Shouldn't he at least say *something*? Using that anger, I turn to a freshly showered Dominic, his dark hair tousled on top of his head, his skin darker from his run. A smug smile on his beautiful bastard face.

"Look, Major Malfunction, I get that you have some sort of personality disorder, but can you, just until I finish my steak, try to play nice?"

Sean throws his head back. "Major Malfunction. Good one, baby."

"Backseat Betty says you fucked her in your Nova," Dominic supplies as my steak catches in my throat. I choke it down and grab my water, my eyes flying to Sean. This man will use everything I say against me, every word.

Sean glances toward me with a raised brow and I flit my hostile gaze to Dominic.

"So, you like twisting words, huh?"

"I like playing with simple-minded people," Dominic sips his beer. "It's a hobby."

"Fuck yourself, Dominic, there's a hobby."

He tongues his upper lip as if contemplating and then shakes his head. "No, I'd much rather you finish that hand job you were giving me before your boyfriend walked in." He turns to Sean. "By the way, I wouldn't get to comfortable with her. She was *really* reluctant to call you her boyfriend earlier. Between that, her staring contest with junior, and the chub rub, I'm thinking she's not the girl you should introduce to Mom."

I slam my silverware down, glaring between them. "Okay, what's the joke?" I fixate on Sean. "Are you not going to say *anything* to this asshole?"

"Trust me," Sean sighs, "it doesn't matter what I say."

I surge to my feet. "Enjoy your dinner."

"Oh, look, she has a breaking point." Dominic tsks as I gather my purse, "How original."

I head for the door; hearing Dominic speak up behind me. "I told you she doesn't have it in her."

"Give her some time."

I'm beyond the bullshit and any attempt to understand their exchange when Tyler walks in just as I reach the door. "Hey, gir—"

"Hey, Tyler, I can't…excuse me," I push past him, tears threatening and slam the door behind me.

I'm fuming mad, standing at my driver's door when I realize Tyler blocked me in. Intentional or not, he's aware of it by now and not even he is going to make it easy on me. I stand in the heat for endless minutes before I hear the front door open and close. Sean appears and I dart my eyes away.

"You plannin' on glaring at the front door all night, Pup?"

I look up at him to see he's smiling which only infuriates me further. "You guys are assholes."

He dips his chin. "Maybe."

"Maybe?" I round my car, tossing my purse on the hood. "Maybe? What is your game?"

"No games. I told you not to play into his shit and you did anyway."

"He's horrible. And what did he mean by, 'I don't have it in me?'"

"Exactly what he said. And you're proving him right."

"Why do I have to prove anything to him?"

"You don't, but if you're going to be taking up space that he's sharing, you'll have to figure it out."

"Figure what out exactly?"

"How to get along."

"With him?" I scoff. "Impossible."

"Not impossible. *Improbable*."

"Sean, cut the shit. Dominic is not going to cut me any slack, okay? That's clear."

"Then step up."

"And what? Kick his ass?"

"Couldn't hurt." His playful tone has my hackles rising.

"This is funny to you?"

"Hysterical. Got to give you props though, you were holding your own for a minute back there."

"So, this *is* a game."

"No, it's a test of wills, and I really do hope you win."

"You did not just say that to me."

"I did. And I'll say it again. You can do this. I know you can. Don't let him scare you away."

"That's it?"

He grips his biceps. "That's it."

"Another decision."

He taps his nose.

"You said you wouldn't turn into a dick. What do you call this?"

He sighs. "Then I guess I'm sorry to disappoint, but I promise I can do much, much worse."

I can physically feel my heart start retreating. I can walk away now, and something inside thinks it would be wise. But this behavior contradicts the Sean I've gotten to know. I'm utterly torn as I stare at him.

"You guys are on some alternate planet."

"It's fun here," he says softly, "but it's a much better planet with you on it."

I shake my head. "I have no idea what to think about you."

"I'm in the same position with you. Makes things interesting, doesn't it?"

I gape at him. "I thought we…"

"You thought what?"

My heart sinks. "God, I'm an idiot. This was a bad idea." I move to grab my purse and he stops me, letting out a harsh breath.

"Cecelia, you're letting shit that doesn't need to happen, happen."

"And you're standing by and watching it, like, what the fuck, Sean?"

He grips my face, leans down, and kisses me. I break the kiss, pushing at him, and he chuckles.

"I want to leave. Tell Tyler to move his car."

His eyes deaden. "Tell him yourself."

"Fine!" I stomp through the front door and find Tyler and Dominic on the PlayStation in the living room.

Typical.

"Tyler, can you move your car?"

Tyler eyes Dominic. "After this game."

"Are you serious?"

"Yeah. Chill, babe."

Sean's behind me now. I feel his warmth at my back as I stand there, hovering over the two of them huddled on the couch, helpless to my situation. I glance over my shoulder at Sean, who watches me intently as my anger builds and builds. Less than an hour ago, my day was perfect. Sean and I were fine, more than fine, and then Dominic took a Mack truck to all of it. The day, my carefully planned dinner and dessert.

Dessert.

Boiling over, I move to the kitchen and gather the carrot cake I had frosted earlier, Sean's favorite, and walk back to where Dominic sits and smash it into the back of his head. He shoots up from the couch as I gather more ruined cake in my hand and slap it into the side of Sean's smiling face.

"Didn't want to leave you without serving dessert. You all can fuck right off."

Dominic tosses his remote down, his vengeance filled eyes attempting to pin me as I drop the pan, snatch Tyler's keys off the coffee table and make a break for the front door.

Sean and Tyler's laughter echoes through the open door as I climb into Tyler's truck, start it, and peel ass out of the driveway, leaving it running in the middle of the street. I run toward my car, where Sean stands waiting, shoving a fingerful of icing into his mouth.

"It's good shit, baby."

I'm just about to lay into him when he hauls me over his shoulder. Suspended, I beat on his ass with my fists.

"Let me down, *right now*."

"Hell no, we aren't wasting this," he walks me back into the house where Dominic hovers over the kitchen sink, peeling his shirt off. His arctic eyes challenge mine as Sean takes the stairs one by one in what seems like a deliberately slow ascent. Choice fingers lifted; I flash Dominic a spiteful smile until he disappears from sight.

Sean closes his bedroom door and sets me on my feet, spinning my back into the door and presses into me. He looks infuriatingly gorgeous with a half-decorated face as he moves in and I turn my head to dodge his kiss.

"Even better," he smears the frosting onto my face and chuckles darkly a second before I hear the rip of a condom.

Chapter Eighteen

TIME OUT.

I'm calling it.

If a man seems too good to be true, he usually is a liar.

That's the stance I took that night I left Sean sleeping in his bed.

I've spent four weeks trying to piece together the dazzling puzzle of Alfred Sean Roberts, and I'm no closer to figuring out what his true intentions with me are. He's not harmless, that much I do know. I don't know if Sean's a good guy or a bad guy.

Maybe he's both.

For two days after I left him without a goodbye, I ignored his texts, and for those two days he left me alone on the line at work. He's been unapologetic.

When I don't respond, he doesn't grovel. It's what I had expected, even though we'd had some amazing angry sex. But it wasn't exactly make-up sex, at least for me. I'm still pissed he didn't defend me. Though with Sean, I've come to expect the unexpected.

It would be easier for me if I understood why he let a man who he considers a brother treat me so shitty.

So for now, I'm fine with mad.

I decide to pull back no matter what. Honestly, getting feelings for someone so soon is dangerous for a girl like me.

Am I creating drama for the sake of it?

I believe Sean about a lot of his observations. One, in particular, is we're programmed in a lot of ways. Of course we are, but another part of me knows that we can program or, better yet, taint ourselves in different ways.

Through patterns of my past, I've learned that I'm drawn to dysfunction, and more so to the men who provide the questions.

I'm determined not to repeat my mistakes.

I have a misplaced theory that if you're not suffering, you're not loving hard enough, deep enough, and that's just not healthy.

I gave Brad my heart and virginity and we broke up because he thought I expected too much.

With Jared, it was the same. I'd almost forgiven him for cheating on me, almost.

But then I chose myself.

The truth is, I do expect a lot out of my love story and the man I'll share it with.

I expect passion and butterflies, and one or two fairy tale moments. When we fight, I want it to hurt. When we fuck, I want to feel it with every fiber of my being. When a man confesses his love to me, I expect him to mean it. I don't want to question the words' authenticity. I want to be claimed and owned and ruled and possessed by love.

Is that expecting too much?

Maybe it is, maybe I've read one too many love stories.

From what I've learned so far, maybe I do expect too much.

Especially if I can't get the man I'm falling for to defend me.

Did I cause the drama? No. Dominic did.

Did I expect too much from Sean?

It breaks my heart to think I might have. That he's incapable of being who I hope he would be because he's given me so much of what I want already.

Should I compromise to keep him? Hell no.

Sean was wrong. Dominic was wrong. I am taking up for myself.

I've lived through two bad examples and know enough to see the warning signs.

Some part of me thinks that my sickly heart was inherited, coded in my genes. Not only that, but I've also watched my mom fall in and out over the years with the same sort of reckless regard for her own well-being, always one-upping her last disaster with a bigger one and hoping for the biggest payoff.

It's only since she started dating her latest boyfriend that she's calmed that part of herself. But inside, I know she's never gotten that payoff. She struggled for years to find a man to give her those feelings but instead settled. She gave up, and we both know it.

Even though I vowed to be different from my mother in the way I live my life, we have the same disease. We crave the all-consuming, soul-stealing, drama-filled romances that are destined to end badly. I inherited my heart from her, and it's relentless.

Though I'm fearful, I can't give up. Finding love is the mecca of what I dream for myself. I have other dreams, dreams enough to hold me. A fulfilling career is a no-brainer but finding that once-in-a-lifetime love is non-negotiable. While my life has been riddled with shitty examples, I still believe it exists.

My greatest hope is to be in all-consuming love. My biggest fear is to be in all-consuming love.

Sean brought out that thirsty girl, only to dry her hopes in the next breath.

Some part of me already knows falling for Sean will end badly. I feel way too much already—way too much for just a month.

But isn't that what I want?

Maybe for now, I should just listen to the voice of reason in my head, instead of the addict in my heart. The voice that tells me there are relationships out there filled with just as much passion that don't have to result in bloodletting.

The truth is, taking this stance has been hell. I miss him horribly.

But I'll stand on principle because to hell with playing the fool. Sean was right in another sense. If I don't stick up for myself early, I'm setting a low bar.

So mad I'll remain.

Fucking men.

I stab at my food, my mood shit as I glare at the side of Roman's head.

Lamb chops with mint sauce and rosemary potatoes. It's the most pretentious dinner I can think of. I *hate* lamb. Roman returns my gaze, unflinching as I stare at him with his own arctic eyes. He's handsome as far as older men go, and for a second, I wonder what he looked like when my mother met him. Was he as charming as Sean, just as disarming? Did he play the game of trust me before he hurt her? Or did his cold exterior only intrigue her to the point she couldn't resist him? She's never told me the details of their story, even though I've asked multiple times. She refuses to visit that part of her life, and I assume because it's painful. If being his daughter is this uncomfortable, I can only imagine what being the woman in his life was like.

"Is there something wrong with your food, Cecelia?"

"I don't like lamb."

"You liked it when you were younger."

"I tolerated it to please you."

"I see we aren't in the business of pleasing our father anymore."

"I've grown up. I prefer to eat what I enjoy."

Roman cuts his chop, dipping it in the green goo before he hesitates. "Cecelia, I'm aware I've missed a lot—"

"Eight years," I wipe my mouth. "Forgive me if I'm wondering what the hell I'm doing here."

"You're in a mood tonight."

"I'm curious."

"I see." His wrists rest on the edge of the table. His cutlery posed just so. The ritual makes me sick. We aren't a family. I'm a part of his corporation.

"You're part of my legacy. You are my only child." No apologies for the years he's missed. No excuses for his extended absence. Simplistic answers with no emotion behind them. I can't even imagine Roman being intimate with anyone. Mom must have had a field day loving this bastard.

"We were discussing your parents last time we talked. Did you grow up wealthy?"

He frowns. "Somewhat."

"Define somewhat."

"My mother had a fair amount of money she inherited when she married my father. But they squandered their small fortune away instead of growing it and died penniless. That's where they made their mistake."

"Were you close?"

"No."

"Why?"

"They were not affectionate people and do refrain from any rude comments. I'm aware some consider that a shortcoming."

"Only people with a pulse."

He chews his food slowly and looks at me pointedly. "My blood is red, I assure you. It's the same blood that runs through your veins."

"I'm nothing like you."

"You have one sharp tongue."

"Don't pretend to care, Roman. Why make me a part of all this at the last minute if you really didn't want me in your life? Why give me anything at all, if you could just write a check and be done with me?"

He slowly lifts his tumbler to his lips and takes a sip. "Maybe I have regrets on how I handled things with you."

"Maybe?"

"I do." He sets his glass down and presses his napkin against his mouth. "Excuse me. I have business."

"Great talking to you, *Sir*."

I'm most definitely about to start my period, and I'm sure this shark smells it. I would feel bad if it wasn't Roman Horner on the receiving end of my attitude. But tonight, I'm over the bullshit pretense.

He pauses at the doorway and then turns to me. He waits until our eyes connect before he speaks. "I gave you my last name because I had hoped to be a father to you. One day, I realized I never would be, and the least I could do was care for you financially. I'm handing you my life's work because of my failure. All I ask is that you play a small part. I know it doesn't make up for it, but it's all I'll ever have to give you."

"Did you love my mother?" I ask hoarsely, damning the budding emotion. "Have you ever loved *anyone?*"

He grimaces, his eyes fixed somewhere in the past as he

stares through me. "I tried." With that confession, he leaves me at the table.

I do my best to ignore the sting behind my eyes and the tear that falls because of it. That was it. I know it in my soul. That will be the one and only confession my father ever gives me about the way he feels about me.

After years of wondering, I finally have my answer.

He tried.

My father just admitted he didn't love me.

I pull the tear from my face with my finger and study it. Roman Horner probably would have preferred an abortion to an heir, and he thinks an inheritance will redeem him in some fucked up way.

I smash the hope-filled tear I didn't know I was harboring between my fingers and finally give myself permission to hate him. Just more proof that the fantasies of a masochistic heart are much better than any experience with the real thing.

With that knowledge, I retreat.

SO BE IT. IT'S BEEN DAYS SINCE THE TEXTS STOPPED, AND I'm still convincing myself I'm fine with it. If Sean can't deal with me standing my ground about his own shitty behavior, we're already a lost cause.

I fell for every line his beautiful lips fed me. Only to feel slapped.

I caught myself just in time.

To make shitty matters worse, my plant bully has taken it upon herself to make my days more grueling, taunting me in Spanish—I can't understand—in the breakroom and all but smashed me into the wall when we punched out last night. She's got it in for me, and she's making it known shift by shift. The last thing I need to do is report it to my supervisor, who I'm actively avoiding.

I smooth on more lotion and kick back in the lounger,

feeling the tingle of the sun on my skin. A much-needed day off alone is exactly what I need to recharge. I just wished my libido would do me the solid of agreeing.

Sean woke that part of me up again, and now it refuses to be ignored. Day in, day out, I'm constantly in a place where the throb won't cease and my new craving reminds me of what I'm missing.

I'll be thankful when I outgrow my teenage hormones, but I have to woman up early because I'm no longer dating boys.

Restless from another uneventful day, I close my eyes after my third attempt to get into a novel, certain it'll take me more than seven days to break my new bad habit.

A tidal wave of water covers me, and I shriek from where I lay, jerking to sit, and when I do, I see none other than Dominic appear from beneath the rolling surface. Water pours from him as he stands to his full height a second before my view is blocked by the man who I spent the last week ghosting but continues to haunt my every thought.

"You think I'd let you get away that easily?" Hazel eyes glitter down at me, along with the dazzling smile I can't banish from my thoughts.

"What are you doing here?"

The slap of the closing gate has me peeking around Sean as Tyler comes into view, hauling a cooler. "Hey, beautiful," he greets, scanning my yard and letting out a whistle, "I can see why you're holing up here."

With the salute of my hand, I cover my eyes, peering up at Sean. "What the hell are y'all doing?"

"We shared our spot with you," he shrugs. "Only fair."

"That may be, but I assumed you could take a hint."

His eyes flare and his jaw twitches. "Don't play bitch. I like you too much."

He takes a seat next to me and I don't know whether I want to kiss him or slap him, I decide on neither.

"Kiss," he says, reading my thoughts all too well. He leans in, and I do my best to hold my breath but fail, inhaling him fully. It's like coming home.

"Get that asshole out of my pool."

"Stop it," Sean snaps.

I rear back. "Who the hell do you think you are?"

"I'm the *boyfriend* you're pissed at."

His statement strikes deep, threatening my progress as Tyler sets the cooler between the loungers and pulls off his T-shirt.

"Give us a minute," Sean asks Tyler who nods, grinning at me over his shoulder.

"Hey, Cee."

I can't help my return smile, especially when that dimple appears. "Hey, Tyler."

"I'm jealous," Sean whispers.

"About what?"

"That smile you just gave him. Did I really fuck up that badly?"

"You hurt me," I decide on stark honesty. "I thought we had a good thing, and I feel like you threw me to the wolf."

"That's what I'm trying to avoid. But you twisted the whole situation into what you expected to happen. You expected me to show my Gemini side, but I'm a Virgo, remember? I had no chance against your imagination. This fight was inevitable. We both knew the minute I pissed you off; this would be your argument."

I gape at him. "I might have a hard time trusting, but you're making it impossible."

He grips me by the neck and leans in, so we're nose to nose. "Tell me you don't miss me."

"Irrelevant. If I can't trust you to have my back when I need you, then what's the point?"

"The point is you didn't need me. You just *thought* you did, and I wanted you to realize that. Instead, you left my bed and decided to punish me for not handling your business."

"*My* business?" I gawk. "You have some nerve."

He refuses to give me space and grips me tighter. "I call it faith. You are a lot stronger than you think you are, and I wanted you to see that."

"Why?"

"Because I want you around, and often," he murmurs. The part of me that wants to fight is growing weak by the sight of him and his logic. My feelings for him scare me. It scares me a lot, and maybe I was looking for a reason to push him away.

"I thought you said it was my decision."

He threads his fingers through my hair. "I don't like your decision. At. Fucking. All. But I'll respect it. If that's what you really want."

He's got his mirrored sunglasses on and I pull them off, sliding them on so he can't see the emotions I'm sure I'm broadcasting. "I won't be treated like that."

"Then don't allow yourself to be, but your point's been made with me. I'm sorry, baby," he murmurs, and I can only hope it's sincere. "You'd better believe I'm going to have your back when you need it." He presses my hand to his chest. "Believe that if you don't believe anything else about me."

I can't deny him. I can't, no matter how much it scares me. I want Sean, I want his words to ring true, and the only way to know is by taking a chance on him, and riding this out.

"I thought I was doing the right thing, but I don't know what that is when it comes to you." He looks torn, his eyes losing focus as he says this.

"What do you mean?"

I feel the shift in his posture, all signs of play gone. "It means for both our sakes, I should probably leave you alone, but I'm not fucking going to." He flattens me to him and kisses the life out of me. I moan, my hands instantly clutching him as he inappropriately deepens our kiss. But that's Sean, and it's one of the things I love so much about him. He kisses me and kisses me, and I take it, giving back just as much. When he pulls away, I'm on fire, unable to hide the rapid rise and fall of my chest.

"Fuck, I look good on you." He lifts the glasses resting on my nose and presses his forehead to mine. "I really wish I hadn't brought these assholes with me."

I peek over to see Dominic perched on the shallow end of the pool.

"My father has security cameras set up everywhere, and he's already threatened me about company. This isn't going to bode well."

"We'll handle it."

"You'll…handle it? How?"

He nods toward Dominic and I groan.

Sean turns back to me. "Look, he isn't easy. But he's here because he wants to be."

"Is that supposed to make me feel better? The guy is a motherfucker."

Tyler claps his hands together, joining us at the loungers. "Cool, Mom and Dad made up. Time to celebrate." He grabs a beer from the cooler, shakes it up and sprays us with it.

"You shit," I smile, just as Sean lifts me honeymoon style into his arms and jumps us into the pool. When we emerge, I'm grinning, no doubt the goofy one that tells him far too much. He gazes down at me and kisses me before he sends me flying. I shriek as I come up, his sunglasses half-on/half-off.

"You ass, I wasn't ready!"

"Then I guess you better up your game," he taunts when I charge him. We frolic in the water as Tyler makes himself comfortable in a lounger, turning up his radio. Sean's phone rings and he gets out of the pool, holding up a finger to me that it's important before answering. "Hey, Dad."

I make my way over to Dominic who sips a beer. I can't see his eyes behind a pair of classic black Ray-Bans, but I know they're on me as I wade through the water toward him.

"I guess you want an apology," he flips his glasses to rest on his head, his thick black hair cradling them easily. Soaking wet, he's even more deadly, his lashes darker, everything darker. It's impossible not to note his appeal. And his venomous smirk makes breathing around him no easier.

"I won't hold my breath."

He holds up a finger, downing his beer and I roll my eyes. "Okay, I think I'm ready." He exhales as if he's about to give a grand speech. "I'm sorry I told Sean I caught you staring at my dick."

I can't help it. I burst out laughing.

He gives me his first genuine smile and it knocks me for a loop.

"You are a rare bastard."

"I prefer motherfucker. At least then, it would be somewhat factual. Isn't that right, Tyler?"

Tyler doesn't flinch from where he lays basking in the sun. "Fuck you."

Dominic grins and I shake my head.

"You had your door open. I was shocked, to say the least."

"And the other five minutes?"

"Do women actually sleep with you?"

"No, never. They're too busy screaming my name," he says without a trace of humor. "Except the last girl, she was a corpse."

"You are unreal. Psychiatrist's dream, indeed." Briefly, I wonder if violence does make this maniac hard. If it's the only thing that makes him hard.

"What you thinking about?" Dominic asks, his lips twitching as he lowers his sunglasses.

"Nothing."

He smirks before pulling himself from the pool and heading toward the back door.

"What are you doing?"

"Have to use the can."

"You could ask."

He turns from me, and his swim shorts dip slightly, revealing the top of his toned ass as he positions himself on the side of the house.

I cover my eyes. "Oh my God, through the door past the study, down the hall on the left. Savage."

"Oh," he tucks himself back into his pants, "I might like that better than motherfucker."

I palm my face as Sean chuckles, rejoining me in the pool. "You'll get used to him. I swear."

"Either that or I'll kill him."

"Or that." Sean corners me where I stand tucked in the corner of deeper water, pulling me into his hold.

"So, you get to use your phone, but I can't have mine?"

"I needed it today for my parents. Sorry, I know that seems hypocritical."

"It is."

"Everything I ask is for a reason."

"Which you *will* give me."

He nods. "When the time is right." His breath hits my skin as he leans in and I go languid, due to his proximity alone. "Tell me something, Pup."

"What?"

"Why'd you give up so easy?"

His eyes bore into mine and one hit of those hazels is like taking a shot of truth serum. "Is it because you don't trust yourself, or you don't trust me?"

"Both."

"Trust your instincts," his tone anything but playful.

"You're being cryptic again."

"I want you, how's that?"

"That's…"

He presses himself against me and a breathy moan escapes me, my eyes darting past his shoulder.

"Where's Tyler?"

"I told him to fuck off for a second."

"Why?"

He kisses me, and in seconds I'm wrapped around him, my bikini bottoms pushed to the side as his fingers enter me. He hooks my arm around his neck. "Because I can't go another fucking minute without being inside you. Hold onto me, baby."

That's all the warning I get before he invades me, thrusting so deep, I bite onto his shoulder to muffle my moans. He grinds into me, my back against the unforgiving cement as he consumes me. He moves the triangle at my nipple and sucks deep, speeding up all the while keeping us connected to the point it's almost painful. He's punishing me in the most delicious way, and I feel it, his claiming. Within seconds, I come with his name on my lips as my eyes search for any sign of Dominic and Tyler over his shoulder. I'm not sure I would make Sean stop at this point, even if they did walk into view.

"Goddamn, I missed you," he grunts and pulls out, biting into the flesh of my shoulder as he comes.

"Missed you too," I mumble before he draws my lips into a

kiss, and then another, and then another. He rights my bottoms after tucking himself back into his board shorts seconds before Tyler walks back through the gate. Sean buries his face in my neck, his breathing labored as Tyler speaks to us both like he has no clue we're post-orgasm. Maybe he doesn't, but what we did was the closest I've ever come to voyeurism. My cheeks heat as Sean pulls back, his golden smile dazzling as I slowly shake my head.

"I promise a lot more than CliffsNotes, later. We good?"

"Sex isn't going to fix our communication issue," I point out, trying to level the playing field.

We stare each other down for several seconds. "I know, but please don't do that to me again," he asks softly.

"Do what?"

"Cut me."

Chapter Twenty

"**G**IRL, YOU ARE GLOWING," MELINDA SAYS AS WE CLOCK out. You must be spendin' all your time outdoors these days."

"Mostly, yeah."

"Well, if that smile you're wearing has anything to do with the one matching our supervisor's…" she pauses, giving me time to confirm or deny, I do neither.

"Anyway, even if he's trouble, he's pretty to look at."

He is, he's beautiful. For the last week he's treated me with nothing short of devotion. His kisses are lasting longer, his looks filled with more. My feet haven't touched the ground since he bulldozed his way back into my space and began ruthlessly chipping away at my reinforced heart. We spend no nights apart, and I don't bother reporting to Roman where I'm going anymore. Most nights with Sean, I spend the night at his house.

Dominic's being his usual charming self, and only once have I extended any sort of olive branch. He locks himself in his room constantly, music blasting until the late hours of the night. In an effort to ease some of our tension, I made some homemade ice cream and brought a bowl up to his room where I found him pacing in front of his computer, if it can be called that. It looks more like a space station equipped with three massive screens and two keyboards. I set my offering on his desk, and he all but slammed the door in my face in thanks. When I asked Sean what Dominic was working on, he quickly changed the subject, and so I dropped it, no closer to finding a piece of the puzzle that is Dominic King.

As a veteran wallflower, I've spent years simply observing people, some more than others, to try and figure out what makes them tick. Though I'm in the midst of shedding my introvert skin, old habits die hard. Dominic is definitely a new focal point for me.

The bigger question in my mind is why is an MIT graduate working at a garage, instead of looking for a job to get him into a higher tax bracket? Surely Dominic didn't get a degree at one of the best schools in the country to replace brakes and mufflers for the rest of his days.

But I keep those questions to myself. One, because it's not my business. Two, because Dominic *is* a motherfucker and still engages me at every turn. However, I've been giving back just as good as I get. Since that day we called a semi-truce, we've grown more playful in our sparring matches.

Despite my curiosity about Dominic, the majority of my attention outside of work belongs to Sean. A few times since that day at the pool, I've felt a little guilty for trying to shut him out, though I got the apology I think I deserved. But some part of me is still holding back. Maybe it's the jaded part that keeps me on edge. I think most of it is because some part of me can't believe he's real. The irony is the cynic in me doesn't want to be right, because even she's falling for him.

The summer nights have been alive, full of electricity as we split our time, going to Eddie's on occasion to throw darts, or shooting pool with guys at the garage, or simply driving around as I try and up my skill behind the wheel of his life-sized Matchbox car.

Tonight, we've decided to forgo all our new norms for some one-on-one. Through a set of unlocked gates, I pull up next to a large barn and park in a space to see Sean waiting for me. I can't help the elation that stirs when he peers up at me with a knowing smile before he crushes out a cigarette with his boot.

"Hey, baby," he pulls me to him, kissing me deeply as I lift up on my toes and return his kiss.

I glance behind him at rows upon rows of apple trees, the angry branches filled to the brim with the blossoming fruit. There are a dozen or more farms in Triple Falls, and the locals take their pride in their apples seriously. Annually, at the start of autumn, Triple Falls holds an apple festival in the square that most townies consider the highlight of their year. Townies, including Melinda, who insists I cannot miss it.

"What are we doing here?"

"Midnight picnic," he turns to gather the supplies stacked on his hood. He hands me a familiar blanket before gathering the rest, which consists of a battery-operated lantern and plastic bags before starting us down a path through rows of trees. It's picturesque, especially under his small camp light, the mountains in the distance silhouetted by the night sky.

"How did you get access to this place?"

"A buddy's parents own it. But it's all ours tonight."

"This is incredible," I look around as I follow him down a

line of trees, and he stops when we're far enough down that our cars are impossible to see.

"Good apples, but I've got the goods here." He lifts a plastic bag.

I eye the lid of the container which reads The Pitt Stop. "From your parents' restaurant?"

"Yeah, it's lukewarm, but it'll still be good. Let's park here." I toss out the blanket and begin spreading it out. "I'll take you there on our next day off."

"Promise?"

He pulls the light toward his face. "Scout's honor."

I roll my eyes. "You were never a Scout."

He chuckles. "What makes you say that?"

"Maybe because of your issue with authority. I can see you arguing with your troop leader about rules and principles you refuse to abide by because they were created by self-righteous assholes."

He sets the lantern on the blanket and pulls me to him, kissing me soundly. "You're getting to know me pretty well."

"I am."

We take our seat on what I now consider my lucky blanket before he carefully unpacks a small feast. Aside from our one fight, it's been almost idyllic with him. At times, I try to imagine life in Triple Falls without him and can't stomach what it would be like if dinners with Roman and shifts at the plant were all I had to look forward to.

He's not just a distraction with a nice penis, although, his penis is incredible. Emotion swells in my chest as I study his profile in the soft glow of the fake camp light. Whatever reservations I have, I want to let them go. But I still have lingering doubts I've kept to myself to keep the peace. Yet one question gnaws at me daily, and if I want to give myself over to him fully, I need an answer.

"Sean?"

"Yeah?" Distracted with his task, he kneels on the blanket, opening the first container. The crickets sing loudly around us and I take in the scene, the gnawing to ask growing at the setting, the sounds around us, a romance addict's fantasy. I've had so many firsts with Sean—at twenty-five, adventurous as he is—I'm sure I would be hard-pressed to give him one of his own. And that's some of where my hesitance lies, with the question I don't want to ask because I know how it will sound. I slip off my shoes and socks and run my feet in the cool grass, deciding it's best left alone for the moment.

"Cecelia."

"Yeah?"

"You had a question?"

"I forgot it."

"No, you didn't."

"You don't want me to ask it."

He looks at me expectantly. "All right, now I have to know."

"How did Dominic know about the waterfall?"

He exhales, putting his hands on his knees, before peering up at me with guilty eyes. "Your real question is, how many girls have I taken there, right?"

"Is that like the place you take all women?"

He shakes his head slowly. "It's a place I love, that I will often frequent with any company. It's kind of slim pickings around here at times, like there are only a few restaurants in town worth a shit. This is a small town. If you stay in one place long enough, you're bound to have repeats."

"Repeats," I parrot, sipping my iced tea.

He eyes me warily. "Shit, bad choice of words. Look," he moves to sit and draws up his knees, his toned forearms resting on them. "No, you aren't the first or second girl I've taken there."

Suspicions confirmed, I try to hide my disappointment. "Thanks for the truth. I guess that day was special to me, that's all."

He chucks my chin. "Then let it be. You think I was thinking about the last girl I was with when I had you underneath me? Fuck no. And I like that you're jealous."

"Eww," I prop up to my elbows and drop my head back dramatically. "I guess sometimes I make it obvious you're dating a teenager."

"Jealousy isn't limited or nullified by age, babe. And you've been hurt. You've told me you have from the start. You're being cautious. You don't want to be fucked over again. Nothing wrong with that. I get it. And I'm not mad you asked about it."

"Do you get mad?"

"Yes," he says softly, so softly, it's scary, "and it's not something you want to see."

"Oooooh," I turn on my stomach, kicking my feet into motion behind me. "Do tell. Were you an angry child?"

"No, I was more like 'Tarzan with Chimpanzee rip your arm off if you fuck with me' tendencies."

I laugh. "I believe it."

"I did get into a lot of fights."

"Why?"

"Because I was a little asshole."

"So, what's changed?"

"Cute. I was going to share my banana pudding, but…"

"Hey, I'm sorry. You haven't given me many reasons not to trust you."

He frowns. "Cecelia—"

I reach over and run my hand down his jaw. "I hate that I asked. But it's been bothering me."

"Next time ask so you aren't wasting your time."

"I did, but we were fighting, remember?"

"My bad, but I mean it, don't let shit eat at you. Ask."

"I will."

"Good, now eat."

And we do. After, we lay back looking up at the stars as his Zippo closes and an unmistakable smell invades my nose.

I grin over at Sean just as he passes the joint to me. I take a deep inhale and release it, already laughing from the act alone.

"You're such a lightweight," he chuckles.

"And proud of it. Why do you smoke?"

"It's as relaxing as a few beers to me. And if you relax, and don't think about anything or anyone but where you are and who you're with, you can control the high and it won't control you."

"Okay, dude," I say as I inhale in my best stoner impression. He grins and takes it back, and I turn and lay back on the blanket, gazing up at the night sky.

He grabs the hand resting on my stomach and brings it to his mouth to kiss the back of it. His eyes close and my chest buzzes from the intimate act.

"I thought I would hate it here," I admit.

"Glad you don't."

"You're the main reason I don't. You know, I have to leave next year. I'm only here until next summer."

He pauses his kiss on the pad of my finger. "We'll make it count."

"You don't sound so sure."

"Nothing's certain."

"Oh, Lord, not this again."

"It's the truth."

"Always so damned cryptic with me. I'm not an idiot, Sean, you've been trying to indirectly tell me something since we met. What the hell is the big secret?"

He leans in, his grin dazzling in the dim light. "You're the secret."

"Oh, am I?" I reach for the joint. "Give me that, God, I'm going to need it if I'm going to listen to your madness."

"You love it."

"The devastating truth and life philosophy according to Alfred Sean Roberts." I take a small hit and pass it back to him.

"Knowledge is power, baby. Strongest weapon out there." He takes a hit. "You know why they outlawed weed?"

"Not a clue."

He props on his side, the cherry glowing brightly as he takes another pull. "Because the powers that be at the time couldn't figure out how to regulate who grew it and tax it. So they created all this propaganda about how lethal it is. Look up Reefer Madness on YouTube when you get a chance, and you'll see just how far they went. And people believed it because they were told to believe it."

He leans down and spreads my lips with the swipe of his tongue so I open for him. He exhales a plume of smoke into my mouth, forcefully puffing out my cheeks. Laughing, we break apart as I sputter and cough swatting his chest.

"Reefer Madness?"

"And I quote," he widens his eyes. "'Marijuana, the burning weed with its roots in hell!'" I giggle as he leans in and slowly starts to unbutton my shirt, "Smoking the soul-destroying reefer," he drawls, pushing away the fabric to reveal my flesh before running his knuckles along my skin. "They find a moment's pleasure," he murmurs softly, before lowering to kiss the swell of my breasts.

Under his spell, I tangle my fingers in his hair just as he inches his fingers along my sides. "But at a terrible price!" The boom of his voice has me jumping before his fingers dig into me and I laugh hysterically, swatting him away as he shouts in his best preacher man imitation. "*Debauchery! Violence! Murder! Suicide!*"

His fingers continue to tickle me as I twist to free myself. "Stop, Sean, I'm going to pee my pants."

He stops and leans in close, his eyes tick-tocking back and forth erratically. "And the ultimate end of the marijuana addict..." he holds up a finger in a 'wait for it' gesture, "hopeless insanity."

"You're kidding, right? Violence, Murder, Suicide?"

"Don't forget debauchery. And no, I'm not kidding, look it up," he runs his fingers through my hair. "Nineteen thirty-eight. Complete and utter bullshit and the masses bought into it. All because the greedy fuckers couldn't figure out how to tax it and control the distribution, they outlawed it. Now all these years later, they're using it to relieve people of pain, stop seizures, to help treat incurable disorders with just the plant itself without the THC. And the mental effects for some can be just as healing as popping a more harmful pill. Can you imagine where we would be or how far we would have come since nineteen fucking thirty-eight if those assholes hadn't ganged up on a plant? Instead, they taught us it was wrong, because some people decided it was and told us it was, and the law-abiding folk went along with it and preached to others it was wrong. And here we are after decades of it being outlawed and it's suddenly safe for medical and medicinal purposes?" He shakes his head in disgust. "Did you ever hear that story about that guy who got stoned before he went and committed mass murder?"

"No."

"Yeah, me neither. And I doubt anyone else has either because the odds are not fucking likely. We have to be careful about who we listen to."

"You're a one-man revolution. Is there anything about this country you do like?"

"The scenery," he exhales, lifting my bra and running a warm hand over my breast. "Peaks and valleys," he slides his palm over my stomach. "The oceans surrounding it."

I get lost in the workings of his hands and frown when he pauses.

"I mean, the idea of America is great, the execution not so much. But we're still a young country. There's still hope for us."

"I like the way you quack," I say honestly. And I do. I love that he challenges me, makes me think.

"I like your quack too, baby," he dips and kisses me soundly.

"You know," I take the joint. "You would make an amazing politician. Too bad you're addicted to the burning weed with the roots in hell."

He tilts his head, his eyes lit by his lantern. "A politician?"

"You've got my vote."

"Your vote," he bounces his head back and forth, mulling it over. "Yeah, well, I don't want to be a politician."

"Why?"

"I'd rather be part of the solution."

"That's a shame. I was just thinking of all the dirty things I would do to you if you wore a suit."

"Ah," he hangs his head, "so she wants a suit guy."

"No, I want *you*, guy."

I can feel his smile against my chest. "That so?"

"Unfortunately."

"Well," he nestles between my legs and sucks my nipple into his mouth, speaking around the peaked flesh. "I'm going to have to make you work for it."

My breath hitches as I speak. "Don't you always?"

"Yes," he pulls back and looks down on me, "but this is

getting serious, you see because any minute we're going to hit our ultimate end as marijuana addicts. We have to make it count."

He hovers above me with the moonless night sky behind him.

"Then we'd better hurry," I say, lifting to kiss him and he dodges it, pressing my wrists into the blanket.

"You're such an ass."

"And you're…so fucking beautiful," he murmurs softly. "So beautiful…" he places my hand on his chest. "Cecelia, you wound me. Why'd you have to be so pretty?" For a second, I see something I've never seen in his expression and an unmistakable flash of fear in his eyes.

"Sean, what's wrong?"

His eyes clear as he gazes down at me. "Not a damn thing."

"You sure?" I run my hands through his hair as he buries his head in my chest.

"Help me, baby. The madness finally got me."

SWEAT SKATES DOWN MY BACK AS MELINDA BABBLES ON, and I silently curse Sean for the absence of my watch. The wall clock mounted above the plant entrance stopped a week ago and I'm most definitely a slave to time during my shifts. "It was his sister," Melinda says, frowning as I gather the tubs from her and stack them at our workstation. "No, no," she continues, "it was his cousin who did it. Girl, I have never in my life seen—"

"No! No! Fuck this!" The outburst has me pausing and brings Melinda's latest report on the extended family to a halt as we crane our necks while a rapid-fire of Spanish and English bursts throughout the floor. Two women argue heatedly a line over and finally appear in the middle of the floor as one tries to restrain the other. It's then I see the source, Vivica. She's fighting with one of her cronies, who's struggling to push her back toward her place in the line. "I'm over it. I'm done!" She shouts, pushing past her, her dark eyes landing on me and narrowing to slits.

Dread courses through me as she begins to make her way in my direction.

Oh, fuck. Oh, fuck. Oh, fuck. Oh, fuck.

I've been in one physical altercation in my life, and it was with an inanimate object, a skirt.

I knew working here wouldn't win me any popularity contests, but I had no idea what kind of a reputation my father had in this town. He's not beloved by *any*, let alone all. No one here seems to respect him in any capacity. The sniggers and whispers I hear at my back are becoming harder to ignore, but I did not think I'd be held responsible for anything concerning matters at the plant. My assumption is clearly wrong because she's coming straight for me, and I know her beef has nothing to do with me unless it's about Sean.

"You!" She yells, gaining the attention of everyone else on the line. I point to my chest like an idiot.

"Are you not the owner's daughter?"

Anyone who didn't know before is aware now as her friend manages to get between us when she's only a couple steps away. "Vivica, you need to stop and think about what you're doing."

"What *I'm* doing?" She snaps at her friend before turning to me. I'm still debating whether to lead with a donkey kick or risk a punch. "Your father is a fucking crook. Did you know that?" She waves a piece of paper I recognize. A pay stub. "I worked forty-two hours last week and only got paid for thirty-nine." She flaps her hand around again, gesturing toward the rest of the workers on the floor. "Ask them, ask them how many times it's happened to them."

"They'll fix it," her friend says, still attempting to usher

Vivica back. The line stops, the noise of the conveyor that was drowning her out before doing nothing now to stop every ear from pricking our way.

"Oh, they'll fix it, and then they'll figure out a way to get rid of me."

I muster up the courage to speak. "Look, I don't have anything to do with—"

"You are his daughter!" She yells at the top of her lungs as more eyes dart my way. "Bet your paychecks aren't short."

"Honestly, I haven't—"

"Haven't looked?" She scoffs. "Of course *you* haven't. Well, allow me to enlighten you, princess. He's been doing this for *years*, screwing us on our overtime, shorting our checks just enough so we don't raise too much hell. We get told over and over it will be fixed, that it's an oversight." She scours me and not in a flattering way. "Are you not rich enough?"

"Ma'am, I'm not..."

"Ma'am?" She harrumphs. "I'm twenty-five years old."

"I don't own the plant. I work here. I don't have anything to do—"

"You're his *daughter*."

I know what that's supposed to mean, but I've never lived any sort of meaningful reality behind that statement.

"It's not as simple as that," I try weakly to start my defense.

"Vivica, he's got his own daughter working on this line, in this heat," the woman says defending me, though the accusation in her eyes doesn't quite match her tone. "I don't think he cares much for her opinion."

"She's exactly right," I finally snap back, straightening my spine to face off with her. "And he doesn't ask for it. I have nothing to do with company polic—"

"It's not policy. It's theft!"

All eyes are now on me as I check out the room and see what they aren't saying. People who've otherwise kept their heads down when I walk by are now looking directly at me in the same way Vivica is, their openly hostile expressions knocking the fight out of me. Maybe they've regarded me this way since I started, and I haven't noticed it as much because I've had my head in the clouds. "I'm just working here because, well, because..."

"Are you here to spy on us?" Vivica squares up, planting her hands on her hips. There's no way to win this battle.

"No," I blurt out honestly, "Not at all. I've been..." I struggle with word choice, but what can I say? That I've been biding my time until I inherit my father's money? Fire rages in my cheeks as I try and will myself out of this nightmare. "I can try to say something to him."

"Try all you want. It won't matter," the friend says, trying to keep Vivica at bay. "Don't waste your breath."

"This is his plant," Vivica argues, "you work here, and you want to tell me you have nothing to do with him?"

Everyone begins to crowd in as my throat dries up. I'm shaking uncontrollably now, figurative walls closing in on me. I feel suffocated, completely unprepared for the hostility directed toward me. And from the looks I'm getting—this has been a long time coming. No one is defending me. They too, want answers. Answers I don't have. "Have you told the supervisor?"

Her smile is acidic. "You mean your *boyfriend?*"

"Vivica, collect yourself and get into my office, *now.*" Sean's voice booms from behind me. "*Now.*"

"You think we are stupid, Sean? You think we can't see what's going on here?"

He doesn't miss a beat. "And what you're doing right now, Vivica, you think that's going to help your case?"

"My case? How many times have we asked you to make this right since you've been back?"

"I'll get it handled," he snaps, keeping his eyes trained on hers. "Everyone, get back on the line, now!" Everyone flies back to their places as Sean turns to me. "Take five."

"I don't need it," I step toward Vivica.

Sean stops me from engaging with the bite in his tone. "It wasn't an offer, Cecelia, take five."

"I'm sorry this is happening," I tell Vivica, "You have my word. I'll talk to him."

"Sure, you're sorry, wiping your ass with my shorted paychecks."

"Off the line. In my office, *now*," Sean barks, and she spins and stomps toward the front doors.

"Too late for me anyway. Fuck this place."

I move to join Melinda, who's working double-time to keep our station clear, no doubt bursting at the seams as the drama unfolds. It's probably the most exciting thing to happen here in years. Melinda bumps my shoulder as I slide back in next to her and try to bury myself in our task, never more grateful for a tub of calculators in my life.

"Take five," Sean's at my side as I fight the emotions warring inside me.

"You're just going to make it worse," I snap. "Let me work."

I can feel his stare on me for a solid ten seconds before he concedes and walks away. When I'm able to speak, I turn to Melinda. "Is that how you feel about me?"

"Honey, I know you," she nods over her shoulder, "but they don't. I wouldn't spend any time trying to convince them otherwise, people only hear what they want to." It's a bitter truth I have to swallow down. No part of the next year will get easier for me here. I'm guilty by association, and these people don't just dislike

Roman Horner because he's the boss, they're aggrieved and have been for some time.

Embarrassed tears threaten as I collect the empty tubs and nod.

"Have your paychecks been short?" I ask, and I see the answer before she speaks it.

"They have been, several times." She keeps her eyes down. "It was today too."

"By how much?"

"Just a half-hour."

My next question, I whisper just before the buzzer sounds and the line resumes. "Did you tell people Sean and I are together?"

"Come on now, that's just obvious," she replies, clear sympathy in her eyes. I know it's true, and I don't argue with her.

The whole plant now definitely knows I'm the owner's daughter, and just in case they missed it, they also know I'm fucking my supervisor.

Perfect.

I never counted on my dad's pull to get me any preferential treatment, but I sure as hell didn't expect to be attacked this way because of it. It's the sad truth that it was Vivica's desperation that started that argument. I have no idea, but she probably needs this job, I'm sure she needed that overtime. Judging by her reaction, she must have been counting on it. Melinda needed that half-hour too, because she's just put her mother into a nursing home, and she's being forced to come up with some of that monthly expense. Her husband is a painter and often takes odd jobs to make up for the lack of steady pay. They all count on this plant, on Roman Horner.

It's then I think of Selma and fight more tears. In a few hours, I can lose my shit. But time is what cripples me as seconds and minutes drag by, an invisible chain around my neck. Sean makes more than one appearance on the floor, no doubt to check on me, but he doesn't engage, he just talks to some of the others and monitors the line as I avoid any exchange. Melinda picks up where she left off, ending with a story about tomorrow's event, a church fundraiser.

By the time I clock out, I'm exhausted, both mentally and physically. It's when I hit the parking lot that fear sets in.

Did Sean fire Vivica? If so, is she waiting for me to deliver her wrath? Surely, she knows I had nothing to do with her short paycheck. But that's a rational line of thinking, and angry people don't always think rationally. Lord knows, she was anything but rational when she left the floor.

What if she's truly decided it's my fault? I make a beeline for my car as Melinda calls out to me. I don't want her putting herself at risk for me, and the truth is, she's the kind of woman who might. She proves my thinking right as she tries to join me on my walk into the parking lot.

"Honey, wait up, I'll walk with you."

"I'm fine, see you tomorrow," I yell over my shoulder as I lose her in the first five rows of cars. Vivica is no doubt the type to 'cut a bitch,' and it's all I can do to pace myself to power walking. The minute I make it to the driver's seat and lock my doors, I burst into tears. I hate that I feel so weak. I hate that I don't know if I would have been able to defend myself if I was attacked. I hate the position being Roman's daughter puts me in. Whether or not I declared I was his kid, someone would have found out, and hiding it might not have been the right call either. Did they really think I was sent to spy on them? That's insanity.

My phone rings from my purse and I ignore it, knowing it's Sean.

Headlights click on behind me, and I look in my rearview to see Sean sitting in his Nova, gazing back at me in the mirror. He was waiting for me, and he saw me crying.

Great.

Done with the day, I jerk my head to keep him at bay while clearing my face as he opens his car door to get to me. I shake my head, profusely denying him the chance and put my car into gear. I haul ass out of the parking lot as the humiliation subsides, and anger begins to smoke itself into my system. I'm not mad at Sean, but I don't want to face him with these conflicting emotions. He can see my crazy when he deserves it. Tonight, he did what he had to do, but I refuse to unload on him, not with the range of emotions I'm feeling. He follows me closely, leaving me when I turn onto the lone road home. There he leaves me, and I'm grateful.

When I pull up, I'm met with an empty driveway and an empty house. My phone rings in my hand, just as I clear my bedroom door.

"I don't want to talk now," I sniffle back furious tears.

"I got that after mile five, but it's not your fault." The tenderness in his voice hurts. I do my best to rein it in, but my voice shakes anyway.

"Did you know about this?"

"I've been working on it since I got back."

"So, this is the norm? He shorts their paychecks?"

"Have you ever looked at your pay stub?"

No, I haven't. I've simply cashed them and assumed they were correct. More anger coils as I make a decision and hit reply on my latest email. I'm typing furiously as I speak.

"Did you fire her?"

"Yes."

"Damnit, Sean. Why?"

"Because it's my job, and her behavior was too severe for a write-up."

"You know it's wrong."

Silence.

"This is my battle. Let me fight it."

"I'm here if you need me."

"I know, and I'm grateful, but you've got to stop taking me off the line, okay? It's already a shitshow, and I don't want to give them any more excuses to come after me."

"You've got to know I won't let them hurt you. I've got your back."

"And I'm grateful, but you can't. This truly is my fight and I'm...really fucking angry and I don't want to take it out on you, okay? I have to go." I hang up, livid about the nosedive my day has taken and intent on making the right guy pay. Vivica's words ring like a chant in my head, with the emphasis changing on each repetition.

He's *your father*. He's *your* father. He's your *father*.

Ten minutes later I shoot off my email, wash the night away in the shower and begin prepping for my morning meeting.

Chapter Twenty-Two

"I DON'T APPRECIATE THE TONE OF YOUR EMAIL, CECELIA," my father starts the minute I come into view and pour my coffee. He must have gotten in late, and I know the reason for his arrival was due to the content of the email I sent last night. More often than not, he's been staying in Charlotte, leaving me the sole occupant of this massive house.

"You put me in this position," I counter as I take the seat next to him. "You wanted me to take my job seriously. Well, this is me, taking it seriously." I lay my pay stubs between us. "I've been shorted a quarter-hour on nearly every weekly paycheck since I started and a full hour on two of them."

"You have a supervisor to report this to." There's no insinuation in his tone which brings me relief that my relationship with Sean is just a factory rumor and hasn't reached corporate ears. He's taken no other interest in me and if he's been monitoring the security cameras, thanks to Dominic, they're now on an uneventful loop.

"We all answer to someone, don't we? I'm sure a particular government agency would be interested to know that your employees have been shorted for years, sweetening your bottom line. Especially if they were tipped off by a call from the CEO's daughter."

His eyes flash with pure hostility as I try and muster up more courage. I'm still on the fence if this is the smartest move to make regarding my future, but I remember all those people that gathered around me, the weight of their accusation. This isn't just about me. This is about thousands of people and the fact that they're living their future out in that plant.

"I have no plans to do that. But I'm certain this is an ongoing issue that you need to take seriously because they're past the point of fed up. So much so that yesterday, I was humiliated on the line for this. Is it really worth it to have your employees loathe you?"

"I couldn't care less how they feel about me. I provide jobs—"

"It's theft, pure and simple, for the people who make," I cut my hand through the air, "all of this possible. You wanted me to get a taste of your business to earn my place, well it's got one hell of an aftertaste, Sir. When's the last time you spent a day in your own factory?"

"Your point's been made, Cecelia. I'll look into it, but don't think your threats are what make a difference to me. I've been running this company since I was twenty-seven years old."

"I was afraid to walk to my car last night. Do you have any idea how that feels?"

"You live long enough, and you'll make enemies."

"Glad to see you're concerned. Did you know about this?"

"I will tighten security if need be. This is an accounting oversight, I'm sure."

"An oversight that's involved every single employee check? Pardon me if I call bullshit."

"You've never been so liberal with your tongue. What has gotten into you?"

"It was a hundred degrees in there two days ago!" I feel like I'm going to burst into flames as I slap my hand on my small stack of paychecks. "A hundred degrees, easy. It's a literal sweatshop and you have me working there alongside everyone else. Did you expect I would just shut up and take my paychecks and play along? Well, you almost got lucky in that respect. I wasn't paying attention, but I got my lids razored off last night."

"Cecelia, stop with the dramatics. I've heard your concerns."

"When's the last time you updated anything in that plant to make it comfortable for the people who run it for you?"

He clears his throat, eyes dropping, voice ice cold. "Again, I'll look into it."

"That's a standard reply and frankly, Sir, I'm not accepting it. Especially, if this is the legacy I'm to inherit. A plant of disgruntled employees who loathe my existence because they can't feed their families? No thanks."

He straightens in his seat. "I will not be lectured to or threatened by my own daughter."

"If I'm being forced to pay, literally, for your oversights, then I will have my say with you. That woman told me over and over that I was your daughter, and I had no idea how to convey that meant nothing!"

His eyes snap to mine, and I feel the full brunt of his narrowed blue-eyed stare.

I tongue my cheek, damning my swimming vision as I glare at him. "Who better to inform you of your wrongdoings, other than your biggest mistake?"

He swallows as the air shifts, followed by a long silence.

Something resembling remorse flits over his features before it evaporates. "I'm sorry you feel that way." For a single moment, I do feel something, something tangible, and it passes between us at that table. A flicker of hope lights in my chest, but I bat it away, refusing to back down.

"You want me to take pride in my job? Pay me. You want my tone respectful? Be a respectable employer. You want me to respect my name? Be a respectable man."

His eyes lift to mine, his voice soft. "I've sacrificed quite a lot to make sure you're cared for."

"I've never asked you for a single thing, aside for extending support to my mother, who worked herself stupid to make sure I had everything I needed, and you wouldn't do that. I'm asking you to make this right, not for me, but for them. If you want to continue to dangle your fortune over my head, then do it, or better yet, take it away and give it back to them. Because if it's their money I'm inheriting, I don't want it."

"Again with the dramatics, which are not necessary. I've obviously made an error in judgment trusting the wrong people. I'll handle this."

"Thank you." I move to get up and he stands with me, stopping my retreat.

"Just so we're clear. You are aware that I own twenty-four factories, ten of which are overseas?" His tone has me pausing.

"I didn't realize you had so many, no."

"Then you are also unaware I trust people with the day-to-day handling of them because I have no choice but to delegate these details, details I can't oversee myself. When they don't do their job, it's my head on the line and it's *my head* that will roll. I'm very aware of that truth."

I've started a tiger fight with a tiger with the same stripes, though his roar isn't as loud, it's there, and just as effective. But it's still guilt I feel when I think for seconds, that maybe, there is some truth to his words.

"I'm sure it's a lot to deal with, but this one is close to you. It's right under your nose." My voice cracks with that statement, and I curse my inability to keep my personal feelings out of it. He opens his mouth to speak and I wait, seconds, maybe longer, before he finally does. "I'll take care of it, Cecelia." I stride out of the room feeling more defeated than victorious. And when the front door closes minutes later, I sag behind my bedroom door and let another lone tear fall.

Chapter Twenty-Three

DOMINIC IS HERE TO PICK ME UP TONIGHT. I HAVE NO IDEA why, but he's in my driveway staring at me as I descend the steps, his features impassable. Nerves fire off as I round his hood. He doesn't have the decency to open the door for me like Sean does before I climb into his passenger seat.

"Where's Sean?"

He takes off in reply while I glower at the side of his head. My day is not improving at all with his surprise arrival. It was Sean I hoped would balm and distract me from my argument with my father. The last thing I want to do on my day off is spar with this motherfucker.

"Seriously, man. Words."

"Sean is busy. I'm doing him a favor."

"I could have driven."

"Well, you aren't."

"You could let me drive now."

"Not a chance."

"I've been practicing in Sean's Nova. I've gotten better."

He smirks. "You think so?"

"Know so."

Wrong words. Those were the wrong words to say.

In zero to a hundred and twenty, the bastard has me screeching at the top of my lungs as he fully opens up his dark horse's capabilities. This driving is nothing like the thrill ride that he took me on the first night. I'm terrified as he flies down the road with absolutely no regard for his life or mine.

"Okay, point made. You're the king, okay? Slow the hell down, please."

He nails the few curves before he hits the straightaway as sweat gathers on every surface of my body.

"This isn't funny!"

He cranks up the music as we pass a small gas station.

"Dominic, please. Please!"

I'm truly terrified, and he glances my way before he crosses the yellow lines and slows considerably.

"Thanks for reducing speed, but we are not in Europe, Dominic!" I shriek, white-knuckling every available surface before he pulls the emergency brake and turns, banking us on a shoulder doing a complete one-eighty. I'm fairly sure I just pissed a little as we race in the opposite direction.

"Forgot something," is his excuse as he slides to a halt perfectly between a minivan and pickup at the beat-up station.

I'm in a full-blown panic attack at this point as he turns to me. "Need anything?"

"You motherfucker!"

"Not in the mood for foreplay at the moment, but how about a Mountain Dew?"

I'm a millisecond from launching myself at him when he graces me with his bored expression. "I'll take that as a no."

He walks toward the store, and I've never seen a more perfect depiction of full swagger as I do in Dominic's gait. I glance around the sketchy looking store and fight my bladder. The drive to wherever we're going will no doubt take twenty minutes. It always does here. I decide to go for it and get out of the car. Dominic is in the cooler section when I walk up to the counter that sits next to an oversized LIVE BAIT sign and ask the attendant for a key. Next to me, a few older men sit perched in outdated black plastic chairs while continually pressing buttons on old lottery machines like their lives depend on it. Taking the key, I exit the building and walk around the corner to the battered door before suffering through thirty of the most disgusting seconds of my life. I wash my hands with syrupy looking soap and exit the bathroom with the oversized key in hand. I'm halfway to the door to return it when a guy blocks my path. He nods over his shoulder to Dominic's Camaro.

"Nice ride."

"Thanks."

"Yours?"

The man has to be in his late forties, his pot belly on full display due to his T-shirt riding up and riddled with something resembling ketchup. He reeks of liquor. I side-step him and he blocks me, his eyes rolling down me in a disgusting and predatorial way. Booze has obviously given him way too much false confidence.

"No, the car isn't mine, excuse me."

"I used to race back in the day. Just wanted to—"

He doesn't get a chance to finish his sentence because olive fingers wrap around the side of his neck, and the arm attached to it launches him into the side of the building. I grimace at the sick smack of flesh to concrete as the man's eyes go wide and he stumbles, his legs twisting awkwardly before he falls flat on his ass. Dominic doesn't so much as glance his way as he snatches the key from me.

"Get in the car." An order that leaves absolutely no room for argument.

Eyes bulging, I haul ass to his Camaro and lock myself inside. I look to see the man still struggling to get up as Dominic joins me and takes off without so much as acknowledging what just happened.

I crane my neck, relieved to see the man stumbling back into the store. "Was that really necessary?"

"Yes. They have to have the key back to let someone else piss on the seat."

I roll my eyes. "You're unbelievable."

We take an unfamiliar route as the sun starts to set and my driver remains mute. After a series of turns, I'm completely lost as Dominic slows on a crowded street full of young thugs and scantily dressed girls huddled on the corners. Government housing lines either side of us as we creep through and every head turns our way before their eyes dip down.

"Why are we here?"

"Errands."

"Look, to each their own, but I want no part of drugs, or whatever business brings you here, you can take me home and come back."

His jaw clenches as a guy in a ball cap salutes him, stepping off the curb. Dominic rolls down his window and lifts his chin.

"What's good, man?" the guy says, eyeing me, his grin growing wider. "What do you got here? New girl?"

Dominic's reply is ice. "Nothing you need to worry about."

I hear the unmistakable cock of a gun next to me. My eyes go wide when I see the Glock in Dominic's grip before he lays it across his lap. I have no idea where it came from.

"I told you I don't like company, RB."

The guy looks over his shoulder to see another man approaching and turns to him. "Step back, right now, motherfucker, I told you I have this." The guy eyes Dominic carefully and steps back onto the curb.

"Sorry, man, he's a young buck, my little nephew. I told his stupid ass to stay put." He reaches into his pocket and Dominic's venom stops him.

"The fuck you doing?"

"Sorry, man, just wanted to get straight."

"Then I guess you need to see *Friar*. I'm not driving back through here again. We clear?"

RB holds up his hands. "Been meaning to. I swear," he nods over his shoulder. "Car is fucked again. See?"

Dominic eyes the Chevy on cinderblocks in the driveway behind him.

"Get it to the shop. We'll work it out."

"Thanks, man. I wanted to ask—"

Dominic jerks his chin and the guy takes a step back from the car before he pulls away.

"So, you are a drug dealer. Jesus, I should have known." I don't know why, but I'm disappointed. I thought better of him and maybe I shouldn't have. But why the hell would a graduate of a prestigious school resort to something so fucking dangerous and juvenile? It's equivalent to a dumb as hell NFL millionaire playing thug games and losing his life in search of street credit. And I waste no time voicing as much. "You know you have a golden ticket out of here. Jesus, Dominic, I thought you were better than this petty shit."

He slows at the stop sign, and everyone within feet of the car takes a step away, keeping their eyes down. Dominic leans over, his eyes on mine and his breath hits my skin, as his finger brushes my leg before he opens the glove box. My neck prickles as silver eyes infiltrate mine and my chest starts to rise and fall quicker. His gaze drops to my lips, and the air crackles thick as I run my tongue along my bottom lip. Adrenaline spikes in my blood when he lingers for long seconds before he smirks and pulls back, tossing a piece of paper in my lap. I pick it up and read. It's a concealed gun permit for one Jean Dominic King.

"Jean, huh? Doesn't get much more French than that."

He rips the permit from my hand and locks both the glove box with the gun and permit tucked safely behind it.

"So you have a permit, whatever. Doesn't change the fact that I want no part of your shady shit."

He takes a left, and then another, getting us out of the questionable neighborhood. "Did you see an exchange of money?"

"No."

"Drugs?"

"No."

"Did I point my fucking gun at anyone?"

"No."

He tilts his head in my direction, brow arched. "Was a crime of any kind committed?"

"No."

"Then the only shady one in this car is *you*."

"How so?"

"Because it's your fucking brain working overtime, making assumptions you have no grounds to make."

"You don't know me."

"Government housing and a corner conversation, and you

drew the worst conclusions." He takes off and drives wordlessly while I search the previous conversation and come up blank. The guy was obviously trying to give him something. Money or drugs, I'm sure of it. But, who in the hell is the Friar?

It's pointless to ask, even though I know I haven't offended Dominic, I doubt anything does. He seems impenetrable.

"Why am I with you?"

"You got better things to do? A Kardashian episode to watch?"

"I don't watch that."

"One more errand and I'll get you to your boyfriend."

"Can you, just for once, be decent to me?"

He ignores me as we pull into a parking lot. I look up to see we're at a medical center. Dominic circles the valet, leaves the car running and rounds the front, opening my door. "Get in the back."

I don't bother asking questions and climb into the back seat, wishing I could shoot off a hostile text to Sean. But I have no phone because I'm following his damned rules while being forced to entertain his maniac 'brother.'

Ten minutes later, Dominic reappears through the sliding glass doors, and he isn't alone. A woman whose age is indiscernible due to her weakened physical state is being ushered in a wheelchair by a nurse. When they get close enough, I can hear the back and forth.

"Pourquoi tu n'es pas venu me chercher avec ma voiture?" *Why didn't you pick me up in my car?*

I can't understand what she's saying, but her displeasure at the sight of his car and his reply—in an endearing tone I've never heard—makes it clear.

"I've got it at the shop, Tatie. I told you this."

Tatie. *Aunt.*

Her eyes find mine as she stands with Dominic's help. Upon closer inspection, she looks aged well beyond her years. I'm guessing somewhere in her early forties. However, it's apparent in her eyes and the pallor of her skin that she's been through it. Possibly by her own hand or the unforgiving hand of sickness, maybe both.

"Who are you?" Her accent is thick, and I make it a point to brush up on my French.

"Hi, I'm Cecelia."

She turns to Dominic. "Ta copine?" *Your girlfriend?*

This, I understand and I answer for myself. "Non." *No.*

She harrumphs as Dominic helps her into the front seat.

"Comment ça va?"

"English, Tatie, and we aren't talking about that tonight." Dominic never speaks French, which is odd because of his 'Frenchman' nickname. Maybe it's for lack of competent company.

He eyes me and shuts the door, rounding the car. Those few seconds alone with her intimidate the hell out of me. Though sickly, she commands an air of respect. I keep my mouth shut and am surprisingly relieved when Dominic is back behind the wheel. A few minutes of silence ensue as I study her and the resemblance between the two of them. It's there, especially if I picture her a few years younger with more life in her eyes, her frame. When she speaks up, her question is directed to me.

"Why did you come?"

"She's Sean's girlfriend, I'm giving her a ride," Dominic offers as we pull up to a pharmacy drive-thru. The cashier greets Dominic, her face lighting up like Christmas. Beneath her white jacket she sports a risqué dress, her face painted up like she's going out for a night on the town, rather than working a respectable shift as a professional. He's mildly pleasant with her which only pisses me off. He pays for the medications and asks for a water which the girl supplies, her ample breasts on display as she graces us all with a view.

"Salope," Dominic's aunt says with clear disdain. I know it's an insult to the girl trying to give us something resembling a window pole dance. I try to hide my grin, but Dominic eyes me in the rearview and doesn't miss it. I swear I see his lips twitch. He's so impossible to read, this man. We pull up just a car length past the window and he opens the bag, palming some of the medication, handing her a dose with the water.

"I'm not a child."

"Take it." His voice is full of command.

Grumbling, she takes the pills and swallows. I see his lips tilt up again as he studies her, his eyes shining with the closest thing I've seen to affection from him. I feel that look pierce the surface of my skin, the warmth and respect he's showing her satisfying some need inside me. Like I knew it was there and needed confirmation.

"How many more treatments?" she asks.

"We've been over this. Six."

"Putain." *Fuck.*

I laugh out loud because I know that one.

"Je ne veux plus de ce poison. Laisse-moi mourir." *I don't want this poison anymore. Just let me die.*

"English, Tatie." He wants me privy to their exchange. Since when is Dominic so considerate?

"Put me in a box and forget me."

"I would have when I was younger. You were a horrible parent."

"That's why *I* didn't have children." She turns to him, lifting her chin defiantly. "I was barely twenty when I took you. You did not starve. You—"

"Hush, Tatie," he gives her the side-eye, "let's get you home and comfortable."

"No such thing with this sickness. I don't know why you take me."

"Because my first murder attempts failed, and you've grown on me."

"That's only because you honor your parents."

He swallows, and we ride in amicable silence for a few minutes before Dominic turns into a small driveway. His headlights beam on a Cape Cod-style house with overgrown plants on the porch, most of them dying.

"Stay," he gets out of the car and points to her where she sits in her seat. She doesn't say a word to me. Dominic opens the door and lifts her easily. I get out and he looks over his shoulder.

"No, stay, I'll be back in a minute."

I ignore him and scramble to the porch to open the screen door.

"Ha, I like her," his aunt says, scanning me in the dim light from the streetlamp. Dominic curses as he holds her against him and fumbles with the keys before he hands them to me. I hold each key up until he nods at one and then twist it in the lock and walk in, turning on the closest light and can't help but cringe at the scattering of a few roaches on the wall. This is the house Dominic grew up in?

Dominic walks her to an old beige recliner, and she sighs in relief when they get there. She kicks back, and he spreads a blanket over her lap before disappearing down a hall.

"You're looking at him the same way as the girl was at the pharmacy."

"He's hard not to notice," I admit truthfully, "but getting easier to ignore with his sunny disposition."

I carefully assess the house while trying not to make it obvious what I'm doing. It's nothing but old furniture in need of a thorough dusting, cleaning, and extermination. I don't know how she expects to get well in an environment that's anything but sterile, but from what she said in the car, she's not intent on a recovery. She examines me from her chair and I return her stare, just as curious. She's reading me, and she's doing it with Dominic's silver eyes. The resemblance is most definitely there. Early forties at most, I decide as I stare her down. It's tragic. She's too young *not* to fight.

"Can I get you anything? More water?"

"Please."

I move to the kitchen and click on the overhead light. More roaches scatter, making my stomach turn. There are only a few dishes in the sink and my skin crawls as I search the cabinets for a clean glass. I open the freezer, which reeks and grab a few ice cubes, tossing them into the glass before turning on the tap. I set the water on the small wooden table with a built-in lamp sitting beside her. She clicks it on and picks up a thick leather book—a French Bible, littered with tattered bookmarks.

Dominic strolls back in with a Monday through Sunday pillbox and a plastic garbage can. He sets the pills on her table, and the can within her reach.

"All separated. Take them, Tatie, or you'll get sicker." He chuckles when he sees the Bible. "Too late for you, witch."

I expect her to gasp or get indignant. Instead, she laughs with him. "If there's a back door into heaven, maybe I'll find it for you too."

"Maybe I don't agree with His politics," Dominic says, his timber full of mirth.

"Maybe He doesn't agree with yours, doesn't mean He can't be an ally. And you forget, I know you. And stop separating my pills, I'm not an invalid."

"You're doing a good job getting there. Don't drink tonight," Dominic orders, entirely dismissing the spiritual part of the conversation. "I'm not searching the house, but if you do, you know what will happen."

"Yeah, yeah, go," she shoos him away. I hear the distinct clink of a bottle beneath her rocker as she adjusts her position in the seat and Dominic makes himself busy with the TV remote. He didn't hear it, but her eyes meet mine in challenge and I quickly decide it's not my battle.

"Should we stay?" I ask her, genuinely concerned. All of my chemo aftermath knowledge has been gained from books or soul-crushing movies, and from what I've gathered, people get violently ill after a round.

"Not my first time," she says. "Go, the night is young and so are you, don't waste it."

"You are too," Dominic mutters, flipping through the channels.

I walk over to where she sits and kneel down on the over-stressed carpet. I don't know what in the hell possesses me to do it, but I do, maybe it's her living situation or the state she's in. Her predominately black hair is pulled back into a braid, her olive complexion deeply etched with life, the small wrinkles around her mouth defined with remnants of her lipstick. She looks breakable, her frame meek, her under eyes outlined by her sickness. But it's her eyes alone that shine with her youth, the same metallic shade as her nephew. They pin me curiously as I lean in on a whisper.

"Romans 8:38-39."

She navigates to the passage easily and to my surprise, reads it aloud.

"For I am sure that neither death nor life," she whispers softly, "nor angels nor rulers, nor things present nor things to come, nor powers, nor height nor depth, nor anything else in all creation, will be able to separate us from the love of God in Christ Jesus our Lord."

She looks up at me, her eyes flitting with emotion, mainly fear. "Do you believe that's true?"

"Those are the only verses I've memorized. So I guess, maybe, I want to believe it." It's clear as she studies me, she does too.

She looks past me at Dominic, who I can feel standing behind me. "Elle est trop belle. Trop intelligente. Mais trop jeune. Cette fille sera ta perte…" *She is too beautiful. Too smart. But too young. This girl will be your undoing.*

My eyes drift up to Dominic whose face remains impassive. Frustrated that I can't make out more than a few words of what's been said, I stand.

"It was nice meeting you."

She waves us away and we move toward the door. I look back at her, just before we clear the doorway and I see it, the slight lift at the corner of her lips. It's Dominic's smile, and a part of me lifts at the sight of it.

A few minutes into another silent drive, I turn down Dominic's blaring radio. "What happened to your parents?"

A muscle in his jaw flexes as he flicks me an expression I can't place.

When he cranks the radio back up and downshifts to gain speed, I know he will entertain no conversation. I observe him, baffled by the shift in his moods, and the utter beauty of the mask he wears along with the secrets he holds so tightly to him. He's very much like Sean in a sense they both give the bare minimum when questioned, like they took and mastered a fucking class on terse responses. My cheeks puff as I blow out a breath, and I hold the rest of my questions. There's no point. He's back to impenetrable, his body language alluding to as much, and I let my thoughts wander until we pull up to the garage.

Dominic parks close to the bay and exits as if he can't get away from me fast enough, and I sit and watch him walk into the shop without looking back. Today was eventful, to say the least, and slightly insightful.

A flash of fire grabs my attention and I look over and see Sean slapping his Zippo closed through the windshield.

He joins me as I step out of the passenger side. "So, I take it that didn't go well?"

"Why would you subject me to that man?"

He chuckles lightly, but the humor doesn't quite reach his eyes. "What's going on in that head of yours, Pup?"

I wrap my arms around him as he exhales a plume of smoke, careful to avoid my face. "I'm just relieved to see you."

"That so?" There's no accusation in his words, but I know he saw me watching his roommate with open curiosity. Then again, he knows Dominic like no one else. He's got to know how just an hour or two alone with him can be exasperating and exhausting.

Sean tosses his cigarette and pulls me tightly to him, kissing the mystery away. When he pulls back, I grip the back of his hair, hard.

"Why didn't you pick me up?"

"A couple reasons, one of them being an unanticipated and mandatory work meeting on my day off."

"Oh, yeah?"

He grins down at me. "You fought well, baby."

It's my first real smile of the day.

A DIZZYING SMILE GREETS ME AS I SAUNTER DOWN THE porch steps to where Sean waits at the passenger door, eyes devouring me in my cover-up, a dangerously flossy bikini beneath. I meet him where he stands and warm, calloused hands cup my ass as he pulls me into him in a way that stakes claim. When he kisses me, diving deep, and a soft groan rumbles in his chest, I'm already starved for more. More of what we've been doing, I'm anxious for what's to come. I'd called Christy last night and filled her in on the details, shamelessly sparing few because she's my person, and she is just as taken in by all that has transpired with Sean.

Being with him makes me happy. It makes my romantic heart sing. Sean's a caretaker and has done nothing since the day we met but do exactly that. His grip strong, he kisses me and kisses me, our tongues dueling, his feel, his smell a new craving.

I feed on him as he takes further control, pulling me further into him, rubbing his erection along my stomach to let me know he's just as needy for me.

When we eventually part, his eyes are lit, a content smile playing on his lips. "What did you dream about last night?"

"Aren't you really asking about who?"

"I don't flatter myself."

"You should. You were in all the ones I remember."

"Good ones?"

"Damn good ones."

"Good to hear. You ready to have some fun?"

"Always."

"That's my girl." Tucked in his passenger seat, he buckles me in and presses a gentle kiss to my lips, as if he can't wait another second to do so.

"Dom's coming. Hope that's okay."

Deflating a little, I only nod. I was hoping to be alone with him, but I don't make a stink of it, because any time with him is well spent. Dominic puts me on edge in a way I'm not comfortable with. My draw toward him is unexplainable, and I only feel guilty for it. I don't tell this to Sean because I don't want him mulling it over the way I have been for the last couple of days. Being in Dominic's proximity is like a slow-motion view of an explosion of metal on metal. With Sean, I feel safer; but when Dominic is around, I feel that every breath I take is laced with something hazardous. Yet with each inhale, he becomes more intoxicating.

I prefer sober and aware, at least that's what I try to tell myself.

Once in the driver's side, Sean grips my hand and runs a thumb along the skin of my thigh. "You look beautiful."

Part of my answer is a beaming smile. "So do you."

"Let's go, baby," he murmurs, taking my lips once more before kicking back in his seat and starting the engine. Southern rock drifts out of the speakers as he taps his fingers on his steering wheel, and I just...watch him. It might not yet be love, but it's definitely nothing short of heady infatuation at this point. We sing along to the classics as he races toward the lake, a cooler packed behind us in his seat.

"Good one," he says, just as a new song begins to play and he sings along. Curious, I glance at the dash and read the title, "Night Moves" by Bob Seger. Completely at ease, he squeezes my thigh as he sings to me, but it's when I really listen to the words that I start to deflate. The more he sings, the more I start to feel sick. The song is about a meaningless hookup for a summer, someone to pass the time with sexually until they move onto better things. He notices my frown just as we pull up to his cousin's property, the picturesque view of the lake surrounded by the mountains rapidly tainting along with my mood.

Once parked, I push his hand off my thigh and slam my way out of the car, seeing Dominic eye us from a tractor tire-sized raft docked at the foot of the lake.

"What the fuck?" Sean asks as I turn and make my way in the opposite direction toward the woods casting shadows a few feet away. I'm already stepping up on to a small hill path leading toward a clearing when I hear Dominic speak up.

"The fuck's her problem?" I don't bother turning back to explain myself, I just charge past a few trees in flip flops that are not at all fit for a morning hike. I'm acting a fool and need to get a handle on myself before I do worse.

"Cecelia."

"Sean...just give me a minute."

"Hell no," he stomps after me, "we're not going through this again."

"Seriously, I need some space," I snap over my shoulder.

"That's not the tune you were singing twenty minutes ago."

I whirl on him, coming close to running into his chest. "Speaking of *tunes*, what the hell was that?"

He draws his brows together. "What was what?"

"The song you sang to me. Are we hinting around to anything here?"

"I played liked seven of them on the ride over. Care to get specific?"

I cross my arms as he racks his brain, and I see the moment it dawns on him.

"It's just a song."

"Is that what I am? Is that what this is going to be?"

He towers over me and grips my wrist, placing my hand on his heart. "I have no idea yet, and neither do you, but I can promise you that only a quarter of how fast this is fucking beating has to do with chasing after your beautiful and crazy ass."

"I heard you share."

He doesn't flinch.

"We have."

Silence.

I snatch my hand away and cross my arms. "Care to elaborate?"

"Nope. And if you heard about that, it's not because we said a thing about it."

"Wow, that's some arrogance talking."

He runs a hand through his golden strands. "It's the truth."

"Is that why I'm here?"

His jaw ticks. "You're adding insult to injury by acting this way."

"Meaning?"

"Meaning, should I be offended you think I'm a fucking sleazeball for taking part?"

I only glare as he steps forward crowding me, his eyes lit with temper.

"You have a thing for Dominic. You can deny it all you want, but I've seen it, I've felt it, and I'm not standing in the way of that, and claiming you as mine is not going to do either of us any good. The truth is, seeing it only makes me want you more. And I *do* get off on it, and I won't fucking apologize for it. Just like I won't make you apologize for your attraction to him. I told you when we first hooked up, I don't do things in the traditional way, neither does Dominic. Giving you the choice is more of a reflection on how I respect and feel about you and what *you* want, and it's much better than denying to myself that I've seen you eye fuck him, more than once."

I gape at him, completely blown away by his brutal honesty.

"Step outside that brainwashing for a few seconds and be honest with yourself. That's all I'm asking. Just be truthful. In your heart of hearts, if you *didn't* have to choose, would you?"

I'm still stunned as he leans in, invading my senses.

"I-I-I'm...I'm with you," I stutter out, hating the fact that he's drawn all these conclusions. His superpower of reading people and anticipating what they want has just blown up in my face. I feel nothing but guilty as he inches closer.

"God, you're beautiful," he drawls, "but completely mistaken if you think I want anything more from you than you are willing to give." His finger runs from my chin to my neck. "I'm not trying to manipulate you into a goddamn thing. And today, when I picked you up, I wasn't thinking about you sinking onto anyone else's cock but mine and *without* an audience." His flecked eyes light up. "But it makes me so fucking hard that you're thinking about it." He brushes my lips with his. "But the choice is always, *always*, up to you."

I stand fish mouthed and utterly speechless. He curses and

reads my expression. "Let's just table this, okay? You were pure sunshine when I picked you up and the last thing I want to do with you today is argue. Let's just try and have fun."

I'm still stunned stupid, reeling, as he tugs on my hand and I jerk it away.

"Are you kidding me? You just told me…" I gape at him. "I thought we…would…"

He turns back and I can only conclude he sees the warring hurt and confusion in my eyes, my expression. "You catchin' feelings for me, Pup?"

All I can do is give him the same honesty. "Yes, of course I am. We… I was hoping… I don't know."

"That's right, we don't, so let's not go around getting offended and slinging drama where it isn't needed. You want to trust me, but you're not letting yourself, and there's nothing I can do about that. I can tell you every day you're safe with me, but unless you believe it, it's pointless. And for the record, I caught feelings the minute I laid eyes on you." I go slack as he brushes a finger over my lips. "You're beautiful, intelligent, kind-hearted, sensitive, and *more*," he drops his forehead to my shoulder and groans, "and pissed off."

Initial shock aside, I decide to try and be completely honest with myself, to give myself the freedom to try and see things his way. There is a lot of truth to his words, but I expect to see hurt in his eyes, and I don't. It disappoints me and, in a way, wounds me. I was hoping at this point he would be possessive when it comes to me, but that's not what I'm feeling from him. "I just don't want to feel…"

He lifts his head. "Used? Degraded? That's you doing it. That's you, baby. Not me." He leans in. "Any judgment being passed right now is yours and yours alone." He's still holding onto my hand and slowly lifts it, kissing the pads of my fingers one by one. "When we started spending time together, I didn't expect…" his eyes pierce me deep, "I have been and will be monogamous with you, Cecelia, *easily*, if that's what you truly want. I have half a mind to lock you up and throw away the key with only me behind the door because of the way I think you're starting to feel. But there's the other side of it, and I don't want to hold you back, because liberation can be a beautiful thing. And you deserve to have whatever you want." He leans in, whispering kisses along the hollow of my neck, his lips trailing over my rapidly heating skin. He grips my hair, his breath warm in my ear. "It's okay to want his dick, baby, I'll watch it go inside you and fucking love the view, and the savage it'll make me."

Pulling back to weigh my reaction to his words, I see nothing but satisfaction before he tugs my lip into his mouth, the act aiding to the rapidly pooling desire between my thighs. He runs his hand down my stomach and dips beneath the material, slipping a lone finger inside of me. My slickness glistens on his finger as he lifts it, forcing me to see just how much his suggestions arouse me and I can't look away as he sucks it into his mouth. On the brink of combustion, my legs begin to shake as he drops to his knees. "Yeah, let's take the edge off that."

I push at his head with urgency as he chuckles darkly while he unties my bottoms. Kneeling before me, his hair tickles my stomach through my hole-ridden cover-up.

"Sean," I moan out his name as he pushes my legs apart and hooks one over his shoulder. "Jesus."

"Open up," he nudges my legs further. "Wider," his deep throaty grunt reaches my ears a second before his tongue lands on my clit. I jump at the contact and he grips me, grounding me in his firm hold as he lashes out with his tongue. It takes only seconds to start feeling the crest of an orgasm as he eats me eagerly.

"Fuck, yes," he murmurs, looking up to me while pushing a finger inside and moving my cover-up so I can watch it glide in and out. He adds another as I gaze down at him, his golden crown glowing in the clearing of trees as he kneels amongst pine needles, his hazel gaze brimming with lust. I'll never in my life forget how good it feels being looked at like this, touched like this. Breaths heavy, I begin to shake in his hold as he coaxes my orgasm with expertise. He's good, too good, and that tinge of jealousy spurs me as I clench around his thick fingers. I just watch him as he does nothing short of worship me. Keeping my eyes trained, he leans down and darts his tongue with perfect pressure, his fingers twisting before I detonate. A satisfied groan vibrates from his throat as he watches me from below, his tongue picking up speed as I come undone.

Quaking in his arms, it overtakes me entirely and he struggles to keep me upright. Unable to control myself, I shriek his name as he laps me up until the surge subsides. When I'm liquid, he re-ties my bottoms, placing kisses on the bare skin on my stomach, trailing his warm mouth up my neck before claiming my lips. In that kiss, I feel nothing but safe and adored. Not judged for my wicked thoughts, not condemned for getting heated by his suggestions.

He pulls away. "Damn, it's all I can do right now to keep from fucking the hell out of you." He shakes his head reading my dazed expression. "There's a battle raging in your head from what you've been taught and what you think you might want, and that's okay, baby. It's okay. Some believe without rules and morals that we're no better than animals." He leans in, his mouth twisting seductively. "But it can be a lot of fun to be an animal, and it's always about the choices you make. But it's always going to be up to you. Understand?"

I nod as he pushes thick strands of hair behind my shoulder. "Good." He turns and crouches down in front of me. "Now, hop on before you blow out a flip flop."

BASKING ATOP OF THE ROUGH EXTERIOR OF THE MAMMOTH float, eyes closed, I lift my chin toward the direction of the sun. Sean to one side of me, Dominic on the other. Both are bare-chested in dark swimming trunks, and I've had a hell of a time ripping my eyes off them today, especially after what transpired this morning. Dominic met me at the float, silvery eyes gleaming with mischief, a devilish smile tilting his full lips, the picture of a dark angel with deviant intent.

"Get it all figured out?" His words were full of insinuation as if he knew exactly what our spat had been about and how it ended, so I just glared at him. And he seemed to glow in it, saying nothing else as he helped Sean get the two coolers on the massive float.

It's where we've been for hours; drinking, talking, swimming, eating, and sun-bathing like lazy cats. Dominic hasn't gone out of his way to be nice to me, but it's become evident as the hours pass that the dynamic changed after the day I spent with him.

Music plays from the small radio Sean brought as we all laze silently, floating in the middle of the lake, anchored in the water, secluded by the majestic mountains above. It's the perfect summer day, the coconut smell of suntan lotion lingering in the air between the three of us.

I flip on my stomach and turn my head in Dominic's direction, opening my eyes when I feel his lingering stare. The sight of him is jarring. He's sprawled out, skin slick with sweat, his gaze darkening as he watches me.

"What?"

He says nothing, just concentrates on me, and I feel the clench inside, the ache, the unfurling, and the truth of Sean's words. I do want Dominic. I'm constantly fighting our draw, all the while trying to make peace with what it would mean to me if I stopped.

Is it wrong?

And is this the only chance I am going to get, to be in a situation with two insanely hot men I share desire for?

Dominic pivots his arm so he's able to brush the pad of his thumb down my spine. I shiver at the contact, my eyes widening slightly, my lips parting as he tracks his finger trailing down my skin. And then I feel the tug on the back of my bikini string as he slowly unravels it, and the soft material slackens at the front of me.

"I'm not..."

Dominic lifts a brow, stilling his touch, a question in his eyes. He's seeking permission. I can feel Sean bristle next to me and turn my head to meet his eyes, light green depths flecked with brown searching mine. He leans in and places a gentle kiss on my lips as Dominic resumes his touch.

It's a choice. My choice.

"I'm not f-fucking…" I sputter out to Sean, thinking that's what he wants to hear while trying to voice my lie.

Can I do this?

Do I want to?

Am I capable of living with it?

Dominic's breath is hot in my ear. He's shifted somehow since I've turned my head, I can feel the skin of his chest at my back when he whispers. "I would never let you fuck *me.*"

I turn in his direction, he's close, so close, just a breath away from our lips touching.

"You know what I mean." I'm breathless. Thunder rolls in the distance as if it's a warning sign, and I lift on my forearms, forgetting I'm topless and look at the clouds just past the mountain peaks. A storm is coming, and it seems to be the case in more ways than one. Is this a warning? It goes against my very nature, and the romantic that dwells inside me. Dominic adds the rest of his fingers as he strokes my back, still on his side while continuing to watch my face with calm focus.

"Relax, baby," Sean murmurs, his lips trace my arm in a light kiss before he boosts me so my lower half is still on the float, and my upper half rests on him. He smiles up at me, nothing but hunger in his eyes before he rises slightly to take my nipple in his mouth. I watch him, consumed by the feel of him beneath me, hard muscle and beauty. I shiver at the caress down my back, all too aware of the fact that Dominic is touching me.

Dominic is touching me.

And I want him to.

Shivering at the pleasure it brings me, I turn to face him and see his relaxed posture as he silently watches me.

His thick hair is tousled and my fingers itch to run through it as my eyes drop to his full lips just as Sean draws my nipple tight.

Gasping out in pleasure, my eyes roll down Dom's physique, he's all hard lines, deep indentations, perfection personified, cut from a god's blueprint. But in truth, he's the all-too-tempting apple, and if I take a single bite, I may be enchanted in a way I'm not sure I can handle.

But I want that bite.

Lost in our static, Dom's hand stills as we draw the same breath.

And that's when I feel the snap on both our parts. He lifts, just as I bend, and our lips meet.

Tiny explosions pulsate throughout before my body shudders on impact.

Sean groans as if he feels it happen and moves to my other nipple, sucking it greedily into his mouth. Thunder sounds again, as Dominic slips his tongue past my lips, and thrusts a hand into my hair, kissing me deep, his tongue stroking, sure and probing, tasting every corner of my mouth. I moan into his, the kiss intoxicating as Sean's mouth covers me, his lips tracing over every inch of skin. Dominic closes our kiss but stills my head with steady hands, keeping our eyes locked.

I want this. I want this more than my next breath. An audible moan leaves me due to Sean's magic, and Dominic's eyes flare as he draws my lips again for another kiss. This one far deeper, more, just…more. I feel like a siren, worshipped, beautiful, sexy. It's the most power I've ever had, and they're giving it to me.

It's a choice. I can stop this at any time. I can stop it now.

Sean's fingers feather in a soft caress up and down my skin as Dominic lulls me into his kiss with his tongue. I could spend eternity kissing this man. It's intense, sinful, consuming, along with a whisper of something else. Moaning, I pull back, surprised by just how much I didn't want it to end. Dominic's stare seems to match the mystified feeling pulsing throughout me—our connection brimming with possibilities.

More thunder, another kiss with Dominic which he seems content to do, as if that's all he might want as Sean suckles my nipples, hands cupping my ass, spreading me, rubbing me along his swollen cock. My clit pulses in awareness, the throbbing going from a steady thrum to raging as something inside of me, an inkling, starts to wake within me as if from a deep sleep.

I have questions, so many questions, but they remain unasked as Dominic makes quick work of breaking our kiss, rising up to sit and then pulling me into his lap so I'm straddling him. We lock eyes for seconds until he dips and claims my mouth fully. This kiss goes deeper as our chests touch, and my breasts graze his solid wall of muscle as he groans into my mouth. This kiss is filled with unexpected passion and longing and seems endless. I can't, even knowing Sean is watching, rip myself away. Tongues tangle, hands roam, we explore hungrily. When we part, our fast breaths mingle, revelation dancing in both our eyes. I feel like he can see mine, and I know his mirrors it. His touch, his presence, his kiss is like being surrounded by a cool, dark cloud, one I'm dwelling comfortably in.

For the first time since I met Dominic, I truly want to know who he is and why his kiss affects me this way. Spellbound, a familiar touch sweeps my hair from my shoulder just before I feel the sting of Sean's teeth and then his tongue. He's behind me now, his hands roaming all over my skin, unhurried as if we have all the time in the world.

The thunder grows closer and I know I should be worried about the coming storm, but I can't stop staring at Dominic. He's still waiting for a decision. And I know he sees it the second I make it. But I put that answer into action as I rub myself along the growing thickness in his trunks.

A crackle sounds in the distance as I let myself go, let my hands and fingers roam freely, my lips explore. Then I'm being lifted up on all fours over Dominic as he cups my jaw, keeping my eyes trained on his. Sean spreads me before his lips find purchase on the inside of my thighs. Dominic drinks in my pleasure, watching my every reaction. I close my eyes against the feel of Sean's traveling mouth and Dominic's grip on my face tightens in command. When I open them, I can see the reflection of the fire raging within me. Satisfaction covers his face as he lifts a hand and cups my breast, his thumb brushing my nipple, just as Sean unties my bottoms and pulls them away.

I fight the distant voice of reason threatening in my head, letting the whirring of my lust drown it out. Dominic's eyes roll down my naked body, setting me ablaze.

I want this.

And they know it.

Sean's lips close around my clit and I yelp at the contact as Dominic soothes me with a stroke of his thumb along my cheek. "I want to hear her." His voice is full of lust and command and that's when I fully let myself go.

Sean begins to lap me up wildly, adding fingers to his assault. Still bare and on all fours, I glance below to see Sean's head resting between Dominic's spread thighs. A second later, Dominic pushes me back to sit on his face. Immediately, I begin bucking, but Dom keeps me in his iron grip, savoring my reaction, his eyes hooded. I can't kiss him in this position. Sean spears his tongue into me, adding a third finger, and I lose control, rocking on his face, my hands braced on Dominic's shoulders.

"She's close," Dominic says, his voice dripping lust. With the hand cupping my face, he traces my lip with his thumb before he pushes it into my mouth. I wrap my lips around it, sucking furiously and I bite it when I feel my body start to quake with the onslaught of my orgasm. Sean spreads me wider, his nose tickling my clit before he moves me up and begins furiously licking it. I move to toss my head back, riding his mouth, but Dominic stills the movement commanding my attention back to him.

"You're perfect," Dominic whispers hoarsely, and I feel it to my toes.

"I want your mouth."

"I know," his only reply. I move to touch him, to grip his cock and he encases my wrist with his free hand, squeezing and halting my movement with the jerk of his chin.

"Goddamn," Sean murmurs a second before he sucks on my clit hard, and I come, crying out as he stretches my opening with his fingers.

The orgasm rips through me as Dominic traps my face with his hand, watching me, watching my body pulse with release until I'm nothing but a pool of submission.

I flood in Sean's waiting mouth as his lapping slows before his head disappears. Dominic and I collide, mouths devouring as he grips me back into his lap. Thunder roars not far away and I jerk in his hold, yet his kiss burns hotter than the fear as he ravages my mouth. It's the hottest fucking moment of my life and I don't want it to end. I struggle with my kiss, wanting, needing to get closer, greedy for more. When he pulls away, we're both panting.

"Say it," he orders.

"Fuck me," I reply without an ounce of hesitation, batting away any sort of lingering doubt. In seconds, Dominic has a condom in hand, and I watch on rapt as he slowly rolls it down his thick dick, my hunger growing unbearably. Behind me, Sean explores my back with his lips, his hands possessive, predatory, claiming.

"You taste so fucking good," he murmurs into my neck and I turn my head and kiss him hungrily, tasting myself on him. Dominic stretches me with his fingers, as Sean thrusts his tongue deep into my mouth, a branding kiss, utterly captivating. He releases me, running a finger along my lips. "You sure?"

I nod, not wanting another second to pass in this time I've allowed myself, freed myself to have what I want.

I turn back to Dominic, whose eyes are fixed on where he spreads me, stretches me. Rolling my hips, I grind into his touch, loving the feel of him, loving the way the desire feels rolling off him.

From behind, Sean lifts me in offering, arms wrapped around me as Dominic lines his cock at my entrance. Eyes locked with Dominic, Sean slowly, so slowly lowers me onto Dominic's cock, inch by rock hard inch, while all three of us watch.

"So fucking hot," Sean rasps into my ear as Dominic clamps onto my hips, while I gasp at the full feel of him. Pussy pulsing, the need to move unbearable, I start to rock my hips and Dominic stops me with the jerk of his chin. He's taking this slow, he wants to watch, and he does, fixated on my stretch around him. I study his face, the hood of his eyes, his damp hair, dark lashes, the muscles rippling in his chest, the tightness of his jaw.

I moan his name a second before his eyes shoot to mine and he thrusts up, stealing my breath. Sean latches onto my neck with his lips and teeth. "Fuck," Sean's voice strains unbearably as Dominic thrusts up again, fusing our bodies, burrowing deeper as I call out to him, scratching at his chest. And in the next second, I'm set free.

My hips rocket into motion, my heart pounding, my desire out of control as I stare down at Dominic, whose jaw has gone slack, the pleasure in his eye spurring me on, the fullness I feel too much.

"Let her go," Dominic orders Sean. A second after I'm released, I'm on my back, the breath knocked out of me as Dominic drives in deep, hitching my leg over his hip, fucking me at an animalistic pace, his eyes feral, curses and grunts pouring from him.

I look between the two of them, their eyes worshipping, their mouths moving with curses, and filthy words. In a small shift, Dominic lifts to his knees, keeping us connected, my back anchored on the float my lower half in his lap as he begins to pound into me, giving Sean a clear view. Sean lowers his gaze and watches Dominic fuck the breath, the life out of me, his eyes pure desire as he keeps his hands moving, stroking, kneading. I cry out, my body quickening as Sean pushes his shorts down and frees his cock, sheathing himself in a condom before taking my lips in a kiss. I feed off him as Dominic picks up his pace, his cock jerking inside of me, his release close. I pull my lips from Sean and gaze up at Dom and what I behold is nothing short of perfection. He's gone, so gone, lost in the connection of our bodies, his eyes untamed. Sean lifts and hovers above me, his hand sliding between us, his thumb pressing against my clit. And I shriek out Dominic's name, my body convulsing with another orgasm, my eyes slamming shut, my heart pounding out of control. Sean backs away, watching me unravel as Dominic thrusts in once, twice, and then groans deeply with his release.

Spent, he leans down, strong biceps next to me and he kisses me for endless seconds before pulling out and away, crashing onto his back, his chest pumping in exertion. And then, Sean is there, kissing me deep, his hunger unfathomable as he pulls me onto him, his legs spread, my back to his front. He fists my hair, pulling my head back to rest on his shoulder as he lines me up and thrusts up into me.

I cry out at the invasion as he fucks me ruthlessly, spreading me over his lap, my clit throbbing in the open air, his free hand covering me, starting at my breasts and then sliding down my navel to where we connect. He circles my clit with his finger as he hammers into me, his mouth ravaging mine as he thrusts and thrusts. I catch my second wind, grinding myself into him, consumed in a haze of lust. When he tears his mouth from mine, I blink down at Dominic, who's riveted, his eyes blazing as they roll down my body with fresh desire.

"Feels so good," Sean murmurs, tensing, his orgasm close. I cover his working fingers with mine and in seconds, I come between our efforts, my eyes fastened on Dominic, just as Sean grunts out his release. We collapse on the float, our breaths erratic, limbs tangled just as the thunder sounds farther away in the distance. The storm missed us entirely.

Chapter
Twenty-Six

BACK ON DRY LAND, WE ALL PACK UP WORDLESSLY AS I TRY and grapple with what just happened.

I chose it. I wanted it. I can't afford to regret it too deeply because if I do, I'll be opening myself up to loathing, my own, for eternity.

Once both cars are packed, Dominic grips my hand pulling me to where he stands, his car idling. He looks down at me for a few tentative seconds before he kisses me, the result—rapture. I clutch him to me, and he takes his time, filling my mouth with his tongue, just as hungry as our first kiss, seeking, searching. It's beautiful, this man's kiss. It's consuming and I can't get enough. When he pulls away, he brushes my lips with rare affection, gets in his car, and drives away.

I peek over my shoulder to where Sean stands, eyes lowered, afraid to meet his gaze. I walk over to where he waits at his passenger door. Unable to handle it a second longer, I brave a glance at him and see…nothing but the same golden boy who picked me up hours before. My heart lifts instantly. I didn't realize it had been so heavy. He stops me before I duck into the seat and leans over and presses the gentlest kiss to my mouth. When he pulls away, I feel the sting of tears.

"Don't, baby. Just don't. We'll talk about it when you're ready, but don't do it."

I nod in understanding, not having any clue how to follow that order. I feel a bit like an alien in my skin. That girl, what she did, I don't even recognize her. I just let two men share me.

And I loved every minute of it.

The weight of that truth, I can never, ever erase.

And the part of me now awake and breathing within me doesn't want to.

The drive home is silent, but Sean clutches my hand the whole way. I'm still battling myself and my decision, all the while glowing in the aftermath. He left the music on just low enough to hear me speak but remained silent, giving me the time I need while occasionally bringing the back of my hand to his lips.

Reeling, my body is tense, even though my core is sore and thoroughly sated, I can't think of a single thing *to* say. And maybe there is nothing to say. His posture remains relaxed as he drives like he needs no assurances in my place with him, and I'm not sure I know what it is.

What *are* we?

That's what I'm supposed to be analyzing, isn't it? But it's not my focus. Neither of them looked at me differently, at least not in the way I was predicting. The change I felt between us all after today is a far cry from the quenched curiosity I was expecting to feel. Their kisses after weren't any different. If anything, I feel more connected to them both.

Could this be real?

I've had sex, plenty of sex in high school, in monogamous relationships with boyfriends I swore loved me, cared for me, but later showed their true colors. All of the pain I assumed I felt when they'd ultimately rejected a future with me felt empty, meaningless, pale in comparison to any experience I'd had with them to the one I had today and to the possibilities of what's next.

I study Sean as he punches in the gate code and the car slowly makes its way down the driveway.

"You didn't do anything wrong," he finally speaks up. He meets my stare. It's full of the same surety Dominic kissed me with before he left.

They truly aren't judging me, something about that eases a bit of the tension in my shoulders.

But why? Why aren't they judging me? Why don't they see me differently?

I remain mute as he parks and slides me over to him on the bench seat.

"Tell me anything."

"I don't know what to say."

"Own it, fucking own it," he says adamantly. "Own it and don't let you or anyone else make you feel like it was wrong." He presses a finger to my temple. "It's going to take some time for you to make peace with it, but fucking own it, Cecelia."

"It was…" I try to mask the shake in my voice.

"Incredible," he answers for me. All I can do is nod. He chuckles at my expression. "I'm a bastard for saying it, but I see your mind is blown."

He chuckles further at my scowl and pulls me into his lap. His hazel eyes twinkle with humor as he brushes the hair away from my neck. "If you're wondering what happens now, the answer is we don't know. Dom, me, or you. We don't know what this will or won't be. And that's the fun part."

"What if someone gets hurt?"

"Chance we have to take."

"Why do I have a feeling that someone will be me?"

"I don't want to... The way I feel about you, hurting you is the last thing I want. But if you're debating on a choice, on choosing, I'm telling you right now you don't have to. Unless you want to, and in that case, I hope it's me."

I blow out an exasperated breath, which only makes his smile grow.

"There's a beauty to keeping a secret, Cecelia. But it can only remain one if you choose to guard it. Years from now, when you're toasting with your friends during Sunday brunch, before the bitching commences, this secret can be the subtle smile that tilts those beautiful lips before you take your first sip of champagne. Everyone has them, but not many can keep them."

He brushes my hair behind my shoulder before trailing his knuckles along my jaw. "It was beautiful watching you come undone, giving in to what you wanted. I don't think I've ever seen Dom so wrapped up in *any* woman."

"Don't...don't say that."

"Why?"

"Because if he feels anything...I want him to tell me himself."

Sean nods, as if in perfect understanding.

"This is really okay with you?"

"You're in my lap, looking at me like you want me, why the hell wouldn't I be okay with that?"

"I don't want to lose you," I manage, my breath hitching, eyes watering.

"Cecelia, I swear to you, you will never lose me over this. Put that thought out of your mind. What happened doesn't make my feelings for you any less real. I'm so fucking crazy about you." A soft kiss, then another. "You gave me your trust today, and I need it." He swallows. "There's very little you could do at this point to get rid of me."

"You are so..." I run my hands through his hair, "different."

"That's a good thing, right?" He nudges me on his lap and traces his lip ring with his tongue. "Whatever it is you want to do, do it right now."

I lean down and mimic the movement of his tongue along the metal, and he exhales audibly and grips my neck, bringing our foreheads together.

"If you're ever wondering what to do, that's what you do. Whatever you fucking want, whenever you want, and you don't apologize for it, not ever."

"This is insane."

"Welcome to my world," he murmurs, before sealing me inside it with his kiss.

It's been days of nothing but texts from Sean and not a word from Dominic, not that I expected any different. He's practically a stranger.

However, now, an intimate one.

I cringe at the thought as I mentally crack a whip on my back.

I've been in a state of "what in the hell did I do?" and "please, my lords, may I have seconds?" for days and hiding in my house for the majority of it. I've been passing on Sean's invitations, reading, swimming, talking on the phone with Christy—who I did not disclose the details of that day to. It's my Sunday Brunch smile secret to keep—if I want to.

The more I question if I should tell her what happened, the more I try to think of words to explain it, how it felt...right, how letting myself go felt better than anything I'd ever come close to in the past. The longer I think about it, the more I know she wouldn't understand.

'Behind closed doors,' 'in the privacy of my home,' there's a reason people keep a lid on their sexual escapades, and I've never had one worthy of keeping despite our act being out in the open, until now. Scraping myself out of bed, I stare out the window into the dark forest beyond and the flickering lights of the cell tower wondering where the two men who have consumed my thoughts are. Have they thought about me?

Did they fist bump when they met back up?

Shuddering at the thought, I close the balcony doors and press my forehead against them. "Christmas came early, Cecelia, and guess what? You're a ho," I bang my head against the door with each word. "Ho," bang, "Ho," bang. Face burning, I send out another mental lash of the whip. My back should be nothing but lacerated and bleeding flesh with the number of imaginary whippings I've given myself. Still, the only thing reddening is my face as I blush and again relive every second on the float. My dreams of them the past few nights are vivid and downright sinful in nature. They've invaded me in both my waking and sleeping hours and I haven't lived a single moment past those minutes I shared with them on the lake.

Sean's texts are vague, they always are, but he sends them often. He's been helping his parents at the restaurant this week, and because of my slut-shaming, I again missed the opportunity to meet them.

What in the hell am I going to say?

'Hi, I'm Cecelia. So nice to finally meet you, Mr. and Mrs. Roberts. Why, yes, I am the tramp ass ho having wild, animalistic sex with your son amongst the trees. Why, just the other day we tossed his best friend in the mix, it was quite delightful. And your green bean casserole is delish.'

With every text, I can tell Sean's making an effort to let me know he's not going anywhere. He doesn't want my head to get the best of me.

And I love him for that.

But what of love?

Thinking of this situation long term would be beyond foolish. But Sean hinted heavily, more than once, if I wanted to commit to him, he wouldn't be opposed to it.

Maybe it was a one-time thing.

The idea of belonging solely to Sean appeals to me greatly. He's more than enough. But did that act set me up to be greedy for more? I've bitten into the forbidden fruit, and with that knowledge comes the unrelenting urge to sink my teeth in again.

Sean knew it was a possibility, and he'd alluded to as much.

Do I really want to let the static chemistry with Dominic go if I don't have to?

And being with the two of them and watching their reactions, I've never been so turned on in my life.

But how many more lashings can I handle? It's only been days, and I've all but burned myself at the stake.

I'm not that girl.

I'm not that girl.

I'm *now* that girl.

The one constant that eats at me is if this is something they do on the regular, can I condemn the women before me?

Hell no, and I hate that. But I want to. So much. Jealousy burns me at the knowledge I'm not the first. Yet in a way, it makes me feel less alone because I share a secret with them.

But what's become of them?

Am I different?

Damn them both.

They have to know what a head trip this is. I doubt Dominic cares, but Sean knows, and he's waiting on my verdict.

It's another decision.

Restless, I turn on the shower and try to drown my anxious thoughts out with the spray of water.

The morals we're taught early on are meant to guide us, and without them, we're directionless. But Sean doesn't follow the norm or the guidelines that most of society adheres to. He's an independent thinker who navigates his life by his gut, living decision by decision.

He lives unapologetically in the grey. So does Dominic. But what can that mean long term?

What of soulmates? Love of your life? One and only? These sayings exist for a reason as well. One.

One man, one woman, or *one* partner for everyone.

Not two. There's 'The One.' Not 'The Two.'

But for some. For some...

Welcome to my world.

There's also 'college phase,' 'that year I was promiscuous,' 'before I met,' these are also sayings I've read about, heard over the years.

Though my experience is limited in the telling of these stories, save the one I just earned, I know they exist. From what I've gathered, the college phase is always about promiscuity, freeing your inhibitions for an allotted time, and same-sex curiosity. Isn't that one and the same of what I've just experienced? Aren't I allowed time to explore my sexual prowess and expand it, if I so desire?

Soulmate and one true love haven't been on my list of priorities since Jared hurt me.

One day. Sometime in the future. But does it have to be now?

No.

It doesn't. I do care for Sean in a way that's too far gone to pull back completely.

And though the arrival of my feelings for Dominic surprise me, along with our connection, he doesn't have to be Mr. Right.

No doubt, he's not. Dominic doesn't seem to be a forever type of man.

Falling for Sean is becoming inevitable. I love the way he cares for me, the way he makes me feel—the comfort his presence allows me to fully be myself.

Own it.

I'll drive myself crazy if I don't.

I can't even bring myself to regret it.

Out of a scalding shower, I study my reflection in the mirror and don't back away from what I see. Skin tinted pink from the water; I let my eyes roam freely, searching for flaws, searching for a reason not to look.

All that I expect to feel, gazing at my reflection, I don't.

This is owning it.

And it's my decision.

At some point in time in a person's life, they have the choice to search for their forever or let themselves off the leash.

One more glide of my eyes down my body lets me know what choice I'm making tonight.

Down the rabbit hole I go.

I slip into my second skin and rub scented lotion on it before pulling out dark washed jeans and an off the shoulder tee from my closet. I brush bronzer on and sweep thick black mascara over my lashes before lining and filling my lips a shimmering blood red.

Then I shoot off a text.

Maybe I'm not in college just yet, but it's clear that my education has started early.

Chapter Twenty-Seven

I PULL UP TO THE GARAGE TO SEE SEVERAL CARS BACKED INTO the parking lot, and hordes of guys huddled around them, most faces unfamiliar, but their shared ink is unmistakable. The shop is pitch dark, locked up tight, the bay doors closed. Sean walks over as soon as I pull up. When I step out, I see his eyes heat when he takes me in.

"Fuck, baby, you look, *goddamn*," he turns away from me, shielding me with his body to block me from the others and I slip my arms around his chest, pulling him into me.

"Miss me?"

He turns and peers down at me, my hand locking around his back. "I wanted to give you space and fuck me, it was hard. But it's going to be even harder tonight." His tone is filled with insinuation, which stirs my memory and I feel my cheeks heat.

He's dressed in his usual attire, jeans, a T-shirt, his hair picked through, delicious. "You good?" He asks with genuine concern, as strong arms haul me tighter to him.

"I'm good." I see him visibly relax with my reply.

"Yeah?" One side of his beautiful mouth lifts. "Made peace with the devil inside?"

"Trying to."

He rubs his thumb along the edge of my lips. "Had to wear that fucking lipstick, huh?"

"You like?"

"You're going to pay for that later, come on." Loosening my grip on him, he grabs my hand and leads me toward the crowd.

"What's going on?" I ask, just as we break through a line of tall, tattooed men, some of the faces familiar.

"Waiting on Dom to leave," Tyler answers, giving me a dimple and a lift of his chin. Of all of the crew, Tyler and I have grown the closest. We have a lot in common and recently bonded over our shared love for all things nineties, while he helped me up my pool game.

"Where are we going?"

"You'll see," Russell chimes in. "'Sup, Cee."

"Hey, Russell." The warm reception from them helps my shaky confidence and I embrace it for what it is. They seem to have accepted me as one of their own, and it's a foreign but welcome feeling.

"Hey, you." Layla appears, breaking through the line and bumps into my shoulder. "Been a minute."

"Hey, Layla," I say, my gaze back on Sean who's looking at me in a way that feeds my soul. A look that says we're still us, and that's truly what matters most to me. It's still very much beyond my comprehension that he could be liberal with me and still look at me the way he does. In a hypocritical way, my romantic heart is disappointed he would, that he did. But so far, he's practiced to the letter what he's preached. He liberated me that day because he wanted me to have what I wanted. And that's a different way, maybe Sean's way of showing affection.

Not only that, it turns him on.

A scenario I never saw myself living in.

But I am, and my heart starts to kick up as we gaze on at each other as though we're the only two people in the parking lot.

"Let's get you a beer," Layla says glancing over at Sean. "I'm taking her for a minute. Girl talk." Sean only nods, his eyes still fixed on me, his tongue tracing the ring on his lip.

She pushes past the wall of men and pulls me into her side as she walks toward the guy manning the keg. He pours us each a beer. And Layla remains quiet as I survey the crowd of at least twenty guys. "What's going on tonight?"

"Waiting on Dom, as usual. He takes his fucking time, on no one's schedule."

"Are we late for something?"

"Not really, a meetup." She looks me over. "You look good, girl."

I tear my eyes away from Sean, who's now talking animatedly amongst his circle, and study Layla. Her dress coordinates with mine. She's in jeans and a tee that shows her toned midriff. Her blonde hair is sleeked back in a high ponytail. "Thanks. So do you."

"Couldn't miss that exchange if I was blind. So, Sean, huh?" She gives me a knowing grin.

And Dom. I hide my flinch at the knee-jerk thought, and she reads my posture.

She draws her brows. "Undecided then?"

I take a sip of my beer. "Can I ask you a question?"

"Sure."

"Do they…am I?" I shake my head, frustrated. These are clingy chick questions.

"They?" She reads my face, my posture. "Ah, oh, okay, I got you," she says through a laugh.

I just told my secret, in a look, with a single stuttered sentence. A part of me is relieved, the other is horrified I spilled it so easily. I'm not good at this, not at all.

In truth, I'm relieved. I've been bursting at the seams for a little female perspective, other than my own.

Layla isn't close to me, so this is as good as it can get. She taps the bottom of my cup, encouraging me to drink. I take a hearty sip and exhale.

"Okay, first of all, don't freak out, I'm no saint. Not by a long shot. Second, I'm the vault. Whatever, and I mean whatever, you tell me will never, ever reach anyone else. That's code. But let's get some distance to make sure I'm the only one who hears it." She walks me over to the abandoned side of the garage, where everyone is out of earshot.

I'm still unsure of what questions I truly want to ask. She helps me by speaking up. "Sean is an open book in a sense. He's going to be honest with you, about *everything* he can, even if it hurts. And you won't have to do too much to try to read into him. Dom, well, he's a different story. He's both bark *and bite* and trust me—you don't want to be on the receiving end of either one. But he's got heart, and we've all glimpsed it at least once, but rarely twice. He's literally the male version of Fort Knox, a born loner."

I sip my beer and she tilts her head. "What do you really want to ask me?"

"Am I just another…" *one*. Just another one. But I can't bring myself to say it.

"That I can't tell you, but from what I've seen, the house has been quiet lately."

"Quiet?"

"*Dom* has been quiet and so has the traffic in his bedroom." She grins at me. "It started right after the party."

Faithful. She means faithful. To me? Before he even had an idea if there was an us? Does it matter?

The tug in my chest tells me it does.

"Try not to dwell on it, but look," she pulls me over to the edge of the garage and scans the gathering. "How many women do you see?"

I examine the crowd, silently counting. Four, five, and the two of us amongst the twenty or so.

"There's a reason you're here." The serious lilt in her tone has me searching her face, though I can't see much due to where we're standing. "And there's a time and a place for *fraternization* and it's definitely *not* on meetup nights."

"Meetup nights?"

"You'll see. But do yourself a favor and keep your wits about you, even though it will be hard. Especially with those two distractions."

I nod and she laughs. "Lighten up, girl, it's a party and you have the attention of two of the finest brothers. Come on."

We're in the midst of crossing the gravel walk when a rumble sounds at the mouth of the driveway and headlights shroud us in light. Bass rumbles from the sleek black car as my eyes drift to the driver. Dominic's gaze paralyzes me, making me a literal deer in his headlights. He greets me by the twitch of his lips, his eyes sweeping me.

"Damn, to go back to the beginning again," Layla sighs wistfully. "I envy you."

Dominic stays in his car and with another rev of his engine the party disperses. Shortly after, engines fire up in every direction.

"Go with him," Sean speaks up joining me where I stand. I glance his way, frowning.

"With him?"

He presses a kiss to my temple. "I'll see you there. And don't you dare smudge that fucking lipstick. That's for me."

I nod as he saunters off and round Dominic's Camaro. He leans over and pushes open the heavy door. The minute it's closed, I turn to him.

"He—" my greeting is cut short as we burst out of the parking lot, my laughter filtering out of the car. The hint of a smile unmistakable on his lips as the cars speed out, following us, and Dominic unleashes every bit of horsepower under the hood. Braced with one hand on the dash and the other on the car door, I squeal as we tear down the road.

This only seems to fuel him as he races down the straightaway for a mile or two before he slows considerably, taking turns, tracing every curve of the road.

I turn the radio down and he glances at me. "Are we ever going to have a real conversation?"

One side of his mouth lifts. "We had a good one not too long ago."

"That's not what I mean."

"Want to start with politics or religion?" He chuckles darkly at my answering scowl before he shifts, pinning me to my seat as we race forward. "Eggs—runny, coffee—black, beer—cold, music—loud, cars," he floors the gas.

"Fast," I say through a laugh.

"Woman," he turns and rolls his mirror colored gaze over me.

Woman, not women. I feel that comment so much I move to grip his hand, and he pulls it away before I reach it.

"I save that for when I can do something about it."

"And you think that's affection?"

"Isn't it?" he takes a turn that has me yelping. That's exactly what it felt like on the float. Like he'd been waiting for an eternity to touch me.

He's the opposite of Sean in a lot of ways.

It's not a fault, but something to look forward to.

"What makes you happy?"

He takes another turn, his forearm flexing when he shifts. "All of the above."

"Runny eggs and coffee make you happy?"

"What if you woke up tomorrow and there was no coffee?"

I feel my brows pinch together. "That would…be tragic."

"Next time you drink it, pretend it's the last time you can have it."

I roll my eyes. "Great, there's two of you. Is that some life philosophy? Okay, Plato."

"You can discover more about a person in an hour of play than you can in a year of conversation."

I gape at him because I'm pretty sure he just quoted Plato.

"I was raised in a way I appreciate the small shit." He looks at me pointedly and it's then I understand his point fully. I saw the house he grew up in, and it screamed of poverty and neglect. He let me see it. My heart melts some at both his spoken and unspoken admissions as he makes a sudden turn and skids to park, cutting off his lights, leaving us shrouded in partial moonlight.

I lean up to peer through the windshield and see a crescent moon hovering above us. "Come here," the order is whispered at my neck as he grips me and pulls me to straddle him, stealing the attention of the moon. I grin down at him as he slinks down in his seat, making enough room for us to fit comfortably between his seat and the steering wheel. The look he's giving me is enough to make me forget myself. I lean in to claim his lips and he turns his head, dodging my kiss.

"He likes the red," he runs his fingers through the hair at the back of my neck down to the ends and repeats the movement, his touch enchanting.

Something about the comment twists me. In just seconds alone with Dominic, I'd forgotten Sean's request not to smudge my lips. I try and squelch the guilt as Dominic's touch travels, inching beneath my T-shirt before he strokes lightly along the waistband of my jeans. The low ache his touch brings ignites the fire in my veins as he gazes up at me, always watching, but relaxed. The pull is undeniable, but he stills my every attempt to touch him, be it by the squeeze on my flesh beneath his fingers or the jerk of his head before he resumes his torture, caressing me everywhere but where I want him.

"How long have you known each other?" I rasp out while his hands roam up my back past my bra line, cupping my shoulder blades, further warming my skin.

"Most of our lives."

"That close?" I say, rocking a little on his cock, feeling the bulge growing beneath me. The friction is delicious. I can't help but rotate my hips for more. His eyes heat in response, but he makes no move to do anything about it.

"We're all close."

"Apparently so."

Sudden and loud rumbling drowns out the chirping crickets just before I get an eyeful of cars speeding past Dom's shoulder. We must have been flying if they're just now catching up, or Dominic must've known a short cut. "They're leaving us."

"We left them." In the shadow created by the half-moon hovering above, I study him. His eyes glint like pools of silver even under the cover of night, his high cheekbones casting twin shadows on his jaw, his lush lips lit fully, taunting me.

"And we left them because?"

"Because," he lifts up as if he's going to kiss me, his breath hitting my lips. I brace myself for the feel of it, closing my eyes and leaning in, and then feel his absence. Opening my eyes, I see he's again resting against his seat, a knowing smirk on his lips.

"You're an asshole."

"That's not news. Anything else you need to know?"

"I don't *know* anything."

"Sure, you do." He thrusts up just so, the friction maddening, rendering me senseless.

"You described most red-blooded men," I pant. "Cold beer? Ah," he thrusts up again and this time I feel how hard he's become, and my blood boils. "Fast cars? Black coffee? Runny eggs and..."

"And?" He prompts.

I can't hide my smile despite the insatiable hunger he's drawing from me. "Me."

"Then you know enough." He lifts my shirt, revealing my bare breasts, I went braless tonight, and I feel him physically tense when he discovers it a second before he sucks a nipple into his mouth. Panties soaked, I clutch his head to me as he feeds, rocking my hips over his erection, picking up speed.

"Dom," I murmur as his fingers explore and he bites my nipple before he soothes it with his tongue. When he pulls away, I'm near orgasm, but he lowers my shirt and stills my hands before again running his fingers through my hair.

"That was cruel," I whine, my body on fire.

"We'll have to pick this up—later." With that, he nudges me up enough to grip my hips, easily lifting and placing me back into the seat next to him before he starts the car, backing up the way we came. Intentional or not, I feel the brush of his fingers on my hand just before we speed off in the direction of the others.

WELL-ORCHESTRATED ANARCHY.

That's the only way to describe it when we pull in. A slew of cars are parked in a circle around a story-high, raging bonfire. The rest outline a large clearing surrounded by a forest. Kegs are hauled off trucks by some while others wait ready, tossing bags of ice around them. Music blares from the speakers of a truck as a few more cars pull up and empty. Fifty heads, at a minimum, most gathered in small groups as if there's some social protocol amongst them.

"Please give me a straight answer, what in the hell is this?" I ask Dominic as he surveys the yard, pulling dead center into the circle where just enough space was left as if it's his rightful place in the lineup.

"Just a gathering of friends."

"I don't have this many friends."

"Lucky you," he says with an edge as he scans the crowd. He dodges my next question by exiting the car and pulls my door open, lifting me to stand with him as I survey the party. Sean meets us at his car, his eyes going straight to my lips, satisfaction brimming in them when he sees they've been left untouched.

"Have fun?" He asks, pulling me into his side.

"We didn't," I can't meet his eyes, "we didn't...do—"

He shakes his head and tips my chin. "That's not what I was asking." He drapes an arm around my shoulder and looks over to Dominic. "They're here. Waiting on you."

Dominic dips his chin, his eyes darting to mine before he takes off.

I immediately look over to Sean as he walks us into the crowd. The scene playing out before us looks like one straight out of *From Dusk till Dawn*, an old Quentin Tarantino flick, and I half expect fire breathers and half-naked girls dancing on poles to pop up at any moment before the fangs come out. "Are you going to tell me what this is?"

"It's a party."

"I can see that."

He chuckles at the arrival of my mean mug. "Then why are you asking?"

"Back home we don't call parties a meetup."

"This isn't the Atlanta suburbs."

"No shit." I look around to see bottles and joints being passed around like free-flowing water before noticing the out-of-state plates on some of the cars. "And not everyone lives here."

He nods. "Good eye."

"Sean, come on, give me *something*."

He gestures in the direction of an El Camino where two mammoth men sit on the tailgate scanning the party, their faces void of any animation. Clearly brothers, their features similar. "See those two?"

"Yeah."

"That's Matteo and Andre, The Spanish Lullaby. Behind them is their crew. They're from Miami."

"They drove here from Miami?"

"Yeah."

"For a party?"

He nods.

"Why are they called The Spanish Lullaby?"

He eyes me. "Use your imagination."

"That isn't scary at all."

"I've got you, Pup."

And I believe him. Sean's face turns to stone as he dips his chin at the Miami crew when they zero in on us. The lift of their chins barely perceptible.

"And that group over there," he points to a truck where one of the guys lands a backflip off the hood of a pickup before downing some Jack Daniels. "That fool is Marcus, and the guy next to him is Andrew. That's Tallahassee, the rest of Florida, and they're fucking shysters. So, stay a foot or six away at all times, if you want to keep your valuables."

He takes his time walking me around the party, or meetup, or whatever the hell it is, and it doesn't take long to notice the slew of raven tattoos marking the arms of everyone in attendance. Some of the girls have a tattoo as well, dainty wings inked on their shoulder blades. A few of them are wearing halters, no doubt to show them off. And it's then I know those wings are a symbol of possession.

Sean leads me over to a freshly tapped keg and passes me a beer. I take it, and a sip, preoccupied with the truth behind this party. Sean merges us in with a few of the groups, easy conversation flowing from his lips as I scan others sitting on the edge of their cars, watching the rest of the party. I press up on my toes after a few minutes and lean into Sean with a whisper.

"Are you in a gang?"

He tosses his head back and laughs.

I scowl. "How is that funny?"

"Do we look like gangsters?"

"No. Yes. Kind of. Then what is this?"

"Just a bunch of like-minded people with similar interests hanging out."

"With the same tattoo?"

He shrugs. "It's a badass tattoo."

"Sean," I grit out impatiently. Though we're in the midst of a mingling with Alabama, he lifts his chin at Tallahassee and turns to me. "I need to go talk to a few guys. You cool here?"

Eyes wide, I search his face. "They won't touch you, Cecelia. You pulled up with Dominic."

"And that means what exactly?"

"It means I'll be right back."

He smiles and shakes his head, moving to abandon me and I grip his arm. "Where's Layla?"

"She's here somewhere. Go find her, and I'll come get you in a bit."

"You're seriously leaving me here?" I whisper yell. "Alone?"

He drains his beer. "Yep."

Shit. Shit. Shit.

"Is this like a throw her in the deep end thing and see if she can swim test?"

He laughs. The bastard laughs. "No floaties. Show me that mean mug."

Furious, I grip at his arm as he begins to saunter away, and he shakes me off easily. "You're fine, baby."

Pulse rocketing, I scan the party for Tyler, Layla, Russell or anyone I know, and see Sean find Tyler just in front of the raging fire before they both disappear behind a few cars.

I decide to bite Sean's testicles the minute I'm able.

Trembling from head to foot, I toss back more beer.

"What's he like?" A feminine voice sounds up from behind me and I spill half my beer jumping out of my skin before I turn to face her.

"Sorry," she laughs lightly. "Didn't mean to scare you. Must be your first time here."

"It is," I take her in. She looks to be my age and has jet black hair with purple tips. She's dressed in black from head to boot, a silver and black raven wing's necklace resting in her ample cleavage. "Are you asking about Sean?"

She's exotically beautiful and jealousy simmers through me to the point that I can't help my question. "Why?"

She takes a step toward me, hesitation clear as she lifts light brown eyes to mine. "Sorry, I guess that was weird to ask his... girlfriend?"

She wants Sean, and she's brazenly telling me within seconds of meeting me. Is that how this works? An even better question is would he be interested to know about her?

"I don't know...what we are." I take a sip of my beer. "We're new."

"Hard to know what you are with any of these assholes unless you get winged," she sighs. She glances at my cup. "You're out. Let's get another one."

I never used to drink, not like this. I blame the new men in my life and the nerves associated with them. She nods toward the guy minding the keg as we walk the few steps to get to him and hand him our cups.

"I'm Alicia."

"Cecelia." She's taller than me by a few inches, definitely not a girl any male eye would pass over. She sizes me up just as carefully. "Did you come with anyone?"

"My brother," she supplies. "We're Virginia."

"Oh." Not from Virginia, no, she claimed a whole state.

"Dominic's never brought...neither of them have ever brought a girl here. I thought you came with Dom, so I wasn't sure which one you were with?"

I fumble with my reply because I don't know exactly how to answer. And I decide I'm not going to. She smiles and does me a solid by taking the question off the table, so I do her one back, even with the lingering sting of jealousy.

"Sean is kind, considerate, smart, so smart, caring, sexy, funny, protective." And mine.

"I thought as much," she blows out a breath, pushing her waist-length dark hair away from her shoulder. The woman has the most beautiful head of hair I've ever seen.

"So, you've got a thing for him, huh?"

I'm graced with an apologetic grin. "He used to come to Virginia a lot when I was younger. I never said a word to him, but yeah, I guess you could say I do. Hope that doesn't piss you off."

It does, to a degree. But she's being honest.

"He's also bluntly honest, like you."

"Yeah?" She smiles.

"But, I *am* with him."

She nods. "I'll back off. I just...he's perfect, but you know that. Dominic too. But he scares the shit out of me."

Me too. But in the way I can't get enough of him.

"Yeah, they're...hard to describe."

"So, come on, girl," she nudges me with her elbow, "what exactly did you do to get in that car?"

Fucked them both on a float. I cringe at my vulgar thought and burst out laughing despite it.

Who in the hell am I? Alicia gives me an odd look.

"Sorry, it's been an interesting week. I met Sean at work and we all just started hanging out."

"If my brother wasn't such a dick, I could too."

"Overprotective, eh?"

"Yeah, to the point I might kill him in his sleep."

"Have you been to many of these?"

"This is my fourth." She rolls her eyes. "Twenty years old and I still have to ask my brother to play with him and his friends."

"So, what is the meetup about?"

She shrugs. "It's just a party."

I harrumph. Third time is *not* the charm.

"You don't find it odd that every one of these men has the same tattoo?"

She lifts a shoulder, her face impassive. "Not at all."

"Please, please tell me what I'm missing."

She frowns. "You don't know *anything?*"

"No. Is this a gang?"

She squelches her laughter after gauging my expression. "No, not like that. But if they were to bust us right now, I'm sure half of these assholes would serve time."

"For?"

"Their crimes."

Questions and evasive answers. It's becoming an infuriating pattern and I can see she's sympathetic. I go at her at a different angle.

"So why do you come here?"

"Because I believe in this."

"And this is?"

"A party."

Annoyed, I glance around and look for a sign of either Sean or Dominic and come up empty. The longer I look around, the less faces I recognize. My garage guys are also nowhere in sight.

She sees my panic and does her best to study me. "You have nothing to be afraid of. This is just a meetup. It happens once or twice a month."

"Like Masons?"

She nods sharply. "Sure. Like a club."

"But you can't tell me about the club? Like rule number one of *Fight Club*?"

"What's that?"

"A movie," I run my hands through my hair in frustration. "Never mind, so this is a club?"

"Sure, and I guess you could say this is the clubhouse."

"So that necklace…"

"Means I belong to someone or am with someone in the club." She grimaces. "Right now, it's my brother."

"So, who is the leader?"

"There's no leader at a party."

"I thought this was a club?" I counter.

"A club *party*."

More evasion, another thousand questions popping up that I have no doubt will go unanswered.

"This is so weird," I mutter as an outburst of laughter sounds behind us.

"I thought so too, at first."

"And now?"

She shrugs, pulling a joint from thin air and lighting it. "It's a way of life." She exhales a plume of smoke and offers it to me.

"No thanks."

"Sure? It's going to be a long night."

"Yeah."

I need to keep my wits about me. What in the hell am I doing here? The question spins in my head constantly as I survey the party. Alicia walks with me as we talk in circles and I get nowhere with answers until commotion breaks out on the other side of the fire. We both strain to search for the reason around the volcanic flames. A second later, we hear the roll of engines.

"Shit, this should be interesting. Come on," she grabs my arm and I allow her to drag me to the other side of the circle to see Dominic's Camaro roar to life along with two other waiting cars. "One of them belongs to one of the Miami crew, the other is Tallahassee's ride," she continues on. Sean appears at Dominic's side as they exchange words and Dom gets a clap on the back from Sean before he steps away and starts his own car.

"Where are they going?"

"To play tag."

"Like a race? On these roads?" I turn to see Sean searching the party for me behind the wheel before his eyes land on the two of us. I hear the stutter of Alicia's breath as he looks from me to her, and I know she's got it bad. The smile he casts in our direction lights me up, and I know I do too. And I'm *not* sharing him.

Even if these weird-ass men belong to a strange club held in the backwoods of Bumfuck, Nowhere.

"So, what's going to happen?"

"They'll race."

"And then?"

"One will come back the winner."

Catcalls and whistles sound out as they collectively pull out, engines gunning as they make their way toward the road. The now-familiar rumble stirs something within me. It's as if new code is being embedded into my genetic makeup. An image of

Sean hovering over me the first night we were together flashes through my mind, along with the stolen minutes Dominic and I shared tonight.

"Anyone ever died?" I ask, the blood draining from my face.

"Twice. But that was years ago before the rules changed."

Years. I wonder how long this has been going on. Unease slithers through me as I focus on at the fading taillights.

And then I hear it, the tell-tale signs, engines roaring in the distance. They're racing. A part of me wishes I was inside that car with Dominic. But mostly, I'm terrified. Sean's more careful, but Dominic is fearless with his driving, dangerously so.

"Don't worry. They'll be back," Alicia speaks up from beside me.

"Let me have that joint," I say, hoping it will calm my nerves. She laughs and passes it to me, and I inhale deep.

Ten minutes later, the sound of an engine has us all craning our heads. Dominic is the first to enter and the bodies around us roar with cheers.

"He won," Alicia lifts her beer toward him in salute.

"Of course he did."

He's hell on wheels and tonight he represents his name well, a king amongst the masses crowding around his car. Pride fills me as I watch him, knowing tonight was the start of something between us. I move to go to him, but the second he's parked, he's out of the car, pushing those congratulating him out of the way to inspect the body, a string of curses erupting from him. Miami comes idling in next, and the second the driver is stopped, Dominic flies towards him, meeting him at his door. Emerging from the car, the Miami driver smiles in a way that makes my stomach roll. A moment later Dominic wipes it off his face with his fist.

"Oh, shit," Alicia says next to me.

Sean speeds in sideways, barely stopped before he's flying out of his car and stalking over to where Dominic is unleashing hell. Tallahassee trails in last, the side of the car caved in as it comes into view under the firelight, wheels wobbling, smoke billowing out of the hood. The driver gets out, a crocodile smile in place as he watches Dominic beat the ever-loving shit out of the Miami driver. Everyone at the party stands by, watching, including Sean, for several punches before he moves forward, barking at Dominic to stop. I can't help myself. I move closer to hear the exchange as Miami finally steps up in defense.

"Ease up, Dom." The guy Sean informally introduced as Andre says, moving in. His expression puts me on edge. These men are dangerous, and as I survey the faces of most of the onlookers, I see amusement. They're clearly desensitized by what's playing out in front of them, which instills some fear in me. I've never bore witness to this type of raw violence. Not only that but by a man who less than an hour ago was lighting my body on fire with tender touches.

Though a little fearful, a foreign but carnal desire begins to course through me as I watch him destroy his opponent. Dominic delivers one last punch and the guy goes down, landing limp at his feet.

Dom steps away, his power rolling like a tidal wave over the crowd as he addresses everyone within feet of where he stands. "Happy to fucking address any objections."

Andre jerks his head and two of the guys behind him lift what's left of the guy on the ground.

Dominic's livid gaze follows him. "You do that again, you're out," he barks as the guy spits out a mouthful of blood. Dom's hand is dripping with it, and I push through the crowd to get to him as Sean speaks up.

"Ease up, man," he mutters just as I reach them.

"Fuck him," Dominic snaps, his rage-filled posture challenging everyone within feet of him.

"You've made your point," Sean takes his place by his side.

Dominic looks over to where Tallahassee stands, surveying the damage to his car. "You all right, man?"

He nods as I reach Dominic, lifting his hand to inspect it. He jerks away from my touch, turning on a dime and rears back, fist drawn. He drops it once he sees my face, which drains of all blood when I witness up close, the rage in his eyes.

"I'm good," he snaps, jerking away from me and I back away, right into Sean's chest just as he hooks a hand around my waist. "Let him cool off, baby."

I nod as Sean pulls me to his side and glance over his tense frame, scanning for Alicia in the crowd, but she's disappeared. "Let's go," Sean prompts, tugging me in the direction of his Nova.

My gaze flits back to where Dominic stands, his chest heaving, his eyes frighteningly feral before he stalks out of sight.

"He's good," Sean assures before he whisks me into his car and in seconds, we're back on the dark road, the eerie quiet a stark contrast to the party we just left. If I hadn't have been there, I would have thought I'd imagined it.

"You're pissed," he speaks up as tension grows in the cabin. I am angry, but these men make it impossible to rationalize a functional line of hard limits and remain sane while doing it. But in choosing my battles, this one I'm not backing down from. I'm done with all the mystery.

"First of all, you left me at a party where I hardly knew anyone."

"I knew enough people to know you were safe, safer than you are locked up all alone in your house."

"Whatever. Second, you went racing—racing—in the middle of the mountains at night."

He grins. "Sorry, Mom."

"It's fucking dangerous and stupid. Look what just happened."

"I love that you care."

"Don't smile at me all sexy."

His grin only grows as he checks his rearview.

"Third, what the hell is all this?"

He expels a breath.

"And don't you dare tell me it was a party, or you can lose my number."

He flicks his gaze on me, and it's unforgiving. I've just pissed him off. Good.

"What *is* this, Sean?"

"It's your explanation."

I focus on the beam of the headlights as I sift through my thoughts.

The phone rule, his dealbreaker. The secrecy. The omissions and half-truths. The subtle hints he's been giving me since the day we met. This is what he's been hiding, and I still have more questions than answers. It's not enough.

"Then explain."

"I just did."

"You have to know how infuriating this is."

"Trust me, I do."

"Yet, you won't give me anything."

He glances my way. "Let me guess, you asked around tonight and got no answers."

"How did you know that?"

"Because that's how it is."

"So that's what this is…like a secret society? Like the masons or some shit?"

He doesn't answer.

"Take me home."

He chuckles. "I am."

"And then lose my number."

His smile disappears as his fingers tighten on the top of the wheel. "If that's what you want."

"I want the fucking truth!"

"You're getting it," he says calmly, "you just don't like what I'm telling you."

"Because it makes no sense!"

"It makes perfect sense."

A minute or two of silence follows before he finally speaks up.

"Can you keep a secret?"

"Of course."

"Too quick to answer," he snaps. "I mean really keep a secret. Can you think of secrets that you'll take to your grave, that you've never confided in anyone, ever?"

"I have a few, yeah."

"And how do you go about doing that?"

"By never talking about it. Or thinking about it. Acting like it never happened."

"Exactly, I can't give you specifics on a history that doesn't exist. I can't give you rules and details or dates about things that never fucking happened."

"So, all of those people back there?"

"Can keep a secret. Nothing about that party, and no one in attendance can tell you who was there or what went down because it never happened." He goes quiet for long minutes and I know it's because he's trying to find his words. He darts his gaze my way. "Masons have walls, out here, it's tree lines. So, when you asked me what tonight was. I told you the truth. It was a fucking party. When you asked what we do, the answer is *nothing*."

240 | KATE STEWART

"Unless I'm *in* on the secret. And even then, nothing ever happened?"

My answer is silence, but I'm starting to think that silence may be admission.

"So why even show this to me? Why not leave me clueless like the rest of the world?"

"Because you're with me." Simple. To the point. And if I want to be *with* him, I have to be willing to be in on his future secrets. He chances another quick look at me. "It's going to be your decision."

"And what if I don't want to be in on it?"

"No choice tonight," he says, gunning the gas. He checks his rearview again and I turn and see blue lights flash from a side road behind us before turning our way. "Hold on," he says as I turn to face him in the seat.

"You're kidding. You're going to pull over, right?"

"No can do, baby, they aren't impounding my shit for thirty days."

Oh, Fuck. Oh, Fuck. Oh, Fuck. Oh, Fuck.

A phone rings in his pocket, and when he pulls it out, I don't recognize it. He answers without looking my way. "Yep, someone must have called in… I figured. Better break it up. I'll take this one." Sean floors it and my eyes go wide. I turn and see the lights are falling farther behind us, he's losing them, but every muscle in my body is screaming with warning.

"We're running from the *police*. You do realize that?"

I sink in my seat as Sean completely ignores me, his concentration solely on the road.

"Sean, this isn't fucking funny!"

Calmly, he says to me. "One more time, Cecelia. Can. You. Keep. A. Secret?"

Terrified, I search myself for the answer. "Yes."

He slows, downshifting and yanks the wheel and I scream,

slamming my eyes shut as we veer sideways onto a gravel road. When I open them, I fully expect to catch a glimpse of my imminent death, but I can't see anything because Sean cut his headlights and we're now running in the light of the moon.

I'm seconds away from pissing myself as Sean guns the gas, leaving us flying down a gravel road. It's while the tires crunch beneath and the silent wind whips through the cabin that realization dawns. These men I've been hanging with are exactly the type that Mom warns you away from and that Dad is supposed to greet at the front door with a shotgun in hand.

Since day one, I've been subtly and not so subtly warned by them to keep my distance—by both them and those who knew of them—and since day one, I've done nothing but walk directly into the line of fire. There's always some basis or truth to rumors. But this? This is so far from what I expected. And it's in the dark where I see the light. I've been running with these secretive devils for the last six weeks, and I'm being baptized in truth in something akin to hellfire.

"Jeremy was serious when he said he'd just robbed someone, wasn't he?"

Silence.

Sean makes another fast turn, and I have no idea how, because I can't see a foot in front of his hood, but his quick side-eye confirms everything.

"You spend *all* your free time crossing invisible lines," I say, knowing it's the absolute truth. "Jesus, Sean. How many secrets do you have?"

His reply is another turn before we slide to a stop. He kills the engine as we sit quietly under the cover of a few trees. I twist in my seat but see no sign of the blue light. I've never been prone to panic attacks before, but I'm positive I'm having something close to one now.

"It's okay, baby. We lost him. We were too far ahead. He never even saw the make of the car. We're safe."

"Safe?" I pant, trying to even out my breathing. "I don't think so."

He watches me carefully as I gather and examine all the red flags that have been piling up in front of me over the last several weeks.

"I didn't expect this. I knew something was going on, but this? Tyler's a United States Marine, and he's a part of this!?"

He nods.

"How far does this go, Sean?"

He bites his lip in contemplation and I glare at him.

I gesture toward the phone resting between his thighs. "That's not your phone."

"Never was." With the quick workings of his hands, he pulls the SIM card out and snaps it in half.

"So, you all are like fucking outlaws or something?"

"Or something."

"All of you?"

"Everyone with the bird was invited to the party. And they can all keep a secret. If they can't…they can't party. And probably never will again."

I shake my head, unbelieving of the truth.

"I don't know you at all, do I?"

"You know me," he swears and moves toward me, but I jerk away from his advance. In the dim cabin, the slight sting of rejection shines in his eyes as he curses and fists his hands at his sides before turning back to me.

"You know me," the gentle timbre of his voice has my eyes watering. "You know my mind and my heart. You know *me*. I made sure of it. But *this* is my world, *our* world, and if you want in, you have another decision to make."

Sean speaks up, jerking me out of my reverie. "I can see I've blown your mind again. And not in a good way." His tone is mournful, and I know he sees the battle I'm fighting. He's put me in a dangerous position with his explanation, but he's also left the door wide open on the other side of it for a quick escape. The problem is, I can't even look at the threshold, because it means losing him. Knowing nothing about the party *is* my saving grace. I can walk away now, no ties. Merely aware of their existence but with nothing that incriminates me.

He runs a knuckle along my wobbling chin, and I look up to see we're parked in his driveway. I've been so lost in my thoughts I didn't follow his route home.

"I thought you were taking me home?"

"I didn't tell you which home."

"You're a good liar."

"You're a terrible one." His beautiful chest bounces. "And you don't really want to go home."

He reaches for me again and I shy away from his touch because it will draw me further in. Right now, I'm toeing a very dangerous line in some sort of alternate reality.

"Cecelia, I tried to ease you into this the best way I could. I had to be able to trust you."

"I still don't know *anything*."

"And that kept you safe from your involvement and all that it implied. But from this point forward, your decision changes that."

Chin set, he looks over to me. "I have a lot to lose, too." He turns his head, looking out the window and I swear I hear "more," muttered under his breath. He rests his head back on the seat and sighs before his head lolls back my way, his expression weary. "You'll go crazy trying to figure it out. Everything we do, we do for good reason. If you choose to stay, a lot of your questions will be answered over time. But everybody at the party has to earn their place. No exceptions."

"Can I ask you a question?"

"Not tonight, and not until you've made your decision. And even then, I can't guarantee I'll answer. Come on, let's get some sleep." He cuts the engine and gets out of his car. I follow him silently into his house and up the stairs to his bedroom. Everything has changed, every part of my involvement. I must be a willing participant in whatever comes next, or I have to walk away from him. I can feel the weight of my decision already weighing heavy on my heart.

When he closes the bedroom door, he pulls off his shirt and slips off his boots.

I'm too exhausted from the crash of adrenaline to fight, and he clearly is as well as he unbuckles his jeans and shoves them off, along with his boxers. The sight of him naked has my fingers itching to touch, my blood pulses more rapidly, but inside all I feel is dread.

I'm already more than halfway in love with this man and walking away will break my heart. He watches me carefully, no doubt reading my thoughts and then goes down the hall into his bathroom, leaving the door open, before turning on the shower.

An invitation.

Another decision.

I follow, shut the door, strip bare and join him. He draws me to him, kissing me for long minutes. Back in his room, we're silent when we towel off and I pull on one of his T-shirts before slipping into bed, into his waiting arms.

"Please understand, there was no other way," he murmurs

into my neck, pulling me snugly into his body. He's hard, but he doesn't act on it, he just keeps me firmly tucked into him, weakening me with his scent.

I should feel betrayed, but I *do* understand the 'why' of how he introduced me to it. And now I also understand that if I'm in, I'll have to become a lot better at lying, and if I can't keep a secret, it will cost me a lot more than a broken heart.

Chapter
Twenty-Nine

SEAN SLEEPS NEXT TO ME, PASSING OUT JUST MINUTES after his head hit the pillow. I lie in his hold restless, my thoughts running rampant.

This could cost me my future.

One misstep, being implicated in any of their shady dealings could cost me my life.

Is becoming tangled up with them worth it?

What kind of future can we have?

This isn't a phase for them that they'll outgrow, this is their way of life. Their purpose. Do I want to be anchored to it by a relationship that may or may not work out?

It's insane, this decision, this choice. One I never thought in a million years I would be faced with.

It distorts the natural order of things. This is a no picket fence life.

But somewhere, deep down I knew, I knew something was off—way off and clearly dangerous. I just didn't realize how off, how dangerous. In a delusional way, I assumed it wouldn't affect me.

The more I fall, the more entangled I become, and if I'm not careful, if I don't choose out, I'll be shackled in by new secrets.

But I'm leaving. In a year, *I am* leaving. That's a definite. I'm not going to skip college or throw away my chances at a higher education for anyone.

How much can really happen in a year?

Tyler's words the day we met come into mind.

"*Crazy where a day can take you, huh? That's nothing unusual around here.*"

"Ain't that the truth," I whisper into Sean's hair. I need to sleep on this. My decision doesn't have to be made today. I can distance myself until I've made it. I've got the willpower.

Liar.

I run my fingers through Sean's hair, and he groans lightly in his sleep in thanks, making me smile.

Sleep evades me, and I untangle from Sean and toss the covers off when I hear the distinct sound of an engine pull up in the drive. Padding down the stairs I find Dominic at the kitchen table, wrestling a small plastic-wrapped package with a freshly uncapped beer next to it.

"Is it broken?"

He looks up from where he sits, eyes sweeping me before getting back to his task. I approach him and take the thick gauze from his hand and gently examine his injury. Both his wrist and hand are twice their normal size.

"Ouch. Could be broken."

"I can bend it."

"You okay?"

"Shitty night," he grabs his beer from the table and takes a long pull.

"Where's Tyler?" I ask, starting on his bandage.

"He's indisposed."

"Did something else happen?"

"He's good. Business as usual."

"Just a party, right?" I can feel his eyes on me as I carefully layer the material snuggly against his skin. "Tell me if it's too tight."

"Why are you going along with this?"

I pause and meet his silvery depths, which threaten to pull me under and dart my eyes away. When I make my decision, I need to be far away from the two distractions that will only make it harder to step away. "I'm not sure if I am yet."

"I didn't think you were the type."

"I'm not, it's just as surprising to me, if you want the truth."

"Always."

One side of my mouth lifts as I carefully wrap his wrist and hand. "Says the deviant liar."

"Some people can't handle the truth," he drains the rest of his beer. "It's best to let them count sheep."

"Always so cryptic."

"You're smart enough to decipher truth from fiction."

I pause my hands. "I'm not so sure after tonight, but that's a rare compliment coming from you."

"I don't let my dick get in the way of my judgment."

Our gazes hold for long seconds as I draw more conclusions. They both made the decision to bring me in tonight. Together. It has nothing to do with our sexual relationship. The feelings that stir because of that make my heart sing.

"You *can* trust me," I say, securing the metal teeth on the bandage.

"It's a lot to ask."

"So is keeping your secrets."

"You don't know my secrets."

"I know what I think I know, and that's plenty."

"And what do you think you know?"

The last few hours I've been staring at Sean's ceiling sorting through his subtle teachings of the last six weeks. He incorporated the 'club's' beliefs into our courting and did so in the most effective of ways, spoon-feeding me until I knew what they collectively stood for, without directly coming out and saying it.

"That you're high up in an organization of backroads' misfits who do bad deeds to carry out good ones."

I'm not at all surprised when my answer is silence.

"So, what happens now?"

He reads my question, and it has nothing to do with tonight's discovery.

"I'm not Sean."

"Meaning?"

"I don't do these talks." He drains his beer as I secure the teeth a little tighter on his bandage. "But I could use a shower." I'm not sure what he's implying. He clearly needs my help undressing due to the injury, but I'm unwilling to go any further until I figure out what I need to.

He stands and awkwardly grabs another beer from the fridge. He uses the edge of the counter to pop off the cap and downs it like water before moving toward the stairs, and timidly I follow. Once inside his room, I glance around taking advantage of the peek into his world. Hundreds of books line the shelves next to his fully loaded space station with giant monitors. Next to it on a small table are three charging laptops. The pained grunt echoing from the next room deters me from taking more of a curious look around, and I meet him where he stands in the bathroom toeing off his boots. He bends to rip his sock off and loses his footing, his beer bottle clinking against the counter as he tries to brace himself. I laugh, steadying his hips with my hands, and between our efforts, he remains upright. He gives me a lazy half-smile, his eyes going glassy. "Fuck, my left hand really needs my right."

"I'm sure the alcohol you sucked down didn't help. We should have iced it first," I free him from his other sock.

"It can wait until morning."

"It really shouldn't."

"Cecelia," he expels a breath that's more like a plea, and I concede. I'm just as exhausted and wish my mind would let me sleep.

Moving in behind him, I unfasten his skinny jeans and tug them down his muscular thighs along with his briefs, before I circle him to remove his T-shirt. He gazes at me wordlessly and I turn on the shower, holding my hand in the spray, he snakes his good arm around me, lifting my shirt to stroke the skin of my stomach.

"Thank you. I'm good now. If you want to go."

The touch is sensual, sweet, and in reply, I lift my T-shirt off. His eyes flare as he drinks me in bare. It's our first time being alone and naked since we had sex, and I can't tear my eyes away. But I have to, so I turn my back on him and rest my head in the crook of his shoulder as the water warms. Once it's ready, he releases me, and we step inside. I tilt the faucet head, so most of the water pours over his body. I've already had my shower.

With another man, Cecelia. His roommate and best friend.

This cannot and will not end well. Unless I believe Sean, unless I believe them both. Too many wheels spin in my head and I decide to let them fly off, along with my lingering questions about the meetup as I suds up his loofah and begin to wash him from head to toe. Taking my time, I start at his chest and work my way down, unable to avoid the sight of his dick when it springs to life. My core begins to ache at the memory of our earlier exchange in his Camaro, my nipple in his mouth, his head slowly working as I clutched him to me.

"Sean was my third," I look at him pointedly. "That makes you my fourth. Before the two of you, I was in two separate and monogamous relationships, which may seem boring to you, but..." I shake my head. "Anyway, my point is, I don't sleep around. And that day...I've never done anything like that. I've never been in this position. I'm a one at a time type of girl."

Silence. The bastard is not going to make this easy on me.

"I know it seems hypocritical, but if you are sleeping around, I can't," I gesture between us. "I'm not...I don't think I can do *this*."

He eyes me without a word, not giving me an inch as I carefully avoid his erection and scrub off the day from his muscular thighs. He holds his injured hand away from the spray as I circle him, going up the same way I came down, daring to look up at him through the streaming water. Not a hint of his earlier smile, just his rapt attention when I rise and tilt his head back, soaking his onyx hair. The water cascades down the cuts of his body, as he hovers above me, temptation personified.

The urge to take another bite is damn near impossible to resist.

I pour shampoo on a shaky hand before raking my fingers against his scalp, feeling his exhale on my chest. It's utter agony being this close to him while clutching what's left of my moral standards tightly to me. Once he's clean, I step out, toweling off before he does, and then I take my time drying him off, not bothering to find him some boxers because I know his sleeping preference. Overly doting, I coat his toothbrush with toothpaste, and he rolls his eyes but takes it as I gargle with some of his mouthwash. Out of the bathroom, I can feel his eyes trail me as I straighten and pull back his rumpled sheets. After he slides in, I bend and press my lips to his forehead, knowing he won't like it. And he doesn't, shaking the maternal act away while giving me the stink eye.

I can't help my laugh and nuzzle him with my wet hair to spite the air surrounding him. I pull back to hover above him and I see his lips twitch before he grips my neck and draws my mouth to his. He goes deep, setting me on fire. A moan erupts from my lips as he thoroughly fucks me with his tongue, before pulling away and adjusting his pillow.

"Do you need me to stay?"

"I'm not Sean."

Nodding, I pull away.

"If you need me, you know where to find me."

Feeling the slight sting of his rejection, I walk back down the hall to see Sean shift in bed, pulling up the sheet to make room for me.

"He good?"

"He's good."

He reaches for me and pulls me into his arms and within minutes, my dreams find me.

Chapter Thirty

SEAN WENT ON A HIKE THIS MORNING AND I DECIDED to stay back to check on Dominic. He's spent the whole of the morning in his bedroom. I know he's in pain. After hours of waiting in vain for him to appear, I walk up the stairs with my arsenal in hand and knock on his door.

"Yeah?" Sounds from behind it.

I open it just enough to get a coffee cup through.

"Coffee, *black*," I say, and he takes it.

I push the plate through. "Eggs, *runny*. Peas, *ice cold*."

I shove my hand through the door last.

"Woman?"

I leave both the question and my hand hanging in the air. "Woman?" I wave it back and forth, a smile on my face.

Chuckling, he pulls me into his room and onto his lap

where he sits at his computer desk, his breakfast situated to the side of his keyboard.

He runs his good hand along my back, and through the tips of my hair as I rest the peas on his wrist. He winces on contact.

"Bad?"

"Hurts like a motherfucker."

His mood has lifted considerably from last night, and I'm thankful.

"Serves you right. Why did you go crazy like that?"

"I have a temper."

"Noooo, not you."

"Yeah, well, that motherfucker almost killed Sean."

"Then I'm glad you broke his jaw."

A tense silence follows and suddenly I feel awkward.

"Just wanted to check on you."

I move to get up so he can eat his breakfast, but he stills me, maneuvering me across his lap before picking up his fork and digging in. His clean scent invades me as I sit locked in his arms.

I glance around his room in the full light of day. Eyeing the private library over his shoulder that takes up one entire wall. "So, I'm guessing reading is a hobby?"

"You could say that."

"One of mine too." I shake my head. "Gotta say, you fellas surprise me at every turn."

"Why, because we aren't illiterates with mile-long rap sheets?"

"Your presentation is deceiving and…effective."

Assumptions from unsuspecting others like me keep them hiding in plain sight. At the most, they come across as twenty-something delinquents, but that's not the whole truth. People believe what they want to. The boys don't fight or negate their reputations because it keeps them in the dark. And the dark is their playground.

"I can't imagine you on a college campus. Did you like living in Boston?"

"It was all right." He dips his toast in the yolk and pops it into his mouth.

I glance over my shoulder as he makes quick work of inhaling his eggs.

"Good?"

He nods. "Thank you."

"Welcome." I glance toward his screen. "What are you doing?"

"Eating breakfast."

"God," I roll my eyes. "I'll never get a straight answer."

"Get used to it." He pushes his empty plate to the side and moves his mouse. The monitor comes to life and lines of code pop up.

"Jesus, it looks like the Matrix. What is this?"

"I don't know, you haven't chosen what color pill yet." He continues to eye the screen. The whole of it is dark, mostly. No browser links, nothing. Just numbers popping up, algorithms, and he seems to be reading them with ease.

"It's a back door," he says, moving his mouse.

"A back door?"

"To where I want to be."

"Is this the dark web?"

One side of his mouth lifts, indicating just how clueless I am. "It's my web."

"You're the spider?"

"With teeth," he bites down onto my shoulder and my lower half pulses.

"So, you're the brains, huh?"

"Don't credit me." His comment leads to more maddening silence. He knows I have zero idea of what we're looking at, and this keeps me safe in his secret.

Still sideways on his lap, I run my hands along his muscular neck and shoulders. He's wearing black sweats and nothing else, giving me the freedom to touch him, and that's exactly what I do. He lets me, his skin silky, nothing but carved lines and muscles. He grows hard beneath me and ignores it, clicking over and over until he situates me so I'm facing forward before he instructs me to type. After my shower, I decided against wearing last night's thong so the only thing separating us is the material of his sweats, which may as well be nothing. Unable to ignore the electricity racing through my veins, I draw heavy breaths, my nipples pulling tight with his every whispered order. He instructs me easily, in a carefully plotted symphony of moves until he seems satisfied. We do this for the better part of an hour, his body priming with my stolen touches, but he keeps his focus on our task, while I twitch in anticipation. In these minutes, I go from wet to soaked, stealing glances back at him to study his dark lashes and the perfection that is the rest of his face. It's too much to ask not to touch, but he nudges me when I lose focus, keeping my fingers working as I start to tremble with need. I'm helplessly seduced by the time he murmurs, "Good, thank you."

"Welcome."

I've adjusted myself over him several times for his comfort, but know he's probably tired of being my chair, and at this point, I'm terrified I made a mess in his lap. Slowly, I move to get up when he buries his nose in my hair, hooking me back into him. I draw audible breaths as he finally acknowledges the bulge in his sweats and the raging current between us. Clinging desperately to my will, I start to speak up when he beats me to it.

"No."

I turn my head, drinking in the lust that greets me and know this 'no' has everything to do with my questions last night. Our eyes stay locked as his grip tightens on my waist.

"I know what I'm holding, I know her worth," he whispers, his words so intimate that for a second, I think I've imagined them. "I'm not a teenage boy with his first hard-on. And even when I was, I've never tried to prove myself to anyone by using my dick as an exclamation point. I told you everything you needed to know last night. This is your decision, Cecelia, don't turn it on me."

I sit stunned, blinking several times before he grips the back of my neck, a harsh exhalation hitting my lips before he kisses me.

Deeply.

So deeply, I struggle for air, for sanity, as he takes and takes and I open for him, my limbs going lax. In his kiss, I lose a part of myself, his words lifting me above ground while his tongue coaxes me into this moment with him. Mouths molding, he lifts my T-shirt, breaking just long enough to bare me fully. And then his lips are back and capture my moan as we fuse. Drunk by the intensity of our exchange, I sink into him, my body lines up with his while he controls our rhythm with his tongue. Cradled, surrounded, my chest rises and falls with him as we drift into the deep end.

Lips drifting, teeth nipping, he latches to my neck and lifts me, pushing his sweats down. Gripping him tight, his grunt hits the back of my throat as I squeeze him from root to engorged tip. He thrusts into my hand before reaching between us to find the evidence of my desire. He groans into my mouth, palming my pussy, the heel of his hand massaging my clit as he presses his finger into me. Breaking from his kiss, a loud moan escapes me as his fingers conquer and my head falls back to fit in the crook of his neck. We work each other into a frenzy before he pulls back, his order clipped.

"Bedside drawer."

I'm up in a second, plucking a condom from the box, I hurry back to where he sits in his chair. Kneeling, I look up to where he watches me, gripping him in my hand a second before I take him in my mouth. His hips jerk at the contact.

"Fuck," Dom grits out. I hollow my cheeks and tighten my lips around the length of him before taking him to the back of my throat.

He traces his finger around the stretch of my lips as I suck him deep before my greed gets the best of me and release him with a pop. Rolling the latex on his cock, I lift to stand and he turns me, massaging my ass, spreading me, his fingers probing lower, dipping to ready me. Taking his cue, I grip the handles of his chair as he lines up his thick dick at my entrance, and I slowly sink onto him, the angle and intrusion, stretching me full.

When I'm seated, a gasp escapes me just as a groan bursts from his lips at the nape of my neck. He pushes us away from the desk, his legs anchoring us to the floor before he reclines us back in the chair so I'm practically laying on top of him. He thrusts up just as I begin to move, and I lose my breath, calling out his name.

"You," he pants, his voice hoarse. The appreciation in that one word is enough. It's all I need.

He runs his good hand along my chest, cupping my breast before sliding it down to where we connect. His strokes are methodical, slow, thorough. The feel of him is incredible and only adds to my elevation from his admission. This can't be Dominic.

But it is.

This is him.

Body tense, my suspended toes curl with every thrust. The sensation of him beneath me overwhelming as he fucks me gently, my body gliding along his chest. Rotating my hips, I meet him thrust for thrust until we both snap, needing more. He roots deeper as his finger coaxes me, running up and down my soaked clit. Collectively working together, our breaths the only sound in the room, he dips his finger lower, adding it to the stretch of his cock, and I shudder.

"Dom...G-G-God."

I'm quivering from head to foot when he bites down on my shoulder. My orgasm crests just as he thrusts up, encouraging me to ride the wave as it rolls through me. It takes every bit of my strength not to go limp once I come down, but the feel of him, his pants at my ear, fuel me and I swivel my hips and dip my hand to squeeze the base of him.

"Damn," he mumbles as he thrusts up, holding us both off the chair, once, twice, his exhale a total surrender at my neck when he comes.

Dazed, I turn my head to receive his crushing kiss, my temple damp, a thin veil of exertion covering both of us. When we break, we just stare at the other wordless, sated. And then slowly, so slowly, his lips tilt fully, knocking me senseless. It's my first genuine smile, and I snap away, knowing it's a mental picture I will never forget.

I stand and head to the bathroom for a towel, soaking it with warm water before coming back just as he discards the condom. He takes my offered towel, cleaning his lap before pulling up his sweats. Completely clueless on how to do *after* sex with Dominic, I brace myself for rude words, a cruel brushoff, but he surprises me by cupping my neck, pulling me flush to him and kissing me. I expect it to be brief, but he keeps our mouths fused and I eagerly kiss him back. We stand in the center of his bedroom as if it's our first kiss all over again, exploring each other. With the advantage of both hands, I run them down his chest to the growing bulge in his sweats. All traces of that smile disappear when silver-grey eyes hood.

"Get on the bed."

Chapter Thirty-One

DOMINIC FLIPS ANOTHER PAGE AS I RUN MY FINGER ALONG his happy trail and over his toned stomach. I note the title, *1984* by George Orwell, as I lay sprawled diagonally facing him where he sits propped against his headboard. The same position I've been in for the last ten or so minutes as he's shamelessly ignored me since I got out of the shower. It's storming heavily outside, the day seeming night in his bedroom. The rain beats on the roof as he flips another page, the only light in the room coming from the screensaver on his computer and a small bedside lamp.

"You just going to ignore me while you read all day?"

"Yep," he says, a hint of a smile on his lips.

"Well then, I have better things to do." I move to get up and he slides his hand down my back before molding it over the curve of my ass. My eyes close in remembrance of the past few hours of being at his mercy. I'm sore, more than sore, I've been fucked to within an inch of living. My afterglow dims considerably when Sean crosses my mind, and in those seconds, I become paralyzed by guilt. I can't for the life of me figure out how this is going to be okay for him, for either of them, when I could never handle being in their shoes while they shared their body with someone else. But Sean's not here, and I don't know if that's why I'm taking such liberties with Dominic. I try and remember the words he spoke to me that day after our tryst on the float, but they bring me no relief. Dominic speaks up behind his book.

"He's not mad at you. And he won't be. And you have nothing better to do."

The wind whips around the house. "He's not back from his hike. It's been hours and it's storming. You think he's okay?"

Dominic flips another page, reading at lightning speed.

"It's rude, you know, to ignore a direct question."

"It's a stupid question. I don't answer stupid questions."

"You are a rare bastard."

A smirk. "A rare bastard you can't seem to stop fucking."

"It takes two," I run my finger along the band of his pants. Apparently, he deems it inappropriate to *read* in the nude. "Why did you hate me?"

His gaze drifts from the page to me. "Who says I don't hate you?"

"I do," I straddle him, snatch his book, and toss it behind me. His eyes flare in annoyance as I dip low and hover above him, putting my hands on his shoulders to pin him down. "And if this is the closest thing I'm going to get to a date, the least you could do is give me a little conversation."

"A date," he chuckles dryly, and it stings. "You're barking up the wrong tree."

"I know, I know, you're not Sean."

His eyes snap up to mine. "I'm not."

"So, tell me who you are."

"You know who I am."

"A closet geek and introvert with horrible manners and excellent taste in music. It was you who played DJ at the party you kicked me out of, wasn't it?"

He nods. "I was working."

"Until you saw me?"

Another dip of his chin.

"Have you ever had a girlfriend?"

"When I was younger and thought getting my dick wet was the second coming of Christ."

"Have you ever been in love?"

Silence.

"That's not a stupid question."

"It is if you find love irrelevant."

"Why is love irrelevant?"

"Because it doesn't interest me."

"What interests you?"

"The book I was reading." I huff and move off his lap to pick the book up before I hand it to him. He resumes his reading as I move for his door.

"Pick one," he says just as I reach the handle.

"One what?"

He nods toward the shelves.

I run my hands over my face in frustration. "You drive me insane."

I move toward the shelf and look over his collection. I pause when I see a few familiar titles. "You have a whole romance section." I giggle and pull a book from the shelf. When I open it, a receipt falls to the floor. Inspecting it, I see he's just bought ten books and spent a few hundred dollars opting for some pricy hardcovers over paperbacks. "You just bought these?"

Upon closer inspection, I see most of them are romance titles by my favorite indies. There's also a few suspense and an older historical, all of them titles from a familiar list that I wrote on a bookmark in my bedroom. When he was in my house, he had to have snooped in my room while Sean was distracting me.

"You looked through my stuff?"

He keeps his eyes on his book.

It's a stupid question. And the answer is so obvious, but I can't help myself.

"You bought these for me?"

Silence.

And again, I'm floating off the ground as he continues to read, feigning indifference. But *I know* differently now, and it changes everything. Beneath that mask is a man who's been paying attention, *very close* attention to me.

He turns another page and pulls an empty pillow closer to his shoulder. He wants me to read, with him, in his bed. And what better way to pass a day in stormy weather than curling up with a gorgeous man and getting lost in the words.

Hours later, he's on his second book, and I'm deep into an erotic suspense, my breath growing shallow as I flip the page and begin to ache. Dominic's scent envelops me as I reach out and tentatively run a hand down his chest. We've been like this, stroking each other's skin on occasion since I sidled up next to him. Desire runs through me as I get to the part where all of the delicious tension explodes and that's when I feel his kiss on my stomach, my eyes drift from the page when he jerks me to the edge of the bed, spreading my legs.

I move to set down my book and he jerks his chin.

"Keep reading." He lowers his head as I attempt to resume my reading as he spreads me, thrusting his tongue into my center. I'm already close when he begins to lap at my clit. Dropping the paperback on my chest, I thrust my hands in his hair and he stops, the command in his eyes clear as I pick up my book, my thighs shaking as I try to read the paragraph for the third time. His thick fingers plunge into me just as the hero starts to pound into her, ripping at her hair, taunting her with filthy words. The words start to blur again as I get lost in Dominic's torture, my mind far more interested in my own story.

He wraps his lips around my clit, sucking hard as I lose the grip on my book. The sight of him alone makes it impossible to follow his order.

"Dom," I beg when he halts all movement, but he doesn't budge. It's only when I grapple for the book that he resumes, running his fingers along my lips to spread me before dipping his head and jackhammering his tongue along my clit.

Hyperaware of his every touch, I come undone on his tongue and lose it altogether when I hear the sound of a condom wrapper before he slowly pushes into me. In seconds, he puts the book hero to shame as he fucks me with ruthless abandon.

He's only a few thrusts in when I throw the book across the room, not giving a damn about the ending.

THE DAY SPENT IN DOMINIC'S BED IS COMPLETELY
unexpected and utterly blissful. We have a small picnic
on his comforter after ordering Thai, and then he rolls
us a blunt. Stuffed and smoked out, we lay on our backs, both
listening to and discussing Pink Floyd. Dominic's enthusiasm
never wavers as he explains his ideas on some of the lyrics to the
more cryptic songs.

We gaze up at the ceiling, our hands brushing, the window
wide open as the music duels with the pouring rain.

It's one of the best days I've ever had, just being at his side,
our shared touches, the frenzy of kisses, the endless fucking, our
laugh infused conversations and the rare, full smiles I draw from
him when he lets me. This day has been astonishingly intimate.
He's let me get a peek into his world. Much like Sean, Dominic
is nothing at all like I thought he would be. Past his remarkable,

yet hostile exterior lies much, much more. He's very much an idealist like Sean, and in conversations I can see the impression, the impact each has made on the other. This trust they have for one another, I envy it. When Sean told me that he needed my trust last night over everything else, I thought I understood, but not in the way Dominic has helped me understand today with just a few comments about Sean in conversation. And some part of me is comforted by that, not only because of the way they have each other's backs but for my own selfish reasons too.

Maybe they can hand me over freely to the other not only because of the way they feel for me, but because of the way they love and respect each other.

Or maybe, I'm using it as an excuse to try and justify taking part in it.

But no matter what, it's there, evident in their bond, their kinship, their intertwined lives.

"Wish You Were Here" floats out of the Bluetooth speaker on his desk, the melody surrounds us, drawing on my sentiment as I grip Dominic's hand and turn to face him. His attention stays on the ceiling.

"You don't hate me." It's a statement, not a question, but he ignores it. "And this *is* a date. You stare at me too. All the time. And you're not as cruel or scary as you make yourself out to be."

Nothing, it's as if he's completely deaf to the words I'm speaking.

Forever a motherfucker.

"Whatever," I agree with myself for my own sake. "Today was amazing, and you're an amazing reading partner." I giggle because I'm high, because this man makes me feel high, because I'm happy. I turn his hand over and brush my fingers along his palm. When I look back at him, I see his gaze follow my fingers before it returns to mine. He's not used to the simple affection, and that saddens me. We hold our stare for a few seconds before I speak up.

"My rainy days are yours, Dominic. If you want them."

"It rains a lot here," he says after a few long beats.

"Fine with me. But my sunny days belong to Sean."

"Making rules defeats—"

"No, I'm not making rules. It's a request," I interrupt, my eyes search his. "I just need some clarity for myself, but I want rainy days, very much."

He bites his lower lip and I click another mental picture. "So, you're in?"

My eyes drop and tension fills the air. "I don't know."

"It's that serious," he warns. "Don't downplay this."

"I'm not."

"Good."

Opening my mouth to speak, I freeze when the sound of Sean's Nova filters into the room through our open window. His arrival has me scrambling around to collect the trash and other evidence of our day. Grabbing the bag from the can next to Dominic's desk, I rush around tossing in our takeout and empty water bottles.

I can feel steel eyes on me, and my guilty heart pounds in an erratic beat while I scramble around the room.

One glance at his set jaw and chilled eyes lets me know he's pissed that I don't believe him. That I don't believe Sean. That I'm still unconvinced this won't blow up in my face. Cowering, I tie the bag just as Sean bounds up the carpeted stairs. I have the door halfway open when he peers in. He's soaked from head to foot and greets me with a golden smile. "Hey, Pup."

"Hi," I say, my eyes drop as he draws near.

I can't do this. I can't.

But if that's the truth, why does it feel like my heart is

capable? My body has given into the idea easily, but the damning in my head never ceases.

It's their words, their actions and reactions that ease my mind, not my own mindset, and at some point, that has to change if this is going to work. Sean waits patiently, but I can't bring myself to look at him. I'm naked beneath Dom's fresh T-shirt, a sure indication that I've temporarily switched sides and beds.

I reply with the only safe line my brain supplies. "You were gone forever. Did you have fun today?"

"Yeah, I did, perfect hike, and then I had some work to do, you?"

I nod, emotion clogging my throat. Unsure of what to do, I don't glance back at Dominic to gauge his read on this situation. After another painful silence, Sean tips my chin and shakes his head adamantly before leaning in to kiss me. His lips are soft, his smell making my eyes water as he pulls away.

"Still trying to make peace with the devil?"

My nod is solemn. "I want to so much."

"I'm all yours, Cecelia." Words, the perfect words from a perfect man I no longer feel I deserve. He nods past my shoulder at Dom before whispering a soft, "Night, man." I open my mouth just as he grips the handle on the other side of the door and closes it with me inside.

Shocked, I stand motionless for several seconds and turn to see Dominic's eyes on me before he pulls the empty pillow closer to his shoulder. Climbing back into bed with him, my smile grows wide just before he clicks off the light and reaches for me.

Chapter
Thirty-Three

"**T**HAT ONE," LAYLA SAYS AS I PUSH THROUGH THE DRESSING room door and step in front of the full-length mirror. Tessa, the store owner, nods in agreement from her position at the register of the small shop as I critique myself in the pale, yellow sundress that hugs my every curve. I've toned up, due to extended hikes with Sean. The color of the dress makes my sun-tinted skin appear darker and brings out the blue in my eyes.

"Yeah, this one."

Layla gives me a sly grin and leans in, out of Tessa's earshot. "Which one is this for?"

"Sean. I'm going to head over to the house after we leave and cook for the boys before fireworks tonight."

She sorts through a rack of hangers and grins. "If I didn't love my shithead fiancé so much, and hadn't watched those two twerps grow up, I would be jealous."

Layla is substantially older than me, having just turned thirty, and I hadn't realized how much older in our previous exchanges. From our conversations, I've gathered she's been in the 'club' since the beginning. She's a true ride-or-die when it comes to the hood, and we've been spending more time together in the last few weeks. She's the only person aside from Tyler who knows my Sunday Brunch smile secret.

The secret that I'm in a polyamorous relationship.

Which is odd and wonderful, exhilarating and terrifying all at the same time.

My phone sounds from my purse, and I pluck it from where it sits in the chair next to the dressing room to decline FaceTime with my mother. I've been avoiding her like the plague, due to my current dating status and the fact that I don't want to share any part of this with her. From the time I hit puberty until now, I've condemned her silently for sharing stories showcasing her blatant promiscuity, and now I have no place to judge. I've never once appreciated the fact that she played more friend than mother with her oversharing in that respect. And it's all wrong. I shouldn't punish her for it now that I better understand it. But some part of me wants to believe my circumstances are different. That my relationships are different. Grabbing my check card from my wallet, I brush away the guilt and see a message pop up when I hand it to the shop owner who's done nothing but helicopter us since we walked through the door.

I just wanted to see your face. Stop ignoring my calls. This is bullshit, kid, call me back or I'll be driving in from Atlanta TONIGHT.

I type out a quick reply.

Sorry. I'll call you later.

That's what you said last week.

I will. Promise.

Once Tessa rings me up, Layla snips off the tag. The dress costs far more than I would normally spend on any one item of clothing, but under Sean's influence, I only shop locally now. Which means I pay thirty dollars more at this downtown boutique for a dress and pump money into my local economy to support small business owners.

But the fear was real in Tessa's demeanor and hopeful eyes when Layla and I walked in and started eyeing price tags. It was so apparent she was desperate for a sale, which made me feel good about what I was buying and terrified for her that it wouldn't last. As I check out, I get some background on how she had inherited her grandmother's store when she died and rebranded it, sinking every dime into refacing the little shop. Tessa's not much older than me, and I can't help but feel for her as she catches herself oversharing, clear emotion leaking from her voice.

I make it a point to tell Sean about it, not for the credit of shopping here, but because I know he can do something about it. Christmas comes every quarter to a few select and local businesses in Triple Falls, mostly businesses owned by hood relatives to keep them afloat. That I learned by a full day of being in on the secret.

As promised, I got an answer to another lingering question. *Tyler* is the Friar. And I figured it out the day he and I were charged with passing out the checks to said businesses, something Sean didn't want me to miss. By the end of the day, I understood why he let me in on it. He wanted me to witness firsthand the why of what they do.

I was a sobbing mess both during and by the end of it when

the store owners burst through the doors with tears in their eyes. Every one of them had grateful words pouring from their lips as they accepted their checks.

But his part was to play the mask for the true culprit, Dominic.

Dominic and his sorcery behind the keyboard had everything to do with it. The source of the money? Large corporations and banks that siphon funds from unsuspecting shareholders and employees. Corporations and banks who could never report the theft for fear of getting examined more closely by the powers that be, the powers that govern and regulate.

That's the beauty of robbing thieves.

More than once, I've asked Sean about his plans for my father's company. Every time he's changed the subject, refusing to acknowledge the question and I wouldn't be surprised if, down the line, my father got a painful dose of justice.

That may be hitting too close to home and my boys are nothing, if they aren't cautious. Not only that, but a substantial hit would also endanger the jobs of their friends and relatives.

I can't, for the life of me, understand how they get away with it, but they do and have, and it's been going on for some time. Sean argues that it's been going on far too long on the other side of things. The government either fines the white-collar thieves heavily or some government official accepts a payoff to help cover tracks. No one gets prosecuted, and no one truly pays.

I wholeheartedly agree with his logic, which made me happy to be in on the secret.

Aside from that significant tidbit of information, Sean's kept his mouth closed about hood business, still waiting on my decision. I've taken my time with it. They've kept me at arm's length, refusing to answer any more questions until I put a voice to it and pledge my loyalty. Tyler is rarely home, if ever, and he, Sean, nor

Dom will give me any details on the why of that. He's still in the Reserves for four more years, that much I do know, so I assume he's keeping up with participation. I have zero clue of what he does with the rest of his time. He's rarely at the garage anymore, either. So, when I'm over, it's just the two men in my life and me.

And when I'm with them, I'm being schooled constantly. Though I still haven't voiced a decision, that hasn't at all stopped them from voicing their opinions. Dominic is speaking up more as well. It's highly entertaining waking up and walking downstairs to see them watching the morning news on every station as I hand them coffee. Both of them tense at the same moments and utter 'bullshit' at the exact same time. In lieu of football, they talk politics and are never in favor of either side. If I wasn't studying the distinctions between them daily, I would sometimes think they are the same person.

But in a lot of aspects, they're night and day, dark cloud and golden sun. And drawing the comparison between them has become inevitable. I stopped beating myself up about it after the first week or so.

I've never navigated my way through dating two men, and I've got more on my plate with them than I can handle. If I weren't so blissed out daily, I would probably give in to the naysayer screaming "ho" in my head. I bat that bitch away like a gnat because I'm sure that many women, given a chance, would tap dance toward either of their beds, roll around in their affection and then vie for my position between them.

Though I am tap-dancing over that moral line, the day at the lake was the one and only time I allowed myself to be shared at the same time.

But that's where it ended for me.

Man, did they ever make it memorable.

Not because I didn't enjoy it. Just the opposite. I enjoyed it far too much. However, my conscience did not, and it cheapens the romance aspect of it for me.

These two men have flipped my world, made colors more vivid, made sounds sweeter, made the world as a whole more bearable. My dreams consist of ray-filled days full of coconut lotion, long kisses, itchy sunburns, floating between waterfalls, and sighs before exhausted bodies collapse against feathery pillows. Other dreams of rainy days and nights filled with flips of pages and old nineties flicks, of cheddar popcorn and lavender scented blankets, of lightning and thunder and the fast pants and moans between the streak in the sky and the ground rattling boom that follows.

But these are my waking dreams, and I'm living them.

Dreaded shifts at the plant no longer bother me. I work them faithfully with Selma's smile. My father's absence no longer affects me in the way it has in the past because I've bore witness to two prime examples that there are good men left in the world. Loyal men. Faithful men. Though thieves they may be because they've stolen my heart.

I'm in love with both of them.

Two men, who make me feel adored, cherished, and respected. Two men, who have no issue which bed I keep warm. Two men, who look at me with nothing but lust and affection. Well, Sean does; Dominic gifts me with rare looks and slammed the door in my face the last time I saw him. I'd popped my head in his room and barely managed to get out before it was sealed tight. I tried not to take it personally, but I lost. We're currently in a fight he doesn't even know about, but I don't let that deter me.

He's a moody one, that motherfucker.

Layla smiles at Tessa while she bags her dresses and thanks us both profusely.

We eyeball each other as we exit the store.

"I'll tell him." I offer as we cross the walkway of the square toward her truck.

"I thought you would."

"It's so sad."

She nods.

"I love that we can help, well," I bite my lip, "you know what I mean." We climb up into Layla's massive truck, parked off Main Street as she looks around.

"Did you like growing up here?"

"Yeah. I'm glad I stayed when I graduated. I see it differently as the years pass."

I consider the bustling square that looks like something out of a Norman Rockwell painting. "I get that."

"Gotta love Small Town, USA," she says softly before turning to me. "Do you think you'll end up settling in Atlanta?"

"Honestly, I don't know. I've no plans past applying to UG."

Layla owns a small salon on the outskirts of town and refurbishes furniture on the side. We spent most of our morning scouring yard sales until she found her new project.

She pulls away and heads toward my father's house where she picked me up this morning. I make sure to sleep at home at least twice a week to keep myself centered, though it's not much help. My dreams are twice as memorable as they used to be.

"What you thinking about over there?"

My cheeks heat with guilt. "I'm so screwed."

"It's okay to be happy, Cecelia. You don't have to apologize for smiling. I don't know who taught you differently."

I look over to where she sits, her hand on the wheel as she winks at me.

"I'm in love with them."

She grins. "I know."

"You think they do?"

"You haven't told them?"

"No. You're the first person I've told."

"I'm glad."

"I can't talk to my mom, or my best friend, ya know? They won't get it. But you do, and I'm grateful."

"Trust me when I say that you're better off keeping them in the dark about everything."

"Trust me. I intend to." I type out a lengthy text to my mother, promising her some one-on-one and toss my phone in my purse.

"Have you ever regretted it?"

Layla and I never directly talk about the hood, it's kind of an unspoken rule between us.

"Absolutely. I've lost my damned mind a thousand times. And when I thought Denny and I were going to break up, it was worse. But I've got a leg up on him. I've been in this longer, secured my place. But the worrying," she shakes her head, "fuck, that can really weigh you down."

"It's dangerous to get so close, isn't it?"

"Honey, breathing is dangerous these days."

"True."

"Remember, you can be as involved with them as you *want* to be. It's all up to you. But I've got your back, babe. Especially with those two shits." She grins. "Dominic seems more relaxed lately."

"He's in trouble at the moment."

She turns to me, a hint of warning in her baby blues. "Keep your wits about you at *all times*, okay? You're taking on a lot, and it's hard enough dealing with one."

I smile. "Thanks, I will. And thanks for the hair." I run my hand through my newly trimmed mane and lowlights.

"Welcome. Let me know how tonight goes, and I'll pick you up for Eddie's next week. I could use a girls' night."

"It's a date."

She pulls away and I charge through the front door and up the stairs, changing sandals and ditching my phone before I gloss my lips. I'm halfway back down, building a mental to-do list when I see Roman standing at the bottom of the steps waiting for me, and I freeze. He's in casual attire with a half-drained gin in hand.

I slow my descent as he considers me with glassy eyes. It's not his first drink of the day. "Do you still live here?"

"On occasion," I answer honestly.

"I knew you would be off for the holiday, so I drove home last night."

I frown, clutching my purse in front of me. "I didn't get an email."

He tilts his glass in his hand, slashing his brows. "I didn't think I would have to send one. Then I saw you weren't home and assumed you had plans."

"I do have plans."

He nods as I approach, the exchange putting me on edge. Even in casual clothes, he's intimidating.

"Is there something that you wanted?"

He sips his drink and clears his throat as I hit the landing.

"I wanted to be the one to tell you that the plant is getting an upgraded AC system today, and I've looked into your other concerns, and it's been handled. Accounting will be handing out additional checks this coming pay period."

"Thank you," I say warily. There's clear hesitation in his posture as he looks down at me. He stands a little over six-foot, but he might as well be a skyscraper.

"It's clear you've adjusted here, and unless you have any

objections, I'll be staying at the condo." His eyes implore mine, and I swear I see a glimmer of hope for an objection, but it's way too late.

"No objections. Is that all?"

With a nod, his eyes drop, and he steps away, giving me a lot more space than I need to get past him. I'm grateful for it and make it halfway across the foyer when he speaks up.

"Don't make her mistakes."

I turn back and catch a glimpse of him over my shoulder. "Sir?"

"Who better to warn you than her biggest one." He tips his glass back, draining it, his deep-sea eyes meeting mine once more before he strides into his office and closes the door.

Chapter
Thirty-Four

CLAD IN MY NEW FAVORITE SUNDRESS, I SIT ON THE counter in the kitchen, my carefully prepared barbecue ice cold as I turn the page of my latest novel. Hours after our planned date, the roar of Sean's Nova goes silent a minute before he enters the house. Not taking my eyes off the book, I lift a piece of lukewarm watermelon to my mouth as he stands at the entrance of the kitchen, gauging my mood and watching me nibble the sweet fruit. After a long stretch of silence, I finally speak up.

"Explain yourself, Roberts," I mutter between bites, glancing over the top of the book, my feet swinging beneath me.

He eyes the cover. *1984.*

"I love that you're reading that, instead of your usual."

I flip the page and try to take one from Dominic's playbook, my voice considerably cooler when I reply. "Don't knock romance books. From the last one I read, I learned how to play a solitary card game, snagged the barbecue recipe I cooked today, and discovered how to bring myself to a proper orgasm, which means I can do all three *without* you. This makes me *fully* capable of entertaining *myself*. Coming here, in this dress, and cooking for you was a *decision*, and like all decisions, it was *optional*."

His growing smile is infuriating.

"You look beautiful."

I bite into another piece of watermelon, setting the book down and raise my hostile gaze to him as he saunters toward me, looking delicious in a white tee and dark denim. Cedar and sunshine encase me where I sit as he leans in for a bite. I jerk the fruit out of reach. "Get your own."

"I want yours."

"Tough shit. Mine was ready six hours ago."

He sighs, clear fatigue in his posture. "All I want right now is a bite of that watermelon and to get inside my woman as soon as possible."

"Not happening."

Frowning, he eases back before turning and fishing a beer out of the fridge. "I got tied up. And you know I didn't have my phone."

"Which is bullshit."

He shakes his head. "No, what's bullshit is that you think *Big Brother* is just the name of a TV show."

"Are you really doing this right now? You're going to twist this to lecture me?"

His eyes flare with warning as I widen mine. "Big Brother is watching, I know, Sean. I know." I roll my eyes. "You're so paranoid."

He takes a long sip of beer and shakes his head ironically. "No, I'm cautious," he declares softly. "And being arrogant will only get us caught."

"You don't think you're being a little ridiculous?" I eye the book and lift it. "You don't think this is a little farfetched?"

"It's fiction, so sure, it's farfetched," he snaps, full of sarcasm as his jaw sets in a hard line. "No, in-depth or massive brainwashing of that magnitude could ever come to fruition in real life, right? Except for, you know, that minor incident we named The Holocaust where millions were executed at the hands of a fucking madman."

"You know what I mean. This is Triple Falls, Sean, not Nazi-occupied Germany."

"No, I don't. And what's ridiculous is that you need to see to believe."

"Excuse me if I think the government has more important things to do than tap you."

He gives me a dead stare. "Everyone is tapped. Everyone. Every single conversation on every fucking device is being recorded by the government, period. And maybe it would be ridiculous if I was Joe Schmo, and my only crime was recording a home porno with my wife's best friend. Shit no one cares about, except for my wife. But you *do* know better." He narrows his eyes. "Ever have a *face to face* discussion with someone just before seeing an ad for it in your newsfeed?"

I bite my cheek.

"Exactly. That should be all the proof that *anyone* with something to hide needs to see to think of technology as a threat. No one is safe. Our information is sold regularly for no other reason than our need for consumption. We're all locusts at this point. But that's only half of it. Our digital fingerprints include a lot more than what we buy, and what we're being sold for, they are fucking markers. So, what's *ridiculous*, Cecelia, is that you need to *see* it to believe it."

"Whatever," I bound off the counter. "Gotta admit, it's the

perfect excuse though, isn't it? 'I'm a secret agent man,' yadda, yadda. Dinner is in the fridge. I'm going to bed."

The coolness in his voice stops my retreat. "You're being awfully fucking flippant about something that means a great deal to me and to Dom. This point, in particular, has been explained to you over and over in painstaking detail. And if you think I'm so fucking crazy, if you refuse so much to believe in what I do, why the hell are you sticking around?"

I swallow at the lividity in his tone. "It's not that I don't believe you, it's just…"

"You're so quick to point out what a goddamned idiot you think I am. Do you know what happens if I'm right?" His voice shakes with anger. "Do you know what happens to caged birds?" I've never seen him so pissed, and I don't congratulate myself for being granted the fight I've picked.

Nerves firing off, I twist my hands in front of me. "Sean, I think you're brilliant, but—"

"I'm not a fucking schizophrenic, Cecelia. These are Dominic's rules too. You think he's ridiculous? What about Tyler? Is he ridiculous? Have you turned on the fucking news lately? How much do you need to see to believe?!"

"No, I just—"

"Everything I do has a reason behind it. I've explained that over and over and tonight, what I was doing was equally as important as what I did yesterday and the day before that."

"Sean," I take a step forward, hating the glare in his eyes, it's the first time it's ever been directed at me. He crosses his arms, cutting me off from getting closer.

"It's just… I spent half a damn day cooking for you. The least you could do was give me a real apology."

"Oh yeah, this is about the *dinner* I missed, right?" He spins, jerking open the fridge and grabs his plate. He rips off the

foil and snatches a fork from the drawer before shoveling barbecue into his mouth. "It's delicious, you happy?" Tears gather in
my eyes as he tosses the plate across the kitchen and it shatters
in the sink.

It's then I realize how weak my argument is, and he looks
me over, shaking his head in disappointment. "I thought you believed in me. You're getting a lot better at lying."

"You know I do." I step forward and he jerks away from my
touch, peering down at me with cold eyes, his face resolute. "If
we're going to continue to fight about trust, maybe we should table this."

"What?" It's physical, the way every word strikes me. I feel
every violent blow down to my freshly painted toes.

"Us. Table this. We should break."

"You mean break up?" Tears fill my eyes instantly. It's at that
moment that I realize how deeply I love him.

He's dumping me because I'm throwing a fit.

At this point, it's deserved. I went too far and insulted him
in a way I can't take back. I have zero defense.

"Yeah, I mean break up." He eyes me from where he stands,
his tone unforgiving.

"D-d-don't do that, don't do that, I was angry."

"Doesn't matter. Anger isn't an excuse. I can't have someone around me who doesn't believe in me and what I'm doing. It
was a gamble with you, and it's clear to me now that you're too
young."

"Don't, Sean, don't. You know I-I believe you."

"No, you don't," he snaps. "Not in the way you need to. Go
home, Cecelia. We're done."

"I'm not trying to manipulate or belittle you, Sean! I was
scared! I didn't know if something had happened to you!" Hot
tears gather and fall down my cheeks as he stands feet away,

284 | KATE STEWART

though it might as well be an ocean. "You've been distracted lately, and I-I just miss you...Please take it back."

He grabs his beer from the counter, tossing it back, his face void of emotion. He's shutting me out.

I refuse to believe it's over. There's too much between us. And I wasted so much time not admitting it. Terrified it might be my first, and last time, I bare myself completely.

"I love you," I whisper through a blur of tears. "And I don't think you're crazy at all. I got upset sitting here for hours romanticizing how I would say this to you, and that it would matter. Instead of admitting it, I got angry and said stupid things I didn't mean. I t-trust you. I believe so much in what you're doing. I think you're brilliant."

He darts his eyes away and slams his beer on the counter, the suds spilling over the bottle.

"I-I'm sorry. I'll go." Sliding on my sandals, I grab my purse from the table, my eyes sting as I try to hold myself together long enough to make it to my car. I make it just past the staircase to the entryway before I feel his chest at my back. A cry escapes me as he flips me around and cups my chin, lifting my eyes to his.

"I take it back."

I burst in his arms, my sobs coming out in a rush as he pulls me to him leaving no space between us.

"I'm so sorry, baby. Fuck, I regretted it the minute I said it." He wraps strong arms around me. "You're fucking crazier than you're acting if you think I want to spend a minute away from you. I missed you too. Today was bad, and fuck, I'm sorry. You look so beautiful."

Hiccups consume me as I tearfully try to speak, and he wipes at my face.

"Shit, shit, I'm sorry," he says softly. "I hate the idea of waking up and not hearing about your dreams in the morning. Hey,

hey," he whispers softly, "baby, please stop crying. You're killing me. You mean so much to me, so much more than I ever thought possible," he murmurs. "So much more."

He pulls the purse from my shoulder and grips me tightly to him, my chin trembling as my heart slams against my chest.

"I-I j-just, I love you," I murmur into his neck and he pulls back, staring at me, drinking the emotions sliding down my face.

"I know, and it's ruining me," he whispers, thumbing my cheeks. "Rest assured. I'm going to make sure you know just *how fucking much* it matters to me." He lifts me easily and carries me back into the kitchen, setting me on the counter. "But first, I *will* have my watermelon."

I smile. It's not at all what I expected to hear, but it's Sean, and so it's perfect. He adjusts me to wrap around him as I sniff into his shoulder, ruining his T-shirt. It's when I inhale his scent that I bury my face in his chest, unable to fully muffle my sob.

"Don't cry, baby. Please stop, fuck," he hangs his head, "this hurts."

"I'm sorry," I say through a snot-filled nose, looking over at him. "It's just. You smell like wood."

He cracks a smile a mile wide and chuckles. "What?"

"I don't think I've ever told you that. You smell like wood, like cedar and sunshine and I love the way you smell, and I would hate it if I couldn't smell you anymore. And I do take you ser-ser-seriously."

He stares down at me, his eyes full of affection as my breath starts to hitch in a way that lets me know I just ugly cried.

"It was just a fight."

"You cut me back," I say, my breath hitching making me do that involuntary head and chest twitch. I'm humiliated I'm reacting this way. "And it hurt. But I deserved it."

"Maybe, but I'm still going to make it up to you," he assures, grabbing a slice of watermelon. He takes a bite and offers it to me as I sniffle and turn my head. "I'm good."

He takes another bite and repeats his offering, and I shake my head, denying him. By his third slice, we're sharing while I start to come down from the most excruciating emotional high.

"I went girl on you," I admit, my cheeks flaming with embarrassment.

"Yeah, well, I went raging dick on you, so we're even."

I palm his jaw. "I'm sorry, Sean."

"Me too, baby."

He presses the watermelon to my lips, and I bite into the juice-laden fruit. He licks the remnants of tears along with juice off my face before he pulls me into a deep kiss. "Sorry about the fireworks."

"I don't care about the stupid fireworks. Just..." my breath hitches again and I can see it pains him. "Just don't forget about me while you're out saving the world."

"Impossible."

I look over at him imploringly. "I need you to believe me. Because I do believe in you, Sean. So much. I saw my father today, and I think he was trying to bridge the gap, and all I could think was that I don't respect him enough to try. No matter what excuses he gives. I don't respect him. And then I thought about you, and I realized I have this respect for you that I've never had for *any man* in my life. I want you to know," I exhale a shuddering breath as my eyes water, "that. I need you to know that."

He tosses his watermelon and palms my face, holding my gaze for long seconds before he presses the gentlest of kisses to my lips. He pulls away slightly so our foreheads touch. "What do you say we make up now?"

"I thought we did."

"We did, but this, right here, this is the best part," he

captures my mouth in a deep kiss. Sinking into it, our tongues dance as I start to lift his shirt, my breath hitching against his mouth, disrupting our kiss.

"Baby," he murmurs, biting his lip and running gentle knuckles across my chin as he gazes over at me. Then he dips, his descent slow and deliberate before he again presses his lips to mine. Leisurely, he slips the straps of my dress down before lowering the material to free my breasts. Nipples tight, he runs a rough, warm hand along the whole of my chest. Following his pace, I unhook the button of his jeans and unzip him, pulling his ready cock free. Eyes locked, I pump him in my hand as he fishes a condom from his wallet, before he crushes my mouth with another consuming kiss. Positioning me, he pulls me to the edge of the counter before rolling the condom on. Pressing his forehead to mine, eyes cast down, we collectively watch as he slowly pushes into me.

"Sean," I rasp out as he exhales a pleasured breath.

Emotions zing between us as his hands flatten me to the counter while the rest of the forgotten watermelon slides to the floor. His strokes are deep, his eyes full of love, as his sticky hands palm my breasts trailing down my new dress. It was worth every penny.

He leaves no place untouched.

Chapter Thirty-Five

TYLER EXITS HIS TRUCK WHEN HE SPOTS ME PULLING UP, that natural swagger of his greeting me at my driver's side door.

"Hey, beautiful." His dimple appears, and I drink in the sight of him. He's let his hair grow a little longer since I met him, only adding to his appeal. It lies in a mess of short waves on his head. His rich brown eyes sweep me as he pulls me into a friendly hug.

"Hey, you, thanks for meeting me."

"No problem. What's with all the secrecy?" He nods, scanning the parking lot of the shopping center.

"I thought secrecy was the name of this game, which is why I need your help."

"Yeah?" Another shot of dimple. He truly is a beautiful man. In the short time I've known him, he's presented himself in a way where I'm convinced his beauty runs well past skin and bone structure.

"Yeah, but it might get you into trouble, if we're caught."

He cups my shoulders and leans in. "Did you forget I'm the problem solver?"

"That's why I need you. You're the only man for the job."

His smile widens. "Well, before we go in, you should know, I also love trouble."

"You're right," Tyler scopes out the house with trepidation from where we sit parked in the driveway before turning to me. "He won't like this."

He again peeks at the house and sighs before hopping out of his truck, gathering bags of the supplies we'd picked up at the store. Once I'd let him in on what we were doing mid-trip, he went quiet.

"That's why it's our secret," I fill my hands with another half dozen bags, weighing his expression. He clearly doesn't want to be here. "Sorry, I guess I could've just asked for her address."

"It's fine," he says, his arms and shoulders bulging from the weight he's carrying before he nudges me forward. "Let's do this."

We head up the porch past a few neglected plants, anticipatory nerves seeming to fire off between us. I steady the brute Marine next to me, whose posture is braced in a way that makes me squeamish. Was this really that bad of an idea?

His unexpected hesitation has me second-guessing myself. But I don't see the harm. It's a gesture, a kind one at that. How much could Dominic possibly resent it? Within a few knocks she answers, but I can tell it was a struggle for her to get to the door. Her hair is a braided mess over her shoulder, black half-moons of sickness lay prominently beneath her eyes. She stands in a pale blue robe and matching pajamas, her gaze filled with clear accusation when she darts them to me.

"I had my treatment *last night*," she snaps, her tone laced with embarrassment, as she pulls her robe more tightly around her. "I don't need a ride."

"Hey, Delphine," Tyler greets as she drinks him in slowly before eyeing the dozen or so plastic bags in his hands.

"What are you doing here?"

Tyler remains mute, looking her over carefully before lowering his gaze. He seems at a loss for words, so I speak up on our behalf.

"Here to see you, we were just at the store and—"

She slices her hand in the air, effectively cutting me off, her unforgiving gaze on Tyler before rolling back to me. "I need *nothing.*"

"You need this," I say softly. "And if you don't, *I do.* So, please let us in."

After a painful silence, she takes a reluctant step back just enough to let us through. Tyler carries the bulk of the load through the living room, setting the bags on the counter. He's no stranger to this house. When I think about it, it's no surprise, Dominic grew up here. Tyler told me during our hood errands that he grew up with Dominic and Sean in the same neighborhood, that they played together as kids. His childhood home is a few streets over from hers, which is why I asked him to help me today. I knew he would know the way.

Sean would've probably tried to talk me out of it, so I went with the safest option. And I'm happy about my choice as a bold roach crawls over the lip of the bag I just unpacked. I jerk back before smashing it with a can of bug spray. Delphine joins us in the kitchen as I shudder and shove the empty bag into the trash. Tyler remains mute, unpacking the rest of the bags, tension rolling off his shoulders. Delphine views me with speculation as I strategically stack dinners in her freezer.

"This will not earn you any points with my nephew." She speaks from behind me, her French tongue laced with disdain.

"Then let's not mention it to him," I reply. I'm not insulted by her assumption. I can only imagine how many women she's chased off over the years. But it's not Dominic I'm the most concerned about at the moment. Tyler either, although he seems pretty ill at ease. I might have asked too much from him.

Delphine hovers in her kitchen, her focus drifting between the two of us, but I can tell her defiant stance is taking some effort as a thin veil of sweat starts to coat her translucent skin.

"Or maybe it's not my nephew you're fucking?"

Tyler snaps his head her way, and I lift my hand.

"No, it most *definitely is* your nephew I'm fucking."

Her eyes drift over my shoulder to Tyler, who seems surprised by her reaction to us. She shakes her head and walks out of the kitchen as we share a weary glance before we resume our work.

Once we've fully unpacked, we divide to conquer. I start in her bedroom, filling a trash bag full of junk under her eagle-eyed scrutiny before I gather my arsenal of cleaners. I'm halfway into scrubbing out a carpet stain that looks like a lost cause when she sounds up behind me.

"Why are you here?"

I decide to give her a dose of Alfred Sean Roberts honesty. Something tells me she'll appreciate it a lot more. I glance over my shoulder and meet her assessing eyes. "Because I don't like the state you're living in. You're not well. You're fighting a sickness while allowing yourself to live in an infested house."

"Who are *you* to criticize me?"

"No one of authority." I stand and face her fully. She's so thin I can see the deep purple vein in her neck. Chemo has taken a scary toll since the last time I saw her. "You can tell me to leave, Delphine. And I will."

She crosses her arms, her thin robe accentuating her gaunt figure. "I'm doing what I'm supposed to. I've taken my meds."

"I'm not here to police you." Simple, honest, to the point. The woman can smell bullshit from a mile away.

"Fine," she flips her hand. "Do what you will."

"Thank you." She frowns at my reply and turns on shaky legs, walking back toward the living room.

I resume my scrubbing as the house remains quiet and the tension builds. She finally speaks up, calling out to Tyler who's working his way through her kitchen. I hear the distinct clink of a bottle to glass where she speaks from her chair.

"Never thought I'd see you again. Are you still a traitor?"

"If you mean a Marine, then yes," he replies, clear mirth in his voice. "You haven't forgiven me yet?"

"No."

"Maybe if I get these dishes sparkling, you'll forgive me."

"Those dishes are older than you. They no longer sparkle."

"Well, you certainly know how to keep hold of things that aren't worth a shit."

My ears perk at his comment.

"You wear both tattoos like badges of honor, but which house do you *really* serve?"

"*This house*, today," he replies without pause. "And I explained to you a long time ago I wanted to serve both."

She huffs, indignant. "They are not one and the same. They're contradictions of the other."

"That's what we're trying to change."

"You know better."

"I refuse to give up, and you have no place lecturing anyone on that."

I can feel the tension his scorn causes. The house goes silent again as I make my way toward the bedroom door and peek out, seeing just enough of Tyler as he kneels down in front of her. I'm too far away, but I swear I catch her features soften as he whispers to her from feet away.

"I'm sorry I haven't been back."

He pulls the drink from her hand and sets it on the table. Tentatively, she reaches out and palms his cheek, and he covers it with his own.

"I had high hopes for you." She pulls her hand away, and he sighs.

"Keep them high, along with your expectations, but you have to live to see me meet them. What in the hell have you done to yourself, Delphine?"

She leans in on a whisper, her eyes finding mine over his shoulder before I jump back into the bedroom and head toward the bathroom to finish my task.

So, Delphine is in on the secret.

Interesting.

But I'll never be able to use this to my advantage. She's just as closed off as Dominic. I'm not enough of a crowbar to try and breach her barriers. I know this without even trying.

After spending endless minutes scrubbing her bathroom and setting out roach bait in every corner, along all the baseboards, and in her closets, I move to join them in the living room. Tyler's clearing a thick layer of dust from one of her floating shelves. "How do you breathe in here, Delphine?"

She lifts her vodka bottle and pours an inch into her glass. "Breathing is overrated."

He shakes his head and peers down on her, his voice full of authority. "Stubborn ass woman."

"Careful, have some respect for your first crush," she says softly.

He tilts his head, his eyes brimming with affection until she averts her gaze.

"Bet you never thought I would end up like *this*."

"I have no pity for you," he clips, "the woman I knew would fight this shit with her eyes closed. You are choosing this."

"I chose the wrong man." Her lips curl into a sad smile as she takes another sip. "You fight this for four years and then come lecture me about it. Cancer is very much like a cockroach. They always come back to the one who hosts them best."

"First of all, he was a piece of shit," Tyler supplies, a sharp edge to his voice. "And secondly—" He stops berating her when I walk into the room.

"By all means, carry on," I gesture, "I heard every word."

Delphine laughs, lifts her glass, and drains more vodka. She doesn't even look phased by the alcohol. Clearly, she's earned her tenure as a drunk. After a long swallow, she nods toward me. "I like this one."

"She's fond of you too. Don't know why."

"Sure, you don't." She smirks, and I see the subtle upturn of his lips. The air grows thick again and I get an inkling, and study them collectively.

"All done in there, Cee?" His eyes drift from me to Delphine and back again.

"Yeah." I bob my head.

Tyler resumes his cleaning as I cross the living room to inspect his job on the kitchen. It's sparkling and reeks of lemon disinfectant—Marine clean. Enough to eat off the floor.

Even if she doesn't appreciate it, I'll sleep better, selfish as it may be. I'm thinking Tyler will be sleeping better as well. He clearly has affection for her. I just can't understand why Dominic wouldn't try to do this for her himself.

Maybe he has, and gave up like she did.

Dom's home is always spotless, and his room is as well. That she lives this way by choice is what's so hard to accept.

Satisfied with our job, I write down an inventory of the groceries we bought for quick reference and leave the list on the counter for her. Delphine's draining another drink when I reach her. Her Bible open on her lap before she lifts her eyes to mine. Her expression is full of hope.

I fight the emotion budding in my chest and manage to school my features as Tyler wipes the debris off the window ledge next to her. He reads the situation and glances back at the two of us in a stare off before he tosses the rag over his shoulder.

"I'm going to hit the other two rooms." He excuses himself, his gaze lingering on Delphine before he disappears down the hall.

However, it's Dominic's aunt who keeps me captive because the fear in her eyes is real, and it makes me just as fearful for her.

Despite her flippant comments, she's afraid to die.

If only that quack were real. The one who has proof of *His* existence, then she wouldn't be so scared to take the journey. But all she has is faith. All she *needs* is to keep the faith of the book in her hands. And that has to be enough. This point right here is when faith becomes her burden and possible breaking point. I might have needed to sterilize her environment to feel better about her situation, but what *she* truly needs isn't in plastic bags.

She doesn't bother to ask, and she doesn't have to. I kneel next to her as she flips through the pages and begins to read.

Back in Tyler's truck, we collectively stare at the house. She'd thanked us and hugged Tyler for several seconds before she'd given me a slight smile and closed her door. I eye the plants on her porch as he turns the engine over.

"Shit, I forgot to water her porch plants."

"You've done enough." His whisper is covered in melancholy. I could have asked for directions because I'd forgotten the way, but I needed back-up. It's a hard situation to deal with, especially letting a stranger in, and I needed that familiarity from Tyler to get through her door. But even with him there, it was still hard, and it's just as hard now leaving her alone to waste away in that house, especially knowing how scared she is. She may have chosen to stop fighting and die alone, but she doesn't want to be alone when she gets there.

"She needs to believe," I look him over. "She's terrified."

"I know." He turns and meets my gaze. "Do you believe in all that shit y'all were talking about?"

"I want to. And if I were told I might die, I damn sure would be praying for my salvation every day. I guess that makes me a hypocrite when it comes to religion. I am because I'm only faithful when it's convenient."

His nod is solemn as he peers back toward the house as we continue to idle. "She's changed a lot, but I can still see her in there." A reminiscing smile tickles his lips. "And you will never be the heathen she was."

"You know I have secrets of my own." I swallow and brave a glance his way. I see no judgment, which only endears him to me. He squeezes my knee briefly and winks.

"You've been corrupted."

"*Willingly* corrupted."

"You are good people, Cecelia." His eyes drift back to the house. "Dominic's tried for years to get her to start living right. They—" He clears his throat and darts his gaze away, "tried." He's in pain. Real pain. And that's when I know I was right. His eyes light up when he speaks. "You might not see it now from the shape she's in, but eight years ago, she was one of the most beautiful fucking women to walk this Earth. Her ex ruined her, and she let him."

"She wasn't just a crush, was she?"

He slowly shakes his head. "I was comfort for her, but she's the one who *crushed* me. Despite being a punk-ass eighteen-year-old, I knew I loved her. He'd left her years before we hooked up. She was already heavy on the bottle and when she sobered up, she made it clear to me I was a mistake. I enlisted right after."

"Oh my God, Tyler, I'm so sorry."

He wipes his hand over his face. "It was never going to work anyway. The military was always my plan, and she was too far gone by the time we happened. I—" He shrugs, though I know the weight on his shoulders is too heavy to shake away. "Can't help who you fall for, right?"

"Ain't that the truth." I study his stark profile. "Did Dom know?"

"No. No one. You're the only one I've ever told. And she... well, she'll take it to her grave. She's the best at keeping secrets. Better than any one of us." He takes one more look at the house before pulling out of the driveway. "She was only twenty when she...became a reluctant parent."

My age. I can't imagine.

"But she did what she could. The irony is it's her ovaries killing her anyway. One big life fuck you. I wouldn't have given a damn about her age, then or *now*, if she would have let me in. Fuck, I hate seeing her like this."

I cover his hand on the seat with mine. "I'm sorry I dragged you into this. If I would have known, I never would have asked you."

"No, I'm glad you did. I thought it was best to stay away, but now that I've seen her...I know better. I'll do better and I won't let her suffer alone anymore. She dismissed us and broke my fucking heart, and then I turned around and gave up on her in return The eighteen-year-old me didn't understand it. I do now." I study his profile as he drives us out of the neighborhood.

"You still love her."

He nods. "I have since I was sixteen. But Cee, this is our se-cret to keep."

"I will. I swear to you, Tyler. Thank you for trusting me with it."

Silence follows and I know he's hurting—I can feel it pour-ing from him. Even after all these years, even in her wretched state, he still loves her.

For the first time in my life, I don't see the beauty in trag-edy. I see the cruelty of it. He drives on, silent and reflective, the whole way back to the shopping center, only addressing me when he turns into the parking lot. He grins, shaking his head ironi-cally. "Life is crazy, isn't it?"

"Never know where a day can bring you, especially around here," I repeat his words from the day we met. "You okay?"

"I'm good. Swear." The light in his eyes returns briefly, along with a peek of his dimple. "And I'm here for any favor you need, Cee. I've got your back."

"Same, Tyler, same."

Chapter Thirty-Six

"**Y**OU ARE ONE LUCKY BITCH." I PALM MY STOMACH, admiring the snug fit of the dress I bought specifically for tonight. I spent half of another shitty paycheck just to see that shop owner, Tessa, light up. It was a reward in itself. It's a dangling two-piece, a halter that shows a little side boob, along with a flowing black skirt. It's a little risqué, and I decide Dominic will love it. The occasion is special. It's for our first date.

A real date.

His idea.

If that isn't evidence of progression, I don't know what is. I try not to question anymore the why of the three of us.

For the life of me, I can't understand why these two gorgeous guys with so much to offer have settled on me. It can't be just the sex, because I've seen for myself just how capable they are of getting any woman within a five-mile radius. I want to believe that their interest is genuine, that they truly do respect me and are okay with this arrangement because I can't imagine having to choose between them. I get no grief in return for this tradeoff, absolutely none.

My rainy days with Dominic are scarce because he stays so busy with running the garage and with hood business, sometimes I have to wait days just to lay eyes on him. That's why tonight is so special, and I'm soaking up every minute because there's an inkling inside of me that reminds me one day this will all end—whether it be the day that I leave Triple Falls for college or whether they leave me for someone else.

I rarely let my mind go there because just the thought of it ruins me.

My dreams are filled with them, riddled with them every night. Lately, I've been brushing up on my French with a new app, and Dominic sometimes entertains me when we're together, though he's rusty himself, the moody Frenchman.

But he does, they both do, they indulge me, and they've allowed me this time to be selfish, and it's been the best summer of my life.

So tonight, I'm going to try like hell to live in the now.

The unmistakable sound of his Camaro tearing down the drive has me smiling as I survey my appearance one last time. Today had been especially hot, but I left my hair down because he likes it this way, constantly pulling the hair ties out when I have it up and throwing them in the trash. He isn't a fan of makeup either, because he also tosses it when I leave it in his bathroom.

The motherfucker.

But there's so much I love about Dominic. About the way he communicates with me without saying a word.

I can read him more easily now, gauge his moods, his dislikes, his preferences. Outside the bedroom, you wouldn't know we are together. Inside the bedroom, he doesn't go more than minutes without his hands and lips on me.

I love it.

Some part of me thinks I should be offended by his refusal to acknowledge us publicly. Still, another part of me knows it's just his way, and that he's probably protecting me from the small-town gossips because Sean and I have been seen quite often around town in a lip lock.

And I am guilty. But I do things often, that I hope show Dominic I'm just as devoted to him.

My time, heart, and attention are distributed as equally as I can spare them, and somehow against the laws of monogamy and human nature, we work. We're working, and I'm starting to believe them.

There's no jealousy, no bickering, and no fighting unless the fight is mine. I've tried daily for the past few weeks to accept that my heart is split and fully capable of loving both of them, but I don't see this arrangement as fair to either.

So for now, I'll take what I can get.

Grabbing my purse, I haul ass down the stairs, leaving my cell phone behind.

I slip outside and smile when Dominic pulls up, his Camaro newly waxed and gleaming.

I slip in and fight the urge to kiss him.

"Hey," I say, and he takes off. We ride for a few minutes in silence, my fingers aching to touch him. He smirks, keeping his eyes ahead, and I know he knows what I'm thinking.

I roll my eyes. "Asshole."

"And here I put on a clean T-shirt just to be insulted."

"We're alone, you know," I point out, knowing the minute we're behind closed doors, he'll be touching me, and I'll be begging him not to stop.

"I'm driving. Show some restraint, woman. And we're never alone."

I glance around the cabin. "You got some imaginary friend in here?"

"Cecelia." His face goes blank, and I wait for what seems like an eternity until he speaks. "We'll be alone later." It's as close to a promise as I'm going to get and I decide it's enough.

"I can keep my hands to myself, you know."

"Sure you can."

Smug bastard.

Lips twitching, he shifts, his muscular forearm bulging due to the firm grip he has on the wheel.

"When are you going to let me drive?"

"Easy, *never*."

"Seriously?"

"Only one other person has a key to this car, and it won't ever be used."

"You know I'll be searching Sean's room from top to bottom, right?"

His chest bounces. "Good luck with that."

"I will drive this car someday, Dominic. *Bet on it.*"

He takes me to Asheville, where we dine on an outdoor patio. The city is nestled in the heart of the Blue Ridge, but it's far more populated than Triple Falls and likely the reason why we drove forty minutes out of our way. But dinner is delicious, and being with him in this capacity is equally as intoxicating. I love being on the opposite side of the table, studying his face, his dark lashes as he scans the menu before ordering for us both. He opens my doors, tips ridiculously, and smiles—really smiles—more than once. The man is no stranger to proper date etiquette, nor is he a stranger to the ways of a gentleman, which only makes me question his initial reception of me. When we met, he'd acted like an obnoxious pig to the extreme.

On the drive home, he lifts my skirt and exposes my panties, slapping my hand away when I try to push it back down. He gets satisfaction in knowing he can glance over and see me vulnerable, and though I feign annoyance, I love every minute of it. He spends the drive describing how he wants to touch me, where he wants to lick, and details exactly what he is going to do to make me come as I sit there listening, rapt, losing my mind, and growing wetter by the second. By the time he parks, I am close to orgasm. The minute he cuts the engine, I fly at him, and he welcomes me, a groan leaving his throat, letting me know he is just as needy for me.

And he is because he fucks me twice before he rolls a joint while I lay back in the seat, my head resting on the door, in nothing but my panties. From my vantage point I'm able to admire his profile, his physique, him. Music drifts from his speakers as I lift my bare foot and playfully massage his side with my toes as he readies the blunt paper.

"What *is this?*"

"David Bowie. Shhh," he releases the weed into the paper and reaches for his dash to turn it up. "The first minute and a half of this song is money. Listen."

And I do, deciding it's definitely one for us to dissect and repeat. It's one of our things now. He plays DJ, and we talk about the music. I'm pretty sure if he wasn't a vigilante/criminal/mechanic, he would have done something in that arena.

"I love it."

He flashes me a rare, full smile. "I knew you would."

A flutter zigzags across my chest. He's trying, for me. "Are you ever going to tell me why you didn't like me at first?"

"Who says I like you now?"

I press into his side with my toes and earn a stink eye when some weed falls from his lap.

"If I say I like you, do I have to take you to prom?"

"I'm not that young."

"You're a baby."

"You aren't that much older." He's just had his twenty-sixth birthday, and I woke him up in a way I hope he'll never forget.

"I'm old enough to know better."

"Yet, you got really *stupid* with me."

"Yeah," he says thoughtfully, "I did."

"What's that supposed to mean?"

"Don't take offense," he cuts in, apparently rethinking his word choice.

"Color me offended," I dig my toes in, hoping it's painful.

"Drama," he chuckles, licking the blunt and sealing it. "Don't be such a girl."

"Sorry, I've been missing you."

He frowns, and I laugh because I know it's not the fact that he doesn't want me saying those things, it's that he feels like an asshole when he's not in the mood to return the sentiment, and that mood comes more rarely than his smiles. There's so much about him I can anticipate now, and I pride myself in getting close enough to understand him. Sean tried to tell me there was far more to him, but I didn't truly recognize it until I got close enough to see, to experience it, for myself.

"Are you ever going to tell me what happened to your parents?"

I immediately regret my question because his eyes dim, his focus shifting past his windshield into the woods. We're at the meetup spot, where he takes me often to work on his laptop when he wants to get out of the house before storms hit. I now consider it more our spot, though technically Tyler owns it. He bought it before joining the Marines.

"They died in an accident."

"How old were you?"

"Almost six."

"I'm so sorry."

Joint in his lips, he tilts his head and lights it, his reply coming out on an exhale.

"Yeah, me too." The now-familiar smell is a comfort as it clouds around me.

"I don't remember a lot, images here and there of a smile. Of her cleaning up my knee after a bad bike ride, the color of her hair, like mine. The way she laughed hysterically. Little things, small pieces of her I keep locked up. But mostly, I remember the music she listened to because she played it all the time." He swallows, his confession taking me by surprise.

"What we listen to? This is all her tastes?"

He nods. "Most of it, yeah." He turns to me, his eyes shimmering with a rare vulnerability. "When I listen to it, I feel like I know her. The older I get, the better I understand the lyrics and understand her, you know what I mean?"

My heart melts with his confession, and I nod, wanting so much to pull him to me, but now's not the time.

"And your father?"

He grimaces. "The same. A flash here and there." He chuckles. "He had red hair."

"No way."

"Yeah, *his* father was Scottish, that's where my namesake comes from, and his mother was French, so he was a half Scottish, half French mutt, raised in France."

"You must not look a thing like him."

"I don't."

"How did they meet?"

He takes another tug on the joint and exhales before passing it to me. "Different story for a different day."

I don't press my luck and inhale deep. "Do you have pictures of them?"

"A few, but they died before the digital revolution." He pulls a piece of loose weed from his tongue. "Tatie has some photos locked away in her attic somewhere, but we weren't much for family photos anyway."

"Why is that? Because of The Ravenhood?"

He grins over at me, his brow lifting, an incredulous laugh in his question. "The Ravenhood?"

I shrug. "I mean, essentially that's what you are. Don't tell me you've never thought of it that way. Tyler *is* nicknamed the Friar."

"It's a lot less storybook to me."

"Because you're living it."

"Get dressed. Let's finish smoking this up top."

"Up top? Something wrong with your current view?" I glance down and back.

"Yeah," his eyes slide down my body with clear intent. "I'm out of condoms."

"Isn't going topless *zee French way?*"

His returning look is laced with a hint of possession and has me smiling as I pull on my dress.

Blissed out, I rest in the crook of Dominic's arm atop his hood as we gaze up at the night sky. I sink into the feel of him, his crisp, sea scent filling my nose. I'm fully lit inside and out with the buzz of the joint we smoked and the feel of his lips, his skin.

Smiling, I turn to him just as he glances down at me, his eyes filled with mirth.

"What?"

"Who the hell are you, and what have you done with my motherfucker?"

He grazes his hand over my nipple before tweaking it painfully. I screech and then burst into laughter.

"There you are." I settle back in and we bask in the breeze. I swear if there's a heaven, it's here with him. "Dom?"

"Yeah?"

"What do you want, you know, for the future?"

He's silent for long seconds, and I assume he won't answer.

"It's not a stupid question."

Another beat of silence.

"Nothing."

I sigh. "I guess it's a good thing you won't be disappointed."

His chest bounces. "Am I supposed to ask you what you want now?"

"Not if you don't care."

"I'm not future centered. Plans don't make the man."

"I know. I know. Live in the now, take each day as it comes. I get it, but isn't there something you want?"

"No, but it's obvious there's something *you* do."

More. More of him. More of Sean. More of this endless summer. But I keep my hopes to myself. Because I'm sure this can't go on forever. That fear is starting to eat at me more and more. And aside from their ambitions, I do have my own and know one day I'll demand more for myself. One day, maybe, I'll choose a life or a path that neither will be able to go on with me. The thought of losing either of them, of that sort of progression is crippling. I've never been this happy. Not ever. My only saving grace is I'm not leaving Triple Falls anytime soon.

"What?" He gently nudges me from where he rests.

"I don't like putting a voice to my fears. Because then, I can only expect them to come true."

"That's bleak."

"It's better than not wanting anything in the future."

"I already know what happens," he whispers with surety.

"What do you mean? You can predict the future?"

"I can predict mine because I make shit happen."

"What is it?"

"Whatever I decide."

I lift from him, and he lets me. "Just for once, can you give me a straight answer?"

"What's the question?"

I switch gears. "Do you ever get jealous?"

He keeps my eyes, his voice even. "No."

"Why?"

"Because he can give you the things I can't."

"I'm not complaining, please don't think that. But why can't you?"

"Because I'm not like him. I'm a lot simpler."

"I don't believe that."

"It's true."

I trace the line of his jaw. "You are anything but simple."

"My needs are. I don't want things like other people."

"Why? Why train yourself for such simplicity when you are worth so much…" I dig in and let myself reveal what I'm feeling. "You are so much more than what you let people see, than what you give yourself credit for."

"That's the point."

"Why won't you let people know you?"

"You know me."

I melt into that statement, the tone giving me life, his words giving me life. "And I'm lucky."

"You are anything but," he mutters dryly.

"Please just stop that...you don't have low self-esteem. What's with this glib shit?"

"There is so much you don't know."

"I want to, Dom. I want to know all sides of you."

"You don't, Cecelia, you think you do, but you don't."

"You think I won't care for you like I do?"

"Things will change."

"I don't care," I place my hands on his chest. "I want in. Please let me in."

He remains quiet and I blow out a frustrated breath. Lately, I'm becoming more and more frustrated with the militant restraint they show, but it's not changing. It's the price I have to pay to be with them both, so I backpedal.

"Okay, okay." I roll back and let my head rest on his windshield and silently berate myself for pushing so hard. "Sorry." I lift and press a kiss to his jaw. "It's hard being with you. It's just hard sometimes."

I reclaim my place back in his hold and run my hand underneath his shirt palming his chest, he grips my bare shoulder, pulling me tighter to him.

"You are in."

Every word hits the innermost part of me. Emotions surface as I crane my neck to look up at him. He places a soft kiss to my lips, deepening it to the point he's pressing those words into me.

When he pulls away, I feel everything at once. I know I'm in love with him. I just don't know how much of him I know.

My computer geek/keyboard warrior, my book nerd who lives like a peasant despite his place in the ranks. A silent hero with a flip switch temper. A passionate lover, who reserves his subtle kindness, a warmth close to imperceptible unless you get close enough to see it. Yet with him I can see it, I can feel it, in his touch, in his eyes, inside him dwells a gentle soul capable of much more than he lets on. I'm so greedy for him that I want him to have everything. I want him to embrace it. I want to see him showered with the love he deserves. And selfishly, I want to be the only one ever to do it.

I open my mouth to do just that when he covers it.

"Don't waste good words on me."

He muffles my objection.

"It's okay, Cecelia. I'm as close to happy as a man like me deserves."

It's his secrets that keep him humble, keep him from letting himself want anything more than what he has. Only a good man would question whether or not he deserves anything more. A part of me breaks at the idea he thinks he deserves nothing more from his future.

"Have you hurt people?"

Silence. But it's not a stupid question. It's just a question he won't answer. It's probable he's used the gun in his car and will do it again. He's a man with too many secrets and no one to share them with.

"Do I make you happy? Even a little?"

I can't help my smile at his silence before he kisses me breathless.

Dominic pulls up to the garage and I grin when I see Sean's Nova. I rush through the lobby, stopping short when I see the look on his face. He meets Dominic's eyes behind me, his expression grave before he gives me his attention, a quick flash of teeth when I reach him.

"You've been up to no good?"

"Always."

"That's my girl."

"Where is everyone?" I ask, looking around the garage. Sean ignores my question and runs his fingers through my hair.

"Cecelia, I'm going to take you home, okay?"

I turn to see Dominic's eyes have gone cold; his jaw set in a firm line.

"But—"

"Not tonight, okay?" Sean says softly. "Me and Dom have to talk."

I know asking what's wrong is pointless, but the tension rolling off him has me on high alert.

"Are you…safe?"

He runs his finger along my nose and peers down at me with pure adoration.

"Safety is an illusion, baby."

"God, Sean, just for once, can you lie to me?"

"I hate the ground you walk on." He deadpans before glancing over my shoulder at Dominic who speaks up behind me.

"When?"

"Now."

"Fuck," he says, his eyes trail over me and then back to Sean. "Get her home."

Sean nods and grips my hand, and I shake my head walking toward Dominic. Just once, I hope he'll make an exception and let his temper take a backseat, and he does. I rise up on my toes as he pulls me to him and kisses me for long seconds, practically lifting me off my feet with the sweep of his tongue. When he pulls away, I'm dazed.

"You gotta go, baby." The term of endearment from his lips instills dread into me. I glance back at Sean as emotions take over and I see it, the worry I've gotten glimpses of since the moment we met.

They're scared.

It's written in the rigidity of their posture as well as their expressions.

"It's okay," Sean says softly, pulling me to him, uncertainty in his tone. "But we have to go, Pup. Right *now.*"

"Okay," we move past Dominic, and our fingers brush. He doesn't look back. He just stands in the middle of the garage, his eyes cast down, and I watch him just seconds before he erupts, the jarring sound of metal hitting the bay doors as Sean rips me from the building and pulls me into the car.

All the color drains from my face as Sean ushers me inside.

"I don't care, do you hear me, I don't care what it is, give me something."

He tears out of the parking lot and I wait, knowing he can feel the anxiety pouring from me.

"Sean, plea—"

"Somebody couldn't keep a secret."

Chapter Thirty-Seven

I T'S BEEN DAYS OF SILENCE, DAYS OF UNANSWERED TEXTS. I've gone from worried, to confused, to angry, and all I want at this point is just a little fucking acknowledgment. Pulling up to the garage, I take a steadying breath. My leaping heart has taken an unexpected nosedive from the place it was seventy-two hours ago, and all of that is due to their deafening collective silence.

I've been patient, given them enough space to handle whatever took them from me without ample explanation.

I don't have to have answers, but I do have to lay eyes on them. I know what they do behind the scenes is dangerous, but their silence at this point is just cruel. I haven't slept at all, and just finished another shift Sean didn't show up for, but thanks to the gossip mill at the plant, I did hear that he called in. I've been tempted more than once to call Layla, but that's not how this works.

Calling for a simple proof of life check for the sake of my sanity would have been the next step if I didn't see several cars outside of the garage, including the two owned by the men I came to seek answers from.

Hood business. All of the last few days had to have been filled with it because the parking lot is more crowded than ever. Virginia is here, so is Alabama. But it's not a meetup. That was last week, which means there won't be another one for at least two. Unless something is really wrong.

Exiting my car in sheer panic, I feel the boom of bass and can't help my relieved grin when I hear the mood on the other side of the door—voices mixed with laughter.

They're okay. You're okay.

I have to believe that hood business is what's kept them away because the alternative is too painful. I haven't let myself dwell on that. Nothing about our last interaction indicated that was even a possibility. But if they're ghosting me, I'm not going to give them the satisfaction of doing it without an explanation— especially after how close Sean and I have become this summer both as friends and lovers. And Dominic, well, I can't even pinpoint which feelings exist due to lust or intrigue or the culmination of both but that last night we spent together, it was love I felt, that I wanted to admit.

Because I truly love them both.

And if they're okay, I'm okay.

Gnawing fear eats at me as I approach the door with shaky resolve. It's when I reach it, that I hear the out of place melody blaring through the garage and I know they were expecting me.

"Afternoon Delight" carries through the air, out of the doors as my chest churns and dread fills the pit of my stomach.

It's a joke. It has to be. And it's not funny. I'll find a way to punish Sean for this.

Standing at the door of the lobby and looking into the bay, I see it's business as usual with the addition of several guests. My guys crowd around the pool table, cutting up, beers in hand as they pass a joint around. Sean watches Dominic take a shot at the table, refusing to look up. He knows I'm here. I'd changed after work and am dressed to impress in his favorite red sundress. My lips painted to match. I stand, a beacon waiting for some sort of acknowledgment as they chatter on and a few heads I don't recognize turn my way. When the next song begins to play just as I step through the threshold, my fight for attention quickly shifts to my threatening nausea.

It's then I know why Sean is keeping his eyes down. He doesn't want to watch the dagger he's slowly pushing into my chest.

"Cecilia" by Simon and Garfunkel begins to play as the door slams behind me, securing my place in the trap.

Every word of the song like a slap to the face.

This isn't happening.

This isn't happening.

But it is. The song, the lyrics, the out of place melody pierces me as my heart rages in my chest, continually slamming into the crumbling barrier, begging to be set free, for a destination anywhere but here. Tears burn my eyes as I watch the two men I came for blatantly ignore me, as more heads begin to turn my way.

Dominic is hunched over the table, taking his shot as Sean stands in the corner, his hands wrapped around his pool stick as Tyler whispers in his ear, his eyes on mine, a smile on his dimpled face. He doesn't know.

But Sean does, and so does Dominic.

The rest of the party huddles around the kegs, oblivious to the fucking knife slicing through me. Dominic takes the shot, before finally, he looks directly at me, a smug smirk playing on his lips.

Lumps of betrayal clog my throat, choking me as that smirk brands me with the scarlet letter, turning all our dirty deeds against me.

Drowning in deceit, I sink further and further where I stand, fighting the bile climbing up my throat while drifting into the wave of despair.

Neck on fire, my heart screams for mercy, beat after painful beat against my chest as Sean finally lifts his eyes to look at me.

That's when I break, utterly humiliated and completely taken aback by the second faces of the men I've fallen so in love with. Each lyric turns every beautiful moment we shared into one of my degradation.

I've been played.

I let them in.

I let them use me.

I convinced myself it was real.

That they cared.

I thought it was love.

But I was a game to them.

They set me up, lifted me as high as I could fly only to watch me fall.

I don't realize I'm sobbing until I can no longer see them, but blurred versions of the men I gave my heart—my trust to—as black streaks my cheeks. And maybe it's best that I don't, so I can erase the old images with these new ones, replace the everything I felt with the nothing they've left me with.

They'd made me feel safe, accepted.

I loved them wholly.

I gave myself to them, and they let me...

One by one, heads slowly turn my way. And little by little, I realize I've gathered the attention of the entire garage. Face hot, sobs bursting from me. I slam my eyes shut, willing the moment away, hellfire in my heart, the damning, the branding, the judgment.

I can't bring myself to open my eyes, to look up, to move. I can't breathe through this betrayal, through the ache in my heart, through the pain searing through me.

I'm *that* girl. The girl I swore I would never be. The fool I promised myself I'd never be again.

But here I am, a goddamn fool.

No better than a hired whore.

Worse, I'd given my heart for nothing. To become nothing.

I played with fire, and now I'm singed beyond recognition.

Opening my eyes, I know only seconds have passed while I scan the faces of those laying witness to my end. In them I see nothing but confusion and pity, especially from Tyler whose eyes volley between us.

Sean takes a step toward me, and Dominic slams a hand to his chest, his lips pulling up, his eyes dancing with amusement.

I was their toy, and now I'm no longer worthy of their time and attention.

Disgust fills me as I fixate on Dominic, remembering the words he said to me days ago, the way he touched me beneath the stars. Worse than that, Sean had been just as convincing, maybe even more so. Images flit through my mind of our beginning, our kisses, our shared laughter, waking up in his arms, our conversations.

In their eyes, I'm nothing. *Nothing.*

In their eyes, I'm just another one.

Destroyed, I'm halfway to the door when I hear a scuffle break out on the other side of the glass. I turn back long enough to see Sean's fist connect with Dominic's jaw before I fly out of the garage, humiliation pulsing at my temples, blood trickling freely, padding each of my steps.

I don't bother to pack, and drive through the night.

Chapter Thirty-Eight

TWO WEEKS.

That's what I asked my father for, and he'd granted them to me without an issue. I went straight to Christy, who'd just leased her first apartment in Atlanta. I spent the first week on her couch, crying in her lap as she tried to soothe me with comforting words.

I don't think Sean wanted to hurt me, not like that, and the fight that broke out seemed to indicate as much. But if he's that much of a coward, and went along with Dominic's plan, even entertained it, I can't allow him to mean anything more to me.

I blame myself. I'd actively taken part in all of it. I'd allowed myself to be passed around like a party favor, all the while begging for more.

And they'd taken and taken, and I'd loved every second of it.

I've since spent my time taking long walks around Christy's

complex, trying to pinpoint where I went wrong, and all of it came back down to the beginning, accepting the invitation from Sean the day I met him.

I'd been played up until the last second. Up until they'd shown me just how much.

I don't know how I expected it all to end, but certainly not like that. If I'm honest with myself, I didn't see myself picking one over the other, even if presented with the choice. But they'd even taken that away from me.

They tossed me aside like trash. And I'd asked for it. By pining for them both, by letting them between my legs, into my psyche, and my heart.

Christy still has no idea what to say to me. I've shared a large part of the relationship details with her, leaving the hood business aside. She'd eaten the details up like it was the most fascinating story, but if I look too close, I can see a little of her condemnation. And I can't blame her for it. I understand it. I've done enough of that to myself to last a lifetime.

I just wish I could regret it.

But the truth is, I can't. And the sickest part? I *still* want them. I still love them.

I'm disgusted with myself. How have I become this depraved?

Daily, I still crave their attention, their affection, their strong arms, their kisses, their quirks. I've memorized them. But it's the fresh memory of those seconds I spent in that garage that keeps me outraged.

Between the cloudy haze of my despair, there's a silver lining. Something is building inside of me that overrules any of these foolish emotions, and it's the need for retribution, revenge. And if given a chance, I'm determined to take it.

Whether they admit it or not, those men did care for me.

For whatever reason they decided to cut ties, cut me, their affection was far too convincing to be completely contrived.

Even if it played out in the cruelest of ways, that affection wasn't a figment of my fucking imagination. They'd confided in me, treated me with the utmost care. It couldn't all be a lie. If so, I'll truly be lost.

Something happened.

Something had to have happened to make them carry out a plan so brutal. Even if Dominic is capable of that type of malice, of masking his feelings so well, which I know he is, Sean is not.

But he deserves just as much of my wrath because he let it happen.

It might not have been love for either of them, but it was something more than sex. Even so, their actions are unforgivable.

For the first time in my life, I take comfort in the fact that I am my father's daughter. Some part of me is capable of being just as callous, just as reptilian as he is. If I have to channel the blood I continually deny, continually curse, that now runs cold in my veins to become something other than a dangling and bleeding heart, so be it.

"What's that look?" Christy asks me as I stare unseeing at a little girl playing on the steps of the apartment pool. We've been out here for the last few days soaking up the last of the summer sun. The little girl squeals in delight as her mother kneels next to her, reapplying sunscreen on her arms.

I remember playing a game with myself when I was her age, a dangerous game. I often played alone, while my mother was busy entertaining friends or whatever boyfriend joined us that day. I'd dared myself to swim out farther and farther away from safety and eventually found myself in the deep end, over my head and alone, bailing myself out while no one noticed I was drowning. And I'd done it. A second before I knew I was going underwater for the last time; I'd kicked my feet so hard I ended up hitting my head on the lip of the pool. Just before everything went black, I found purchase with my palms on the concrete and pulled myself up to safety before sobbing, hysterical with relief. That's when my mother finally noticed. I got hugged, and then spanked, hard.

Even when I was a kid, I always had a sick fascination with the deep end, with putting myself at risk. The sickness that resides inside me isn't new. But I'd let it out, and in Sean's words, I'd made peace with the devil inside. I let that devil rule me for one summer, and it was just as reckless with my well-being.

This is that time, where I can sink or sob in relief. It's time to kick and pull myself out of it. But it's my heart, my memories, my lingering sickness that weighs me down, threatening any sign of progress, leaving me helpless in the deep end.

Time to kick, Cecelia.

"Cee?" Christy prompts as I keep my eyes on the little girl, splashing around before leaping off the step and into the safety of her mother's arms.

"I'm thinking it's not okay. I'm thinking…" I need to find that concrete. At the same time, I'm thinking I need to kill the curious part of that little girl, so this never happens again. I don't credit myself much for the life I've lived, but maybe I should. I survived raising an adolescent and slightly neglectful mother. I put myself through school, kept my head above water without supervision. I've made it this far on my own without the true guidance of the people I was supposed to count on, and I did a damned good job of it, up until a few months ago. I made it through nineteen years of kicking, and I'll make it nineteen more. With new resolve I turn towards my best friend. "I'm thinking I forgot who the fuck I am."

"Atta girl," she says. "Had me worried there for a minute. What are you going to do?"

"For myself, move on. To them? I don't know. Maybe nothing. But revenge is a dish best served cold. I'll know it when I see it. For now, it's about getting my head straight. I don't completely trust Karma, so if I'm ever in the position, I'll make sure she delivers."

"Damn, to be a fly on the wall," she says, "you've got this, baby."

All I can do is nod.

Christy twists from the cheap plastic lounger, planting her long legs on the deck between us before reaching for my hand, her light brown eyes full of empathy. She's a beautiful girl, my best friend. Medium-length, wavy brown hair, an athletic build, soft, full features. Seeing her after taking that sledgehammer to the chest made breathing possible when she met me at my car in the late hours of morning, arms wide open. "I don't blame you, Cecelia. I might not fully understand it. And I'm telling you now, I can't say I wouldn't do it myself, but God, girl, two men? I can't even pretend to imagine what it would be like."

"It's not that uncommon anymore."

"I know," she says, "but," she shakes her head. "You really went *all in*, huh?"

"I believed them, you know? I thought they were enlightened. Thought they were some rare breed. What a fucking idiot."

"But you are now. *You* are enlightened. They might have been preaching some bullshit, but you believed it, and you still do. You liberated yourself. You can be proud of that."

It's the truth, the absolute truth. Hypocrites they may be, but with them, I'd unleashed the truth about myself, about my nature. I've changed, and my mind's changed too, despite their slut-shaming hypocrisy and damning cruelty.

"You better call me every day."

"I will." I turn to her, my only true friend. My only real family. "Let's go visit my mom."

Chapter Thirty-Nine

CHRISTY SNIFFLES AS HUBBLE WALKS AWAY FROM KATY before they glance back at each other. "W-w-wait, they don't end up together?"

The credits roll as Christy shifts murderous eyes from the screen to me. "They don't end up together?!"

"Nope."

Christy's jaw drops as Mom and I laugh at her where she sits on the couch, tossing Milk Duds at us both. "What kind of shit is that?"

"Not all love stories have happy endings," my mother says softly. I glance over to where she rests in her recliner, the only piece of furniture she moved to her boyfriend's place. He's absent today, his excuse 'fishing' to give us a day together. She's gained a little weight, and there's a little color in her cheeks, which was absent before I left. I can only be happy for her. She'd been a shell when I moved to Triple Falls. But her last statement piques my curiosity.

"Who did you love like that, Mom?"

"*One* too many."

I nod in perfect understanding.

"I. Cannot. Believe they don't end up together!" Christy exclaims, exasperated as we both turn to her.

"It's called *The Way We Were* for a reason. First of all, he cheated," Mom points out. "More importantly, he couldn't handle her personality or her beliefs, or her strength; therefore, he did *not* deserve her. And given the choice, he didn't have a damn thing to do with their daughter because of it. You still think they should be together?"

"But—" Christy objects.

"That's the truth," I add, "people don't want the brutal truth in love stories anymore, but that, there," I gesture at the screen, "is the brutal, *ugly* truth."

"Right on," my mom says with clear pride in her eyes. "And *that's* a story that will stick with you, too."

Christy sighs. "Well, shit. That was awful."

"No, it wasn't," My mother laughs, lighting a cigarette. "You ate it up." She gives me a conspiratorial grin. "Should we totally ruin her?"

I nod. "Absolutely."

"You two are masochists." She glances between us as I grab the remote. "Making me watch all these old sad movies that *hurt*."

"The best ones," Mom replies, a hint of sadness lacing in her words.

"That may be the truth *for some*, but I still believe in Prince Charming," Christy declares, "no matter what brutes you are to me."

"As you should," Mom chimes in, "but just know, the picture

in your head might not match your reality. There are very few men worth the hell they put you through. So be very careful about who you give your heart and body to. They might eventually take more than you can handle."

Touché, Mom. Touché.

"Brace yourself," I say to Christy, grabbing the remote. "This was made in eighty-one."

"Oh, God." She sinks beneath the blanket on the couch. "I don't know if I can handle it."

Mom winks at me, stubbing out her cigarette as I press play on *Endless Love.*

It's there in that living room I find some strength. It's not the movies I grew up watching with my mom, that she shared with her own mother that gave it to me, though I'm sure they didn't fucking help my warped perception of love. The strength I draw is from the women surrounding me. For months, I've lived for nothing but the men that consumed me before throwing me away. Despite my best efforts, I'd lost myself in them, allowed my affection for them to take up my existence. I made no friends outside their circle, and when I get back, I'll have no life beyond them. I might have discovered a few things, but mostly all I've become is co-dependent. And I'll make it a point to rectify that.

The only thing I have left to do is grieve and get angry.

And though it hurts like no other pain I've felt, I did what I set out to do.

I can safely say Cecelia Horner is a wallflower no more.

I leapt, and now I have to decide if this pain I'm feeling was worth the trade-off of one unforgettable summer.

Time to kick, Cecelia.

Brooke Shields comes on screen, beautiful, naïve, innocence intact as she takes the steps down the stairs to her lover, untouched by the bitterness that I can't help but feel, and I want to warn her, to tell her that look she's giving that boy as they fuck by the firelight is going to cost her. Instead, I ache with her and grieve the innocence she's letting go of because deep down, I'm still addicted to that all-too-familiar feeling. My heart curses me as I watch on rapt, reliving my days and nights beneath the trees and stars.

As I watch, all I can do is feel the sting of loss and mourn the girl she was before love took hold of her.

My phone buzzes on the table in front of me and Christy's eyes meet mine as NEVER ANSWER crosses my screen.

I silence it without hesitation, and she gives me a proud smile before her gaze darts back to the movie, her eyes love drunk.

But mine are wide open.

It's the addict in me fighting to keep me in the deep end, and so, I do the only thing I can.

I kick.

Chapter Forty

THE DAY I RETURN HOME TO TRIPLE FALLS, I CHANGE THE gate code and trash the bikini I wore the day at the lake. My phone buzzes with a lone text and I ignore it. I haven't permitted myself to check Sean's messages yet. There's no excuse, no reason I can fathom that will ever be good enough for what they've done to me.

I've trapped myself in my bedroom and spent the majority of my day reading up on career possibilities and the majors that coincide with them. I'll have the first year of school to seriously mull it over, so I rest easy in that knowledge but decide to get a jump on my pre-requisites and sign up for fall classes. Between my time at community college and working at the plant, I'll stay busy enough to keep my nose clean.

Back to square one.

And I'll use my time here productively. With a clean slate, trying my best to erase the last three and a half months.

After a few hours locked into my cell, I decide on a better plan. And it has nothing to do with getting even and everything to do with eradicating any lingering curiosity or attachment to my summer.

Sometimes the best revenge is piquing the curiosity of those that fucked you and moving on. I've learned well enough over the past few months that silence can be the best weapon. So, if Sean wants to be heard, my retribution for his betrayal will be to shut him out. Although he's been doing all of the calling and texting, I swore I heard the distinct sound of a Camaro on the lone road when I walked the grounds of the garden this morning. But these men are bold, they've raided my home more than once unannounced, and if they want to get to me, they will.

Roman's permanently moved to Charlotte. He's no threat. If they want my attention so much, they know where to find me. And I have to be ready because odds are, if Sean's calling and texting, and I continue to avoid them, they'll be coming.

What could they possibly want or have to say?

If they regret it, why did they take so many pains in making such a show of it? And not just in front of locals, but other chapters of the hood.

I can't afford to care. My head and heart can't take it.

It's over. Whatever it was, it's over.

Spell broken or not, I attach to the burn and let it have its way with me.

Tomorrow is my first day back at the plant, and I have zero doubts I'll have to face Sean. He'll find a way to corner me, to get me alone. After hours in the silent house, and organizing my life to the point of insanity, I decide to take a drive to clear my head. Setting out down the long driveway, I listen carefully for the sound of a Camaro and decide it was the result of my overactive imagination, hating the notion it was more like wishful thinking.

Quieting those thoughts with a spoonful of those agonizing seconds in their garage, I head out on the road. I breathe a little easier when I reach the end of it, and I ease into the three-way stop looking left and then right, my eyes landing on Dominic when he comes into view, waiting on the shoulder.

Fuck.

He watches me, intent from where he sits feet away. Snapping our connection, I spring into motion, gunning my car past him where he's parked before hauling ass down the road. In seconds, he's on my tail, my sedan no match for the lightning beneath his hood. Nerves firing, anger building, I steer through winding roads leading down the mountain towards town. He keeps his distance but remains close enough that I know he's there and not giving up. I gas my car well above the speed limit, but he keeps the same amount of distance.

"Fuck you!" I roar as I race down the now-familiar roads, driving like a lunatic to evade my old spellbinding captor. Rage boils through me as I replay that night over and over in my head, making good headway toward town. Dom remains hot on my trail until I'm forced to slow at the first stoplight. I check my rearview and see he's laid back, posture relaxed, the same smug expression on his face that was there the day I met him. I speed through one stoplight and then the next before crossing through to the opposite side of town. Sure he'll eventually tire, I take him through twenty minutes of winding roads, but he stays right at my bumper.

Fed up with the charade, I skid to a stop at an abandoned camp parking lot, and he narrowly misses a tree, jerking the Camaro in after me, fishtailing and skidding to a stop on the asphalt. I'm already out of my car charging toward him, and he barely makes it out of the driver's seat when I deliver the first slap.

He tracks the tear sliding down my cheek. "I have to let you go for now," he grimaces, and for the first time since that night we spent alone, his emotion shines through. "But I don't fucking want to."

He leans in again and presses a kiss to my forehead before releasing me.

The slash across my chest is enough to have me in full preservation mode. "Stay the fuck away from me."

"I don't have a choice. But everything I do now, it's for you."

"You're right. You don't have a choice. And make no mistake, it's *my decision*."

I stalk back toward my car and tear out of the parking lot, refusing to look back.

When I get home, I take a scalding shower but deny the raging in my chest. I let my tears blend with the water, but refute their existence—my decision.

Chapter Forty-One

HALFWAY THROUGH MY FIRST SHIFT BACK AT THE PLANT, I get summoned over the PA system. Pausing our line, I feel the full weight of Melinda's attention. It's been hours of working in silence, it seems even she couldn't ignore my need for solace, and she let me retreat inside myself during this shift, which only further alludes to the fact I look as broken as I feel. I feign ignorance of why I'm being called off the line, but we both know better.

I'm done playing games. I march down the corridor of the first floor into the secluded office at the end of the hall batting away the memories it dredges up—stolen kisses, lingering looks over private lunches, a late shift quickie with his hand clamped over my mouth while he thrust into me, whispering filthy words in my ear. Closing the door, I lean against it and keep my gaze averted. Eyes cast down, his tan boots come into view, and I exhale just as the scent of cedar threatens to cloud my judgment.

you, and…I'll fucking hate myself forever for this." He grips my face tightly in his palms. "I knew from the get-go you were more," he murmurs. "Just think it all through, okay? Think it through. Think about everything I've told you. Push that night aside and believe me when I say that was all about protecting and distancing you, rather than hurting you. But I blew it. I blew it because I couldn't stand to see you in so much pain."

When he threw that punch at Dominic, that was his breaking point.

"Trust me and trust Dom, and no matter what happens from here on out. Don't look for us. Don't look for answers. I'll find a way to work this out. I'll find a way."

"You're scaring me."

"I know. I'm sorry. You wanted to know, now you do. You wanted in. You're in. It's time to keep your secrets." He grips my jaw, leaving no room for argument before his possessive lips claim mine. We both whimper into the other's mouths as he invades— drinking, taking—his kiss going feather-soft before he pulls himself away in what feels a lot like goodbye.

Briefly, his eyes lift, shimmering with emotion. "I love you," he whispers hoarsely before opening the door and walking out. It lingers open briefly, suspended behind him before clicking closed and detonating the bomb he just dropped.

Chapter Forty-Two

GOOGLED FACTS ABOUT RAVENS OUT OF CURIOSITY LAST night and wished I'd done it a lot sooner. Even with their cloak firmly in place, it would have done me a hell of a lot of good just to recognize their traits are very much like that of their mascot.

A group of ravens is called a conspiracy, the irony of that not at all lost on me.

The birds band together in adolescence to form a bond as rebellious teenagers—which I'm sure is when The Ravenhood was formed—until they finally mate out. And the theory on Ravens is that they mate for life.

The wings Layla has on her back are permanent, a branding, a branding she volunteered for. At this point, I'm too hard-pressed to believe any man in my life is sincere enough for that type of commitment, let alone capable of it.

Let's stay in touch!

Facebook
www.facebook.com/authorkatestewart

Newsletter
www.katestewartwrites.com/contact-me.html

Twitter
twitter.com/authorklstewart

Instagram
www.instagram.com/authorkatestewart/?hl=en

Book Group
www.facebook.com/groups/793483714004942

Spotify
open.spotify.com/user/authorkatestewart

Sign up for the newsletter now and get a free eBook
from Kate's Library!

Newsletter signup
www.katestewartwrites.com/contact-me.html